ENTANGLING THREADS

THE WEBS OF FATE
BOOK FIVE

C J WALLINGSFORD

First edition 2025
Print ISBN: 978-1-954426-14-6
Ebook ISBN: 978-1-954426-15-3
Cover design by CJ Wallingsford
Interior Artwork by CJ Wallingsford
Chapter Header design by CJ Wallingsford
Editing by KillingItWrite (Gina)

For more information: cjwallingsford@outlook.com

For my babe, Eric.
The love of my life,
The irritant in my eye,
I mean this with all of my black heart,
I'd chose myself.

TRIGGER WARNING

This book is intended for mature audiences. This series will contain explicit content and dark elements that may be triggering to some. It will include a magical race of beings known as the Seraphinus that has two factions with extreme prejudice against each other.

Additional warnings:
Violence / Mature Language
Contracted Servitude
Emotional / physical abuse
Substance abuse
Sexually explicit scenes
*including a M/M/F relationship

RUNE DIAL

The Continents Calendar

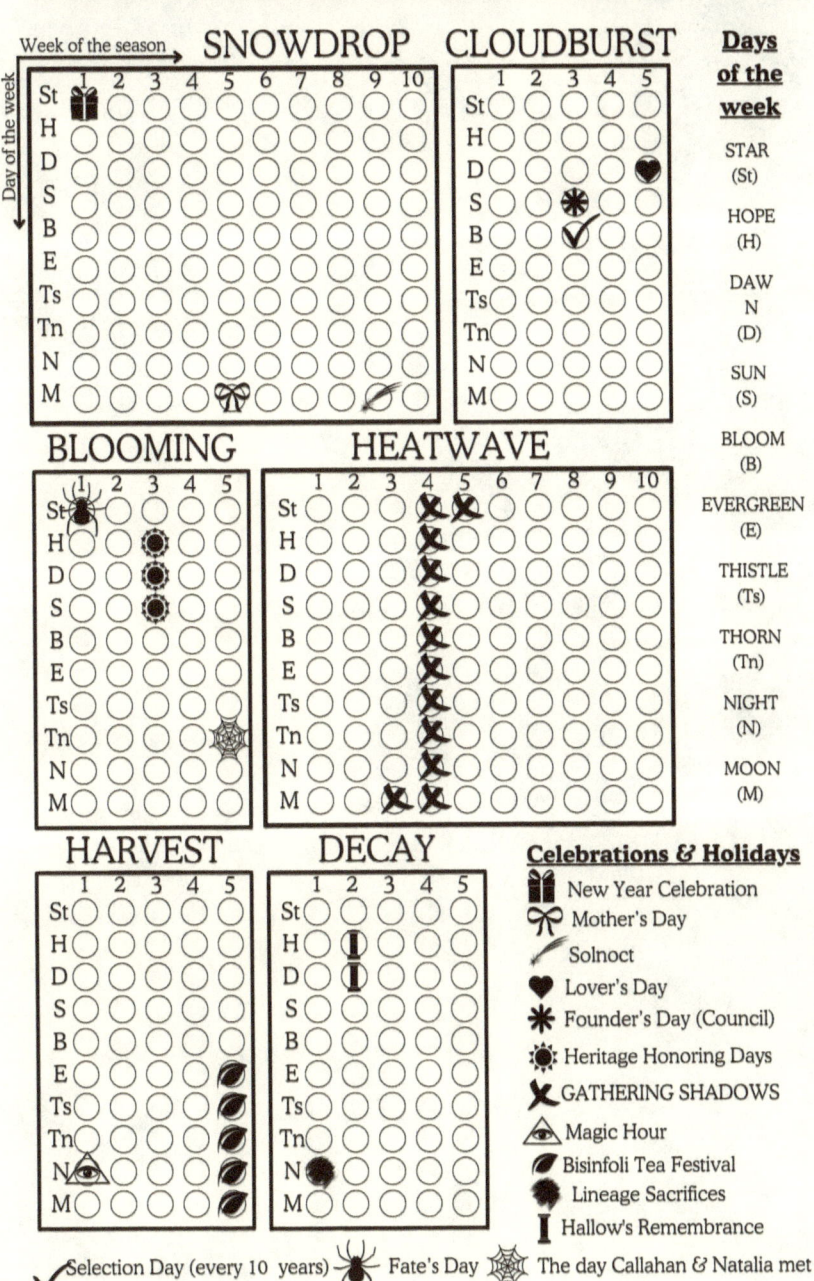

Week of the season
Day of the week

SNOWDROP
CLOUDBURST
BLOOMING
HEATWAVE
HARVEST
DECAY

Days of the week

STAR (St)

HOPE (H)

DAWN (D)

SUN (S)

BLOOM (B)

EVERGREEN (E)

THISTLE (Ts)

THORN (Tn)

NIGHT (N)

MOON (M)

Celebrations & Holidays

New Year Celebration

Mother's Day

Solnoct

Lover's Day

Founder's Day (Council)

Heritage Honoring Days

GATHERING SHADOWS

Magic Hour

Bisinfoli Tea Festival

Lineage Sacrifices

Hallow's Remembrance

Selection Day (every 10 years)   Fate's Day   The day Callahan & Natalia met

"My father used
to tell me that if ever
there was a way
to find a mate,
it was to wish upon
the stars and
ask Adontis for love
mirroring her own."

CHAPTER I
CALLAHAN

1ST STAR'S DAY, BLOOMING, 4050, 6TH MILLENNIUM

I sit in the dining hall, breakfast dwindling to an end. I cradle Natalia in my lap on the head seat, Sterling next to us. My chest hurts, every breath like lifting a ton of rock. Muscles scream and pulse and twinge.

It had been a long night of nightmares, dosed on the toxin that induces that very thing. I'd jerked awake, soaked in sweat, hallucinating smites and cats, after dreaming of being buried alive. I'd woken up too many times to count. The first time, Sterling had shoved Natalia over me, forcing her to my other side so he could pin me between the two of them.

Not even being stuck between the two strongest individuals I know had been enough to calm me.

Lucius had locked me in a cage, using some form of magic to restrain my Dark. I'd been helpless to stop him as he induced agony. Then Pierre came, infecting me with nightmare toxin only to take Lucius's place, inflicting pain. He'd sacrificed his life to set me free, but it was days without end of torment and little sustenance.

It'll take time for the poison to work its way out of my

1

system. I need a few days to recover, to heal. I still have a pulsing wound in the middle of my chest that Natalia couldn't mend with her magic.

I didn't have the energy to please my mate last night. Sterling had been useful, almost delightful.

Picking up my coffee mug, I stare along the table, most of its occupants quiet. Absent are Ashley and Tony, while Alexander sits with Zander in a conversation with other glowing Light Bats. Their presence is odd, to say the least. Lights don't often come into Ilbuio.

Or didn't. Things change.

Zander meets my gaze. Like all Light Seraphinus, his eyes are empty whiteness. His blond, shoulder-length hair is trussed into a war braid, a common fashion for the Light. Without a word, he inclines his head, pressing his thin lips and returning to Alex to speak.

He'd dragged me out a window and carried me to the sky, leaving Pierre to die. It bought my freedom, Thames and Jacques dragged right along with me. Pierre giving his life in sacrifice for the Dark is strange, but that he would die for me is unfathomable. We could barely speak to each other.

I kiss Natalia's temple. "Little Star, you're in trouble."

"What did I do?"

"You have two mates."

Sterling cuts his eyes to us with a grin as he takes a drink from his mug. "At least it's not the Glow Fuck?"

I narrow one eye in annoyance, then focus on my mate.

I'd been unconscious when Sterling sank his teeth into her neck. He marked her over my mating mark, a fact I will never unsee and am trying to ignore. It smolders in my veins like smoking sewage.

I mated Natalia. She's my star, my woman, and Sterling mated her.

I can't kill him. I should. I mock a frown.

He mated my mate. The problem—problems—I have are simple. One, if I kill him, I'm no better than Pierre, and I won't degrade myself in that way. Two, I like Sterling.

I'll give her the choice. If she wants two mates, I'll accept this. If she doesn't, then it's her decision that sends Sterling to the afters. My hands will be clean. Metaphorically speaking, anyway.

I tap her slender, regal nose. I adore that nose and abhor that I do because she inherited it from Pierre. "Did you enjoy last night?"

Her big, wide-set eyes stretch open, and her cheeks turn pink. "Um..."

"Do you want to keep him?"

Ducking her head as she bites the side of her lower lip, she flicks her silver eyes toward Sterling and then winces.

That's a yes.

He swivels his head toward me, but his posture is rigid. Eagerness rolls off him, his ears back and his facial features stretched with glee. "Is that an option?"

I look to Natalia again, her head low. She shifts and fidgets with less enthusiasm than Sterling.

Remaining perked like an excited bird with a worm, he says, "We need a damn answer here, Firefly." He pokes his finger into the surface of the table. "It's a matter of life and death."

She glances at me and then turns her head away. "I'm Cal's mate."

My Dark rumbles, twisting with glee around her. It hisses, going lax.

I frown, pulling my eyebrows together. It's not talking to me, even if it's shifting and pulsing. I raise my eyebrow, eyeing the strands tangled around Natalia. Sterling's Dark has spun around her as well, mixing with mine.

3

Natalia admitted to thinking about sexual activities with Sterling. She's not saying no.

She's not saying yes, either.

Brushing her long, silver hair away, I turn her face toward mine, but she jerks her chin from my grasp. "I'm your mate."

That's her choice. Me. My heart soars, and my Dark vibrates.

She might want him, but she is choosing me. I'll take that answer.

I pull her head to my shoulder, smiling. "I will not leave you again, Mate. I will find you. I will *always* find you."

Snuggling closer, she turns her lips up at the corners with a happy hum.

Sterling looks from her to me, back and forth several times. "Someone tell me if I'm going to the afters."

I shake my head. "We'll see how it goes, but I reserve the right to change my mind and kill you for mating her when I'd already mated her."

Laughing, he picks up his mug and slumps back. "I'll find you in the afters."

"A fatum sewed my soul." I lift my hand, stroking it along Natalia's legs dangling over the armrest.

Sterling chokes on his coffee. "A fatum sewed your soul?"

"Lucius says I'm like them now, a proper blending. He said I'd survive the destruction of the subtorque and subsequent death of my Dark. I didn't misunderstand that spell. I have a soul lock, which locks my soul in my body, so it seems I will likely not find my way to the afters anytime soon. Natalia is an Ancient. I don't know what that means for her if she'll see the afters unless she's killed."

"What the fuck? You have one, too?"

"Too?"

"Tony."

I shake my head. "It lives in Bellasom, an Ancient in the Avgora Mountains I encountered when I fetched my kin."

Sterling pulls his jaw to the side, the corner of his mouth yanking down with it. "Bellasom is dead. Mallafic killed her. Soris, the fatum, took Tony as a new host." He tucks hair behind Natalia's ear. "Soris wanted our woman, but—"

I laugh, cutting him off. "Talia is never going to let Soris near her."

Sterling snickers with me. "No. She screamed her head off, sprouted wings, and floated in midair, curled in a ball. Soris settled for Tony instead."

Natalia frowns, pressing a finger to my chest and tapping it against me. "That's why I couldn't heal you."

I tap my chest near the throbbing pain. "This. Explain."

"My Light is keeping the wound closed, like stitches." She sticks her arm out for me to inspect a thin slice scabbed over on her forearm. "Esme, the crystals, the wounds cannot be healed by Ki for a blended soul."

"Crystals?"

"The ones on the tree," she says, beaming at me. "I made Sterling find it for me so I could be with it. I told it hello for you."

The way her eyes stretch in an innocent gaze melts me. My Dark simpers, whimpering and pleading to corrupt her. We want her writhing beneath us and begging.

I press my lips to her forehead. "The hysterium crystals can hurt the Ancients?"

"I think so, but we can't pull them off." She shakes her head. "You can't. It hurt the tree. It screamed and started to bleed."

Twisting to face us, resting an elbow on the table, Sterling nods. "That cursed thing shook the world when Hiro tore a crystal off."

Natalia nods in short jerks of her head. "Uh-huh, and it has a soul. I used Ki, trying to heal it, and it echoed back. That's what happens with a soul. It echoes."

Drew and Erlak rise from the table.

Eyeing them, I tell her, "We'll deal with that later, Little Star. Right now, we deal with the contractors."

"O'tay." She rests her head on my shoulder.

I take her hand, and the physical contact eases the dull pain in my chest and sends sparks of pleasure across my skin.

Drew and Erlak push their chairs in.

As much as I want to bask in her embrace and scent, I can't. We can't. I take a deep breath to lift my voice. "Where are you going?"

They freeze, and the table falls silent, faces turning toward me.

Erlak sneers. "Where we want."

"No. Sit down."

"You're not the Dark King."

"No. I am her mate and her Dark Queen. Therefore, I get the same respect and command as the Dark King."

Drew sits.

Erlak rests his fingertips on the table, glaring. "She's a fucking piss poor excuse of a Dark King, so I don't care if you have her respect. You were the one who brought her into the contest to let a Glow Whore take our seat of power."

"I chose a weapon. Do you understand the purpose of a weapon?" I wait. "Answer me."

"It's a tool for you to use."

"Yes, which means you select the best weapon you can. I did just that, and my weapon won the contest for the throne. If any of you don't like your Dark King, I don't give a fuck about your pathetic feelings. If any of you think yourself more capable, stronger, harder to kill, more powerful, or even a more skilled fighter, then you are welcome to challenge your Dark King, as is our lawful right to ensure the strongest holds the crown. Are you challenging your king, Erlak?"

"No."

"Then sit the fuck down and shut the fuck up."

Erlak sits.

I rest back, cocking my jaw and considering them. This was always my father's forte, not mine. I look to Natalia, gleaning strength from her belief in me.

Lifting my head, I say, "I don't know what has been going on in Ilbuio in my absence, and I don't care. We are the Dark, which means we survive by our strength, we are honest in our words, and we earn respect through our actions. You made an empty threat to revolt rather than serve Natalia as your Dark King, twisting Sterling into challenging her in an moronic attempt to keep the Dark unified. It's pathetic at best if not a deplorable action deserving of disgrace."

Faces flicker with winces and distaste, most ducking or turning away rather than meeting my eyes.

"His idiocy isn't my concern, and I won't be following him into stupidity. I can't disgrace all of you, but if one of you steps out of line again, I'll revoke your standing. As for Natalia being a piss poor Dark King," I pause, smiling at her, "Sterling was a contender. He's one of our strongest, and he still couldn't kill her."

He says, "I got close."

"She wasn't fighting back, or you'd be in the afters," I snap, turning to glare at him. "It was a lack of judgment on your part and a waste of your life and skill if she had done as any other Dark King would have and sent you to the afters. You were a contender. You should have known our tenets and our laws well enough to point out the lunacy of their demands. You never should have challenged her knowing she's been twisted by Mallafic into an Ancient. You barely stood a chance against her as simply a Magia and Light Seraphim mix, and you displayed an utter lack of diplomacy and thought, allowing the Dark to dictate your actions instead of leading them. Natalia was more Dark than you in her refusal to play their game, and she glows, for fuck's sake."

Sterling hangs his head. "My concern was for keeping the Dark unified to face the Ancients. I never expected to survive her or my challenge, instead seeking to show them the proof they need to accept she is the strongest of us."

"She proved enough." Glaring down the table, I say, "If you want to revolt, then revolt."

"Exactly what I was trying to prevent, and he's encouraging it," Sterling mutters under his breath.

I twist my lips to the side in humor. "Do it." I shrug. "Revolt. Turn your back on the crown. We won't stop you. I'll hold the door for you on your way out, but..." I stroke my knuckles along Natalia's bare shinbone. "The Dark King holds the strongest of your kind in contract. The Mandolux will stand with us. My kin are stronger even than I, and they won't hesitate to protect me or my mate. Sterling won't be stupidly manipulated a second time, and none of you could kill him in the games. Hiro and Thames are as deadly as they are charming. Hiro has always been an example of strength and our tenets, deserving of his standing as a contractor and now an adviser to the Dark King, and Natalia and Tony are the only ones who can stand against an Ancient with any success."

The table remains silent and still. I take a deep breath, holding it for a fraction before releasing it. "I would prefer you skipped the bloody chaos and accept that the strongest already leads you. I ask that you not divide the Dark or our attention. Stand together with us and the Light to defeat the Ancients that threaten our existence."

I take a drink, draining my mug. "You also need to be made

aware that I am also the new Light Queen. The Mandolux are a branch of the Hallow heritage and, therefore, in possession of the Light's crown. As the Barraco lineage was the firstborn of the Mandolux, the crown is mine. I will be unioning with Natalia. The crowns of Dark and Light will come together for the first time in history, which means Dark and Light will merge into one society."

The Dark starts yelling, the words a tidal wave of fury blurring together without any semblance of understanding possible. I let them scream, leaning forward and looking to refill my mug.

Sterling's Dark closes around the pot and drags my cup to him for a refill. He sets it in front of me.

I add a dash of milk, ignoring the roaring rabble.

Hiro chuckles, pushing the longer strands of black hair from his face. "You do not give a fuck."

"No." I lift my coffee. "Thames isn't here?"

"Recovering."

I draw my eyebrows together.

Hiro waves me off. "Recovering from me. I pushed too hard on him last night in my need after his abuse. He's not as strong as you."

"I had help." I cut my eyes toward Sterling. "Not sure how I feel about it."

He trails his finger around the edge of a teacup, frowning at me. "I'm in possession of information I'd like to discuss."

"Whatever Thames said is true."

Sterling puts two fingers in his mouth and whistles, cutting the air with a shrill note. "Quit shouting, it's giving me a headache and serving no purpose."

Natalia pokes a finger into my chest. "Tell them about the shadows word."

"*Ifferentiti?*" I lift my eyebrows.

"Tell them about the overlap between two things and how it

makes shadows," she holds her hands apart, cupping them and rotating from top to bottom. "How two fit together and find the beauty in their differences." Her gaze lifts, and she stares at me with shining hope.

I smile, my Dark melting into shadows and cooing. Natalia is so adorable this morning it hurts.

I face forward. "The Dark and the Light are of the same origins. We differ. We are opposites in nature, but those differences can be advantages. The Dark survives on strength and skill, letting those two things decide who gets respect." I hesitate, turning to Natalia. "What does the Light survive on?"

Natalia shifts. "I'm just as bad at being the Light as I am the Dark King, but I can tell you the Magia survive on balance and practice."

Zander says, "The Light is about harmony and simplicity. We strive for dignity and beauty, honoring others and therefore ourselves."

Someone yells, "Self-righteous and arrogant bastards that don't know what it's like to earn respect, having it handed to you."

Another glowing man yells back, "We aren't vile beasts clawing our way through the dirt."

I send a burst of flames into the air for attention. "The Light is going to learn how to earn respect, and the Dark is going to learn how to give it. Neither side can live without the other, so we need to learn to live with each other. With the crowns of Dark and Light unified, the Seraphinus will be as well."

Gannon asks, "How? Our laws are as different as our magics."

Erlak bolts to his feet and slams a fist on the table. His chair topples and clatters. "It doesn't matter how. This is blasphemous! The Dark and Light are enemies. The Light was made to hunt us down and slaughter us."

Natalia laughs, her humor ringing through the air. "You! You are the reason the Ancients want to kill the Seraphinus. The Light might have been made to hunt the Dark, but the Dark was made for entertainment. Do you exist to amuse others, Erlak?" She waits, and the silence stretches. "I'll assume that is a no. If you can be more than you were created for, then so can the Light."

Sterling chucks a sugar cube down the table. "The next time you refuse to answer your king, I will assume you don't require your tongue and rip it out."

Natalia says, "That seems harsh. He'd have to work twice as hard to please anyone in bed ever again."

Swallowing my laughter, I grin at her. "Then he should have proper incentive to answer you."

"Every single one of you has reason to hate the other side. What is being asked of you isn't easy, but the easiest way is rarely the right way."

Erlak scoffs. "What would you know of easy or right? You're a child."

Sterling frowns at Natalia as I growl in the back of my throat.

Natalia sighs and stands. "Those are fair questions."

I reach for her, but she steps away, her face crestfallen. I've seen that expression once before, when she explained to me her arrangement with Tony. I've learned enough about her. Whatever has started spinning in her mind is vulgar.

"Talia, you don't have to explain anything to them."

She starts walking down the table toward Erlak. "I was born a Magia, raised as a Magia, and lived as a Magia. We are taught to hate the Seraphinus and trained to kill your kind. I was an heiress, my ancestry linked back to the originals who were created by the Seraphinus. For that fact, my bloodline was directed by our Assembly to union with another to preserve our power, or rather breed it, as I've come to learn."

Stopping next to Erlak, Natalia faces him. "I was a middle

child. I had an elder sister, Sasha, and a younger brother, Nicky." She picks up the sugar cube Sterling threw at Erlak, cradling it in her palm. "The Magia have a ceremony, we call it initiation. You must pass initiation to begin your full training and earn your marks."

She turns away, frowning at the cube with her back to Erlak. "I'll briefly explain that initiation is drinking poison that you have to burn out with Ki. If you fail, you die. Sasha didn't pass her initiation. It should have been *easy* for her." Her shoulders drop as she closes her hand and her eyes. "I passed my initiation, but then Nicky..."

I look to my fist as I squeeze tighter, my Dark whining that our mate is in pain.

Natalia says, "Nicky failed his initiation even as I fought for his right to abdicate. He was terrified to go through initiation because Sasha failed. He wanted to back out of initiation and training. I challenged the Assembly members. I attempted to heal Nicky. I fought with every skill I possessed at the time, but I couldn't save him. My brother died because *I couldn't save him.* That is the second time I learned about loss and the first time I felt the sting of failure."

She opens her eyes, twisting to Erlak again. "For my attempt, I was punished by a whip, dosed with a toxin we call Ki-blocker to prevent healing, but I could still heal. I didn't understand at the time that the blocker works against my ability to funnel Ki, but my Light had learned the skill as well, and my Light was healing me. Because I was still healing, they whipped me until I was drained of magic, and left me to suffer for days."

She faces the table, frowning at those opposite Erlak. "No one was allowed to heal me. I was incapacitated from wounds and pain, and I had been drained of Ki. I had no energy to even move, and so I starved with no way to recover my Ki, and still, for my interference, I was forced to heal myself, or I would continue to suffer."

I grip my fists, taking a deep breath to restrain my Dark from lashing out. That's not how I know the story. It's worse.

She tosses the sugar cube and catches it. "To the point that I don't know what's right, fighting for my brother, despite the fact that his initiation had been rigged by the Assembly to ensure he would fail, was the right thing to do. I would have fought knowing he was doomed because he was begging for his life, and I wouldn't let him face that alone, even knowing what the price would be. Eventually, I learned the truth, that the Assembly knew I was a blend of Light and Magia. They intentionally killed my siblings in their initiation to ensure I would continue my bloodline and provide them with power. I lost my sister and my brother, and their deaths rest on my shoulders. My father learned that truth as well. He learned that I was not his daughter, and his two children had been killed for me, and so I lost my father in a different manner."

Natalia resumes walking along the table at a slow pace, her head low. "When I passed my initiation, I started my training. I began to learn how to use Ki and earn my marks. I reached a level that the Assembly deemed to be enough. I refused to accept that, challenging their right to refuse me from reaching Pinnacle, the highest rank we can achieve. They gave me the right to try, but punished me for that, too."

She stops next to Sterling, still focusing on the sugar cube. "The marks we wear for each skill we learn form a bridge. It helps to channel the Ki. I was refused any marks toward Pinnacle until I proved I could accomplish all skills without the marks first. It made everything twice as difficult. I was given more severe tasks than others to prove I had mastered a skill, then had to present to each member of the Assembly separately when everyone else had to present only once to the Assembly members as a whole. Everything they did was to make it almost impossible for me to reach Pinnacle. You see, I was to be a breeder for them, and they didn't want me to have the knowledge or skill to refuse them or fight back. It wasn't easy, but because I did it, I was able to leave the Magia."

I meet her eyes. "You wouldn't accept the easy way, and it saved me from the afters."

Tony slips into the room through the main door.

Her eyes lower to the sugar cube, and she twists to place it in front of Sterling. "Gathering Shadows is brutal, but there wasn't a thing you threw at me that was as bad as what the Assembly made me do for my last trial to earn all of my marks."

Tony's lazy pace turns brisk as he approaches her. "Tal." She turns to him, and he hugs her. "What did I miss? Why are you talking about your training?"

"I'm answering a question."

I ask, "Where have you been?"

"Ash. She's mourning Pierre and needed a shoulder to cry on, but she's asleep now, and I'm starving. What question?"

I reach for my mate, my Dark wrapping around her and pulling her away from Tony. "Talia, what did they do?"

Tony shakes his head. "Buddy, you don't need to know anything other than it was fucked up. It's enough that I would have refused, skipped out, not done it. I would have settled for the embarrassment of being an heir that couldn't make Pinnacle."

"What did they do?"

Tony runs a hand through his hair. "You're an asshole to make her relive that."

She shrugs, leaning on the table to face me. "They drained me of Ki. I'll spare you the how, but the Assembly already knew a blocker didn't work. When I was drained, they broke my bones and dislocated my joints. Then they all blasted me with Ki at the same time over and over. I had to absorb their Ki and heal to prove I could take in and use the magic of another." Looking away and up, she sighs. "It was unpleasant."

Tony claps his hands together, rubbing them, then turns to face the others. "She's not giving you the details, and you're all ignorant, so let me explain this fucked up shit. First off, absorbing Ki is a lot like trying to catch smoke. It's elusive, not like absorbing Light and Dark. That's like catching a ball. Easy.

"Second, it hurts. It stings and burns like getting set on fire from the inside.

"Third, absorbing magic is easier when it's one at a time. When you get hit with two or three at the same time, it's a lot harder. You're grabbing at the first while getting hit with the second, so you grab for that and let go of the first. When you get hit with two at once, you might try to grab both, and that's like choking and not being able to breathe. It sucks.

"Fourth reason this is so fucked up? You have to center to absorb the magic of another, which is hard to do when you can't move or are in pain. You can't relax or straighten your core to center, so the fact that they broke her body kept her struggling to center."

He takes a deep breath. "And the fifth and most fucked up thing is that trying to heal with someone else's Ki is...difficult. It's— Your soul conflicts with working another soul in that manner. It takes twice as much Ki of another to do what you can do with Ki of your own. So, all the other reasons that made it so hard for her to absorb their Ki, to begin with, were compounded by the fact that she needed twice as much.

"What they did is revolting. They never made me do that to earn my final marks. I just had to find a Seraphinus, steal some of its magic, and show I had it. Plus, she didn't even have the marks that would help her connect the Ki for everything to absorb the magic, which is a sixth reason. They wanted her to fail and tried to make sure she did. That test goes far beyond proving she could intake the magic of another in grotesque abuse."

Natalia hangs her head. "It took me a few tries, but I earned my marks."

"I know, Tal. I can't fucking imagine how much it hurt or how you didn't give up. That you went through it three times... But you have your marks, and it's not because you're a Swan." He rubs his jaw. "Now that I think about it, it's twice as fucked that Ben and the others were always going on that you had your marks just because you're an heiress. Fuck, I'm more of an asshole every time we talk about the Magia."

Natalia walks away, patting Tony on the chest as she steps by him. "Sasha deserved to live, and I'll apologize again that I killed her."

"You didn't kill her," Tony yells as she moves down the hall toward the door. "The Assembly did, trying to force you to have my babies."

She doesn't answer, her head still low as she leaves the hall.

Tony turns to me. "What were you thinking dragging all of that up? Don't ask her about Magia. If you need to know something, ask me. I know more about their workings and how it actually works than she does because of everything they did to her." He sits in an open chair while pointing to Alex. "Don't get any ideas. You're not going through that shit they did to her. You'll earn your marks the traditional way, not regrowing a finger in a rune or holding a shield for one."

Alex goes white. "They made her do those things?"

"Didn't she just tell you?"

"No, she told us about Sasha—"

Tony flinches.

"—Nicky, and just that last bit you heard. She regrew a finger in a rune?"

"They cut it off and watched to time it. I've regrown a few

fingers, it took me a couple of days, and it was the fastest I could stomach it."

Sterling turns to me. "You killed everyone involved with orchestrating all of that already, yes?"

"I'm not sure." I clamp my jaw.

Tony shoves back from the table, leaning over with elbows on his thighs and his face in his hands. "Fucking Mother, what they did to her. The High Assembly would have had something to do with all of that. I don't believe it was just the City Assembly, so when we kill those fucks, they're mine. They killed Sasha, they broke my sister's heart when they killed Nick, and they more than tortured Tal. Fuck those bastards to the burning afters of misery."

Sterling looks to me again. "Did you know all of that?"

"Some, in less detail than that." I pull my mouth to the side in disgust. "Talia doesn't talk about things when it involves emotions, and the Magia are a lot of emotions."

Tony lists his head. "I'm going to throw up." He groans, dropping his face in his hands. "Cal, my family... You still have them waiting in Narwal. Can they be here yet?"

"No."

"They can sign contracts, be useful."

"They will, when things are settled. I have enough problems with Dark and Light; I don't want to add another enemy to the mix. They're safe, and they'll be taken care of in Narwal until then."

Sterling shoves away from the table. "I'm going to find something to punch until I feel better."

Tony says, "If you don't mind me punching back, I'll let you swing at me."

They walk to the side of the room, Sterling's posture stiff.

I rub my face, lifting my voice. "Any other stupid questions or comments about the validity of your Dark King?"

When there's no answer, I look to Hiro. "You wanted to catch up?"

He lifts his chin toward the men. "I want to see this."

Sterling squares up and swings. Tony blocks and counters, and Sterling evades. They exchange a few swings, and Tony spins and kicks, sending Sterling into the wall several feet away.

He hits the floor on all fours and groans. "Gods, you're just as strong as she is."

"The fatum sewed my soul and mended my bones. I am like her."

I scowl, making a note to figure that out later. At least I'm not alone in that puzzle to unravel.

Sterling rubs his chest and gains his feet. "While you kick my ass, I have a few questions."

"What do you want to know?"

"Tal. The Magia."

Tony stretches his neck. "Go for it." He swings, and Sterling blocks. "Tal's shit for talking about things, but I'll tell you."

"How much do you know?"

"A fair bit. Probably not everything. I keep learning all kinds of shit now that we're out. Getting Tal to talk is a trick."

Sterling feigns and jabs. "How do you get her to talk?"

"Vodka." Tony counters, but Sterling dodges past the attack to strike Tony in the face.

I sip my coffee, wincing and laughing as Tony beats on Sterling. I get a much clearer picture of Natalia's life in the answers Tony gives.

Everyone lingers, watching the fight and listening to the details Tony provides. He highlights the differences in her training and his with illuminating clarity. My little star was made to be stubborn, and with every attempt to make her fail, the Magia made her stronger than any other.

CHAPTER 2
CALLAHAN

Hiro follows me into the royal chambers, and I step into the office, inspecting it. Natalia hasn't organized this in the least, but I'll manage it.

I face Hiro, crossing my arms.

He leans against the doorway. "Matteo mated Aurora, Pierre Bordeaux's mate, and conceived a child with her. Pierre killed his mate and your sibling seed before it could be born."

"True."

"Pierre took all the contenders hostage to enact revenge on Matteo. He dosed them with nightmare until they were breathing corpses."

"True."

"You killed them all."

"True."

Hiro rubs his forehead, looking to the floor. "You lied to Lucius that Thames and Jacques didn't know anything about the subtorque, then lied to claim you knew where it was."

"True."

"You lied so Lucius would leave them alone."

"I did it because they were there for my mistake. It was the only thing I could do."

"Lie. You could have let them be tortured."

I grin, sucking air in as my lungs seize. It's like humor stuck in my chest, refusing to release. "I couldn't. I didn't have it in me to not do something, so I lied. It was the only thing I could do to shield them for my failure." I lean back, my smile fading. "Eugene is dead. It wasn't pretty, and it was the first thing Lucius did. I couldn't do anything to stop it, and we had to watch. I couldn't..."

Hiro smiles, meeting my eyes. "You're twice the contractor I've ever been, even without proper contracts in place."

"I have no idea if that's true."

"It is. I won't enlighten others, but I will express my gratitude for your actions that protected my mate."

I incline my head. "I did it for Thames."

"I know." Hiro lifts an eyebrow. "Sterling mated your lightning bug."

Curling my lip, I turn away, searching for a seat. I'm saving face, but I'm crumbling quickly, still hazy and weak. "He did." I drop into the chair behind the desk, legs quivering. "I'm figuring it out."

"If someone else mated Thames, I'd rip their throat out."

I prop my chin. "Thought about it."

Hiro rocks back on his heels. "He's still breathing."

I strum on the desk. I didn't want to kill Sterling when we faced each other in the contest. That hasn't changed.

I'm pissed he mated Natalia. If I set that aside, I want Sterling around. "Last night wasn't awful."

"Sex is sex. I've never understood the preference or care some have for one gender or another."

"Not my issue." I wave my other hand at him. "I don't like sharing my toys with others, or so I thought."

Hiro fights a smile. "Thought?"

"Are you asking me how it was? Because I've done it once, and I was half dead." I fake a grin. "My father and Pierre started this mess because they couldn't share. I'm thinking I'll do it differently, try the other option."

He rubs his mouth, looking up. "If you want Sterling, keep him, but why do it just because of that?"

"The child my father and Aurora conceived was the child of Mallafic and Beenin, destined to unite the Dark and Light. Pierre killed it along with my father and the mate they couldn't share. That's why we're fighting for our lives."

Hiro steps away from the threshold into the room. "I don't understand."

"The child would have been Dark and Light and brought our sides together."

"Then you're the child. Mandolux are Dark and Light. You and Tal are bringing the Seraphinus into one crown."

I open my mouth, then give him a glare of terror. "Fuck no. There have been thousands of other Mandolux. I'm nothing special."

Shrugging, he hums. "I signed with Natalia on the belief that I would be serving you. You're to be the Light Queen."

Pierre's letter flickers in my memory. I stand, doubling over to catch my breath and leaning on the desk. "Give me a fraction." I head for the bathroom, yanking the letter from the front pocket of my soiled pants and returning to the office to throw it on the desk before reclaiming my seat. "All right, go on."

"You will be the Light Queen."

"I will be the Dark Queen, too. Stay signed to her. She needs your support. The contractors are unruly."

"Very well. What is that?"

"Pierre gave this to me right before he shoved me—or maybe Zander dragged me—out of a window and away from the

21

Ancients. He stayed behind to give Zander time to fly high enough that we were free of the Ancients. They don't have wings."

"Useful information."

I bob my head.

"Is that useful?"

I shrug. "I haven't bothered to read it yet."

"Your webs have a sense of humor. You'll share a mate when Matteo and Pierre fought over theirs."

"You've summed up that mess neatly into words." I fiddle with the corner of the envelope, staring at it. "Anything else?"

"Thames requires a contract, but that can wait. You'll want to find your mate. She seemed distressed."

"My Dark is whining like an injured puppy." I rub my temple.

"The mating bond is complicated. My Dark is pissed that we left Thames in bed and are talking to you instead of tending to him."

"Does it get easier to manage?"

Hiro laughs. "No, but you learn to. The benefits are worth the pitfalls."

I lift my eyebrows.

"The mating mark is sensitive. Play with it."

I've heard the mating mark can be played with. I'm waiting to try that still.

"Mm." I fight a grin. "Is that why you marked Thames *there*?"

Hiro's face turns pink as he runs his hand up the back of his neck and then back down, looking to the floor. "I didn't consider the removal of clothing during Gathering Shadows when I did that. It never crossed my mind that everyone would be informed of my decision."

I've seen all the contractors naked at one point or another, most several times over.

The only place players are allowed to shift for games is in the arena. That often means players discard their attire while waiting for the gates to open. New players are always funny to watch at those times. The seasoned contractors have lost all sense of shame, but the new ones squirm and try to hide.

"Go. I'll wrangle Talia to get him signed by the end of the day. Jacques needs a contract, too. He wasn't at breakfast either." I rub my face. "I'll check on him. If someone needs anything in the meantime—"

"I'll fetch Thames and be available."

The room brightens, and we both glance at Zander, shadows cast from his glow.

Adrenaline courses through me. My Dark hisses and wraps around me. I frown, but he steps inside.

"Callahan." He approaches the desk.

As his emittance of Light increases, so does my fear. Every muscle in my body tenses as I go rigid. I try to clamp my jaw tighter as the world pops with bright colors.

Hiro frowns, stepping closer. "Cal?"

I should run. Zander is capable of smiting without warning and without end. I breathe through my nose in short, quick pants, never filling my lungs.

The air hums, brilliant blue sparks filling the air with sharp *zzts* that indicate coming attacks.

Several smites drop, blinding me. I shove away from the desk, flailing for safety. I get under the desk, gaping at nothing.

My pulse skips in my neck with painful jabs. The beating mass in my chest thunks in wild, frantic spasms.

The air in the room is sucked away as bolts of electricity burst in front of me.

Clouds of shadows begin to close around me, the outside being swallowed. The wood and metal contraption around me shrinks, everything going black.

I'm buried alive again.

"Cal!" Hiro's face floats before me. "Cal!" He shakes me, and my brain snaps.

I'm cowering under a desk like an idiot.

Fuck.

Hiro grabs a fistful of my shirt, dragging me into the open air. "Cal?"

I push him away, sitting on the floor. I stare at the toppled chair, everything from it to the bookshelves and walls highlighted with a golden illumination.

I push fingers through my black hair, my scalp damp with sweat. "Fuck."

Hiro balances on the balls of his feet in a crouch. "Nightmare toxin." He smirks. "It takes us all down, every time without fail. That shit works."

I curl my lip. "Define works," I drawl.

"It induces full-blown panic, then provides hallucinations that prey on fears. Between the toxin's ability to trigger the fear response, it screws with the ability to discern reality to leave the victim susceptible to hallucinations. Everything it does is to ensure you're scared out of your mind and increase your terror. The more toxin one is infected with, the worse the symptoms, and with enough nightmare toxin, the heart can be stopped through pure fear." He shrugs and stands.

I glare up at him. "I was being rhetorical."

"You're still high on nightmare."

"Say something useful or get out of my sight."

"Zander is still waiting to speak to you."

I grind my teeth. This detour in my morning was more than humiliating.

Shoving off the floor, I spin to face him. "What do you want?"

He furrows his brow, his lips puckering as he stares at the floor. "How long will it take for the venom to clear?"

Hiro crosses his arms. "Depends on how much he was given.

From what Thames said, my best guess is a day or two more of that," he explains, waving at the chair. "Then another day or two of anxiety."

Zander bobs his head. "Callahan, I offer you my services."

"The fuck does that mean?" I ask. "I thought I already had them."

He makes an attempt to smile, but it's more of a sneer. "When a Light seeks a contract, we offer our services. The responses can vary. However, they usually graciously accept the services offered and provide a contract, or you regrettably decline the services and provide a reasonable explanation, such as no need for another vassal or the vassal's inadequacy. You'll find I have no inadequacies, and I see no other signed to you."

Hiro says, "Arrogant of you."

I lift an eyebrow. "I actually can't find fault in his abilities."

Zander inclines his head. "I am a Fulgur. We are contracted in service to the crown and the trinity heritages for services of protection. It is an honor for my heritage, as we are the strongest of all heritages."

"Then why weren't you the royals?"

"The Light acts as a collective to provide structure and support, all working toward a common goal. We serve the Light best as avengers of the highest rank by protecting those who do rule. It is a high honor of my heritage."

Hiro drags a hand down his face. "The contractors are correct. This is never going to work. Everything different about us conflicts with that statement."

I lean back in my chair. "I expected to drag the Light into the ways of the Dark." Zander narrows his eyes, his face pinching, but I cock a half smile. "I think I need to reconsider."

The Dark isn't collective, we're individuals. We stand and survive on our strength, on our own feet, with the ability to do so. We pursue our desires, taking what we want, not serving another's purposes.

I search the desk, finding a page of ligan pagan, only one of two. "Hiro, find Raz. I'll need ligan pagan. Zander, I accept your offer of service, but it will not be a role strictly as protector. Are you acceptable to a worn contract?"

Hiro leaves, and Zander watches him go. "Was he excused?"

"He has an order."

Lifting an eyebrow, Zander faces me. "The Light does not operate that way, nor does a contractor ask a contracted for input in the contract."

I laugh. "For fuck's sake. That's going to change for the Light. Contracts are negotiated. Both parties will agree to terms."

Zander steps forward, frowning at the desk. "I can choose what I want to offer?"

"You can try. What do you want?"

"I will protect your life. You will not force me to endure you with Natalia in intimacy or acts of adoration."

"You don't dictate a fucking thing about me and my mate."

He lifts his chin, his face hard. "She had accepted me, and yet she returned to you and has now mated you. My affections will change and die in time, but I will not subject myself to suffering."

I study him. Zander is taller than me, with a lean face and long blond hair. It's braided, typical for a Light. I won't be adopting the fashion, Queen of Light or not.

He's not unattractive, with high cheekbones and a strong angle to his jaw. Unlike me, it's not a mask. His face is his face.

Gripping my fist beneath the desk, I say, "Fair enough. You get to walk away any time you want to avoid me with my mate... or Sterling."

"It's abhorrent that you seem to be accepting another mating her. The idea of you two sharing in intimate acts is revolting."

"Then don't think about it." I shrug. "He did it. I can't undo it, and I'd kill him, but then I'd be just like Pierre."

"A high honor if ever you could be."

I stare at Zander, cocking a smirk. "Fuck that. I'm twice the man he is."

Zander turns away, a corner of his mouth pulling down in contemplation. "As he is dead, that claim can be made by most. As for negotiations, I expect twice as much free time, and—"

"Free time?"

"Personal time."

"You're a contracted. Your life and time are mine as I see fit."

"No. By law, a contracted gets at least one rune of personal time a day during the sun's illumination and that which is not to be expended during sleeping runes."

"This is going to be tedious." I point to a chair near the wall. "Sit."

His Light picks up the chair, and he takes a seat. He smiles, running a hand along the armrest. "I'd like to make a request. When you merge the Seraphinus, grant the Light the freedoms of the Dark—allow us to use our Light outside of the arena so long as it's not in combat. My Light has enjoyed the ability to flex and stretch, and I find it useful in tasks."

"Natalia mentioned she had to have complete dominance over her Light and keep it locked within herself."

"That is the way of the Light," he says, lowering his gaze. "I've been around the Dark too long and have grown accustomed to doing differently. Seeing how your Dark stretches and provides use has enticed me and my Light into doing the same."

I scoff. "Natalia's Light about strangled her life in warning it wouldn't accept that when she escaped Izul. Let your Light fucking breathe." I shake my head, flexing my hand as shadows twist around them. "It's cruel to refuse its right to live when it has no choice but to exist within you."

"We are the host, and we are in control. We exercise our dominance instead of allowing the Light within us to be unruly."

"I never thought I'd pity the Light." I snort through my nose in humor. "What a miserable fucking existence it has."

He laughs. "It's awful. My Light has declared it will drag itself from me if I return to stifling it."

"Don't. I'll put it in your contract if you'd like." I shake my head. "I won't be keeping my Dark locked up at any point, and I won't expect a Light to do so either. It may even get stronger at the chance to truly live."

"It's already grown to fill me. Any more growth and it will outgrow me. I doubt the possibility of it becoming much stronger."

"It can't outgrow you." I strum my fingers, muttering, "Poor fucking Glow Webs locked up with stupid hosts."

Zander curls his lips. "A contracted is protected by law from its contractor. We are not property."

I hum. "I can accept that. There are contractors who abuse that law and take it far too literally." I focus on the ligan pagan.

I have a chance to change everything, not just unifying the Dark and Light, but to change the world. It's daunting, my chest sinking into a collapsed sinkhole, but there's a spark of excitement.

"I'll accept you as a protector, but you'll stand as my adviser. I will need to intricately understand the laws and customs of the Light."

"Ash is intending to assist in that manner. She and the rest of the Light are presently in mourning over the death of Pierre."

"Understood. How long is your mourning period?"

"Forty days."

I nod. "The same as the Dark."

Forty days to create life and forty days to mourn it. At least that much will be easily agreed to by both sides. There will be more. We are of the same, despite the hatred.

The forty-day mourning period is a tradition that stretches back to the beginning of our creation and beyond. It's one of the basic ways of life we adopted from the Ancients, like tracking time in runes and the calendar of seasons.

I strum my fingers, considering Zander. He's the only one as tall as Sterling, handsome like Sterling, too, though their features differ. "We don't have forty days. Mourning is a luxury I can't afford. I'll give her four days, then she—"

"You cannot interfere."

"—can mourn when the Ancients have been eliminated." I glare. "We don't have time on our side. I won't be coddling any. Swallow the pain and focus on the problem."

Zander's brow furrows. "The Ancients declared they would allow the time for mourning, as they would be doing the same."

"It's an advantage they granted, and I'll not waste it. Welcome to the Dark. Suck it up, Buttercup. You're getting dragged into a world of survival of the strongest."

He sits back. "There will need to be compromises made."

"At times, yes, but not this one. The Ancients threaten our existence. We use this time to build up numbers and strength to face them."

He shakes his head. "It's a private and personal experience granted by law."

"Fuck the laws we know. We are going to alter the world. Every law, every custom. We tear down the walls and rebuild. No more Dark and Light. We exist in the *ifferentiti*. We become shades and shadows, not two sides of a coin but a single entity. The Light will gain some freedom, and the Dark will have some structure."

"You've lost your mind, drunk on power."

I flash my teeth. "Maybe, or maybe I finally have an imagination." I grin for real, laughing. "We'll start with your contract."

CHAPTER 3

CALLAHAN

Zander lifts his right hand. His features twitch as he stares at his forearm, lines of black magic spelling out his contract. My Dark is stark against his fair skin, spanning from wrist to elbow along his inner arm, intricate to detail his commitments and my agreement to his demands.

He rises, bowing to me. "I appreciate your time and look forward to..."

I lift one eyebrow, waiting.

"...serving..." His long face creases with a forlorn expression.

I point to the door. "Just go. I don't want to break your mind if you have to finish that statement."

With another curt bow, Zander leaves.

I scan the desk. This office is a disaster. Pierre's letter sits on the desk, a neat script spelling my name. He'd shoved it into my pocket right before Zander freed me from Lucius's grasp.

I register that I'm staring at a letter with angst and contempt. It's parchment and ink. It can't hurt me, and I'm capable of turning it to ash.

Pierre has a way of eating his way into my soul like acid.

I tear the parchment open and pull out the contents—several pages folded together. I drag my hand down my face, then read.

Callahan,

Since the day I was born, I carried the name Bordeaux and a seed of its heritage. As a Bordeaux, the expectations of others were immense. I was to act and look as they believed I should, held to standards that, for a very long time, seemed impossible to achieve. The respect I was given was not a jest, nor were the obligations I fulfilled, but allow me to honestly say I was never more than the binds of my rank.

A Bordeaux is a pillar of Light within our society. We are to guide others in our customs and set an example. A Bordeaux helped Renave Lamont bring the Light into a collective society, founding the Light as we know it and bringing the Dark together into a society of its own while forging the Council. My ancestors did this all through a grace and ability I am a representation of and held to. My fates were forged in the very act, the terms and conditions of my life etched into the opal marble of the foundation of the Light from that moment.

I am a Bordeaux, and that comes with responsibility for all of my kind. It's a path I did my best to prepare Ashley for, one I wish could be easier.

I was raised in stature, and, as they say, heavy is the crown. I had a duty to the Light and all my kin, one I saw as an honor and did my best to fulfill in every way. I know well the weight of responsibility and the demands it lays on the shoulders of an individual. It's an imposition as much as a gratifying labor of love.

For nearly two centuries, I struggled to meet the demands my position imparted. Acting in honor is not always easy. It can steal a piece of your soul to turn away from your desires. What I wanted did not always align with the best actions for all, something I am certain, if you are the man I believe you to be, you understand.

When I met Aurora, she understood. She was everything I could ever have hoped for in a partner, in a mate, and I loved her. I loved her more than my seed of Light or my very life. I believed I would have forsaken the Light and my obligations for her if she had asked me to.

Aurora gave me a continuation of my heritage, and for that, I could not be more ebullient. She gave birth to a beautiful baby who grew into a beautiful woman. My daughter and my mate became my world, and the name Bordeaux became a second thought. I was happy.

Aurora's actions decimated my soul. My mate betrayed me. I lost all sense of purpose, of honor, even of the definition of 'man.' My mate had given a piece of herself to another, and to me, that was unforgivable. I could see nothing but the black teeth marks on her skin, and that I had failed for the first time in my life to meet expectations, and they were of my mate.

I broke to my very core.

I saw her act as a defilement of what we were—the Light. I saw Matteo's mark as a symbol of her turning her back on everything I had sacrificed my life for. I saw my mate take another in replacement of me with a radiance of happiness in her eyes.

She spoke words of a seed made of Light and Dark, of a man with a code more rigid than mine, of unity, begging me to accept that I had given my life to honor in vain. I reacted as a beast of Nehil without logic, incapable of understanding. I reacted with violence, ending not only Aurora's life and that of an innocent seed but, ultimately, my life as well. I was no longer the Bordeaux I had been raised to be.

I faced Matteo last. Took him last. When I came, he was unsurprised. It rattled me for my enemy to be so consciously aware. I prided myself on forethought, and here was a man who bested me. In every way, it seemed.

For your father's faults, he offered me a drink. He extended a hand to me, speaking words I would

*not hear. I was deaf, blinded even, with humilia-
tion, pain, and rage. I became the monster I
believed the Dark to be.*

*When you arrived, it goaded my fury. I had been
careful, cautious of everything, and acting as one,
not even implementing vassals to aid me. I'd been
determined that none would know, and I would
incur pain until I felt something, anything at all
beyond the shattered remnants in the wake of our
actions. Had I been a better man, I would have
admitted then that I was impressed by you. I
could not, for that would be giving credence to
what both Aurora and Matteo said, that the Dark
is not what I believed them to be, and giving platitudes to the man who raised you.*

*Callahan, you impressed me that day not only in your
discovery but also in the way you fought. In truth,
I barely survived you, and had I stayed long
enough for you to get up, I doubt I would have.*

*I will refrain from apologies, as is your custom, but
know my actions were based on my own pursuits,
and I lacked the rationality to see the ripples of
pain it would cause. I took a father from a young
boy who so clearly adored his father, and I nearly
left my daughter without hers. Your arrival into
my world of life rattled me, and I returned to Izul
a changed man, but at least a man once more. I
returned to my obligations, finding distraction in
a human I found entertaining much later.*

The webs of fate do seem to have a sense of humor, do they not? When I came to Ilbuio to reclaim a seed of Light, I knew not that you were involved or that the very seed was mine. I was sent by my queen and was diligent in honor of the Light.

Natalia stood as a Light should, with her head high and glowing brightly, but declared herself yours. I knew what had become of Aurora in her dalliance with your kind. I was terrified of what that might do to my daughter, and I would do anything for my daughters, even become a beast once more.

In full disclosure, Aurora died by my hand, but had she not, it would have been a public execution at the order of our Queen. The actions she took would have become public knowledge. Her heritage would have been removed from rank, and her brother, Logan, who is a dear friend of mine, would have suffered for her actions as well. It would have tarnished the Bordeaux name, perhaps causing grievous misery for Ashley, too.

The seeds of Light were sown in rage and hatred to eradicate the seeds of Mallafic. This hatred seems to have been imbued into our very magics, and for far too long, we have been blinded by our own glow. I see that now as we face a common enemy.

In the few days I've spent among the Dark, I have learned more than I ever did viewing from afar. While the Dark is every bit as volatile as I believed on the surface, your society is far more complex than I understood. The individuals are hardened and crude, but there is an affection for that strength of character, allowing logic to dictate your morals. I will not lie, I see it as cruel to be so unfeeling, and yet, my daughter Natalia claims compassion and guidance are at the very heart of it. This I cannot understand.

Sterling told Zander to respect himself more. I reeled at that comment, insulted on behalf of my adoptive son. He is, without doubt, respectable in all ways, and yet, for pouring me a cup of coffee, he appeared degraded in the eyes of the Dark.

I was given respect for a name. You had to earn yours. I had to rise to and uphold the respect given to me while you did the same. Which is worth more, I ask? We are not the same, and yet we both carry responsibility the same, with vigor as we put it first above all else. The difference, I believe, is that although I earn the respect given to me, it is not the same as how you earn respect.

I saw the way yours followed you even when they had been told not to in formal, legal disgrace. I watched carefully as you navigated that decree. Had it been handed to me in the Light, had I been removed from rank, I would have been left without anything. The Dark, however, in a very loud and resounding statement, seemed to ignore the words of your king. Your lineage assets were left untouched, and your servants remained loyal.

It was astounding how much you commanded respect among your peers.

You, Callahan, are an exceptional man, though I may not ever speak those words to you, they are no less true.

After your departure from Ilbuio, I came into possession of a relic that had been lost within its library. It is a journal that I took to Izul as an object of the Light to be immortalized, but it belongs not to the Light nor the Dark. This journal opened my eyes far more than any other act or individual for the secrets it held.

Allow me to be brief in explanation. A Hallow loved a Dark. Your origins are born of love when our two sides attempted to join together, not to face an enemy, but to establish a unification, albeit in limited terms of the Council.

The Mandolux were not made by Mallafic but are kin to both the Light and the Dark, born in myth the same as the Eternums in a blending of our two sides of the whole.

The Hallow was executed as a traitor. The reasons were mere conjecture since his death, though widely acknowledged as a blight upon one of our highest respected heritages. I found the reason in the pages of the journal. Barroco had loved Lenora with passion. He died for it.

It is confounding to think that love warranted an execution, but then I realized I was as guilty as the father who executed his son. The son's only crime was love, and for that, he was deemed a stain upon a legacy. It is abhorrent to know, and that is the true marring upon the Hallow heritage.

This world is said to be made of love, and I believe that. I know firsthand the power love holds. Only a fool like me could think of it as a crime or something to destroy.

Love is precious and should be celebrated. The boy should never have been executed, nor the mother hunted, nor your kind shunned and despised. I never should have acted so rashly with Aurora or Matteo. That I followed in those same footsteps and stood between my daughter and you is, in hindsight, vulgar. My webs might have been very different. The world itself might have changed. Our kind may not be threatened with extinction. My act weaved webs of unfathomable destruction, and it was my hand that sewed these fates.

My daughter, Natalia, has glowed for you. She glowed for you, even believing you were dead with the gifts you sent. They were thoughtful pieces of her that you had known, where I did not. You made her happy, and I was a fool to ignore the truth in it.

My son...

I know the detest you'll have of that phrase from me, but allow me to use it with pride. Take your place in the Bordeaux branches. It is yours. Have care for my daughter. For all the strength she has, she is young and fragile, susceptible to the evils of this world that you and I know well.

You are her mate, and it has taken me more time to realize than I care to admit. I watched her beg for you to be spared, offering herself in your stead to be subjected to incredible suffering without hesitation. In my threats to you, you begged for her benefit, not yours. I see in the two of you a reflection of the love I held for Aurora. It is enormous. Please be mindful to deserve it each day, lest you succumb to my same fate.

Now allow me to set aside the webs of Sirius for those of Soris and what presently is. You exist within the branches of the Hallow heritage. You are the descendant of Barroco Hallow and Lenora Renfaire. The journal has been authenticated in age. It is irrefutable facts that bring clarity to documented history.

You make your choices based on what is rather than blind beliefs. You hold within you the Light and the Dark, not bound by either Mallafic's desires or Beenin's. Even our history did not influence your actions or attitude toward my daughter.

You saw past my daughter's magic to the woman she

is, and you have protected her. I cannot express enough gratitude for that.

You could have destroyed her for possessing the Light in blind hatred, merely ripped the Light from her for your benefit, then discarded the host or used her as a food source without tending to her with care. I am aware of your options and, therefore, your choices for my daughter's loyalty and adoration. Despite every reason for you to abuse her for the Light and my wrongs, you did not, nor did you change your actions when you learned she was my daughter, regardless of your threat to do so.

I know you attempted to reach past my guard to reclaim her. I saw this as the belligerent actions of a man attempting to hurt me. I will admit I was wrong, and again, you have my gratitude for providing my daughter with items she cherishes.

I know not what will be, that is Saris's skill alone, but I beg of you, take your place as a Hallow within the Light's eyes. I give you my blessing to mate Natalia. I offer you the crown of Light as a Hallow. I give these two things to you, knowing the weight of responsibility they will have. I presumed you were a better man than me, but Callahan, you are a Hallow, a heritage that is my better, and without a doubt left in my mind, my better in every way. I have belief in your ability to wear these responsibilities without failure.

You have earned the respect of the Dark and will be given the respect of the Light. You, and you alone, can bring our sides together as one society. Take your place as the Light Queen and union with Natalia to be her Dark Queen. Mate her, as she intends to mate you. Weave the webs of fate in a different direction than I did. Be the man I believe you to be, better than me in every way. Save my kind in a way I never could and prove to them all that you are an alpha.

Brightest regards and highest respects,
Pierre

I TOSS the pages to the desk, glowering at them. "Fine, but fuck you all the same."

Getting up, I go in search of my mate.

CHAPTER 4

NATALIA

I sit, staring at the hysterium tree as wave after wave of memories blur and overlap like a twisting downward spiral in my head.

Cal kept waking in the night, thrashing around. It afforded me little rest between the abrupt jerks to consciousness and the stress of my mate in a tortured condition.

I'm exhausted far more than lack of sleep. I'd stolen the crown of the Dark from Cal, then he'd left me in Sterling's care while he attempted to end the threat from the Magia. The plan had been derailed by the Ancients taking him hostage in an attempt to force me into compliance.

I'd accepted Cal's contract knowing it was against Magia law, and that set off a chain reaction from war to breaking Ness's heart.

She hates me and is now gallivanting around with Mallafic. He'd taken her as a gift to himself, but she doesn't seem to mind.

Someone approaches, my Light yawning. *"Friend."*

Warm hands trail down my upper arms as the man crouches at my back. Sterling says, "I assumed I'd find you here."

I hum, staying on the ground, curled in a ball.

He kisses the back of my head, Dark tendrils sliding around me as he sits, tucking me against him between his bent legs. His arms wrap around my shoulders as he holds me close.

The urge to rip away and move grips me. I'm stuck, torn between the urge and contentment to stay where I am. Being alone is easier.

He asks, "Do you hate them?"

"I don't know if I know what hate is. I don't even hate spiders even though I'm terrified of them."

His lips drag across the top of my shoulder, "You seem fractured."

I sigh, tipping my head back against his shoulder. "Where's Cal?"

Chuckling, Sterling says, "I don't know. He left while I was still in the dining hall, swinging at Tony to work off my rage. Tony is as difficult as you to inflict punishment on. He put me down more times than you." He nips the shell of my ear. "You weren't trying, though."

"No."

"I asked a lot of questions. He had a lot of answers, except one. I showed up at the restaurant to collect you with the others seeking to do the same. Tony says you'd already negotiated a contract at that point, but Cal was there with the same intentions I had. Why?"

"Because we negotiated, and I refused to accept the contract."

"Why?"

The breeze sends the branches of the tree dancing, several loose petals falling to the ground, the sweet scent wafting across my senses.

I close my eyes, whispering, "If I took a contract, I knew I could never go back. It was uncomfortable to think about. If you hadn't all shown up, if Tony, his mom and mine hadn't been pushing so hard for me to be something I'm not... For the first time, I tried to do what I thought was the right thing instead of doing what I wanted, so I refused the contract. But when everything pushed too hard, I did what I always do. I made a mess of what I wanted instead of what anyone else wanted or needed. I cracked under the pressure and put myself first."

He grins against my neck. "Such a beautiful, selfish asshole."

I laugh. "You should have met my sister, Sasha. No one looked twice at me when I stood next to her."

"I doubt that." His Dark tightens around me as he rumbles with a delicious growl. He runs his nose along my skin, inhaling deeply. "When I started to pay attention to you at Gathering Shadows, I began to drool. I wanted you. I wanted to use you in every way, to know what you looked like glowing in the Dark, all of you on display for my use."

I roll my eyes. "You Dark have a sick fetish for the Light."

He bursts with laughter, leaning back to howl. When he curls into me again, he shakes with humor. "What's more arousing than something that will kill you?"

"Everything."

"Mm, there's something about fucking your enemy that's delicious. There's a little hate in the sex, a little torment with your pleasure, a little fear with your desire. A little bit of knowing you shouldn't, but it's so irresistible that it entices you." He bites my shoulder, pressing his teeth into me with a sharp sting. "The forbidden desire seems to make the pleasure that much sweeter, and the danger of it makes it more exciting."

I smirk. "You're weird. I just want something attractive to look at."

"Letting my Dark wrap around you, the danger in letting it tie you up and expose you, isn't enjoyable?"

I swallow and shift, my Light panting in my head. *"Tell him you need a demonstration."*

Laughing, I say, "That's so wrong."

"What?"

"My Light said we need a demonstration to decide, but he sounds like Cal, so it was like hearing Cal turned on by you."

Sterling laughs. "Speaking of a little bit of hate in the sex, I'm jealous of him, and I had to look at him naked last night. His body is perfect."

We chuckle together, and I snuggle into him. "It really is."

"Fucking Barracos are bloody impossible to compete with, even if they screw up everything." Sterling moves, pulling me to my feet. "Let's agree to not tell him he turns me on. He's already insufferably arrogant, and I can't find a reason to contradict his ego as it is."

"He's too serious."

"Ah, yes, being serious. It does nothing to ruin the pretty face and cut muscles or make him weak. How foolish of me to disregard it." Sterling pulls me against him, swaying.

I giggle, letting him turn us in circles. "He doesn't explain anything, ever."

"It's frustrating that he knows everything and is never wrong."

"He's really impressive."

"Mm, yes. I hate that." He spins me away and pulls me back against him with a grin. "I don't stand a chance at sharing your heart, but I'll settle for your bed."

I stop smiling, looking away.

He presses his mouth to my ear. "My little wicked, burning firefly has a heart of ice."

"It's difficult for me, sharing parts of me. His contract almost killed me because I wouldn't."

Sterling frowns. "You're too stubborn for your own good."

"Cal dug my heart out of me that night, and it's been his ever since."

"Then I'll see what I can do." Sterling takes my hand and twirls me, grinning. "I was watching you earlier."

"Me?"

He draws me in, my back to his chest. His arm slips around my waist, holding me close as he sways. "Yes, you. I watched you with Cal."

"And?"

"It's adorable the way you become childlike, all wide-eyed and sweet when you're with him." His mouth grazes my ear, his voice lower. "Why are you never like that with me?"

Cal steps in front of us, facing me. "She knows who her alpha is." He extends his hand.

I take it. Instead of pulling me away from Sterling, he steps closer, tilting my chin up with a finger. His lips curve as he lowers his head and kisses me.

Sterling chuckles, kissing along my neck, his arms slipping away for his hands to grip my waist as Cal presses against me to deepen the kiss.

My heart throbs, and the walls I've built that were already crumbling dissolve away. I never thought I'd have a love that was mine. I believed I'd be married to Tony, who would always love Sasha. I didn't expect I'd have someone who saw me instead of her, and when I gave Cal my heart, I thought I was a fool, not an equal, just his toy to be owned and used as I pined away like a silly girl.

Standing between them, pinned from both sides, my heart cracks and grows in the freedom of my chest. Cal loves me. He and Sterling both mated me and mated me for me, not a bloodline, a baby, or a use.

Love.

I can't breathe, dizzy from the overwhelming adoration.

47

Pulling away from Cal's mouth, I press my face to his chest and sob.

He wraps his arms around my neck and head, holding me tight as cool strands of Dark lash tighter around me. Sterling shifts closer, pressing me tighter between them as I cry.

Sterling whispers, "I think we broke our mate."

Cal's chest rumbles. "I don't know what we did."

"Is she usually this emotional?"

"No."

I sniffle, trying to catch my breath. Sterling massages my shoulders, Cal dropping his hands to my hips.

Cal presses his lips to my head. "Little Star, what did we do?"

I blink, trying to push away. They both flex and shift to keep me between them. I manage to get a hand on my face, wiping my cheeks. "Nothing."

Sterling says, "No lying, Firefly."

I sigh. "I'm not lying. You didn't do anything."

"We did something."

I rest my forehead against Cal's chest. He chuckles. "I can find other ways besides a contract to make you talk."

Sterling opens his mouth against my neck and drags his teeth across the thin skin, making me shudder. "It'll involve fewer clothes and a lot more begging."

Clearing my throat, I shove and wiggle my way to freedom, turning my back on both of them and rubbing my tight eyes. "You both mated me," I say. "Not just one, but two."

Sterling says, "Oh, it's my fault. Me, not we."

"I can rip his throat out."

I choke on a laugh, turning to face them—Cal glaring as Sterling moves back with a grin and his hands up.

Smiling, I shake my head. "No, it's both of you. I—Sasha was the perfect one, not me. I never had much interest from men."

Cal lifts an eyebrow, but Sterling says, "That has to be a fucking lie."

I hold my hands up. "There were a few, but not like all the men falling over themselves for my sister." I shrug. "Then I got engaged to Tony, and I thought that was it. I didn't think I'd ever have someone of my own, and now there are two of you." I fling my hand at them.

Cal smirks. "If you don't want two, I'll send one to the afters."

Sterling laughs. "Please want two."

"It just... It just hit me that..."

Cal closes in on me, his Dark wrapping around me to keep me from stepping further away, and he yanks me into him. "You're free." He lifts my chin, kissing the tip of my nose. "They can't hurt you anymore."

"Stay," I whisper.

"The beautiful lie you gave yourself." He squeezes my hips.

My Light winds around him, tangling with his Dark. It whines in my head, terrified his love will leave again.

I reach for him, pressing my palms to his chest, pushing to feel him push back, leaning into my force with an equal strength of his own. It's everything I need: a partner in this world who can stand by my side and fight with me. The power exuding from his core courses from him into my hands and through my arms, a subtle stream of similis threading into me and back to him, weaving us together as a sweet agony searing my soul to meld it with his.

The branches of the hysterium sway around us, everything falling away until there is him and him alone.

Cal's grip on my waist tightens. "You don't need it anymore, but I promise you I will stay."

I can't blink, can't take my eyes off his. Everything in me is screaming brighter than ever, my Light winding with his Dark, tying us together as a second heartbeat echoes in my ears.

49

He tips my head back, crushing his mouth to mine as he holds my face. A fire burns through me as I give him my whole heart, every cracked inch of it. It's fragile, but he won't drop it. He'll keep it wrapped in his Dark like the rest of me.

Pulling back, I smile. "I wanted love. I wanted someone to see me, really see me for me, not babies or a bloodline or as a use, and they robbed me of that."

Sterling stands at Cal's back, off to the side, and rests his chin on Cal's shoulder as he smiles at me. "Firefly, you're wrong. They gave you love. They trained you, which let you save Cal and be his partner in the games, his weapon in the contest, and hold the crown of Dark."

Cal lifts an eyebrow. "They gave you to me with every decision they made."

"And this idiot," Sterling says with a laugh, "gave you to me for just long enough..." He steps next to us, tucking hair behind my ear and pressing his curved mouth to my cheek.

Cal shoves him with a hand to his chest. "Go away." Sterling and I laugh together, but Cal says, "Talia, what you said this morning... I have one question. I thought your mother healed you after the Assembly punished you. Vanessa said so."

I wince. "I lied to her. My mother gave me the antidote for the Ki blocker. I knew Ness had tried to heal me, and I was under orders to heal myself. I knew Ness would have tried, possibly pulling too much on her spirit in any attempt, given how much damage they did. And if the Assembly found out, she would have been put to death. I lied to her that my mother had healed me, but that's why I made it forty days without food to create the Ki-cha. I told her that it was vodka, so I didn't have to explain to her what I'd done."

Sterling slides his arm around me, pulling me from Cal and off my feet as he spins me in circles, "Lying Little Firefly." I shriek with laughter as he sets me down, shaking his head. "What an absolute disgrace you are to the Dark."

Cal says, "What happens away from society and the crown is at contractor law discretion. Natalia wasn't even part of Dark society at that time and cannot be held liable for her actions then."

"Yes, I see what you mean. He's so serious all the time." Sterling shakes his head as I giggle.

Cal holds out his hand. "Come with me, Little Star." I accept his hand, lacing my fingers into his. Puckering his lips, Cal says, "You too, baby."

Sterling laughs, jumping at Cal and clinging to his side, arms around Cal's neck and his legs bent to cling to Cal's hips. "Where are we going?"

Cal turns his head, glaring at Sterling. "You can walk."

Sterling jerks his head forward and kisses Cal. I widen my eyes, struggling to not laugh as I hold my breath. Cal's eyes are wide as he stares at Sterling, whose eyes are closed with much more feeling in the lip-lock.

Sterling pulls back with a wide grin. Cal sighs. "I'll fuck you into submission later. Right now, get off me. Talia has to sign contracts, and we have work to do."

CHAPTER 5
CALLAHAN

I flex my hand, opening and closing it to watch my skin flex and wrinkle. My Dark spells Jacques's contract on the back of my right hand.

Respect and protect. Answer my questions. Jacques Daniel Sarpa.

I hug Natalia closer. "I need you to do something."

"*Mhm.*" She rolls and straddles me, sliding her arms around my neck and kissing me.

Not what I had in mind, but I'll enjoy this before tackling responsibilities.

I deepen the kiss, cupping her jaw and tilting her hand as I lick along her tongue. Need begins to throb in me.

She leans back, rocking on my growing erection. "You can do anything you want to me."

I grin, keeping my mouth closed as I laugh behind my lips. My little star knows she belongs on my cock. It's the perfect place for her.

Sterling drops on the couch next to us with a hard expulsion of air. "What are we doing?"

I look to him. "Do I need to find you something shiny to entertain yourself with?"

"You seem frustrated. Too much energy? Do I need to take you for a walk?"

"Should I request worms for your meal tonight?"

Sterling scratches at the side of his neck. "I prefer fish. When do we have to give you your flea medicine?"

I laugh. "You fucking dick. I don't have fleas."

He reaches over and pats my head. "I know, that's because you're a good boy, and take your medicine."

I shove him to the side. "Go eat rocks."

"I'm good on gizzard stones."

Natalia looks between us with her lips folded between her teeth. Her eyes opened wide.

Sterling chuckles, reaching over to put his hand on her jaw, yanking her sideways to kiss her.

I'm not sure I can handle not ripping his head off.

She pushes away in a hurry, ducking her head.

He chuckles. "So shiny."

I gave a glowing woman to a bird. No wonder he's fascinated.

Squeezing her thighs in my hands, I lift my chin at the wall. "Think I can knock that down?"

He considers it, tilting his head. "Probably. Want help?"

"Later. I need to know what has been going on."

"Did you sign the union contract?"

Cutting my eyes at him, I answer curtly. "No."

He lifts his eyebrows, excited. "Oh? Firefly, why?"

She rests her hand on my chest, stroking me with a finger and talking to my stomach. "Not my fault. I didn't do anything this time."

I say, "I went to draft it, but union contracts, as I know them, contract one to the other. I can't be subservient, and neither can she. I'm deliberating."

"Fair enough." He rubs his nose between his eyes. "Gods, how do we do that?"

"We?"

He rolls forward, snaking an arm between Natalia and me to drag her between us. She goes limp, and I growl at Sterling.

Laughing, he tucks her between us. "Mallafic took Ness."

"Why?"

"We don't know. You saw the Dark's lack of adoration for their king," he sighs. "Jakobo challenged her before she ever touched the crown."

I shift, angling toward Natalia. She leans into me, rubbing her nose against my chest. "Did she refuse that challenge too?"

"No. It was quick, and she didn't set him on fire or use her Magia skill to wield his Dark."

I kiss her forehead. "Good girl."

She hums, and Sterling gets closer, mirroring my pose with a hand on her hip. "The hysterium tree. We need the crystals from it. We haven't determined how to do that yet."

"It's a vine." I press my mouth to the top of Natalia's head.

Sterling says, "I am the center of gravity and reside in depravity, in with thieves and thrive."

I lift my head and stare with confusion.

He shrugs. "I thought we were giving less than helpful answers."

I will not laugh at that.

I chuckle, but I'm pissed that I do. "What else?"

"Eloise is dead."

That catches my full attention. "How?"

"Mallafic."

Natalia nestles in. "He's a dick."

Sterling snickers. His features stick, and then he hangs his head. He pulls her away from me, the touch of her skin to mine, the warmth of her gone. I rumble and reach for her.

He shifts closer, with her in his lap. It brings her to the edge of my senses, my Dark brushing against her in tendrils to stroke her neck and stomach. It's better than out of reach, but I want her on top of me.

I'm tempted to rip his head off again.

She makes an attempt to move, and he tightens his arms around her. "You need to tell him what you did."

Her head tilts, and then her features go lax as the color fades from her cheeks.

As much as I adore my mate, she's unpredictable and wild, disregarding rules and logic. I thought she learned her lesson when I wrangled her into behaving once.

It didn't stick. I told her to stay on the steps. She took the crown of Dark.

"What did you do?"

She wiggles away from me, further into Sterling as she speaks to him. "You were pissed. He's going to be beyond pissed."

He taps her nose. "I'll protect you. That's why I pulled you away from him."

I raise one eyebrow. "That's why?"

He holds my gaze, the lines of his face drawn. "I'm sharing."

The urge to get my claws out and rip him to shreds grips me. My Dark tightens around me with greed. We don't share. We don't have to. We are an alpha; we take what we want, and what we want is our mate to ourselves.

Flexing my shoulders back, I ask again, "What did you do, Talia?"

She winces, looking to Sterling with big, pleading eyes.

He sighs. "Tell him."

Her throat works as she swallows and turns to me. "You know how I'm stupid and stubborn?"

I hold her gaze, waiting.

"I yelled at Pierre."

I cock my jaw, waiting.

"Um..." She takes a deep breath, her breasts rising while she rolls her eyes to the top of her head. "I yelled at him about what he did, killing his mate and the baby she was going to have with your father. Lucius says it was the child of Mallafic and Beenin. It's what brought the Ancients back, and when he realized Pierre killed the child, he decided to destroy the Seraphinus because not even fate could make them exist in peace."

I almost laugh, the tension in my neck and shoulders subsiding. "That's all?"

Sterling shakes his head, and Natalia winces.

"I was so pissed," she whispers, her voice turning fragile. "Lucius told me all that and that he had you, that he was going to hurt you until I gave him the subtorque. Pierre had already hurt you—he killed your father—and it was his fault that Lucius was seeking to destroy the seeds and was hurting you. It was all Pierre's fault, and I screamed at him as soon as I saw him."

I reach for her across Sterling, shifting closer with my shoulder pressed to Sterling's. I cup her face, smiling. "You're protective of me."

My mate is rash, slamming into immovable objects in stubborn stupidity while ignoring logic to go around. It would be less desirable if she didn't manage to move what she wanted in impossible ways.

Sterling says, "She did it in front of the contractors."

The adoration and softness in me vanish as fast as a candle flame can be extinguished. I go rigid against the urge to break something.

Sterling chuckles. "Beyond pissed doesn't cover it, Firefly." He drops his head back on the couch. "She didn't say much, just Pierre killed his mate because of his hatred of the Dark, but I know how to put the pieces together."

The secret I had for centuries is slipping from where I buried it. I told Natalia. I told Sterling. I told Jacques, and Thames heard it all thanks to Pierre. Hiro knows. I don't know how long I have before word spreads.

It's eaten its way through the cage, demanding to be known. I've swallowed the guilt, the nightmares and the pain for too long. I trusted Natalia, regurgitating the truth for the first time in my life.

Sterling keeps blathering. "You needed to know if anyone makes inquiries. Oh, and I informed Hiro. That's on me. I fucked up."

I assumed Thames informed him. Perspiration collects on the nape of my neck. "I'm fucked."

Natalia mewls, scrambling across Sterling and throwing her arms around my neck, clinging to me.

She did it. She drafted the death warrant, and now she cries.

I turn my head away, showing my teeth in a silent snarl. Natalia didn't care about the threat to me, my life, and my existence in this world. She doesn't care about me.

My own mate betrayed my trust, handing out my secret. She'll leave me for Zander, for Sterling. One of them will get her heart.

The world blinks in and out of focus, stars dancing in the air with mockery.

Sterling curses, "Fuck."

In one swift move, Sterling spins, straddling me at Natalia's back, pinning her in my lap between us.

"Get the fuck off me."

"No," he says, shifting closer. "Hold him, Firefly. Cal, breathe. None of us is going to expose you."

"My mate did. My fucking mate—"

He reaches around her, wrapping his hand around my throat.

I think he's going to squeeze, cut off my airway, or dig talons into the soft flesh. I thrash.

"Cal, stop." His long fingers rest against my skin, his palm a gentle pressure. He's holding me, protecting a soft, weak, sensitive spot on my body. The place an executioner will slice open for all my faults and wrongs.

Natalia asks, "What's wrong?"

"He's fucking dosed on nightmare."

I'm back in the cage, the glow of Pierre's Light stinging my eyes as he gloats. He didn't kill them. I did.

"What? When?"

"Pierre dosed him for days. It's still in his system."

"It didn't last this long for me."

"You barely got infected by Marius and Basileus. Not like him. You don't have fear like us. You don't know what it does to you. The maze, the games, the laws that let anyone challenge you, the hatred the Light has for you, and being hunted like animals. You have no idea what fear is. Cal, can you hear me? She exposed Pierre, not you. He's dead, and you are the Queen of Light. This can't hurt you anymore."

"I killed my father. I did it. I pulled the blade across his throat. All of them."

Natalia shakes her head. "It's Pierre's fault, babe."

"It doesn't matter," I bellow, clenching my stomach. "I did it. I fucking did it. I murdered my father...the contestants. I did it. I killed them." My words come out thick, warped by the blockage in my throat.

Sterling uses gentle pressure, guarding the open side of my neck with one hand and using the other to force Natalia into me. "I know."

"I..." I croak, "I did it, but I couldn't kill P—Pierre. I held something I couldn't take rightfully. I shouldn't have ever had this life."

Sterling shifts, sitting on my thighs and leaning into Natalia, their weight compressing me into the couch.

I put my hands on Natalia's shoulders, ready to push them away.

I can't hold this down or in or out of sight. I can't stand on my own. I shouldn't have ever been a contractor.

I fall, a pit yawning open beneath me. I've always stood in a house built of sand and debris I used to bury the truth of what I'd done. It's shifting and crumbling.

All my arrogant belief in myself, I used to hold it together, that I'd been in the right, that I'd deserved what I took, dissolves. The construct can't hold itself together without the insistent delusion.

Sterling grabs my wrists, his Dark lashing around me and binding Natalia into me harder. "Pierre and Lucius really fucked you up."

"I'm not..." I'm too weak to even confess that I'm not the man anyone thinks.

"Those of us who know the truth do not care."

"I don't deserve—"

"Shut the fuck up, you pretty, perfect bastard." His voice is edged. "I have too much gods' damned respect for you to look me in the eye and lie to me."

I swallow, trembling with stinging eyes. I killed my father and took everything from him. I wasn't entitled to it. I destroyed it and sent my sister to the afters because she saw the facts before I could.

Relaxing, Sterling's shoulders drop, and his grip eases as he wraps my arms around Natalia, telling me, "Hold her. Hold your mate. She's got your blind spot and your back, probably your front, too, and if you ask real nice, I'd wager she'd cover your cock." Sterling grins with a wink.

"I do," Natalia says, burrowing into me. "I have you covered, babe." She nestles closer, her nose against my collarbone. The warmth of her breath tickles my skin, hot ropes slithering across my skin, under my shirt.

Sterling presses his hands to my shoulders, forcing me into the cushions. "You're still dealing with the nightmare venom. It's fucking with your head. I don't give a fuck about the law. You deserved to inherit everything. You've proven that. You command others with your mere presence. I was fighting to keep them from revolting. They threatened to if I didn't challenge Tal. You told them to, and they didn't. Fuck you."

I choke, like a laugh that I can't find a reason for.

"You're stronger than any of us, and we fucking hate you because we can't beat you. We are the Dark, and we are pack creatures. We know an alpha when it stands before us. It's instinct."

My eyes burn. My throat clogs. I blink, unable to look away.

Everything is frayed. My standing in society, my ability to be a contractor or even act as an alpha, shielding and guiding others, is all coming apart. The grip I have on who I am is slipping.

My father was right, I am nothing like him. I don't even know who I am anymore.

"I killed my father and stole his life. I told lies to Lucius. I've shown weakness."

Sterling sighs, trying to smile with one side of his face. "You lied to protect Jacques and Thames, not for your benefit. You spared your father, my uncle, and the others from further misery. You have never, not once, been weak in my eyes." He glides his hand to the back of my neck, guiding my head forward. "Hold your mate and trust in those of us willing to follow you."

I turn my face into Natalia, inhaling the scent of hysterium and starlight. "She almost condemned me to death."

She grips my shirt, tugging as the strands of her Light tighten around me. "I didn't mean to. I didn't think. I was so mad, and I knew you were being hurt because of him. *Again.* Do you have any idea what that does to me? It's like my lungs are full of sand and water, and I've been stabbed in the heart."

I believe she screamed at Pierre. I'm more shocked she didn't draw blood or attack him.

The problem isn't that she yelled, it's who heard. She goes blind when she's made up her mind. It was a lack of conscious thought, not callous disregard. I need to break that habit.

Sterling says, "He left soon after she did it. I thought she risked the alliance between our kind. It's a safe assumption that what she did spurned Pierre's actions."

Solid ground is coming back, the world no longer streaking colors and whirling around me.

One question is unresolved, though.

Sterling mated her. He covets my star and claimed her, marring my mating mark with his. My actions can get me executed, and he knows, yet hasn't revealed the information.

I look to him. "Why were you pissed?"

He laughs. "That's not obvious?"

"I'd be sent to the afters."

Natalia tightens around me. "No."

He chuckles, hanging his head. "Why the fuck would I want that?"

He knows. I won't dignify that with a response. With me in the afters, Natalia would be his and his alone.

It tempts me to be like Pierre, to kill the one who dared to steal my mate from me.

Running his hand across the top of my shoulder to my neck, he says, "I really need to educate you on the definition of sharing, baby."

Jacques skips into view, halting a few paces into the room. "Group hug, or am I interrupting foreplay?"

I try to sit up, but I'm too weak to lift the two on top of me to accomplish the task. "What do you want?"

"Well, I'd really love to have that brilliant beauty on her knees with her mouth around my cock."

"Pick something I can manage to do."

Jacques closes one eye, tipping his head to the side as he surveys us. "You know, I think I owe your lightning bug appreciation for letting me live. Between you and Sterling, I knew I was going to die in the contest."

Sterling laughs. "You and me both. We all were. Mallafic had decided Cal would be the Dark King before it ever began."

I gape. Jacques opens his mouth to the fullest, his jaw hanging low.

Natalia nods against me. "That's true. Mallafic told me."

Jacques recovers. "Then I really need to show my appreciation. Can I put her on her knees to—"

Sterling whirls to his feet, claws out as he slashes at Jacques.

Jacques evades and laughs. "No? Fine, fine." He straightens his shirt, holding his hands up to ward away Sterling with a watchful gaze. "Down, birdie. My kind eat yours."

Sterling moves between Jacques and me and my mate, his back to us. "Back off. She's our mate, and you don't get to fucking sink your fangs in her, snake."

"Third choice it is. I bring you to dinner with the contractors."

"Try again. Cal's in no condition to be dealing with them. He's still flushing that nightmare shit from his system."

Jacques leans around Sterling, scrunching his face. "I'd kill that Glow Fuck if he weren't already dead." He looks to the floor, rubbing his forehead. "I'll deal with the pricks in the dining hall, then. They're all gathering to yell or something. I'll take it."

Natalia shoves up, getting to her feet and adjusting her clothes. "I'll go."

62

I try to stand, floundering and collapsing. She helps me sit, a hand to my jaw. "Stay down, babe."

"No."

She wrinkles her nose. "I'll just listen."

"No, you won't."

Sterling steps next to her. "I'll go." He pivots to her. "Stay with him, Firefly. He needs you."

I roll and tense my core, gritting my teeth as I manage to stand. "I can—"

"Can, but don't have to. Perks of sharing." Sterling shrugs, turning to Jacques. "You and me, let's go."

CHAPTER 6
CALLAHAN

IST HOPE'S DAY, BLOOMING, 4050, 6TH MILLENNIUM

Rotting, damp wood splinters into my fingers as I claw for freedom. There's not enough room for me to shift, but I break my fingers, turning them into claws that cleave and chip away at the wood. Dirt rains down on my face, and a worm falls into my mouth.

It slips and squirms against the back of my throat and along my tongue. I choke and gasp, coughing as I try to dislodge it.

I sit up, spitting it out, panting for air. The world is dim, my Dark curling around me and quivering.

Pulling my knees to my chest, arms braced on my knees, I hang my head, trying to catch my breath.

It was a nightmare-induced memory. Nothing more.

From the shadows, Sterling whispers, "Cal?"

I swallow, my throat as gritty as my tongue. "Go back to sleep."

I'm not even sure I know why he's in this bed. He'd gone to dinner with Jacques.

I'd gotten enough mettle to carry Natalia to bed. With her

64

close, her silver shine present from her Light twisted around me, I'd found security and calm enough to rest.

He wasn't here when I passed out.

"Why are you here?"

"Mate."

"I won't kill you, but you're pushing it."

He chuckles, rising to adopt my pose. "We all have nightmares."

"Shut up."

"I don't answer to you."

"You answer to Talia. She's my mate. You answer to me like her."

He chuckles. "You'd think."

"What is your contract?"

Sterling shifts, shaking his head. "Serve the Dark. I don't answer to her, ergo, I don't answer to you either."

He doesn't answer to anyone. I'll fix that with everything else. Natalia will rearrange that contract into proper adherence. Sterling took advantage of my absence.

"That comes to an end now."

"Piss off. She's my contractor."

"She gave you an illegal contract."

"You're the last individual who gets to lecture me on what's legal."

Curling my lip, I glare into the room before me. "Shut up. Go away."

"No. I'm not sleeping on a couch. We've both done things that aren't legal because the law was wrong for the circumstances. We did what was right even if it was illegal."

"You have a room."

"Jacques took it."

I turn my head, opening my mouth.

He chuckles. "I'll move my things in tomorrow."

"No."

"Yes."

I look around, then tip my head back, gripping my wrist in my hand to lock my arms together. "The fuck are you doing?"

"Sharing." Dark snakes around me and tugs as he tells me, "Lie down."

I lower to my back, but the Dark yanks on me, rolling me to my side. I face Natalia, at peace in sleep.

Reaching toward her, I hover my hand over her face. She's beautiful, her silver hair falling about her head and shoulders.

He lies on her other side, propped up on one arm. "Go to sleep. I'll watch over you."

I grumble, squeezing my eyes shut. "Can't."

"What's at the end of a rainbow?"

I stare at him. "What?"

"What's at—"

"I heard you. I'm starting to think you're mad."

"No."

I can't sleep, adrenaline coursing through my veins. "What is that, a riddle?"

"Yes."

I groan. There are a few myths about the colorful streaks in storms. I can't recall a single one. "No idea."

"The letter 'W.'"

I go back through the riddle and glare at him. "Fucking, really?"

"What word do we always spell wrong?"

"I don't know."

"Wrong."

Staring at him, I say, "I hate this game."

He snickers. "The contractors were loud. Gave me a headache."

"What do they want?"

"Natalia's head and separation from the Light."

"No."

"I said as much. I told them to challenge her and take the crown if they wanted it. Otherwise, they could all be silent. Things got a lot quieter."

"Should have done that the first time."

He smiles, displaying dazzling white teeth. I've always searched for that grin on bad days during the games of Gathering Shadows. I counted on it. It's a great smile, and it—he—brings me comfort.

Natalia murmurs and shifts, wiggling closer to me.

He strokes her head, collecting her hair and twisting the strands before setting them at the back of her neck. "Fire," he whispers. "It scares me, and yet, I'm in bed with two that can conjure it."

I've run into him in the maze dozens of times. It's agony when I do. It's always on fire, the whole cursed thing.

"I've never asked, but I'm curious. Does it start burning the moment you enter and never stop?"

"Mm, pretty much. If you can't sleep and don't want riddles, we can always wake her up."

I grumble, but it's better than any idea I have. "Why are you awake?"

"We all get nightmares."

I find his eyes and hold his gaze. I didn't wake him. He was already awake.

"Fire?"

"You would think. I watched a Light murder my father, then it gave me this." He points to his neck, the gray scar on the left. "It was Caligo, a Firebringer. Burned my father alive."

"Talia is Caligo."

"I remarked on the irony of that already." He stares over me, out across the windows at my back.

Moonlight washes across his face, the features highlighted. His ropey locks are loose around his head, his brown skin stretched tight over muscles carved in the illumination. It's eerie to stare at a man who's handsome and ripe with strength and know he's afraid.

He asks, "Dreaming of an execution?"

"Buried alive."

He focuses on me, eyebrows coming together. "The games, our way of life, it makes us strong." He sighs. "It can be as barbaric as the Light says it is. You killed your sister. I killed my brother."

The Dark erases tenderness and softness to eliminate weakness. It tears apart men and women to rebuild them with stone hearts and thick skin, prioritizing strength and logic over emotion or kindness.

I dip my chin, lowering my face toward Natalia. "We bring the two together. We'll keep the best and hope to be rid of the worst."

"I need a lineage seed, but I never wanted to bring one into this society."

I hum. "You get my mate pregnant with your fucking seed, and I will rip it out of her and make you fucking eat it."

He sighs, rolling to his back and goes silent.

"You mated my mate, asshole."

He sits up and looks to me, his features weighted low. His full mouth is turned down at the corners.

I stare back without mercy. Natalia isn't fond of the idea of having children. I won't force her to endure any but mine, and even then, when she does, I'll be on my knees to praise her and appreciate her for the deed.

Sterling shakes his head, twisting away to slide off the side of the bed to his feet.

He takes two steps toward the door.

"Where are you going?" I whisper in a harsh expulsion of air.

"You told me to leave." He exits the room.

I assume to find a couch. The door in the front of the chamber clicks closed.

He didn't leave the room to find a couch; he left the royal suite.

My stomach turns rancid, acidic breath in the back of my throat. I didn't want him to go that far.

Fuming, I roll off the bed and stalk to the front door. I open it and search the hallway. Sterling is absent.

I'm not putting in that much effort to chase after him if I have to seek and find him first. Closing the door again, I turn my back to it, crossing my arms as I lean my shoulders against it.

I wanted him to go away, yes. Another room, at most. I want him to stop touching my mate. I did not want him gone.

I glare at the stone beneath my feet. Conflicting desires yank on me. I can't decide what I want, so I don't.

I return to bed and lie next to my mate, watching her sleep, trying to ignore the guilt and nagging sense that I miss him on Natalia's other side.

CHAPTER 7

CALLAHAN

I'm exhausted, my eyes tight and hard to keep open as I sit at the head of the table. Natalia sits in the chair next to mine, Sterling still absent.

I've been back for over a day, and I have accomplished little. Lucius said he'd take time to mourn. It's an advantage I don't intend to waste.

Hiro and Thames are nestled close, Hiro keeping his arm around Thames. They sit first on Natalia's side. On my side, Jacques glowers at Zander, sitting next to him but tilting away.

Tony and Ashley are both absent again.

Falsion meets my gaze on Thames's other side. I haven't managed to have a conversation with him yet. Shame fills me.

"Galain..." I clear my throat.

"Tarlwin didn't come back."

"No."

He bobs his head. "I've deduced the fact."

I cost the life of my kin, stealing a brother who survived for centuries despite the odds. I did it.

Galain inclines his head. "We followed you. He made his choices."

I swallow hard. I made the mistake of bringing them here, beckoning Tarlwin to his death.

Galain speaks to Fallon, who slips from his chair and hurries to me, throwing himself at me. Trying to hug me with his whole tiny body, he looks up at me with a wide, beaming smile. "Uncle Cal, I ate the Light!"

I lift my eyebrows. "Did you?"

Natalia laughs. "He bit Pierre's leg."

Chuckling, I scoop Fallon into my lap. "Well done, Young Man."

Fallon claps his hands. "I have a friend now. A real one like Uncle Mass."

A knife twists in my side, but I won't damage a child with the pains of the world. I'll admit my failures another time.

I try to smile. "Is it a good friend?"

"His name is Thomas, and he's really tall." Fallon puts his hand over his head. "He's real nice, too."

I look to Galain, who smiles and nods. "Your boy."

Zander cuts in. "I was unaware that you have a lineage seed. You must introduce us. I will need to know whom I must protect."

I keep my eyes on my plate. "Thomas is not my lineage."

"I misunderstood. My apologies."

"He's my son, just not a seed of my lineage."

"Then he is not your son."

Natalia leans into me. "That's not true." She nudges me with her shoulder. "I should know. My dad isn't my sperm donor, but still my dad."

I need to tell her. "Talia, your father, Eugene. He contacted me. He'd found the High Assembly. He's why I knew where they were."

She frowns. "Where..." She glances around, then falls still. "Oh."

"Lucius," I manage.

Nodding, she hangs her head. "Right."

Tossing a berry in his mouth, Jacques says, "I liked Eugene. He didn't deserve what Lucius did."

I warn him with a sharp glare. She does not need to know those details. "He refused to share their location, insisting upon coming with us."

Natalia sighs. "It would have been the easy way out." She folds her arms, resting them on the table and leaning over them. "He wouldn't have accepted the easy way, and he always taught me that if I wanted something or wanted something done, I had to take responsibility instead of expecting someone else to give me what I wanted."

"He..." I brace myself. "He said to tell you if it's too easy..."

"It's never right."

I tuck hair behind her ear. "Talia, he insisted. He wanted—"

"It's not your fault. They were his last words?" She looks to me with glassy eyes.

"Yes."

"They weren't for me. Whatever you walked into, it had been too easy. He should have realized it wasn't right and backed out. He wanted you to know he was taking the blame for what happened. He was saying it was his fault." Pushing away from the table, she walks away.

My Dark whines. I console it.

Natalia has feelings. She struggles with them, maybe all of them. I'm in no condition to force her to lean on me.

I ask Fallon, "Want to see your friend? I should say hello to him."

I carry Fallon on my shoulders, listening to him go on and on. I'd forgotten how chatty children can be in their whimsy. Still, there's a warmth in my chest as he rambles while I locate Thomas.

He hugs me, holding on longer than usual.

I ruffle his hair. "Missed you too, kid."

"I'm supposed to die before you."

A father shouldn't have to watch their son die. It's a coin toss with present circumstances on which of us will see the afters first.

I catch up, make sure Thomas has everything he needs, then leave a rambunctious Fallon with him as I return to the main dining hall.

Natalia hasn't returned, but Sterling sits in her stead. I reclaim my seat, picking up his coffee mug instead of mine. The one I'd been using is stale and cold; his will be fresher.

He eyes me with ire but says nothing, consuming his breakfast.

Taking a drink, I say, "The next time I tell you to leave, you'll go to the next room, not vanish."

"The next time you talk to me like I answer to you, I break your jaw. I offered myself for purchase. You declined."

"Try it, sweetheart."

He throws his fork down and stands, his chair screeching across the stone floor.

I stand, turning toward him.

He swings.

I shy back, block with my forearm, and throw my weight into my palm as I slam the heel against his chest.

He stumbles back, tripping over the chair and hitting the floor. As quick as he went down, he's back up, swinging again.

I step away from the table, blocking and ducking the hectic attacks. This isn't friendly fire. Sterling is pissed.

He catches the side of my jaw with his fist. I see spots of dancing colors as I stumble back.

I don't think it's broken, but he gave it a fair try. I rub my jaw, opening my mouth to work it side to side as Sterling glares.

Zander rises from the table. "Do it again, Dog, and I send you to the afters."

Sterling sneers. "Not sure who he's talking to."

I turn my head but maintain focus on Sterling as I yell to Zander. "Sit down and stay out of it." I curl one side of my mouth back. "You sit down too, Birdie."

He narrows his eyes. "I don't answer to you, and unlike the rest of these fucks, I can handle you, so you're going to quit giving me orders, or I finish what I started."

"You mean try again to do what you failed to do?" I lift an eyebrow, daring him to press my temper.

Jacques whistles. "I need popcorn for the show. Someone get me popcorn."

I rock back on my heels, motioning to Sterling's chair. "Pick it up and sit down."

He steps forward, leaning over as if to grab the chair, then rushes forward, swinging upward into my stomach.

I double over, the wind knocked out of me. I bare my teeth and swing back.

He feigns to the side, rounding to slam his fist into my jaw.

This time, it cracks, blood filling my mouth. I spit at him, lifting my hands as he presses his advantage.

I block and spin, catching him on the side.

He recoils, breathing hard with a smirk. "Now it's broken."

Growling in the back of my throat, I advance, swinging in lazy strokes and quick jabs. He goes on the defense, pushing my attacks to the side and dancing backward.

I feign, giving him an in, and he tries to use it. I get close and grab the back of his neck to force him over, then ram my knee into his chest and drive my elbow down into his jaw.

I'm rewarded with a satisfying crunch and fling him away. I

clench my teeth, regretting the action as pain lances through the side of my skull and neck.

Panting, I rub my chest, the wound pulsing in time with my heart. Pain is fine, but I didn't consider the possibility of ripping myself open again.

He gets up, falling one step to the side.

It's my turn to gloat. "I did it," I manage, my jaw clicking with sharp stabs of pain, "first try."

He snarls, rushing at me.

Zander shouts, "Back off, Dark."

I whirl, shoving my elbow into Sterling's side and yell at Zander, "Stay out of it."

"You are—"

Sterling gets his arm around my neck.

"—the Light—"

Sterling yanks me off my feet, dragging me to the floor.

"—Queen and—"

I thrash, breaking Sterling's grip.

"—I will—"

"Shut the fuck up, Glow Whore," Sterling shouts as we both get to our knees.

I glare at Sterling. "Back down."

He snarls and lunges at me, shadows engulfing us. Claws drag across my stomach, and I kick him away, rolling across the floor.

If he wants to be an ass, I'll shift too.

My skin splits, spikes and bone rising from beneath my skin. It always feels good to shed the mask for this form.

I lash out with my tail as Sterling lurches forward. He evades, and we go blow for blow, trading hits and kicks until we're both panting.

He isn't attacking with his Dark. He isn't going for any mortal injuries. He's just beating on me.

I smack him with the side of my tail barb, dragging his feet from beneath him using my Dark at the same time. He hits the floor with a groan, slower to get back up.

I don't press, waiting for him to reset. With my bone armor, he's doing more damage to himself than me with every attack, and his intensity has begun to dwindle.

I need to get him calm enough to figure out what this is. I'm not interested in doing irreparable damage, and I can withstand a plethora of pain and injuries long before I have concerns.

He lifts his hands, circling me. We shuffle. He steps into a few jabs, testing me, waiting for an opportunity.

My Dark manages to slip past his, wrapping around his ankles. Sterling flails as he topples, and I pin him.

I slam my fist into the stone next to his head. It cracks and fractures, chips flying loose. I growl, both in warning and at the tearing sensation across my sternum. "You want to talk yet?"

He sneers, getting his leg between mine and jerking, using weight to sling me to the side.

I kick and claw, getting free to reclaim my feet.

The air crackles with electricity.

Without looking over, I shout, "Zander, stay the fuck out of it."

Natalia steps between Sterling and me, facing me with murder in her face. "Not Zander."

Sterling takes a step forward.

She rounds, holding her palm to him. "No."

He snaps his teeth. "Stay out of it, Firefly."

"Stop."

I stomp forward. "Talia, go. You can't interfere. It breaks the rules of engagement."

She faces me again. "You fucks both know I do whatever the fuck I want."

"It's the law." I fling my arm toward the table. "Go."

Her Light streaks for me.

My Dark hesitates.

Vines of heat wrap around me, and I flail at them, cursing my Dark.

It pouts. *"It's our mate."*

She drags me backward. Damn her, she knows it's a weak point for me. I hit the stone, squirming to get the right way up. My spinal spikes drag across the floor, reverberating in my skull in irritating shrieks. Rolling over, I get my legs and arms under me to push upright and find balance.

Sterling starts forward, and she shifts to him, pressing a hand to his chest. Light flashes.

I blink, my sight adjusting to clear vision once more.

Sterling snaps his teeth several paces away, down on one knee. "I don't answer to you."

Natalia laughs, low and cold.

Fuck that sound. I nearly piss myself. I wane, waiting.

Sterling is furious. Why is a mystery. I didn't steal his mate, and I haven't killed him for taking mine. There's no reason I can think of that he should be this enraged.

Sterling tries to stand. Silver Light erupts from his hand. He roars as it races up his arm and across his chest in dozens of needle-thin tendrils that thread in and out of his flesh.

I growl, "Talia."

Sterling hits his knees, and it stops. His black skin glitters with threads of light stitched through his arm and torso as he pants. "Fuck you."

He gets upright, and the Light intensifies.

He drops to one knee, growling and groaning.

I stalk forward. "Talia."

She faces me, saying, "Stay on your knees, Sterling, or you'll be in contempt again." Dropping her hands on her hips, she pinches her lips into the center of her face. "He's my contract."

"Stay out of this."

"He's my fucking contracted." She waves behind her. "I'm responsible for him."

I taught her well. Yelping in short barks of humor, I crouch in front of her. "He started it."

"I'm ending it."

"He doesn't need you to protect him."

"Babe." She reaches for me.

I lower my head toward her hands. They are so small against my face.

She scratches behind one of my ears, and my back leg thumps against the floor.

I whine, looking back at it. I tell my Dark, *That was uncalled-for humiliation.*

"I liked it."

Natalia giggles. "The only time I should see this face is when I get to sit on it."

My Dark dissolves into a drooling knot of shadows. *"Mate likes me."*

I lick her neck, dragging my tongue across my mating mark.

She shudders and gasps. "Oh, fuck," she whispers in a pant. Shivering again, she steps back. "That, um, okay." She stretches her eyes.

Turning her back on me, she steps to Sterling, offering her hand.

He sneers at her, not taking it. "Am I allowed to stand, Your Majesty?"

"Sterling," she sighs, tipping her head back. "Don't."

He smacks his hand to hers, but it's twice the size. His talons click as they close around her forearm.

She squares up to him. "Okay, now, tell me what the fuck?"

He lifts his hand, looking to the back of it, shrugs, turns, and walks away.

Natalia throws her hands in the air and spins to me.

I howl in humor. My chest burns and protests. I sit back on my legs, snarling and yelping at the ceiling with glee. Not even my fractured jaw stops me.

She shakes her head at me, lips twisting to one side. "Laugh it up, asshole. Go ahead. I deserve that."

For the headaches and stress she has given me, I'm thrilled Sterling is giving it all back.

I knew I liked him, but I might love him.

CHAPTER 8
CALLAHAN

Natalia heals me, cursing at me for tearing the wound in my chest open.

Her Light weaves through me, the flesh and bones stinging with each stab and yank of her magic, sealing me closed.

She taps near the reformed stitches. My skin twitches and burns from over-sensitivity.

She lifts her eyes toward my face. "Babe, what the fuck was that?"

I open my mouth, wiggling my jaw. At least one injury has been corrected. I shrug, rolling forward.

Picking her up, I stomp down the hallway, ducking and angling my body through the open double doors, heading for our room.

"Cal. What—"

"Sterling's pissy."

"Why?"

My Dark stews, my mind grasping at smoke. I stomp up a flight of stairs. "I don't know. You interrupted."

"You two were trying to kill each other."

I bark in short yelps, shaking with laughter. "No."

"You were both shifted."

"He was blowing off steam."

"That was..."

"Not quite friendly fighting, but he never used his Dark. The next time I tell you to stay out of it, don't interfere."

"I'm not going to—"

"You are. I know Sterling. I know what he's capable of, and he was working out frustrations, not trying to kill me. You got in the way before he started talking. He walked away, still pissed off, which means I still don't know why, and he's still injured. You broke the rules of engagement and got in the way when you had no business involving yourself."

"You're mad at me?"

"Yes," I snap. "I don't need you to protect me. He doesn't, either. He and I were working it out between us."

I shift in the hallway before our suite, knowing I won't fit in the cloistered rooms, then take her hand to yank her inside.

She digs her heels in and pulls against me.

I glance over my shoulder, "Talia."

"I'll go find Sterling. I can at least make sure he's healed."

She's leaving me for him.

My sight goes out of focus. Spots of color dance in my vision even as the edges haze over in gray clouds that encroach further, blinding me.

"Cal," Natalia calls for me, but I can't see her. "Cal?"

No smites. No cats. No small spaces. There's nothing but emptiness stretching before me and Natalia's voice. Even that begins to fade in a mocking echo. I'll lose my mate.

My Dark quivers and whimpers.

After everything I've done and the man I've become, it's a wonder I held her as my mate even once.

My stomach churns, bile bubbling into the back of my throat

to mix with noxious gas. The thumping pounding in my chest accelerates, fear closing like a fist about my neck.

Nothing has ever terrified me so much. I can't breathe. I can't face the thought.

My knees buckle as my Dark thrashes, and everything goes black.

CHAPTER 9

VANESSA

I dance in the light filtering through the trees with my head tipped back and my hair dancing in the breeze. I tread the ground, soaking in the warmth of the suns and the kiss of shadows, embracing the beauty of balance. There is nothing more beautiful than the harmony, a song all its own, audible to only those who can hear the whispers of gods.

I've long desired to walk this place again. The rustle of leaves, the spotted patches of illumination interweaving with patches of shadows from the canopy above. I stop, pressing my hand to the massive trunk, the bark cracked with fine lines of age. Its soul speaks of growth for thousands of years, still so young and ever-augmenting.

With fresh air in my lungs and the warmth of life-giving light raining down on me, my rage renews. It beats like war drums in my chest, singing in my veins with the promise of vengeance and vindication. For too long, I've been caged. For far too long, I lie in wait, suspended in hollow echoes of my mind as a prisoner condemned for the sanctimonious vile lies of another.

I frown. Not me. For not the first time today, I'm losing reality, the overwhelming knowledge and memories of Mallafic repressing me.

I drop my hand, taking in my surroundings. I know this place, though I've never been welcomed so deep within this jungle. It is sacred ground, guarded and harvested by the Brish.

My father was Brish, raised in Jaloquinn near the Brishmam Rainforest. He had brought me to the outskirts, but I was forbidden from the heart of the place as an outsider, not truly one of them because of my mother's bloodline.

Mallafic steps next to me, his black hair and jet eyes darker than any shadow or shade of night. He presses his hand to the tree, looking up along its thick trunk. "A young one, still growing, and yet the tales it has to tell..." He trails off, staring with a kind of sonder. "Nature always finds its balance, but the seeds of the Gremalvis, its children spread across this world, mirroring that of which are the very roots that hold together the land and are the most flagrant displays. Their limbs reach high, and their roots seep low, half in light and half in dark they grow."

"Why are we here?"

"Another piece of me is near." He looks to me, his thin lips curled up at the corners. "So many of them buried in darkness as if I were too dangerous to be illuminated, but my torment is nearly undone thanks to you, my sweetest darling."

Reaching out, he slides the backs of his fingers along my jaw toward my ear.

The way he looks at me with adoration feels nice. I trace the cracks in the bark. "We should hurry."

"Fear naught." He chuckles. "We will finish your story in due haste, but there is a pleasure in lingering in life."

I shake my head, turning my back to the tree to scan the area. "The Brish don't like outsiders. They've killed people for entering their sacred lands."

"They shall not kill me." He holds out his hand, level to the ground. His fingers contort, shadows pouring from his hand and elongating into the air in several directions, tasting, testing, searching for echoes. "Still too far, but closer."

He moves, heading deeper into the forest as I return to marveling at the golden wood and vibrant green foliage. Vines hang in thick ropes from branches and curl around trunks like stoic serpents protecting the forest. The humid air clings to my skin. For not the first time, I find myself yearning for the peace stolen from me.

She did this. She robbed me of my heart and my life, of my nature and my very name. I was a thing to be used for her amusements. Her actions took no heed of my wants, of my soul. Nay, what she did tore me apart, and no matter how I sought to heal, I stitched myself back together wrong. The threads pull too tight, inexplicable and inescapable as fate itself.

As we wander deeper, further into the forest, anxiety coils around my throat in cool shadows. I've dreamed of this place, longed to be allowed to tread within the most sacred lands of my birthright, but I know I'll find no welcome.

I start to notice huts and bridges in the canopy. I slow my pace, but Mallafic doesn't notice, or more likely, doesn't care. Why would he?

A path becomes clear, several Brish huts on the ground woven between thick trunks. I quell. We must be very near the sacred hearth.

Several Brish warriors drop from above, landing before Mallafic. He flicks his hand to the side, and they fly out of his way. He never breaks stride.

I scamper after him, unsure of what would happen to me without him. The thought sends a cold trickle of apprehension down my spine—to be away from part of myself.

I catch up. "We aren't welcome here."

"What do I care? They hold no threat to me, and they have

what I want." His tone cuts the air, a sharp whisper full of malice.

A warrior steps in the path, spinning a spear and taking an aggressive stance. "Be gone, evil."

Mallafic lifts a hand, closing his fingers.

The warrior throws his head back and yells, dropping the spear and falling to the dirt. He thrashes and goes still.

Mallafic opens his hand, dropping a bloody lump that falls beneath his feet. He steps on it, then over the body toward the lingering and growing crowd.

I stop at the edge of the clearing, my mouth hanging open.

It's beautiful.

The canopy is full of rugged dwellings and rope bridges around the open glen, and in the middle is a village of thatched roofs around a monolith.

The sacred hearth.

I'm frozen in awe and reverence.

I finally made it.

But I've been here before—long ago. It's a distant memory, one I have no reason to visit. I wandered, lost and broken. I felt nothing then. With fresh eyes and a new life, the veneration washes over me.

What this has become... Unlike Di Auratis, this hasn't been lost. All these years, and it's been protected, cherished.

In an instant, I'm before the stone, running my hand along the scarred surface. The deep gouges left from Nehil's claws. This was the first, the rock that split to release Nehil from his prison.

"Where is it?"

I drop my hand, turning to the ring of Brish warriors closing around me. Mallafic stands at my side, staring down the warriors with ease.

There is no response. The warriors press inward, raising spears.

I square my shoulders and lift my chin. *"Dontes tola?"*

The warriors don't stop.

I have been forgotten—lost to time—abandoned by them all. There's no respect shown, no recognition of me.

I'm not asking a second time. It's pointless. Defeating ignorance is tedious and, at times, impossible. These fools don't want knowledge.

That's fine. I have the knowledge and will to use it.

I let my eyes slide out of focus, seeing the light raining down and the shadows dancing in the breeze. Of all the places, this is not the one to test me. Here, I am more connected to the father than anywhere. His magic still lingers in the stone that encased him.

I press my palm to it and siphon the power. It ripples through me, a familiar echo in my soul. Nehil birthed us all, but me? I am his only son.

These fragile creatures aren't any of his creations, so I care not for them. It's easy, with the essence of my father, to break them apart and return them to what they once were.

Dark races in threads around the warriors, undoing them. Wet slop slings, the pathetic structures falling into pieces that unravel and decay as mud.

Mallafic applauds. "Well done, my sweetling."

"From mud I am made, to mud I can return," I snarl, my voice twisted.

Chuckling, Mallafic surveys the world. "So long ago. So much forgotten." He shakes his head, his black hair shifting, the small horns dully gleaming under the illumination of the suns. "Kill them all. I'll find my piece."

I shrug. It will be easy to unleash my rage.

CHAPTER 10
CALLAHAN

I'm floating, coming to the surface drenched in cold sweat. My body aches, my chest pulsating with hot pain.

"At least he's not thrashing anymore."

I know that voice. I've heard it say those same words several times over. Jacques.

Someone hums, probably Thames. Thames is the only other it could be with us locked in this gods' forsaken hole, stuck behind bars of unyielding metal.

Maybe it's Pierre returned to inflict pain and humiliation.

Digging deep for fortification, I open my eyes, prepared to face whatever else he's concocted to make me bleed.

I stare up at a ceiling, not rough, rusted metal. I'm flat on my back, a mattress sinking beneath my weight. Reality crawls into my mind.

I'm in Ilbuio, not at the mercy of Lucius or Pierre's sadistic acts.

I sit up, bending my knees toward my chest and wrapping my arms around them, grasping one wrist to lock my arms in place.

Jacques lifts his chin at me, standing at the foot of my bed. "Welcome back to the real world, sweetheart."

"How—" I manage, my tongue dry and thick in my mouth. "How long was I out?"

Sterling glances over his shoulder at me. He's sitting at the end of the bed facing Jacques. "This time?"

I stare at Sterling.

He shrugs. "Tal says you lost consciousness right after you shifted. That was this morning. It's about Night's rune."

Jacques checks the watch on his wrist. "Half past, actually."

I lost another day.

Jacques lifts two fingers. "You're sane again, and I'm tired. Sterling," he lifts his chin, "good luck."

Sterling nods back, getting up to face me as Jacques exits the room. Sterling asks, "Need anything?"

"Water."

"I can play fetch. Wake Tal if you need something before I get back." He spins on his heel and departs.

I look to my side to see Natalia sprawled out in bed. My Dark reaches for her, spreading across her. She doesn't move, likely asleep.

I leave her in bed to shower, soaking in the hot water to wash away the haze and grime. No matter how much I scrub, I can't remove the stains of the past, but they are just that—the past.

I turn off the water and dry off. In the end, I managed to kill Pierre. It wasn't how either of us would have ever imagined, but I am the reason he's dead. The rest is history.

Hanging the towel to dry, I take my first real, unrestricted breath since I woke up in a cage. When I exit the bathroom, Sterling offers me a bottle of bourbon and a carafe of water. My Dark ravels around the liquor, and I chug the water.

I set the bottle aside near the door to return it to the kitchen tomorrow and move toward the end of the bed, intending to go around to my side, but stop, gazing at Natalia.

She's still here. I can't tear my eyes from her, peaceful and beautiful at rest.

Sterling moves around me, pressing his torso against my back. He puts an arm under mine, his hand in the middle of my chest. He rests his chin on my shoulder, his Dark snaking around me.

Mine fizzles, cranky in fatigue but absent of ire. It's more accepting than I am.

He reaches around with his other arm, snagging the bottle of bourbon. Using his Dark, he sets it aside on the nightstand. "We need to talk."

I cock my jaw. "You're a pain in my ass."

He chuckles. "You're cute."

I twist my face toward his, glowering.

"You keep snarling and snapping."

"You swung first."

"You didn't send me to the afters. You could have tried. You pinned me, but hit the floor."

Curling my lip, I return to gazing at Natalia. "I could send you, but..."

Sterling's mouth skims my bare shoulder. "Why?"

"I'd be just like Pierre."

Grinning, he shakes at my back. "The Light fuck is saving me? I'd rather you send me to the afters."

"You mated my mate."

"I expected her to kill me."

"I know you're brilliant, so explain to me how you were that stupid. Natalia only ever does what she wants."

Sterling is silent, unmoving.

"Answer me."

"I wanted her, and I watched you two mate. I assumed if she didn't kill me to serve the Dark, you would for mating her."

"You wanted to die?"

"You left her to me," he whispers, his voice twisted with vehemence. "I knew she was yours, but you walked away. I could see the cracks in her, but she wouldn't quit. She fought Mallafic for you, bled for you, and yet she'd already forgiven you when I was still pissed. She signed contracted into service of the Dark, but never gave thought to commanding service of herself. She showed genuine signs of what an alpha is to be. I have seen her bend her body into knots, and her tits are perky. I didn't understand how you could walk away from her."

My guts turn rancid. I clamp my jaw and swallow the bile, but he doesn't wait for me to respond.

"I knew her heart belonged to you, but you handed her to me. I never intended, never wanted to or expected to fall, but I did. I plummeted faster than I can get my claws out."

"You love her."

"Yes," he says. "You gave me a star and thought I wouldn't hit my knees and worship her? I was on my knees before I even realized it."

I lift my chin, tipping my head back into him. The moment I saw Natalia naked in a bed in my house, she was mine.

When I pulled her onto my bike, everything changed. The world turned brighter, and my senses heightened. Natalia put me on edge with a need—to protect her, to have her. From the very start, I positioned her as a partner, not a vassal. I deluded myself into believing it was to encourage her cooperation and service, but I never wanted her to be another vassal, just another tool. I wanted her to be mine.

I sigh. "I can't fault you for that."

"You'd be a hypocrite, and the world will end before a Barraco ever fails to be beyond reproach."

"Quit stroking my vanity."

"Would you prefer I stroke your cock?"

I choke on a muffled laugh, hanging my head and vibrating as I clamp my jaw against releasing the humor in worry of waking Natalia. "I'm pissed at you, at having to fight for my mate."

Sterling shifts, his arm tightening around my shoulder. "I presumed one of you would kill me, but I saw three options. She killed me, you killed me, or..." He pushes air out of his nose, a smirk in his voice. "I could have both of you."

Those words shock me upright. "Both?"

"Both." He presses me closer, his Dark constricting as he nuzzles my ear, chuckling.

Being held instead of the other way around is strange. I flex my shoulders back, my Dark squirming and my skin itching.

He grins against my shoulder, his tone teasing. "Relax, baby."

It's pleasant, but I am more comfortable as the one in charge and on top. To accept the role reversal is difficult.

Sterling opens his mouth, licking my shoulder. He holds me closer, the hand on my hip gripping tighter. "Trust me."

I have asked so many for the same thing. As a contractor they put their lives in my hands, giving themselves over to me in the belief that I will take care of them. I stand on my own, taking care of others. I am served but not sheltered by any. That is the curse of a contractor.

"It's not weakness," Sterling whispers. "How many times have you told others the same thing?"

He was a contractor. He knows. I didn't have to say anything for him to understand.

"I know you take care of yours. Even when you were disgraced, they served with fierce loyalty."

I sigh. "That's the job of a contractor."

"Gods, you're insufferable. I've tried to break your pretty face in jealousy, and I have tried to knock you off your pedestal in annoyance. I haven't ever once managed either. You're impossible to beat or even measure up to. None of us can compare. It's not fair that you're so pretty and capable." He sinks his teeth into the shell of my ear. "How could I not want you?"

I exhale, letting the tension in my chest slide away. "I didn't realize..."

"You're made of fire and bone. Your mask is pretty and perfect. You've followed our tenets, and you never seem to falter. There's not a fucking thing about you, other than walking away from Natalia, that I can find fault in. And even that...I know why. I heard her say those words, but, baby..." he snickers, "she lied."

I turn my face away from his, staring at the wall. "I thought you wanted *her*."

He drags his curved lips over the top of my shoulder. "Our second Gathering Shadows, I went into the games that year knowing you were my biggest competition, and the second day, when I drew to face you in wall-ball, I was nervous because we were on opposite sides."

I smile. "It started to rain. We were sliding in the mud all over the place."

"It was just you and me left in the game, and neither one of us could beat the other."

"Or would kill each other."

He chuckles. "Basileus came down and beat us bloody for it."

I grin, shaking with silent laughter as I rest my head back on his shoulder. "You had one eye swollen shut, couldn't stand right, and asked if we were supposed to finish the game with a straight face like you were dead serious about the inquiry."

"You picked the ball up and dropped it in your basket."

I snicker. "You earned it."

"I think I fell in love with you for that, although I hated you just as much for that same act. Proper fucking bastard, acting all noble by giving me the point."

"I gave it to you for that quip. I almost pissed myself trying not to laugh."

"That night at dinner, I sat next to you." Sterling's voice changes from humor to a hoarse whisper.

Those words slaughter my mirth, a rock dropping in the pit of my stomach. Sighing, I deflate, hanging my head. "Don't. I remember."

He hums. "I'll be nice. I won't repeat the words that made me get up and walk away, but you made it clear we weren't friends."

The game of wall-ball was my first real interaction with Sterling, and he'd stolen my admiration and my breath. For a moment, I hadn't been aware of the rest of the world, not the contractors watching or the reason for the game. When I walked away from the field, I'd been hoping for a friend. I wanted to find Sterling for a drink after I got clean. He'd been tempting to get to know. I wanted to laugh with him more.

I came to my senses.

The world seemed to shatter like fractured glass that tore me up when Massimo asked why I didn't kill Sterling, pointing out several instances where I could have.

Massimo asked if I was trying to get sent to the afters. I'd delayed Eloise from healing the wounded, risking his life.

He said my head must have been in the clouds.

It had been. I was at Gathering Shadows. I wasn't making friends. I was proving my strength and surviving.

I drag a hand down my face. "I didn't want to be friends and then have to kill you."

"Gathering Shadows makes it hard. Being contenders is even harder." He chuckles. "We still had fun sometimes when we were on teams together."

I grin. Those games were always my favorite. Working with Sterling was as easy as breathing. We were in sync, and I never questioned if I'd lose or even had a consideration of possible death. "We did."

"When the game was over, though..." He trails off.

I wince.

"I often wondered if you hated me."

"No. I went out of my way to avoid you."

"Every year, I felt like a fucking lovesick idiot begging for your attention. You wouldn't even look at me." Sterling lifts his chin, replacing it with his mouth.

Closing my eyes, I lean back into him. "The others...there wasn't one I cared about. Even with the contest starting and players marked, the idea of killing them didn't bother me. I just wanted to survive no matter who I had to kill. Chlem was an ass, Marius, a coward, and that new one—whatever his name was. Even when Telra was on the list..."

Sterling grins against me. "We've been sharing a woman for longer than we knew."

I groan, dropping my head to his shoulder and staring at the ceiling. Neither he nor I really wanted Telra. She was insane and sadistic and injected her paralytic toxin into us to use our bodies without consent.

My Dark whispers, *"We take what we want. Maybe we want both?"*

I narrow one eye. Sterling is strong. He's always been my biggest competition, a struggle point for me.

I could take him. He could be mine, answering to me.

My Dark coils around me, drooling with the thought.

I did enjoy fucking Natalia with him. He's attractive, lean, and well-built. He's useful, too. I could use a partner like him. I need a partner like him. I just want Natalia as unsuitable as she is for wearing a crown in most aspects.

My Dark says, *"Both. I want both. Mate likes it, and its shadow web is fun to play with."*

I smile, tension ebbing from my soul. "I always thought we could have been friends."

"It's your fault we weren't."

Picking my head up, I twist my face toward him, lifting one eyebrow as I cut my eyes to him. "I put up with enough sass from our mate."

"Ours?"

"Mm," I hum, twisting my lips to the side. "You mated her too."

"Knowing full well I'd be sharing if you'd tolerate me." He presses his face into the crook of my neck, drawing his hand down my center. "I know who my alpha is."

I chuckle under my breath. "Keep sweet-talking me. I like it."

He shakes with contained humor. "I thought you told me to stop stroking your vanity?"

I lean my head into his. "Don't..." I fight to keep my voice even, but I'll stoop to begging if I have to. "Don't take her."

He twists his head back and forth, his mouth curved as it brushes across the top of my shoulder. "I *never* wanted to *take* her. I won't stand between you. I won't keep her from you. I don't want to separate you. I want to worship both of you as my gods."

The world seems too heavy to hold up, fatigue burning in my legs. For the first time in my life, I don't have to stand alone.

I will have two mates who balance me. Natalia is raw power but brash and ignorant. Sterling knows everything from contracts to being a contractor, our laws, and more.

I doubt I deserve either of them, but they want me anyway. Even knowing my truths, things that should destroy their belief in me, they still want me.

It never occurred to me that I wasn't going to have to fight him for her, that he was positioning himself not between me and her but with us.

I sag against him, trusting his strength rivals my own. "I didn't realize you were vying for her *and* me."

"I told you I was expensive." He presses his face into the crook of my neck again. "I pointed at you both."

"I thought you were pointing at her."

"Idiot." His chest swells, and he opens his mouth on my shoulder, pressing his teeth into me.

I twitch at the sting of his bite. My throat clogs. The act is useless, but the intentions are everything.

I close my eyes. "We can't," I manage, although my words are faint, hard to push past the lump in my throat.

"I would if I could," he whispers. "I'd mark you both, sink my teeth in you and tie you to me for eternity."

"We can be friends."

He laughs, free and loud. "You can shove friendship—"

"Mate." I elbow him as Natalia stirs, warning him.

"That's the word I wanted."

Natalia pushes up, blinking and looking to us as she rubs her face.

She focuses on us, tipping her head toward her shoulder.

Sterling says, "We didn't mean to wake you, Firefly."

I nudge him again, this time with less force. Letting go of me, he steps away, and I move to my side of the bed.

I lay on my side facing them as Sterling settles into his place on Natalia's other side.

My Dark stretches out, tugging Sterling against her back. It threads around them both, tethering them together for safekeeping.

He grins at me and winks. "Thanks for tucking me in."

Natalia snuggles her head into my shoulder, "Babe?"

I brush her hair away from her face to kiss her forehead.

My Dark vibrates in pleasure as a thread of her Light twines with my Dark, another echo rippling between them as Sterling's Dark braids itself into them. I close my eyes, content with my mates. Both of them.

CHAPTER II
CALLAHAN
1ST DAWN'S DAY, BLOOMING, 4050, 6TH MILLENNIUM

I wake, shuddering and shivering as my heart pounds against my ribs as if it's trying to break free of its cage.

I sit up, working to catch my breath.

The bottle of bourbon floats into view, offered by tendrils of shadows.

I snag it and chug until my lungs burn.

Sterling chuckles.

I wipe my mouth on the back of my hand and screw the cap in place. "What are you doing awake?"

"Getting a laugh at your expense."

I twist and set the bottle aside. "At least someone is getting a benefit from this."

"You'll get through it."

I don't know if he just lied. I close my eyes. "I feel like I'm getting worse."

"I'm shocked at the idea of the amount he must have given you, and yet you survived." He hums. "Is this what my uncle and your father were like?"

"Worse," I whisper.

Shadows twist around me. "Guess I can't be too much of an ass toward you for it."

I splutter on a strangled laugh. "They were mad. My father had his hands shifted and had shredded himself apart." I shudder at the memory of damage he'd wrought upon himself. There had been so much blood. "They were all screaming and thrashing in chains."

I hadn't been able to talk sense into any of the five. I'd given up my father for the worst but tried every trick I could think of. I'd sought to save one—just one—any one of them would have been better than none.

I had been too late. I had failed to help them in every way. I hadn't saved a single life. I didn't get revenge. I kept the secret of what they suffered.

Losing my mind to nightmare toxin and dying the same way would have been cruel justice.

The liquor threatens to expel from my stomach. I clamp my jaw, squeeze my fingers into fists, and hold my breath. "Keep me sane."

More Dark coils around me. Mine slips out, shy but curious, as it weaves itself into the shadows collecting around me.

"If... If I..."

"You're fine, Cal."

"Don't let it be her. If I lose my mind, if—"

"Cal, stop." Sterling rests his hand on my shoulder, giving it a squeeze. "You're fine. You're stronger than this."

"Zander, have Zan–"

"You'll purge that shit out and recover."

"He'll want to."

"Piss off. It's not happening."

I hang my head. "What I did—"

"Your web was weaved. You did what was necessary. I

don't know if I could have. The rest? Fine. But my uncle... He raised me as much as my father. Maybe more because the Light fuck sent my father to the afters when I was barely a man. The kind of fortitude that must have taken? I don't know if I have that."

I blow out hard. "You would have."

He scoffs. "The games are hard enough. Knowing a face and name is bitter satisfaction when you kill them because you survived, but the man that gave you life and everything he had to make you who you are? I'm not certain."

Tipping my head back, I sigh at the ceiling. "We've learned to act for preservation without thinking. Doing it wasn't the hard part."

He squeezes my shoulder. "If, a hard if, and I'm only using that word to humor your stupid idea, it'll be me, baby." His Dark drags me back to lay flat. He rests his hand on my chest. "But it's not going to happen. You're going to get your head right."

"If I can't..."

"The only thing that can break you is what you decide to let break you. I had to mate your mate to get your attention. Don't quit on me now that I have it."

I laugh through my nose, smiling as I slip back to sleep.

I WAKE to Natalia running her fingers through my hair. The air is ripe with mouth-watering bacon and her scent of hysterium.

She smiles down at me, propped on an arm at my side. "Hi, babe."

I grunt and squint. "I don't recall Ilbuio ever being this bright."

She shrugs. "Mallafic gave me the crown of the Dark, and the haze lifted."

"Mm."

Sterling tucks his chin over her shoulder, wrapping his arm around her. "Come on, Firefly. He needs to eat."

My skin twitches. I roll off the bed to my feet, searching for pants.

I stumble, getting them on. Strands of silver and black streak for me, helping to keep me upright.

Natalia steps to me, running her hands across my chest. Her touch leaves sparks of pleasure in their wake, calming my racing heart.

She kisses the middle of my chest. "How's this? Getting better?"

I bob my head.

Sterling moves behind me, clapping his hands down on my shoulders to dig his thumbs into aching muscles. He forces me forward, walking me into another room across the hallway from the bed.

He directs me to the couch, pushing me onto it as I survey the dishes on a low table.

Natalia sits next to me to pour a cup of coffee with one leg tucked under her. She and Sterling are fully dressed.

I eye them as I take the mug. "Eating with the contractors?"

Sterling crosses his arms. "Already did. We let you sleep."

Natalia snuggles into me, her head on my shoulder. "*Mhm.*"

"What else needs—"

"I'll take care of it," Sterling says, straining his eyes at me.

"I can—"

"Eat your damn breakfast and take a nap." He shrugs, dropping his arms. "Two queens are better than one."

I pull my mouth to one side in a wry smile, then take a drink of coffee. He has a point.

Sterling comes closer, leaning over to press his mouth to Natalia's head. "Stay with him, Firefly. Make sure he's okay."

She nods. "I will."

Sterling departs, and Natalia remains curled into me while I eat.

I refill my mug and settle back with it. "Little Star."

She lifts her head, beaming. "That's me."

"What do we know about Mallafic?"

"Oh." She gets smaller and tries to get closer. "He... He's pieces of his soul, not whole. The codexes do have his soul contained within them. That's the subtorque, him—his soul—and he's got Vanessa. He might be collecting the codexes."

"What did he do to you?" I brush back her silver hair. It's longer than I've ever seen. Dragging my fingers through the strands, I ask, "Was this part of it?"

"No. I did that with Ki. All I know is that he sewed my soul with a piece of his. I am the subtorque now, too, or have some of it."

Widening my eyes, I pull my ears back as I process that information. It's the first decent news I've had. If she holds the subtorque, we can keep it safe and damn the rest.

I tap her wrist. "Can other Magia present like this? With silver threads?"

She shakes her head. "Not that I've ever heard of."

I sigh.

"Why?"

I frown. "Lucius can. I assumed you'd have the same magic, but he calls it Aggika, not Ki. He can create threads. I thought it was Light. He said it's his magic."

I drink my coffee, enjoying my mate snuggled into me. My eyelids grow heavy as I review information.

The Magia and the Ancients are blended souls, but the Magia are blends of the Dark and the Light of Seraphinus magic. The

Ancients refer to those as Sube and Sune, not true Dark and Light, but variations of them twisted by their creators.

The Ancients are blends of pure Dark and Light, born of Nehil, the nothingness, and Adontis, the spark. They are similar to Magia, but they differ. The magics they have seem to be as different as their origins.

I let my eyes fall closed, too exhausted to fight to keep them open. Sterling can handle anything, and I have my mate close.

WHEN I MOVE AGAIN, I clean up and then bring Natalia into the office. I sit in the chair, pulling her onto my lap.

"Our union contract," I tell her. I push hair away from her face, collecting the white iridescent strands to one side. "We need to write one and sign it."

I study the ligan pagan on the desk, still there from yesterday when I set it out. It's waiting.

She says, "You weren't sure how to write it."

"I'm not still." I hang my jaw over her shoulder, opposite her hair. "I can't serve you, and you can't serve me."

She puts her hand to it, her Light scrawling across it. When she lifts her hand, my Dark picks the page up for me to read.

I will stand at your side. I will share a crown, a throne, and a bed with you for as long as we live. We work together to serve the Seraphinus unified in one society built on respect.

Smiling, I turn my face into her neck. "Little Star," I whisper, "do you want Tony to perform your ceremony?"

"No." She sags into me. "There are fatum in this world. The webs of fate are real, and I've realized that my religion is a hoax. The Mother, whoever or whatever that is, isn't real."

"Some Ancient that played god." I shrug. "I don't give a fuck if it's real or not. Marry me in whatever way you need for it to be real."

Turning, she straddles my lap, her fingers locking behind my neck. "You're my mate. That's all I need for it to be real."

I rub my nose to hers. "My little mate." I kiss her, opening my mouth to taste her. "My shining, guiding star." I press my mouth to hers again. "My glowing, beautiful home."

"Stay," she whispers against my lips.

I pull back to meet her eyes.

The ceremony between Massimo and Vanessa was simple. Tony tied them together with a yellow ribbon, tethering them together with Ki. The main piece was exchanging vows, promises made to last a lifetime.

Her religion might not be real, but I offer her a vow.

"Talia, I will let you sit on my face anytime you want. I'll even shift just so you can sit on either face you want."

She giggles.

I go on. "I will get my claws out to protect you with the intensity of a furious alpha, even when you can handle it yourself, because I would rather face your ire than ever consider living in this world without you. I will be your home, sharing this life and any other we have. For however long I have, every last broken piece of me is yours. Until the bitter end, be what it may, I will stay."

"Oh," she tilts her head. "Really, what I need is for you to explain things to me."

I stare, deflating. I was attempting to be romantic. It's not a proficient skill for me.

She takes my face in her hands, her fingers curling around the corners of my jaw and yanking my face closer to hers. "I promise you my heart and jokes. I will try to not be a pain in your ass and to make you laugh at least once a day.

Fuck the classics. You can do better, and I'll take it any way you want."

I choke on a laugh.

She grins. "Babe, I promise you I will always choose you."

I know she will.

I crush my mouth to hers, forgetting about the union contract and the rest of the world as I explore her curves with my hands and Dark.

Into my mouth, her tongue flicking against mine, she breathes, "I need you."

My balls catch fire, tightening as my cock throbs.

She rubs her hands down my chest and then back up. "Babe," she turns her head away, breathing hard. "I need you."

"I heard you." I grip her hair, forcing her mouth back to mine.

"My alpha."

I'm fully erect, throbbing with desire in a single fraction. My little mate needs, and I will fill that ache.

One article of clothing at a time, I undress us, taking my time to savor her mouth and skin before bending her over the desk.

I thrust into her, groaning. This is my home. "I missed you."

She whimpers, clenching around me. I grab a fistful of her hair at the nape of her neck, my other hand pressing her hip as I yank, arching her backward.

She makes a pathetic mewl, trembling and tightening around my cock, embedded to my balls.

My woman feels so good. It's not enough. I need to feel her come, to have her come on me, have her come undone in pleasure with my name on her lips.

My Dark works between her legs, stimulating nerves that flush her around me with heat and moisture, Natalia whimpering again.

I pull back and thrust, easing her into the long, hard strokes I want.

She hisses.

"Still like hard?"

"Cal." She quivers from head to toe, getting tighter and wetter.

Taking my time, I drag her to the edge, trying to balance her there. It feels too good to end. I want to exist like this forever, balls deep in my mate.

"Cal," she moans.

I feel her orgasm and rock my hips at a slower pace. "Good girl."

She shudders, still making soft noises. My Dark isn't letting her go, working to stroke her through the orgasm, drawing out as much pleasure as we can.

I find her ear with my lips, dragging a ragged breath in through my nose. "We're not done."

She moans, arching further. "Cal, please."

My little star is insatiable. All the raw power she has, and I can still bring her to her knees begging. The high that gives me is like no other.

A low, sinister chuckle draws my eye to Sterling in the doorway, leaning against it with one shoulder, his arms crossed. His gaze meets mine before it lowers toward my mate.

"Don't stop on my account."

I twist my lips with glee. "Didn't plan on it."

I return to slamming in and out of her, ramming her over the desk. She's trembling and making delicious noises, letting me know she's enjoying herself as much as I am.

Sterling sits on the opposite edge of the desk, twisting to slide across the surface and put her between his legs, to put us between his legs. He props her head up, helping me keep her in position with his hand under her jaw as he starts to kiss her neck.

Her pussy clamps tight around me. My Dark purrs, "*Mate likes that.*"

I move faster, Natalia crying louder.

My Dark whispers to me, "*It's touching our mate again.*"

"*No shit.*"

"*His shadow web is as capable as the host.*"

"*I'm about to come. Do you mind?*"

Natalia comes first. My eyes damn near roll into my head with ecstasy. I'm going to—

My Dark turns curious. "*Wait.*"

"*Fuck no!*"

It laughs. "*Mate likes this. This shadow piss has ideas.*"

I'm less close to an orgasm now, growling in exasperation. "*Shut. The. Fuck. Up!*"

I keep thrusting. Natalia keeps moaning. I'm back on track.

My Dark twists and vibrates. "*Oh?*"

"*No.*"

"*Yes.*"

"*Shut up.*"

"*Mate is going to come again. This is fun.*"

"*I have never hated you more.*"

It laughs, but it was right. My mate cries out, my name clouding my senses. Pleasure empties out of my balls through my abdomen.

I go still, my muscles twitching and burning with fatigue. My chest pulses in sharp stabs of complaint.

Sterling snickers, "My turn."

My afterglow is chased from existence. One concept screaming in my soul. I'll share, but she's mine. He doesn't get to enjoy her without my involvement, and I need a moment.

My Dark hisses. "*Let him. Mate likes it.*"

I groan and squeeze my eyes shut. "*I don't fucking care!*"

Fury radiates through me, and my lungs and esophagus

catch fire. My Dark coils inside of me with rage. *"Don't care about mate? Don't care what mate wants? I will fucking kill us both if you won't make mate happy."*

I give in, going limp, and it eases its grip on my ability to breathe. *"Fucking shadow piss!"*

It laughs again. *"Let's watch."*

Sterling nuzzles Natalia. "How much more can you take?"

She moans. Damn her. She's only supposed to make that sound for me.

Sterling starts to tug his shirt over his head.

I step back, pulling out of her. Sterling is quick to push her upright, standing to remove the rest of his clothes.

Grumbling, I move out of the way, collapsing in the nearby desk chair.

I watch him lift her. I watch her legs wrap around his hips as he spins them, laying her on the desk. Her perky tits are on display, her skin sparkling at every stroke of Sterling's hands across her flesh.

He pins her wrists over her head, his Dark binding them and anchoring her hands in place as he lowers his head.

I lick my lips, arousal building in me as the scene unfolds. My little star is tied up in shadows, helpless and exposed to Sterling's whims.

My Dark hums as Sterling starts thrusting.

I want to rip his head off. Natalia's enjoying herself, though.

My cock throbs, anticipation building in me. *"Fuck. I like this?"*

My Dark churns within me. *"We've never done this before."*

"His shadow piss is all over her."

"It looks enticing."

"Are we really enjoying watching our mate get fucked?"

"Yes."

Natalia gets louder, and I grit my teeth. Half of me wants to tell Sterling what to do to make her come. The other half hopes he fails.

Sterling doesn't fail. She doesn't say his name, though. She's still mine.

He groans, going still. I relax in the chair, staring at them. I've always liked Sterling, and had an appreciation for his skill and style. He's as effective with our mate as anything else.

Watching has me half-hard again. Rubbing my mouth, I roll forward to my feet and step to them.

Sterling lifts his head, working to catch his breath.

I eye Natalia, her skin flushed and glittering with a silver sparkle. It's not the customary lace. Her Light isn't warding away my Dark or Sterling's.

"Let's see how much she can really take."

He laughs on a breathless pant. "Isn't that half the fun? Seeing how much she can take before she breaks."

I grin, sticking my tongue against my lower lip. He's not wrong.

He releases a heavy breath. "I need a fraction, though."

"You can't keep up?" I hold his gaze, daring him to show a weak spot and bare his throat to me.

He grins. "I'll keep up."

Pulling one side of my mouth back, my chest fills with pride. He won't back down, standing his ground as every bit of the man I think he is.

Natalia moans, trying to squirm away from Sterling. "No." She presses a foot to his chest, trying to force him back.

I widen my eyes, fury, possessiveness, and shock ricocheting through me. "Did you just tell us no?"

Sterling snags her ankle, yanking her closer again. "Oh, Firefly, you're in trouble."

"I can't," she whines.

Sterling looks to me, a dark smile claiming his lips. I like that look.

He steps away, moving around the desk. I wait, watching.

Natalia sits up, dazed, as she looks to me. She's in more trouble than she realizes. I doubt Sterling likes being told no as much as I do, and she's going to have to satisfy both of us.

Sterling stands on the other side of the desk to her back, even as she leans forward to hang her head.

He reaches across the desk, massaging her shoulders. "Spread your legs for him." He moves one hand into her hair and pulls. "Sit up straight, legs apart, and let him see what belongs to him."

She whimpers but spreads her legs.

The way Sterling has her in his grip, she's on display. Her perky breasts are in the air, her back slightly arched. With her legs apart, I see her swollen lips and perfect pussy. Like this, everything I claim is visible.

He presses his nose to her ear, nipping at her. "You don't get to tell us 'no,' Firefly."

Stepping between her legs, I run my hands down her arms, snagging her wrists in my grasp. "Not now. Not ever."

She gapes at me. "Cal."

I pin them together in one hand, lifting them over her head. I don't want to look. I want to touch. That requires binds and an extra set of hands and limbs to hold her down and force her to take everything.

Sterling is about to be very useful.

"Cal. I can't."

Sterling wraps his hand around her hands, his Dark winding around her forearms as he takes control of them for me. "You're going to lie back and let him have you." He nips her ear. "And you're going to take it like a good girl and come when we say."

"No." Her voice is thin, breathless. "No, I can't."

Sterling pulls her back, flat on the surface of the desk, pinning her hands. She gasps, her breasts rising for Sterling to lick and suck.

My Dark ravels around her legs, forcing them further apart.

I lean over her, Sterling moving out of my way. He slides a hand along her abdomen to wrap around her hip as I take her lower face in my hand. "You wanted us both."

Her eyes grow wider, fear glistening in them. It's not about what we're about to do to her. I know that. It's me.

Sterling chuckles. "I don't know if she was prepared for the reality."

She thinks I'll leave her again for wanting him.

"No." I ease my grip, pressing my mouth to hers.

I pull back, looking to Sterling. I'll find a way to drag him to his knees. He'll answer to me, and my mate and I will get what we want.

My Dark snarls in agreement. "*Ours.*"

I HEAD to dine with the contractors, Sterling at my side. Natalia has already gone to bed.

She'd been a limp, quivering doll before Sterling or I let up. When we had, she tried to get away, and her legs hadn't been able to support her. She'd crawled as Sterling laughed.

I can't blame him for that. It had been downright pathetic in an adorable way. I'd grinned, thrilled she was so broken.

I enjoyed seeing my mate pushed to her limits and couldn't bear to wake her for this.

I nudge Sterling into a turn. "Your contract is going to change."

He stops, crossing his arms. "She's too inexperienced to be able to override me."

"I'm not."

"Have you signed a union contract yet?"

"No."

"Then you're not my contractor and don't have the ability to dictate fuck all about my contract." He drops his arms and continues a few steps, passing me only to double back and glare. "Why haven't you signed one yet? What are you waiting for? Tal's a nervous wreck thinking you'll walk away again. Give her the damn contract."

"I'm cognizant of that, but I haven't been functional. It's not as simple as drafting a standard union contract, and you know it."

"Figure it out." He turns, heading down the hall.

I catch up. "I was working on it. Talia distracted me."

He pushes air out of his nose with a smirk. "This cursed mating bond is intense."

"It might be a good thing we don't share one."

He laughs, deep and free. "I'd do it anyway."

I shove him to the side, shaking my head. "Idiot. None of us would ever get anything done."

"Hiro and Thames manage it. Oh," he falls in step with me again. "Hiro has the same contract I do."

I cut my eyes at him. "What the fuck was going on in my absence? Did everyone lose their mind?"

He swings his hands together in front of him, one balled to smack against his open palm. "You put a Light on the throne of Dark, then left. Yes, everyone lost their mind, including you."

I breathe out through my nose and glare at the ceiling.

When we reach the dining hall, I take the seat at the head of the table.

Jacques lifts a tumbler at me. "Congratulations on being upright again."

Hiro lifts his chin. "Did that letter say anything about trying to kill you?"

I shake my head. "It was too many words to explain what I already knew." I focus on Zander next to Jacques. He's the only Light present in the room. Narrowing one eye, I ask, "Aren't there others of you here in Ilbuio? Or did I hallucinate that?"

"There are four others, my closest friends and the strongest of our avenger ranks." He inclines his head, his long gold hair styled into a complicated war braid. "They opted to eat earlier to avoid mingling with the Dark this evening."

"That ends tonight. They'll eat with the rest of us or not at all." I glance at Sterling. "Who is head vassal?"

He rubs his jaw. "Raz, Tam, or Sarina. They've been working together to manage my estate, Hiro's, and yours. They know our vassals and are best equipped to orchestrate coverage."

I look down the table, searching for Sarina. She's a small, pretty woman. Thomas was in love with her for a while, and worked closely with her. She never showed interest in my adopted son, but I couldn't fault her for that. I love the boy, but the Dark is all about strengths. He has a severe disadvantage as a Seraphim.

I spy her off to the side, directing a man.

I stand, heading for Sarina to give the order. She inclines her head, welcoming me back. She accepts the order, and I pivot, stopping mid-turn as Tony approaches.

"Cal."

I jerk my head. "Sit. I have questions."

"Do I take orders from you and Tal now? Or still just Tal? Not sure how these contract things work."

"You have a contract with her?"

He rumples his honey-brown hair. "Yeah. Protect the Dark

and train Magia allies. I presume a contract means I follow orders by default."

I cock my jaw as Sarina giggles.

I wave her off. "Go be useful." I drag my hand down my face, staring at Tony. "You're obligated to only do what is assigned in your contract."

"Oh." He yanks back, blinking a few times. "Then I don't have to take orders at all."

I send my Dark to drag him to the head of the table and shove him in a chair next to Thames. "Sit." I take my seat and glare at Sterling. "He doesn't have an orders clause?"

Sterling shrugs. "No."

I wag a finger at him, Hiro, then Tony and back a few times. "All of you are getting new contracts."

Tony holds his hands up. "I'll do what Tal says. No big deal."

Hiro shrugs. "Get fucked. My contractor is Tal."

"You all took advantage of my departure, and it ends now." I focus on Tony as vassals begin serving food. "Magia."

He laughs. "Fuck. This again? Am I going to have to oink for you?"

"I already asked Tal, now I'm asking you. You said the High Assembly knows more magic than the rest and you got additional training. Can you create tangible silver threads with your magic?"

"No."

Jacques leans forward on crossed arms. "You're trying to figure out if they have the same magic? That Aggika stuff."

I nod.

Tony shakes his head. "Don't know Aggika. Hey, parasite, what's Aggika?"

I frown. "Parasite?"

"Fatum." Tony points to his ear. "She can't exist without a

host. That's the definition of a parasite, and she says it's the magic of Eternums." He lifts and drops one shoulder.

Jacques lifts his glass at me with a laugh. "On a bright side, we send those fucks to the afters, and I never have to experience that much pain ever again."

Sarina brings me a glass and a bottle of bourbon, placing them in front of me then backing away. I fill the glass, and Sterling snags it, taking a drink.

I steal the glass back for a drink then set it down between me and Sterling to share. "Less good news, we still don't know how to combat it."

CHAPTER 12
CALLAHAN

1ST SUN'S DAY, BLOOMING, 4050, 6TH MILLENNIUM

When I wake, I roll to my back, stretching out. I wave my arm, but the sheets are cool and barren. Reaching further, I find solid warmth.

Opening my eyes, I twist to my side, frowning at the empty space between me and Sterling. I curl my lip and shove him with my Dark.

He snorts and jerks awake, blinking at me.

I point to the vacancy between us.

He groans, closing his eyes but sitting up. "Fuck," he whispers, rubbing his face.

I get up and look around the room. No Natalia.

Sterling stalks across the end of the bed toward me. I glare. He points out.

Turning, I spy Natalia on the balcony. I should have known.

Sterling opens the glass door, stepping out and leaving it open behind him for me to follow.

He steps to one side, leaning against the railing, bent over with his forearms on the banister.

Natalia has her weight on one foot, the other bent, toe-tapping against the floor. She's wearing one of my shirts. The hem flirts with the bottom of her butt cheeks. She'll have nothing but that on her body.

My cock twitches with excitement.

A chuckle from Sterling wafts through the air.

I step out, moving to her other side. "Didn't I tell you when I go to sleep with you, I expect to wake up with you?"

Sterling laughs. "I owe you coin."

Lifting my eyebrow, I look to him.

He shakes his head. "She wagered twenty coin you would come out and say exactly that."

"Then yes, I have told you that?" I tuck hair behind her ear, sliding my hand to the back of her neck for a solid grip. "I hate waking up and not knowing where you are."

She turns her head to me with a wide grin, too forced for sincerity. "I never go far."

I hum, narrowing my eyes. "You intentionally vex me."

"No?"

Sterling snickers. "I'm more irritated that she can walk this morning."

I smirk at him. "We can change that."

He's upright, swinging Natalia into his arms before I can blink.

She focuses on me, her face lax and eyes wide.

My smirk twists into a grin. Pivoting on my heels, I walk back into the bedroom.

Sterling tosses her on the bed.

Dark races to her, tugging my shirt off her shoulders before tossing it aside to leave her bare.

I grab her, flipping her to her stomach and gripping her hips to pull her against mine.

Sterling slides onto the bed, settling in front of her.

I align my cock, rubbing the head against her slit. It's already slick.

Sterling lifts her torso, winking at me. "Let's get you wet for him, Firefly."

I narrow my eyes. "You think I need help?"

Tangling his fingers in her hair, he pulls her head to the side. I inhale sharply with understanding as his face lowers toward our mating marks on her neck.

I get the crown of my cock into her, starting to stretch her around me as he licks. She tightens, her hips rocking, and her pussy sucks me further inside as she comes.

Sterling forces her over again.

I thrust, lifting her hips. My Dark twists her legs out into a full split, letting me thrust deeper into her.

Sterling groans, "Look at me, Tal."

She whimpers, arching her back, trying to lift her torso. It's a perfect angle for me, and I ram in and out.

Sterling hasn't moved, his hand fisting her hair. "You look so pretty with a cock in you."

She really does.

Sterling binds her hands, holding them in one of his above her head.

Dark strands wrap around her torso, streaking toward the ceiling to anchor her in suspension.

She's helpless, clamping around my cock as she gags on Sterling's. I enjoy that.

Her mouth will be busy. She won't be able to lie with words like "can't" or "too much" as we force her to come for us until we're satisfied.

NATALIA IS STILL in the middle of the bed. She hasn't moved. I stand at the foot of the bed, contemplating what a privilege it is to have my bed occupied by my mate.

Sterling knocks a closed fist against my bicep, then slings his arm around my shoulders, leaning into me. "Aren't we lucky?" he asks, a smile in his voice.

Pulling my mouth back in glee, I chuckle.

She'd whimpered, squirmed, begged, and claimed she couldn't handle more before either Sterling or I finished wringing orgasms out of her. We used her until she quit fighting, making sweet noises of pleasure in surrender to us.

He rests his chin on my shoulder, sagging into me. "Tell me I'm not dreaming."

"You're not dreaming."

"Mm, still feels like it."

I glance at him with a raised eyebrow. "Why?"

He snickers. "Stupid question, baby."

He must be thinking about sharing Natalia. I flex my shoulders back with a disinterested hum. I've accepted this, sharing her with him. He'll figure it out.

I have one great annoyance. I don't have a lot of experience in sharing. I spent years learning how to fuck a woman. I know how to fuck two women at the same time. I have never once invited another male into my bed.

I must find new ways involving another cock. It'll take time to try new things and figure out what works and what I enjoy.

Two annoyances.

I have a union contract to draft.

I got a full night of peaceful sleep. The nightmare toxin is loosening its grip and may be out of my system. It's time to focus.

Shrugging off Sterling, I head for the office. He follows, stopping in the doorway to lean against the framework as I sit.

He jerks his chin. "Union contract?"

I nod, picking up the crumpled, stained ligan pagan with Natalia's concept. I wrinkle my features in disgust, finding a fresh page.

I set it before me, staring at it.

Sterling comes closer, dropping into the chair in front of the desk. "I had an idea."

"No."

Sitting forward, I instruct my Dark. It wraps around a pen, writing. Natalia's concept is perfect. It just needs to be polished.

When it's complete, my Dark signs my name and then throws the pen at Sterling.

I lift my chin. "It needs to be signed."

He laughs, tossing the pen to the desk. "I'll go fetch—"

"Sign it," I say, adding heat to the words.

He frowns. "Tal's in bed."

"I'll get her to sign when you're done."

"Union contracts are between two." He holds up his first and middle finger.

"And contracts one into submission of the second. This isn't a union contract as we know, and we're bringing Dark and Light under one crown. The world is fucked. While we're busy remaking it, we might as well take advantage of it and make it what we want."

He stares at me.

"We *are* lucky. I won't piss on my good fortunes. Will you?"

He picks up the pen and spins it in his fingers, pulling the contract closer for inspection. "I will stand at your side and be an equal partner in decisions made and enforced." He looks to me from the tops of his eyes. "You sure about that?"

"It's incumbent on me to acknowledge your lack of brain for the last few days, but you're usually more intelligent. I expect better from now on. Keep reading."

He returns his focus to the contract. "I will herein be bound in contract to my two mates for the duration of this life. No contract may interfere or disrupt the duties I accept alongside my mates, nor may remove any participant of this contract from the other or others."

"No one in the contract can remove another. You are legally binding yourself into a relationship with Natalia and me."

"Using the contract to ensure I don't pull you two apart. Eloquent."

"Convenience."

"Bound and fucked for life."

I hum. "In more ways than one. I should have put that verbiage into ink."

He opens his mouth, moving his jaw side to side and scratching at it. He mumbles, his lips moving with muted words below the sound of a whisper as he continues to read, and then he laughs.

"I will share a bed, a crown, and a throne with my chosen mates." Meeting my eyes, he says, "You're certain about me signing this?"

"I don't like being questioned."

"You can't be rid of me."

"Being a contractor, having to stand alone on your own and survive on nothing but your own strength—"

"Is exhausting and lonely."

"I love her."

He snickers. "She's a fucking nightmare to manage."

"I'll have you both."

He signs by hand, setting the pen aside, then stands, stretching his arms over his head, pulling them to one side. "I think I pulled something. How the fuck does she get into some of those positions?"

"I have no idea, but speaking of convenience..."

He laughs. "I'll go wake up Tal." He hesitates in the doorway, turning to face me. "Figure out how to ask her to sign that thing nicely. If we tell her, she'll fight."

I shrug, resting back. "She answers to me...most of the time."

"Lucky bastard." He knocks on the door frame, slipping away.

He returns, cradling Natalia in his arms. Setting her in the seat, he leans with one hand on the desk, offering the pen.

She pulls my shirt closed tighter around her, shifting in the chair. Running her fingers through her hair, she looks at the pen, Sterling, and then me. "What am I signing?"

"Union contract. Equal partners responsible for deciding together, protecting each other, and working together as a single unit. You'll be bound legally to your mates for life."

She takes the pen, puts it to the ligan pagan, and then withdraws, leaving the document unsigned. "You and Sterling signed this."

He taps the page. "Now it's your turn."

Her eyes snap to mine.

I smile, nodding. "Sign it, Talia."

She rolls her eyes up and to the corner toward Sterling.

I strum my fingers, propping my chin on my other. "I'm fucking tired of repeating myself. The two of you are going to quit making me say things twice."

Leaning forward, she signs the contract.

I slip it off the desk and slide it into the back of the cabinet with the other contracts. It can rot there for eternity. I'll never burn it to release either of them.

Legally, I can't contract them into submission, but I'll make sure they know their place is beneath me, answering me. I have to rely on subtle manipulation, twisting their minds into subconscious obedience instead of forcing compliance outright. I'll condition them, ingraining the behavior I want.

My Dark fills with smugness.

I pull another page out. "Talia, dissolve Sterling's contract."

They both jerk to me with shock.

I cock my jaw, not deigning to repeat that command. Instead, I send my Dark across the fresh page. It's two words, but it's complex.

I sign my name below it in magic.

Sterling scoops Natalia out of the chair and then sits in it with her in his lap. "All right, Firefly. Tell your Light to withdraw itself." He moves her hand on top of his.

When her hand falls away, the skin is vacant. She frowns at me. "Why?"

Because I want them worn by me, and I'll take what I want. I turn the page, saying, "Sign."

Natalia's hand hovers, and her eyes well up. "Cal."

"Don't make me say it twice."

She sniffs. "Ha. Not this time, babe."

Once she's signed, Sterling puts his hand to it. "Someone explain this to me."

They both signed, so I draw the contract off the page into the palm of my hand. I cradle it, considering, then slide my hand across my ribs on my left side near my heart.

I watch them form on Sterling, black words, two black names on either side of a silver script.

He says, "Now tell me how I comply with this." He points at his side.

I shrug. "You'll know when you're in contempt, and I'll have Natalia play the song for you later. Breakfast first."

CHAPTER 13
NATALIA

I'll Stay.
Callahan Matteo Barraco
Natalia Swan
Sterling Jason Wellsly

I was close to bawling when I read the contract. Two little words that mean so much.

I'm already exhausted and weak. I lost count of the orgasms they forced. I can't handle emotions, still half delirious in afterglow.

And Cal wrote the contract. It's not Shawn Gettemier's version. It's mine. My beautiful lie is a reality I hold.

I've been a selfish, stupid, and stubborn asshole most of my life. I jump first and think second. I let my temper get the better of me, and I refuse to acknowledge that I ever need help.

It doesn't matter.

There hasn't been a single word spoken about children, about use, about power, or control. I'm not a puppet dancing for someone else. I am me with two men and more love than I ought to be entitled to.

Cal and Sterling see me.

They bound themselves to me in a legal contract of union. Cal gave me vows. He signed the three of us into a worn contract, not for service, but for love.

No one is in contempt. That scares me. Cal's going to realize my affection for Sterling. I can't breathe at the thought.

I sit at the dining table in a chair between them. Sterling has his arm draped over the back. Cal's hand is on my thigh.

I should run. I should flee, far and fast, and never look back. This can't last.

The safest choice I can make is to break my heart first. I could throw it to the floor and shatter it into a million pieces, hang them in the night sky as new stars to tell the tale of what could have been and warn others of the agony love brings.

Daring to keep them both will ensure I keep neither. I'm conflicted between what I know and what I want, but I've been adamant with Cal. I am his mate, not Sterling's.

As if reading my thoughts, Cal sets his mug aside. He squeezes my thigh, kissing my temple. "To the bitter end, whatever it may be, I will stay."

He knocks on the table. The occupants in the room begin to fall silent, heads turned toward us.

Cal lifts his voice, addressing those at the table. "Your Dark King, Natalia, I, the Light Queen, and Sterling have joined together in a contract of union. This legally binds us together and signifies the merge of Dark and Light."

The Darklings and Lights all bristle. One leans forward to sneer at us. "We won't accept this."

I lean forward, propping my chin. "Every single one of you just raised your hackles." I motion with my other hand at the table. "Dark and Light." I point at a man wrapped in gold, then a woman in shadows. "You're in agreement on this."

He opens his mouth, jaw flapping.

I smile. "Go ahead, be contrary for the sake of it; agree with me instead." I bat my eyelashes.

A woman laughs further up the table. "The Light will just for spite."

Zander shakes his head, standing. "No. The Light is built on respect. We will follow a Hallow for their strength and their honor. Pierre died for this. We may not like it, but we will honor Pierre's last wishes and stand with the Dark under one crown." He bows to Cal.

Cal points, motioning downward with his finger. "Sit down and quit bowing to me. It makes me twitch."

Zander sits but says, "It is a show of respect."

Cal lounges back. "There is a long list of laws to go through. This will take time. We will forge new laws, a new system, one of compromise between our kinds to exist in shadows between us. The Dark will change. The Light will alter. Our two kinds are going to both give in exchange for the new world, but while the new world is established, we'll start small. As of this moment, slurs like Animal or Glow Whore will not be tolerated. We'll use the terms Darkling and Lighter, or, if you want to show respect, learn a name."

Plenty sneer or curl their lip, displaying disgust.

I twist my upper body. "Darkling and Lighter?"

He shrugs. "I like your Magia terms. Simple, non-insulting descriptors." He rolls forward, picking up his mug, saying, "Lucius and the rest of the Ancients intend to destroy the seeds of Dark and Light that root out magic. If they succeed, we all die, and your pathetic feelings about Dark or Light will cease to exist with you, so we focus on the threat."

The table remains silent.

"Tomorrow morning, and every morning until the Ancients are sent to the afters or placated, every single one of you is going to report to the main lawn to train. That's an order for Dark and Light, and I will assume any who refuse to comply has accepted death instead of fighting, and I will send you to the afters myself."

The order isn't one I was aware of. I almost make a quip about the "we decide" portion of our contract, but stifle myself. I don't have reason to argue his decision in the matter.

Cal drains his mug. "Serve yourself. If you won't fight for another, fight for your life because we need numbers. If you won't protect the Light because you are Dark or the Dark because you are Light, then do it for your existence. The threat to one kind is a threat to the other. We survive in balance as two halves. Serve yourself by saving others."

His Dark slings the mug across the surface of the table, where it clatters and spins in the silence. Turning to Zander, he asks, "Who are these Glow—Lighters?"

"Avengers." Zander motions to them. "Wyham, Liam, Hailey, and Palak. They are those I call friends, as well. You'll find they lack nothing."

I scan their faces. Two brunettes, one black-haired and one blond. I've met them and shared meals and conversations with them. Zander introduced me to his friends. I had forgotten them, discarding the memories of my time in Izul and on Zander's arm.

I never did feel at home standing next to him, and his height wasn't the reason. Sterling is as tall as Zander, dwarfing me.

I turn my head away from them and Zander, studying Sterling. For the attraction we share, a pull drawing us like a thread connecting us, demanding to stitch us together, I barely know him.

Not like Cal. My wicked Darkling is brutal and merciless,

strong, but beneath the carved muscles and clamped jaw, he has a gooey, fragile center.

The hauntings he endures from the past send a quiver through me. He's been drowning, and I haven't been able to save him. Desperation doesn't begin to describe the helplessness engulfing me these last days.

He'd offered me every broken piece of him. Until recent days ago, I would have laughed. Cal? Broken?

The cracks that radiate in him do nothing to tarnish his beauty, adding value instead. They allow him to radiate with strength, proving every misery he has endured without breaking apart.

Cal stands, offering me his hand. "Let's test that proclamation, shall we?"

Taking his hand, I rise, lifting an eyebrow.

He smiles, running his fingers through his black hair, leaving it a rumpled mess, the straight strands falling in front of his eyes. "We're going to measure their worth, Little Star."

I press my fingertips to the pendant I wear, the jewel-fashioned star.

The barest kiss of a smirk turns up one side of his pouty lips. "The rest of you, call on every fighter you have. I want every player, the partners, and every vassal worth its weight who can swing a fist or spin a blade. Bring them here. We start building an army. Sterling, get the fuck up. You're coming with us."

He stands. "Bound and fucked for life."

Cal puckers his lips, mocking a kiss. "You wanted it, baby."

Sterling laughs, cracking his knuckles. "Where are we doing this?"

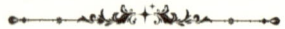

BEHIND THE PALACE sprawls open green, flat for an expanse before rolling into hills. The mountains sit beyond, the grass rising to meet the stone as they tear into the sky as jagged teeth.

I hadn't realized the beautiful gemstone green of the grass here. It had been too dim, hazy with mist and fog during my first visit.

Cal and Sterling bump fists and throw signs with their fingers a few times. Sterling points at the largest Light.

"I want that one."

It transpired without a word between Cal or Sterling. They seem like the best of friends, age-old and battle-worn allies in sync without effort. The two of them together make my heart flutter.

Ardent adoration consumes me. Sterling is half a head taller than Cal, but Cal's shoulders are wider. They're both carved works of art. I can't wait to get back in bed to trace their hard edges and feel their hands on me. They don't hesitate. There is nothing tender or gentle about the way they touch me. I am theirs and they let me know it without remorse. I enjoy it—enjoy them.

Embarrassment flushes my face. I look to the grass, shuffling my feet.

Wyham steps forward, bowing with disdain as he introduces himself.

Sterling has him in the dirt within fractions.

Cal takes down Palak just as quickly.

I thought I'd get a turn, but Sterling chose the third, facing off against Hailey. She does a bit better, but Sterling pins her.

Cal swings with Liam, kicking him away.

Cal rubs his jaw, using the hem of his shirt to wipe his brow. "Fucking pathetic." He twists to Zander. "These are the best you offer?"

Zander frowns, sparing a glance at his friends. "I believe they deserve another chance. I doubt they were prepared for your ferocity in a friendly challenge."

"Not one of them is worth my exertion."

I lift my hand. "Why am I here?"

"I don't know. I presumed at least one would be an equal, given the boast I was offered, that you'd have your try. I could have left you in the hall."

Palak waves his hand toward the other side of the lawn. "May I make an inquiry as to the structure over there?"

Cal, Sterling, and I look. Cringing, I shuffle a step further from it.

Cal cocks his jaw, twisting his features with disgust. "It's the maze. Stay away from it."

Wyham takes a step forward. "May I ask for the reason?"

"Quit asking me to ask what you want and just fucking ask. It's the maze. That's why."

I shudder. "It's made with nightmare toxin and a death trap that makes your fears come to life. Leave it alone, don't go near it. You'll regret it if you do. That thing is awful."

Sterling sweeps me off his feet, spinning us in a circle before smiling down on me. "You don't have to be concerned about doing it ever again, Firefly."

"Once was enough."

Sterling laughs. A strand of Dark strokes my cheek. "You have no idea."

He rubs his nose against mine, pressing his lips to mine.

I shouldn't. I do, anyway. Parting my lips, I tilt my head.

His tongue licks against mine. Then he pulls back, setting me on my feet. "Cal."

"Mm." He stays focused on the others. "Zan, find me fighters that glow for all our sake."

Wyham rolls his shoulders. "I'd like another try."

"I'm not wasting my time."

Sterling scoffs. "I'll go another round. I could use the exercise. I've been sitting around getting fat and lazy."

Wyham takes a step forward. "With Tallie."

Cal tenses, and Sterling snarls. "You can't put me down. You haven't earned that right."

Wyham glares at me. He was the first one Zander introduced me to, the closest confident to Zander. The request isn't about proving anything.

I pat Sterling on the arm. "It's personal."

"How the fuck could anything be personal? You don't even know each other."

Wyham lifts his chin. "We are acquainted. Zander formally introduced us. Hello, Tallie."

"Hi, Wyham."

Cal asks, "Is this some shit about serving the Dark?"

Zander rubs his forehead. "Wyham, this is unnecessary."

Sterling points. "You have something to do with this?" He turns incredulous to me. "What does the Glow Fuck have to do with this?"

Cal swings at Sterling, catching him in the chest, knocking Sterling back a step and putting his palm to Sterling's center. "Non-insulting terms or names."

"Old habits and personal feelings."

"I don't care. Use the terms. If you won't uphold the rules, I can't enforce them on others."

Sterling meets my gaze, scowling. "What don't I know?"

I lean my head to the side to indicate the Lighters. "They're all friends to Zander. I had accepted a relationship with him while I was in Izul."

Sterling bares his teeth. "You said you had history, that he fucked you before you knew better, but not that."

Hailey snaps, "That is uncalled-for language and revolting terminology. Tallie would have been fortunate if she had taken Zander for her mate."

I run my fingers over the pendant around my neck. "He gave me this," I tell Sterling. "They do this thing where if you give a gift, you get one in return. In exchange for agreeing, this was my gift."

"Figured it came from Cal."

Cal snickers. "It did. That fuck used my gifts against me."

Zander lifts his voice. "I had no knowledge—"

"That fuck being Pierre."

The Lighters all turn acrimonious. Palak yells, "Show respect to your better."

Cal waves them off with a laugh. "He knows why he's that fuck. He's not my better, and he wouldn't argue the term. As for the star *my star* wears, it was never Zander's or even Pierre's gift. It was mine."

Wyham feigns a step back. "Excuse me?"

Cal faces him, rippling with fury. "You lied. You each lied to her or at least concealed the truth. You couldn't hold her on merit, so you stooped to falsehood. The pendant wasn't Zander's gift to give. It was mine, and she never would have consented had she known the truth. So back off my mate. She's mine. She has always been mine from the moment I found her."

Sterling chuckles. "I'm going to the afters." He trails his fingers over the back of my neck. "You're going to be the death of me, Firefly."

I really don't want that.

Stepping into him, I wrap my arms around his waist.

He chuckles. "Cal."

"I'm not sending you anywhere."

Sterling says, "I thought about your visit. When you bought the guitar for our woman."

I step back. "Guitar?"

Sterling nods. "Cal came to me for help. He wanted access to Shawn."

Cal moves closer, cupping my face and stroking my cheekbone with his thumb. "He made sure Shawn complied."

I look from Cal to Sterling, then back. I push my finger to Sterling's sternum, asking Cal, "I owe him for my guitar?"

Sterling shakes his head, his thick, twisted black locks shifting. "No, I helped. It was Cal's idea. He paid. I just made sure he got what he wanted."

"Why?"

"I've always had a weak spot for Cal, and I wouldn't cheat him." He tugs my ponytail, turning to Cal. "Yanri. We made a deal, and not quite how we thought things would go, but I still want to deal with that."

"We will. Contracted will no longer be property. We provide rules to ensure contractors meet a minimum standard."

Sterling tips his head back with a smile, sighing at the sky. "Thank fuck."

Hailey laughs. "I'm afraid of what 'minimum standards' means to you. You lot abuse your own kind, beating them and using aggression to force your dominance."

Cal and Sterling pivot in unison. Cal's face scrunches on one side, his lips parted. Sterling's whole face creases. Both stare in confused disgust.

I giggle behind my hand. "No, they don't."

Cal shakes his head, rubbing his face. "Some, I'll admit that. It's abhorrent absurd abuse of contracts. I won't accept it under my reign." He turns to Sterling, jerking his head. "They get designated free time, coin in payment, and protection, all denoted in the laws of the Light."

"Responsibility of the contractor."

"I can legislate so much."

"We."

Cal smiles. "We can—"

"Fine." Sterling scratches at his neck. "I still want Yanri's head."

I poke him again. "Who is Yanri?"

"A slippery fucking prick who has an illegal contract."

Cal turns to Zander. "We need fighters. Any glowing man or woman who has mettle, skill, or willingness to learn. The five of you get them here. The Dark will train them."

Zander's brow furrows. "Ashley will need to make the decree. While I recognize your stature, you remain uncrowned. Until then, a Bordeaux will merit moderate obedience. However, I cannot make a guarantee your demand will be fulfilled."

Cal takes my hand. "Fine. Get Ashley to do it. We're going to take care of Yanri."

Palak steps in the way, chin high. "I beg pardon for overstepping my place and rank, but if I am to consider obeying your commands, I want to see how you handle yours. Will you grant me access to insight?"

"You're welcome to take what you want if you're capable of it. Don't ask for permission to do something."

"That is not our way."

Wyham presses a hand to Palak's shoulder. "We wouldn't even make the request by our customs, allowing our contractor to decide."

I ask, "Who is your contractor?"

Palak nods to me. "The crown. We are here at Zander's behest. I believe your kind is vulgar. We know the way you treat your kind. It's a prominent lack of respect and care, even for kin. I will see how you manage one before I determine my allegiance in a contract of service."

Cal's fingers tighten on mine. "Your kind has a lot to learn. You're welcome to watch, but you won't interfere."

Cal pulls me forward, rigid and his hand clamped tight on mine. In the past, I'd have demanded he let go, the force too excessive for me. My hand pulses, but the pain is minimal. Mallafic changed so much.

He's sour because of the goads, questioning his ability to be an alpha. What the Light thinks that role is differs starkly from the reality of Cal's definition. He taught me a contractor cares and protects.

Whoever Yanri is, I don't envy him. Cal's even less forgiving when he's cranky and Palak just insinuated Cal's a piece of garbage.

CHAPTER 14
NATALIA

Cal pulls me through the palace toward our rooms. When we get to the outer wall, where we usually turn right to our rooms at the end of the corridor, Cal goes left.

This hallway ends abruptly at a set of double doors. Cal's Dark opens one. He guides me inside, saying, "The Dark King's private hall. It's for the throne's personal use."

He lets go of my hand. "I'll summon Yanri."

Sterling shoves him back toward me. "You stay here and deal with that." He waves at the Lighters. "I'll skip the burns and play fetch."

Pivoting, he walks out of the room, whistling with a bounce in his step. I smile after him until Cal tries to tuck a wisp of hair behind my ear.

I meet his eyes.

The corners of his eyes crinkle as his pouty lips curve. "Mate."

With a squeal of delight, I jump at him. He catches me, laughing.

I tap his chest. "This. How's this?"

"Better every day."

A throat clears. "What did he mean burns?"

I look to Zander, but Cal answers. "The Light burns out the Dark until it can no longer exist. We say those words—you say those words as a truth, but you don't know how true they are." He sets me on my feet. "Your magic will burn us just by being in proximity."

Palak frowns. "Then how could a Light and Dark be friends?"

I point at Cal. "I've never burned him, not once. I've never burned any Darkling I've encountered, as far as I know. Sterling said it was because of animosity—that your magic, on instinct, tries to destroy the Dark for no reason other than hatred."

"Then...it's...possible?" Palak lifts his hands, looking at them with a forlorn expression, then to Wyham.

Wyham shakes his head. "No."

"But..."

"Whatever he thought, a Dark killed him."

"I should have gone with him when he asked."

Hailey steps closer, putting a hand to Palak's chest. "My brightest Light, there is no fault in you. The Dark will snuff out the Light on instinct."

Cal scoffs. "For all our sake, put aside what you think you know about the hatred and open your eyes. Dark and Light have found common ground before, it's found love between the two. We are two halves of one whole, and we can choose to end the divide."

I step into Cal, wrapping my arms around him, wanting to be wrapped in his embrace. His Dark winds around me, snaking in cool tendrils that caress my skin and stroke across my shoulders and hips.

Footsteps draw my attention. Sterling nods at Cal, coming to stand next to us. "Raz will summon Yanri and Oscar."

Dark tendrils of shadows and smoke twist around Sterling, but they are a thin haze rather than thick, opaque strands. I reach out, curling one around my finger. It stretches, coiling around my wrist and stroking my forearm. No matter what the truth is deemed, Dark and Light aren't enemies.

My skin sparkles brighter, another shadow elongating from my shoulder to meet Sterling's. A thread of my Light pokes out from my skin, both shadows racing for it. They twist around my Light as it winds itself between the two.

A knock on the door breaks the moment. Cal moves away from me, calling out. "Enter."

Sterling draws me toward the table, turning to lean his butt against the edge and cross his long legs at his ankles as he grips the lip of the wood.

The Lights shuffle, taking seats at the table as I turn my back on them to stand at Sterling's side. Cal will handle this.

Raz leads two men into the room. One is well-dressed and a bit shorter than average. His glossy brown hair is combed over, and he smooths it in place as he steps closer.

The other is lanky, with withered skin and bones, his face gaunt, and his blond hair is worked into a matted, frazzled braid down his shoulder. Dirty, threadbare fabric hangs from his body.

My stomach churns. It hurts to look at him.

Cal pushes from the table, taking a step forward. Both men stop, the haggard male remaining a pace behind the polished.

"He looks worse than ever," Sterling whispers.

Wood cracks.

I turn my head to stare at Sterling, who drops a large splinter of the table to the floor before crossing his arms. "Firefly, promise me that fuck suffers if you get the chance."

I frown, turning forward as Cal says, "Yanri."

The clean, full-of-vitality male inclines his head. "Callahan.

You have gumption, addressing me. I was summoned by my king, not you."

"Queen." He shrugs. "Oscar, sit." Cal jerks his head at the table.

Oscar doesn't move. Yanri glances at him, then returns his attention to Cal. "He's a worn contract and doesn't answer to you."

I move forward. "Oscar?" I point to the dilapidated male.

He lowers his chin, eyes to the floor.

I lean back on my heels. "I know the Light has customs about who can speak and when, but I'm not familiar with that in the Dark."

Yanri shrugs. "You're an idiot."

Cal opens his mouth, but I hold my hand to him. "The word is ignorant. Why is Oscar silent?"

"He got mouthy too many times."

I eye Oscar, then turn to Cal. I get mouthy. He calls it sass. I'm not dressed in rags, starved thin or silent.

"Why did you want to see him?"

Cal's face softens. "Because property or not, we have rules." His focus shifts. "Yanri, did you negotiate a contract with Oscar?"

"Of course." Yanri slides his hands in his front pockets, stretching up on the balls of his feet. "That's the law."

"Did you use it as a worn contract without Oscar's permission?"

Yanri twists his head, sneering at Oscar before answering. "This isn't your business."

"Don't fucking lecture me on contractual law. I've had contracts for centuries. I'm aware of the rules. As a crown of the Dark, I cannot embroil in a contract unless that contract is illegal." Cal steps closer. "Did you, yes or no?"

"You have to prove it's illegal before you can do anything. Can you prove it?"

"A prior contracted of yours informed me."

"Ah, yes, Oscar's wild conjectures that have no basis in fact. He's a liar, but my contracted are mine to deal with outside of court. Now you see why he has no right to speak."

Oscar winces, ducking his head.

"Did Oscar agree to a worn contract?"

"I wrote the contract in my magic."

"A failure to refuse is not an agreement."

I frown at Cal. I was a worn contract. That hadn't been negotiated. I hadn't known better. I was a lineage contract without ever knowing it. Cal's an asshole. We both know it.

He had warned me it was a contract beyond what I'd negotiated before I accepted it. I blame the Magia, Tony pressuring me for marriage and children, but I'd thought about taking Cal's contract, dreaming of him from the moment I turned him down. I'd wanted Cal.

He didn't make me regret it—much.

Yanri objects, making stupid sounds I don't give credence to.

Pivoting, I stare at Sterling. He had no reason to stand at my side, but he had all the same. He accepted a worn contract, knowing full well what I could do with it if I had any imagination. He even suggested I wear the contract.

He lifts an eyebrow at me.

I shift my gaze to Zander. He's leaned back in the chair, his arms crossed and covered in thick gold ropes of his Light. He's handsome, I can't deny that. His face irritates me, though. Those lips lie and lie, and lie. For a moment, I had trusted him. It was a misplaced belief.

I face Oscar, cutting off Yanri's agitated words. "Can you speak at all?"

His mouth twists to the side in a grimace.

He's sickly gray, sickly thin, sickly everything. Even his black eyes are hazy. I stare at him, and my bones ache.

"Okay, no. I'll ask yes or no questions. Nod or shake your head."

Oscar's gaze shifts to Yanri.

"You can't even do that, can you?"

Oscar holds my gaze.

I sidestep in front of Yanri, fury burning in me. "Let him speak."

He spits at me.

Cal snarls, and I round, intercepting him. I eye Sterling to stop him several paces away. I hold his gaze, then Cal's. I don't need their help.

Facing Yanri, I wipe the spit from my cheek. "Let him speak."

He spits again, but this time, my Light shields me.

I crack my knuckles, bending the fingers back. "Third time, and last. Let. Him. Speak."

"You can't dictate my contracts."

"No? Oh, I'm sorry. Did you confuse me with someone else?" I move closer.

He takes a step back. "You're the Dark King."

"I am annoyed, and I have a habit of doing whatever the fuck I want. You'll let him speak to give his side to determine the validity of the contract, or I take your tongue in payment."

"You can't do that."

"Watch me." My Light twists around me in thin vines. It's buzzing at the disrespect and lack of obedience.

Yanri rolls his shoulders back, looking behind me.

None of them says anything. There isn't a rustle of clothes or a sigh of annoyance.

He straightens. "The law is the law, and it is clear. You cannot involve yourself in my contract. Without proof, there is nothing you can do. It's one anonymous word against mine, and as I am in good standing without evidence to disgrace me, you cannot question my word."

I face Cal. "There must be a reason he's denying Oscar the right to speak, like a lie, and he's too much of a coward to confess. That's a disgrace to the Dark in multiple ways."

Yanri hisses through clenched teeth, leaning closer as he says, "I haven't—"

"I agree." Cal inclines his head. "It's your decision. If you—"

"You can't do this!"

"—want to disgrace him. I have the word of one in good standing that the contract is illegal, and while you cannot dictate contracts, you aren't overreaching by demanding the truth. I see no reason other than a lie that Oscar would be forbidden to speak and confirm the words of Shawn."

"Shawn?"

"Shawn Gettemier. He informed me for no specific reason, having no motive to divulge the information other than speaking the truth."

"No." Yanri stomps his foot, pointing at Cal. "I don't know what you think you know, but I didn't break the law."

Cal lifts an eyebrow, stone-faced. "Shawn Gettemier informed me that you have. You refuse to allow Oscar to speak."

"He's my contracted. I can do whatever I'd like to him."

"You've left Oscar to die and tried to sacrifice him for yourself in the games far more than any contractor can pallet."

I blanch.

Cal shrugs. "It's always borderline cowardice. We all see it. We all ignore Oscar because you leave him to die, and the rest of us follow the tenets. There would be no respect earned or honor found in sending him to the afters when you queue him up to be sent."

"How dare you? I use a partner in the intended way."

Sterling laughs, but it rings hollow. "You have no idea what a real partner is."

Cal remains calm, his features relaxed. "A partner is enlisted to prove the strength of those that answer to you. The stronger the individual who *willingly*," he stresses the word, dragging it out and pausing, "contracts themselves to you proves the strength you have in being their leader. In the games, the partner is not a weapon to be used or discarded."

"He came to me for a contract willingly. He signed the contract willingly," Yanri gloats. "The stupid wretch was undesirable until I hardened him in the games, made him a sharp tool to be used. It's the only purpose he suits."

The way Yanri speaks of Oscar makes me nauseous. Cal would never be so disrespectful or cruel to one who answers to him.

"I've heard enough." I square up to Yanri. "You won't even allow him to speak, too afraid of what he'll say. You're a coward, and your contract is illegal."

"How I manage my contracted is not your concern, and you can't prove anything. I wrote a contract in my magic. I took what I wanted because I could."

Folding my arms across my stomach, I lean my weight on one leg, sizing up Yanri. "Then allow him to speak freely and confirm."

"Get fucked, little girl. You cannot command this."

Cal steps to my side. "Do you want to handle this?"

I tip my head back, beaming at him. He's always had belief in me. Looking to Yanri, I say, "Poor Oscar looks starved. Do you feed him?"

"He's a man. He can feed himself."

"I'm pretty sure your vassals feed you. What does that make you?"

Oscar chokes.

I smirk at him. "I get mouthy, too."

Yanri sneers. "You need to be taught a lesson."

Cal snickers. "Good luck."

Shaking my head, I look to him. "How do I do it?"

Cal looks to Sterling. "Do you know?"

He laughs. "I finally know something you don't?"

Cal snickers. "Verifying you could if I need you to. Yanri Horonnon, you are hereby disgraced."

"No!"

"By law, all written contracts you have are to be destroyed," Cal decrees, whispering a single word I can't make out and snaps his fingers.

Yanri yells, "You can't do this."

I laugh. "He did."

Yanri bares his teeth, leaning toward me and clenching his fists.

"Go ahead," I dare him.

He spins. "Oscar, come." He whistles.

Oscar ducks his head like a beaten dog obeying its master.

Disgrace doesn't alter a worn contract, only written.

"Yanri," I call out. "We aren't done. That addressed your cowardice and lies, but there's still an illegal contract in place. Dissolve it."

"No."

I smile, showing my fangs. "Dissolve your worn contract."

"You can't make me."

"No?"

"No." He turns and shoves Oscar. "Move, useless mutt, and don't think this changes anything. You're still my property, and I'm going to make you fucking pay for this."

"Hm, maybe you're right, but..." I walk forward. "I gave you a choice."

"What was that?"

I reach out, my Light streaking for him. He flails, Dark racing toward me. The shards pierce into me, radiating cold.

My Light hisses, turning brighter. I close my hand around his throat.

A garbled scream releases from him as I rip the flesh.

Blood splatters my face, and I recoil, a lump of heavy, wet gore in my hand.

Yanri puts a hand to the hole, gurgling as blood gushes down his front and out of his mouth.

I stare at him, then tilt my head to inspect the mass in my hand. I weigh it, rooting through it with my thumb. I don't know if I succeeded in my intentions.

Yanri tips sideways with a whimper. He chokes, spasming on the floor.

I shrug, toeing him as he goes still.

Oscar gapes at me.

I toss the lump of flesh at Yanri's body. "I told you I'd have your tongue."

Lifting his hand, Oscar runs his fingers over his forearm, then lifts his eyes to mine. They glisten, bubbling over as beads of wet fall. He stumbles a pace closer, his knees buckling as he wraps his arms around me.

I go stiff, and Oscar drags my body to his knees, sobbing.

I get one arm free, patting his head and looking for Cal.

He steps next to me. "I don't think that was his tongue."

Oscar cries, sucking in wet breaths.

"He said I couldn't make him dissolve the contract. I proved him wrong."

"Little Star." Cal shakes his head. "He deserved it, but that wasn't legal."

Sterling helps Oscar to his feet. "Up. On your feet like a man."

Oscar pants and shudders, throwing his arms around Sterling and crying harder.

Sterling puts an arm around him, clapping him on the back. "You're free."

"I— I did–didn't agree."

"Not one of us thought you did. We know what kind of man he was. That was more than enough to know the truth."

I shake my head, wiping my hand on my shirt and wrinkling my nose. "Oscar."

He jerks to face me.

"Come with me." I motion with two fingers, step over Yanri, then turn back and put my hand to him, setting him alight with firelight.

When he's ash, I straighten and look to Oscar. "Please follow me. You need food, and I'm hungry just looking at you."

Dragging his wrist under his nose, Oscar bobs his head. "Five times a week if you behaved, less if you so much as sneezed wrong."

I freeze. "What?"

He swallows. "That's what we got."

"You... He really fucking starved you?"

Oscar hangs his head. "I got more than the rest for one month in preparation for Gathering Shadows."

Cal groans, "Sterling."

"I'll agree to whatever you want. Fuck it, use Light Law. This shit ends now."

Thomas warned me Cal was one of the best contractors. I could have been like Oscar, bound in a worn contract without hope.

I could have been starved, gagged, abused in every way. I've never once shown appreciation for Cal as a contractor.

He doesn't need me to inflate his ego, and I'm not feeding the idea that I will ever sit, stay, and be a good vassal. But I'll be extra compliant sometime soon.

I sigh, moving to get under one of Oscar's arms to prop him up. "Dude, one foot in front of the other. That's an order. We go straight to the kitchens, and you eat all you want. I'll give you a contract with that command if I must, but you need food."

"I'll take a con–contract. I'll serve. I'll do anything you want."

I drag him forward as he blubbers. He weighs nothing. It's sick. He's taller and bigger than me, even as a skeleton with skin. "What I want is for you to eat."

CHAPTER 15
CALLAHAN

I watch Natalia lead a gimping Oscar toward the door. Rubbing the back of my neck, I look to Sterling.

He jerks his chin at them. "You taught her well."

"I'm just glad she learned. She doesn't like to."

She laughs as she disappears. "I heard that."

I smirk as she leaves, muttering about food and being hungry all the time is miserable. She would know. Her eating habits have cut back, but I've watched her inhale my body weight and be hungry a rune later. She mentioned she couldn't afford to eat before I took her as a contract.

I focus on Sterling. The gods help anyone who goes after my mate. I wave at the floor. "Illegal as fuck."

He shrugs. "I have—had—a few of his old contracted. I'd rather exist as Telra's plaything than be Yanri's contracted. He was foul."

"Still murder."

"We're not Dark and Light anymore. Make it legal. It was an illegal contract, and he refused to comply with an order from the king. She did meddle in a contract, but only in the pursuit of truth. Yanri got what he earned."

I laugh. "Fair enough." I puff my cheeks and blow out hard. "We can't change current contracts, but we can establish law to protect new ones."

"Contractors are alphas."

"That needs defining in literature."

"It really fucking shouldn't." He throws his hands up. "For fuck's sake, five times a week? How he fucking talked about Oscar?" He groans. "Just no."

I chuckle. I can't make a contractor know the names of their contracted or force them to learn about their contracted in order to make them happy and give the contracted what they need, but I can offer protection. I can set guidelines for how to be a contractor in the way I demand, and a high level of care and shelter for those who serve.

My mate signed my contract in ignorance. I could have done anything to her. If someone else had latched on first, stolen her away before I held her in my claws, she could have been like Oscar.

My Dark snaps and snarls. It would rip anyone apart who dared to silence her jokes or starve her perfect body to death-like appearance.

Turning to the table, I say, "Zander. I want a full, detailed set of Light contractual law."

He inclines his head. The top portion of his hair is in stylized knots and twists, but the long, loose strands slip over his shoulders. "Contractual law references other law."

I shrug. "Then get me all of them."

I need to spend time with him—figure out what makes him tick and who he is as a man. It's the last thing I want to do, but I'll set aside my feelings for truth. I am his contractor.

Wyham stands. "I knew the Dark mistreated theirs. This has confirmed my belief."

Sterling snaps his teeth. "There's bad Dark as much as there is bad Light. Yanri was one, and we corrected the rotten limb, amputating it from our society. Don't pretend like the Light doesn't have a list of contractors to avoid."

Palak winces, ducking his head. "He has a point."

"More to the point, we," Sterling says, motioning between me and himself, "do not and will not accept others harming or abusing contracted."

Wyham sneers.

"Cal was disgraced, and vassals still served without contracts. Don't fucking tell me he even once hurt them or so much as disrespected them. They would have run at the first chance."

Zander nods and stands. "I'll provide you with what you seek." He checks his arm with our contract.

I tell him, "I didn't change it. You'll know if I do."

Facing the others, Zander says, "I went to Callahan willingly. I offered him my services. He asked if I would accept a worn contract."

Wyham draws his features together. "Contractors don't ask."

"They negotiate. It's their custom."

I say, "Law. A contracted has the right to decide and agree to their contractual services. Worn contracts aren't subject to law as they are rooted in magic, but an agreement to one is required given their nature."

"That is not our law."

Sterling knocks a closed fist on my shoulder. "We keep that from Dark Law."

I bob my head. "Contracts will be agreed to and negotiated, but the law will protect them. I'll make a law that they are to be fed and cared for properly. I'll make sure there are proper guidelines in place. I need to find Thames."

"Why?"

I point at the doorway. "Did you fucking see him? Rags, cheap, ill-fitting and dirty."

"Hair matted and half dead." Sterling winces. "I didn't want to look at him. It was worse than usual."

"Thames can get him cleaned up and in order any Seraphinus deserves." I rub the side of my face. "I need Jacques, too. He's a social one. He'll want to be involved. Marius might have been a coward, but he was a good contractor. Jacques will have opinions."

"Hiro will be with Thames. We'll get his input, too."

"Draft up new laws for contracted, then run them past Falsion and my kin."

"They don't know fuck all about contracts."

"Precisely." I shrug. "They don't. What they'll know is it's fair to them without being tainted by previous contracts."

"Fair enough."

I turn to the table. "Why are you still here? I gave you an order."

Zander says, "You haven't dismissed me to deal with it." He waves his hand across the others. "Any of us."

This is going to be tedious. I meet Sterling's gaze. Broad forehead and wide nose with full lips. At least I have help.

Shaking my head, I look to the ceiling. "If I give you an order you don't need my permission to go do what I ask. You have three rules. You answer to me, you protect me, and you serve me. None of that requires my time to tell you to go do what I said. Go comply, or I change your contract to force you to break that custom."

Zander stands, inclining his torso at the other men. "Excuse me, please."

He leaves the room, the others remaining.

I turn to them, cocking my jaw and pulling my lips to the side, arms crossed. "Wyham?"

The man bows his head. "Your Majesty?"

"Don't call me that. Cal or Callahan is fine. *If,*" I say sharply, as he opens his mouth, "you want to show respect, do it through actions. Don't question me, answer me, do what I say, and don't call me dog."

Sterling steps to my side, wiggling his eyebrows at me. "But you're such a good boy."

I throw my arm into him, trying not to laugh. "Quit, Birdie. They'll think it's okay."

"Starting with contractual laws is good. We rewrite them to establish how contracts are treated by both sides for equal treatment. It'll help show who we are in how we decide others are taken care of."

"Are you just going to keep voicing my thoughts at me? Or are you going to be useful?"

"You need the crown before we can do anything legally." He takes a step closer to the table. "Zander said coronation happens before he officially has the power to rule. Let's start there. How?"

The occupants at the table sneer. Wyham braces his hands on the table as he stands. "Who are you? We do not know you, and you are not a Hallow."

"Sterling Wellsly, and I'm his mate." He jerks his head to me, dreads shifting.

Wyham cocks his head, leaning back slightly, then rights and stares at me. "You have two mates?"

"Yes," I say, pulling one side of my mouth back.

"That's sacrilege."

I hum, looking to Sterling. He turns his head, wincing over his shoulder at me.

Stepping to his side again, I tap the side of my forearm to his bicep. "The mating bond is sacred, but we are both mated to Natalia. I do not have two separate mates, but rather, the three of us are mates."

"It's revolting, spitting upon the very idea of what a mate is."

"How about fuck you?" I lift my eyebrows. "I'm not spitting on anything. I'm embracing my fortunate webs. I have two mates. Some don't even find one."

"A mate is a counterpart. You can't have two."

Sterling snickers. "Don't fuck this up for me, Glows. It's taken me centuries to get his attention." He slings his arm around my shoulders, bending it around my neck to pull me into him.

I chuckle. "You had it."

"You wouldn't so much as look at me."

"You hate pineapple. It makes your throat itch when you eat it."

His lips part as his eyes haze over. "What?"

"I'd join any conversation about you. I paid attention." I shrug.

He laughs. "You fuck."

I hum. "The crown of Light. What do we need to do?"

Wyham shakes his head. "The coronation will take place at the palace in Izul. It requires the presence of the most influential and powerful heritages. It must be planned. All involved will need formal attire, typically designed, made, and worn only for the coronation."

Palak stands and bows. "Additionally, it is usually the royal family and heir who makes the plans. As there are none but you and you lack the knowledge of how might I make a suggestion? Confer with Ashley. Allow her to make the arrangements and heed her guidance."

"Quit fucking bowing. You're contracted to the throne?"

"Our heritages are signed as avengers. That is why we are friends. Duty binds us, and we are suited company."

Sterling turns his head. "The fuck is that shit? Suited company?"

Wyham narrows one eye. "It does not do to interact with lesser. It will only degrade your station. Seek your equals, but do not overstep your betters."

"No. Anyone can talk to anyone. If you earn respect, you get it. How many do you deem as lesser that might be your better?" Sterling asks, holding up his hand as Wyham starts to argue. "No. If they don't get a fair chance, you don't know if you are they're better."

"The Dark is inconsistent with skill and power within your lineage. We assume it's from inappropriate crossbreeding, unlike the Light that will breed and mate only within acceptable ranges, like a Bordeaux and a Hallow, not a Hallow and...Wells."

"Wellsly," Sterling repeats through clenched teeth. "I was a contender like Cal, damn near as strong as him. I'm suitable."

Palak scoffs. "You're Dark. That's unacceptable, and I don't care about contender status. Those barbaric trials you have, take no place in the Light or our regards. A second mate is confounding at the politest, but a Dark is reprehensible. When you are crowned, leave the Wells here in Ilbuio. Use tact if you won't refuse to sever the union in its entirety. Never flaunt it or its status within Izul or bring it there during duty."

Sterling snarls.

I grab his shoulder and yank him back, even as I step toward the table. "You come here, seeking me, to serve me and pursue the unification of Dark and Light while spitting daggers without commitment to anything, then insult my kind, my mate, and my choices? My answer is no, politely, and get fucked in honesty. Sterling is strong. He is capable. He is everything I cherish about the Dark. He is my equal, and you'll show respect, or I beat you into submission."

Hailey flares to life. "You cannot—"

155

"I can and I will as necessary. When he speaks—when either of my mates speak—it's as good as me speaking. If we are going to bring the two together as one, we are going to have to learn to respect the differences instead of criticizing them. Forget preconceived notions and open your fucking eyes and ears. If you can find fault in Sterling, go ahead. Voice your concerns, and I will listen to rational thought. But if you can only find fault because he carries a seed of the Dark, you can fuck right off."

Wyham sits. "You two fought to kill each other a day ago."

Sterling bursts into laughter. "No, we didn't. Cal and I have never tried to kill each other, or one of us would be dead."

I grin. "He was throwing a tantrum, like a child who needed attention."

Palak makes a face as if he bit into a sour fruit. "It was deplorable actions."

"He needed to blow off steam." I drop my hands to my hips. "How my mate and I handle disputes between us is beyond your reproach."

"It endangered the life of a Hallow." Palak flings an accusatory finger in Sterling's direction.

I lift my shoulders. "My life was never at risk from Sterling. He stays. He stays at my side regardless of where I am or who I deal with. Accept that or give me logical proof I've made an error in his judgments or character."

They make disgusted faces but no further response.

Sterling drops his arm over my shoulder, pressing to my back. "I'm not asking for favors. We stand on our strength. Give me the chance to earn respect before you pass judgment." He puts his mouth closer to my ear. "Our mate has been out of sight and reach for too long."

"Mm, we should deal with that."

He chuckles. "It's cute how they think I'm the problem."

"She carries the heritage of Bordeaux. They're blinded by a

name. Am I correct in assuming because you are all contracted to the throne, I do not need to contract you?"

Wyham shakes his head. "Every queen has their own contracts. Our heritages are contracted to the throne, not us personally. You will need to sign us into your specific service."

Sterling squeezes me. "That includes service to me."

The Lights hiss.

My mate chuckles. "I assumed. As Cal isn't officially the Queen of Light, stay tethered to your throne without contractual obligations specifically to Cal, which excludes me and Tal as well. Take this time to deliberate on what you'll offer in a contract because we will ask what you want. Give me a chance to earn respect until then."

I shrug Sterling off. "Go to the kitchens. I'll find Thames."

CHAPTER 16

NATALIA

Vassals sneer as I request food. They respond in refusal, stating Cal had given an order that none were to eat outside of designated meals.

"He what?" I bristle. "No. No, absolutely fucking not. If anyone is hungry, they can eat."

I help Oscar onto a stool at the kitchen island, facing the vassals. "He needs food. Yanri has starved him, and I don't care what Cal said, you're going to feed him this instant, and you're going to give him as much as he wants."

They stare me down with crossed arms and cold indifference. "An order is an order, and we won't refuse."

I stare around the kitchen at them. "You're all signed to me." I point to my chest. "You're going to do what I say."

None of them move.

"Fine." I push through two of them to start scouring for options.

As I finish frying up breaded chicken, Sterling steps into the room.

158

We make eye contact, and his widens with shock. "The fuck are you doing?"

"Ignoring Cal's stupid order because it's stupid." I shrug.

Sterling snaps his fingers at a woman. "Go finish that."

She ducks her head, and I push her away. "I'll finish."

"Tal."

"Sterling." I flip the chicken and find a plate, transferring the meat to the dish.

I set it in front of Oscar, Sterling sitting next to him. I turn to mash boiled potatoes with butter.

I scrape them from the pan onto the plate, hesitating. "You're not eating."

He winces, trying to pick the chicken up with his fingers.

"Oh, Mother." I sigh. "Stop. One fraction."

I set the pan on the counter and search for a fork and knife.

I offer them to Oscar. "Okay, now eat."

He cuts a piece of chicken and lifts it toward his mouth. He pauses, looking to me.

"What?" I ask. "You think because you're Dark and I have the Light that I poisoned it? I'm just as bad at being the Light as I am being the Dark King. Eat."

He takes a bite, chewing slowly. His eyes grow larger, and he whips his head to meet my gaze. "You—you know how to cook?"

He shoves the rest into his mouth in a hurry.

I lean on the counter. "It's Ness's recipe." I wince, ducking my head and clearing my throat. "We were just useless humans. We didn't have vassals, and we had to feed ourselves. Plus, we ate more than you can imagine."

I smile, memories of Ness and food spreading through me with warmth. She's made this recipe for us drunk in our shitty little kitchen more nights than I can recall.

He stabs the second piece of chicken with the fork and lifts it whole to his lips, taking a large bite. "Human?"

"Magia." I point to myself. "Light Seraphinus sperm donor to my Magia mother, anyway. Didn't learn that until last year. I lived my life like any other human, paying taxes and taking care of myself. Then Cal found me." I smile. "After I accidentally won the contest for the crown, Mallafic sewed my soul with a piece of his. No idea what I am now."

The chicken is gone.

I lift my eyebrows at the depressing look he gives the plate, starting to poke at the mashed potatoes. "Want more?"

He licks his lips, slumping in on himself.

"It's okay, Oscar." I push away from the counter. "There's plenty, and I'll make as much as you want."

I'm on my third batch when Cal walks into the kitchen with Hiro, Thames, and Jacques.

The growl Cal emits rumbles the room, and vassals cower.

"Babe." I sigh and shake my head. "What stupid idea did you have that you gave an order that no one gets to eat outside of a designated meal?"

His face goes lax. "The Lights were causing extra work to eat outside of dinner to avoid the Dark."

"Make a new rule." I wave at the vassals and plop the chicken on the plate. I deliver it to Oscar. "I won't let anyone be hungry. It's miserable."

Cal bobs his head. "I should have been clearer in words. The order stands to prevent Lights from hiding, and no other reason."

Several vassals murmur acknowledgment.

Cal frowns at the plate. "You cook?"

Oscar groans. "It's so good."

I hold Cal's gaze. "Human."

He chuckles, stepping to me and wrapping his arms around me. "No."

"Then give me my taxes back."

"You spent it on decade-old bourbon to send my soul to the afters before I was dead."

I giggle, jumping.

He catches me, holding me against him. "You think that's cute?"

I yank on the back of his neck, leaning in to kiss him.

He swirls his tongue with mine, one hand squeezing my butt. The other works into my hair, cupping the back of my head.

Time stops. Nothing exists but my mate, and I tighten my legs around his hips, needing to hold on as if I would fall into an abyss if I let go.

Every scar, every agonizing moment of training for my marks, of Mallafic carving me open is worth this kiss.

He pulls back, the corners of his pouty lips turned up as he meets my eyes.

I draw my finger over the middle of his mouth, staring at it, ready to kiss him again and again until I'm breathless and dizzy.

Lemon.

The thought rises unbidden. I bolt upright in his arms. "Shit!"

"Talia." He tightens around me.

"Ness is gonna kill me. I forgot the lemon juice for the chicken."

He closes and opens his eyes, setting me on my feet. "No." He smacks my butt, grabbing to squeeze it after the initial impact. "Behave."

I lean into him, grinning. "I mean, I'll try."

He hums. "Oscar, when you're finished, Thames will ensure you're cleaned up and appropriately dressed."

He bobs his head, his face to the plate like a broken toy.

I knock on the table. "Head up, Oscar. I'll go with you. I can heal you, too."

THAMES CLEANS OSCAR UP with a haircut and clothes, *tsk*ing and shaking his head, fussing over the fit.

Oscar keeps wincing and shuffling, saying everything is fine and nothing's a problem.

He keeps his head down, his voice low if he speaks at all.

Once that's done, Thames has tea delivered and sits with Oscar and me.

Oscar doesn't touch his cup until Thames starts his second and remarks that it's rude to force him to drink alone.

We whittle the fractions by, Thames and I conversing.

I finish my cup of tea and ask, "You and Hiro?"

He lifts his eyebrows.

My face warms. "Um, how long did it take for you to fall in love?"

"Interesting question, baby." He lifts his cup, smiling behind it. "Are you concerned about Cal?"

"No." I laugh. "It's a long story. I told Thomas you and Hiro fell in love in three days."

Thames bursts into laughter.

"I know." I bob my head, grinning with him. "I didn't know the truth, and I was testing if a Faeling would know a lie, whether it was intentional or not."

"No, not three days. I was young, in my second century. I wasn't sure about being a contractor. My mother had just died in the games, I inherited the lineage estate, and I met Hiro..." Setting the cup down, he taps his finger against the handle. "He convinced me to be contracted to him. He wanted a partner for

Gathering Shadows. I could get experience in the games and learn how to be a contractor. I accepted."

Oscar fidgets.

"The contract was half his standard twelve years."

"So, it took twelve years?"

Thames smiles, lips closed with an ease to his features. "No. I was hopeless at the end of our first Gathering Shadows." He looks away. "You're aware of the bond forged in the games, in watching someone's back and having them shield yours. Complete trust."

Flexing my shoulders back, it's my turn to shift with nerves. "I am. I've never trusted anyone the way I trust Cal."

Oscar winces and hunkers lower over his cup.

Speaking of trust in front of him feels wrong.

Thames says, "It's a unique relationship. Hiro took what I saw as interest in dabbling between us, flirting with the bond we shared. I wasn't his only interest."

I sit straighter, abhorred at the concept of Hiro being with someone else. Resting my hands on the table, I open my mouth to stare. "No."

Wrinkling his face, Thames scrunches his nose in an adorable display of humored disgust. "Several other interests, in fact."

"No, you're..." I point, wiggling my finger. "You're his mate."

"I am. I'll remind you that you are Cal's, and he's had many other interests."

"Yeah, Telra." I roll my eyes. "But you and Hiro, you're... You're so cute together and you are so bloody perfect and pretty and sweet."

Oscar coughs, wheezing on air.

I pat him on the back.

Thames grins, but it's cold.

Oscar gasps and manages, "He's so dangerous and deadly."

"I am, baby, but I like that I can be both of those things. I never could understand how some believe being cruel or overly aggressive is a merit of toughness." He lifts his cup at me. "My contract ended, and I left. Hiro pursued me. He didn't like the fact that I left. He seemed to have the impression it was unfathomable, and I wasn't allowed to do that."

We chuckle together. "I think that's a required trait of a contractor."

"Alphas are possessive. I can't tell you when for Hiro, maybe not until I left, but that's when he mated me."

I put my hand to my neck, covering the mating marks of Cal and Sterling. I know when I fell for Cal. Sterling is a mystery. It's inexplicable.

I guess love is.

Thames puts two fingers against his lips, studying me. "Love is magic, and we all seek it. Whether we possess the capability to see it for what it is or grab hold is another matter entirely." He rests back, the corners of his lips turning up. "Hiro is my mate. He has always been my mate, regardless of how long it took for him to realize it. As his mate I couldn't force him to accept that or me. I'll do anything my mate requires, even if that is to wait for his webs to finish weaving far enough that I could possess him as I desired."

There's a knock on the door, Raz saying, "Thames?"

"Here, darling."

Raz steps into view. "Dinner."

I help Oscar to his feet. "Are you hungry?"

He sways. "I'll eat in spite."

Snickering, I get under his arm. "I like that attitude."

Thames guides me, and I shuffle, keeping Oscar upright.

He stops at the threshold, looking down on me. "Lightning Bug?"

"*Bzzt*, flash, smite. That's me."

His thin lips curl. "I need to walk in there on my own."

Stepping away from him, I nod. "Do what you have to."

I enter the dining hall, Thames in step with me. Cal and Sterling are sitting at the head of the table, but Sterling is in my seat, laughing at Cal.

Sterling has a great laugh, and he uses it more than Cal uses his.

Sterling looks my way and grins, nudging Cal before he shifts to his seat, leaving the chair between them open for me.

Thames sits next to Hiro.

I brush my fingers across Sterling's shoulders as I slide into my seat.

Cal slips his hand to the back of my neck, his nose to my head as he inhales deeply. "You smell as good as you taste." Kissing my temple, he sits back. "Where is Oscar?"

"He wanted to walk in on his own strength."

The table falls to a hush as he enters. He walks slowly, his head up. As he moves, he curls his fingers into fists.

He strides along the table, stopping at a vacant chair next to Thames. He nods to me.

I smile back. He has a chance now. At the root of everything the Dark is, it's all about having a fair chance. Prove your strength, and you get respect.

CHAPTER 17

NATALIA

Dinner passes by in leisure, Jacques at the center of attention with quick words and wide grins.

When after-dinner drinks are winding to an end, Sterling knocks on the table. "As a reminder, you are all to report to the field in the morning. You'll report at half past Sun's rune. All new arrivals can see Raz for quarters and lodging as necessary."

Cal says, "Yanri Horonnon was found guilty of an illegal contract."

That gets the attention of the occupants at the table.

Gesturing to me, Cal's breath hitches. "Your Dark King decided to disgrace him. He refused to terminate the illegal contract, and so your king did it for him by ending his life."

A fist slams on the table. Wood screeches. A man stands.

Oscar jerks to his feet. "Don't." He hangs his head, pressing a fist to the table and leaning on it. "Would any of you question me?"

The other man standing lifts his chin. "Was the contract legal?"

"I never consented to a worn contract. During negotiations, I asked for confirmation that my contract would be written as he was configuring it in his Dark. He ignored me, and before I signed, I told him I would not agree to be a worn contract. He insisted he drafted all contracts with magic as a personal choice. I didn't agree, and he lied."

The table growls in unison.

"Natalia gave him the choice to let me speak before she made any judgment. He spit in her face, and all she did was ask again. My contract kept me from speaking, even answering with nonverbal gestures. All our king demanded was the truth. When that was refused, she acted."

He sways.

I lurch to my feet, my chair toppling. Strength be damned. He needs help.

I'm halfway to Oscar when gold ropes wrap around him, catching him before I can.

Wyham and Palak both withdraw their Light as I steady Oscar.

"Sit," I tell him. "I can take care of myself."

He collapses into the chair. "I—"

"Shush." I tuck him under the table. "The amount of Ki I pushed through you was enough to take down a smoragon. You need time to recover. That's not weakness, Oscar." I lean on the table, meeting his eyes.

"Heh."

"You want me to feed that much Ki into someone else and watch them hit the floor? 'Cause I will if that's what it takes to get you to rest."

Sterling laughs. "Cal volunteers."

Palak leans forward. "If I may comment on your intolerable condition, no one should pass judgment on you for the deplorable state given it was brought down upon you by another."

Some nearby mutters, "Who cares what a Glow says?"

Palak sneers. "This Glow is the son of a man who dared to befriend a Dark and paid for it with his life. Yet here I sit among you, ready to defend your kind in pursuit of honor and saving my own kind."

I jerk like I've been poked with a sharp stick. "Befriend?" I glance at Cal.

He frowns, but Palak says, "Yes. I know better than to trust anything of the Dark, and yet I am doomed to try. I fully believe this will kill me, but here I sit in vain hope."

Someone approaches, and I straighten, turning to stare down a man.

He lifts an eyebrow at me and faces Palak. "You are Palak Jean, the elder son of Jean-Paul Delacroix."

Palak stiffens. "Yes."

The man stares for several heartbeats, then bows, one arm across his stomach, the other behind his back. It's a high honor in the Light instead of a common gesture. "I am Matthew Bernine, and Jean was my friend."

Palak shoves to his feet. "You?"

"When I was in my first century, still a boy, I played in the forest on the edge of Lukette and Fromier. Lukette belongs to my lineage. Fromier belongs—"

"To my heritage." Palak points at his chest, his face contorted in rage.

"Yes, that is an overlap unclaimed by either of us. I fell prey to a human trap devised for hunting. I wasn't able to break the metal teeth sunk in my leg, nor the chain staked into the ground attached to it. Jean found me, gave me aid."

"Then why kill him?"

"I did not."

"You did!" Palak slaps his hand to the table.

Matthew scoffs. "I do not lie. By Jean's strength, I survived, and no matter how I've grown, how strong I've become, I live because of his strength, not mine. For that reason alone, though I had many, I would never harm Jean."

Leaning back on one leg, Matthew props his foot on the table, exposing his shin. "That day left me with these scars and Jean's friendship. We would meet every other month. Then it became once a month or every other week at times when our responsibilities were less. I always brought a bottle of Trilam tequila, a gift for him in return for the gift of his time, as is your custom. I cherished him."

"Then why? Why did you—"

"I did not. You insist I am a liar, and it tries my patience." Matthew's chest rises, and he says, "I was late that day. I found him with another, or so I thought. The other ran when he saw me, and I found Jean dead."

"Other? No. No, my uncle told me—"

"Jean was proud of you and of his heritage. I had seen many pictures. I knew the man who ran to be Jean's brother, Louis."

"Louis told me himself. He was bleeding, injured. He had been with my father in the forest and attacked."

"My kind will not look upon me with mercy for my admittance of weakness, of surviving by the Light's grace and kindness, or of maintaining a friendship with one, but you deserve the truth. I knew not that you were aware of our relationship nor this deceit you believe." Matthew swells, sighing on a long exhale. "When I realized Jean was dead, I pursued Louis. Yes, I tried to kill him. Yes, he ran, and I dared not draw the warrants of the Council by following him into Fromier, and so he bled but did not die."

I can't breathe. All this time I thought Cal and I were an anomaly. I thought the Dark and Light could never come together. I thought hatred was sowed too deep.

There might be others, like Matthew, maybe more than will

even admit for the shame of the disgust others will hold in prejudice.

Palak shakes his head, collapsing into the chair. "I don't believe you."

Matthew shrugs. "If I have the chance to repay Jean's gift of friendship by giving the gift of my life to save that of his eldest son, I will." He walks away, reclaiming his seat down the table.

Palak grips his head, staring at the table. Hailey leans in close to him, whispering.

I focus on Oscar. "Do you need anything?"

"I will survive on my strength as we are to do."

Palak lurches to his feet again. "Why?" He twists to turn toward the other end of the table. "Why would my uncle do it? He wouldn't. There's not a single reason I can conjure to believe your tale."

I laugh. "Are you so blinded by the glare of your glow?"

He gapes at me.

"It's the same reason you all lied to me, concealing Cal's life from me when I believed he was dead. It's the very fucking reason that the Dark hates the Light. You're self-righteous, you're arrogant, and Louis wouldn't have accepted the friend-ship, seeing it as spitting upon your heritage for even helping a Dark. Ashley said it was a disgrace to the Bordeaux heritage that I would be loyal to Cal and the Dark. It's the reason Pierre did so many things, why he tried to keep me from Cal. It's blind hatred for the Dark for being simply what they are—Dark and for no other reason. You." I wave a finger at the Light. "You are the problem. Cal was never bothered with me being the Light because I saved his life. Sterling's father was murdered by a Light, but he held no prejudice against me because I'd earned respect. Hiro killed Charles, one of his vassals, for refusing to serve me because even though I glow, I'd earned respect. If you earn their respect, they treat you with respect. That is their way of life."

Palak stares at me, blinking a few times. His rounded features are scrunched, a tinge of pink to his nose. "Are we so pernicious?"

I drop my shoulders and the harsh tone. "You've spoken highly of your father in the past. I believe he would have had compassion for an injured man, regardless of magic. You kept Oscar from hitting the floor for no reason other than seeing the damage he suffered. I'm sure it's a trait your father instilled in you."

"That other, Yanri, abused him. We can all see that. His plight isn't his fault. He's a man that required aid."

Oscar groans, "I'm a disgrace."

I squeeze his shoulder. "Don't lie to me, Oscar."

He looks to me with tears in his eyes.

I kneel next to him. "You need time to recover. Cal did, too, after he was held prisoner and tortured. Would you question his strength?"

Oscar sniffs and swallows. "Fuck no."

"You'll have the chance to stand on your feet again, but I will not fault you for the time required to heal from that ordeal nor abandon you to fall until you have."

He drops his face into his hands. "I'll take a contract. I'll wear it even."

I stand. Patting his shoulder, I say, "I think you've had enough of worn contracts for a while, but I'll sign you if you want a contract. You have until you've regained your strength to make your decision, and if you choose to stand on your own, I will have no ill feelings, even if you simply refuse to serve the Light."

He coughs, rattling as he gasps. "Light? He spit at you, and you didn't care. You demanded he let me speak in pursuit of truth. You didn't have to protect me. I'm not one of yours. Still, you prop me up and tend to me even if I'm useless to you without the promise of service. You sparkle rather than glow and defend the Dark to the Light. You're not the Dark, that's true. I don't know what you are."

"Stupid and stubborn," I say with a smile. "I have the Light." I wiggle my fingers, a thread of my magic slipping between them. "However, if I ever catch you saying you're useless again, I'll get my claws out like a Dark."

Oscar winces. "I don't know if I want the ability to speak anymore. You ripped Yanri's tongue out through his throat."

Thames spits out his drink, a cough coming from somewhere at the head of the table like strangled humor.

"I gave him his choice. He chose not to speak, so I figured he didn't need the appendage. He wouldn't let you speak, so I assumed he was a liar and didn't deserve a tongue. He told me there was nothing I could do to make him withdraw the illegal contract and threatened you in front of me. Honestly, I should have cut it out and made him eat it before I sent him to the afters." I shrug. "I don't think before I act sometimes."

"Yanri was pissed you're our king. I think I'm starting to like it."

"Are you a Flurry?"

"No." He screws up his face. "I'm a Venominx."

"Oh." I widen my eyes. The only Venominx I've had personal interactions with is Telra. She was sadistic and sick. Recovering, I smile. "My mistake. I assumed you just liked that I'm shiny."

A lot of snickers and chuckles break out around the table, although one woman nearby narrows her eyes at me with ire.

The female next to her nudges her, laughing behind a hand. "Don't pick a fight you can't win, Becca."

CHAPTER 18

NATALIA

After dinner, I took Oscar to an empty set of rooms next to Hiro and Thames. They both agreed to take charge of him for the evening and see to him in the morning if he required anything.

Hiro commented on my ability to be an alpha. I laughed him off. I answer to Cal and we both know it.

When I make my way into my bedroom, Cal is lying back on the bed in a pair of casual pants, one arm behind his head.

Sterling rests at Cal's side, tossing the orb he'd stopped me from throwing away. His Dark throws it up, the glass spinning, only for his Dark to catch it again.

Cal crooks a finger at me. "Come here, Mate. Sterling, get the guitar."

"Where is it?" He sits, setting the orbs on the bedside table with a collection of other baubles.

I straddle Cal's hips. "Under the bed. What did I do wrong this time?"

He rolls up, taking my jaw in his hand and kissing me. "Nothing. You did well with Oscar." Resting back on the pillows, he drops his hands to my thighs. "I just wanted you on top of me."

Sterling rolls off the bed and thumps to the floor.

I reach up with both hands to detach the clasp of my necklace, letting the chain slide across my skin as I remove it. There's something I want.

Cal tenses, widening his gaze as he goes still.

Sterling rises to set the guitar case on the bed. He snaps the clasps open and flips the lid back to reveal Shawn Gettemier's guitar.

I didn't understand how Pierre had attained the instrument. He claimed connections and coin. I knew that wouldn't be enough. The moment I held the guitar, I should have known Pierre lied about how it came into his possession to offer it as a gift to me.

Cal had sent me so many gifts like the guitar—pieces of myself. He'd stolen them when I wasn't paying attention, gathering up the shattered fragments of my soul one at a time until he held them in the palm of his hand.

Sterling lifts the guitar out of its case. "Shawn damn near bawled when I made him sell this."

"That I believe," I say, bobbing my head.

He sits behind me, setting the guitar on the bed beside us to wrap his arms around me.

Cal isn't breathing, staring at me with trepidation welling in his black eyes.

I drop my gaze to his bare chest. "I know it's stupid."

Sterling asks, "What is?" He nuzzles the crook of my shoulder, then lifts his head. "What did I miss?"

Cal swallows hard, putting his hand on mine, clutching the pendant.

I try to smile. "It's so stupid. It doesn't matter, but..."

He stares, a bit of fear slithering into his shocked expression.

"I was in Izul when I got this. Zander handed it to me and..." I look away, wincing. "And he put it on me."

174

Cal makes an odd noise somewhere between a whine and a groan.

"Would you...?" I dangle the chain between my fingers in front of him.

He jerks, sitting and taking the necklace. He kisses me again, long and slow, as if stealing the life from me for himself.

If he wants my life, it's his to take.

Pulling away, he secures the necklace around me, trailing fingers along the chain to the small, clear gemstone star. He taps it, meeting my eyes. "My little star."

I curl my fingers around his jaw, yanking his face to mine. I taste him, my tongue against his, as I steal the air from his lungs. We exist together, impossible to separate. My soul has been woven in fate with his.

Cal settles back. "Play the song."

My Light positions the guitar in my lap, Sterling wrapping his hands around my waist to make room for the instrument.

I find the right notes, strum, and pluck the strings. For the first time, I sing, not in resentment or longing, but with ardent hope.

As I play the version of "I'll Stay," I smile at Cal. His Dark twists around me, along with Sterling's. His mouth skims the top of my shoulder, and when I've finished the song, he opens his mouth, pressing his teeth into my skin.

"Firefly," he whispers, his voice raw. "You have the most beautiful Light."

My heart flutters. "Thanks for not hating me for it."

He chuckles. "I couldn't breathe because I was laughing so hard at your comment earlier about shiny."

I find a new note, strumming. "Yanri said Oscar got mouthy."

"*Mhm.*"

"I get mouthy."

Cal's eyes crinkle as he laughs. "You're worse than mouthy with the sass, sarcasm and jokes."

I swallow, bobbing my head. "You could have silenced me."

Cal puts his hand over my fingers, stretched for the chord. "I never wanted you broken."

"But you could have."

He pulls his eyebrows together. "Yes."

When he was negotiating a contract with me, he'd said I'd find his treatment better than others. He'd warned me. I didn't understand that at the time. I thought he was trying to scare me into cooperating.

"Why?" I ask in a whisper.

He didn't have to do any of it. He didn't have to let me speak or grant me the ability to be sassy and fight his control. He hadn't even had to feed me, let alone buy me a guitar or vodka. It wasn't even cheap vodka, and it was more than I could want for.

"I'd forgotten what it was like to laugh."

Sterling snorts through his nose.

Cal narrows one eye. "I told you I wanted something else. I was looking for better than I had—a sassy star."

He had. I'd joked about it, not trusting the words.

"I never wanted you broken, and you...your jokes, they helped me forget a lot."

I flash my teeth. "Can I be honest? I almost peed my pants when Oscar told me he was a Venominx."

Sterling chuckles. "They aren't all bad. Like cats, they have a wide array of temperaments."

Cal grins. "Stay. Stay with me, fight even if you feel like dying. Hold onto me, and don't let go."

"And let you fuck me any way you want." I giggle, leaning into Sterling with my tongue between my teeth in a wide grin.

"That too."

Sterling rumbles with muted humor. "Take my hand, trust in

me, and guide me home." He presses his mouth to my shoulder. "Always, Mate."

Cal almost smiles, his black hair a mess, his eyes creased at the corners. Contentment grips his pretty features. The angles soften as he gazes at me with Sterling to my back. "You'll know when you're in contempt, but it's not in contempt of service."

Sterling nods against me as Cal's hand falls to my thigh.

I start strumming again, singing "Taste of Sugar," then "Honey High," followed by "Blush Haze," then "Glittering Blue."

Shawn Gettemeir would hate me. I don't care. I have love.

I play every song I know about falling in love, of being in love, and promises of forever until Cal takes the guitar away.

Sterling asks, "How do you want it tonight?"

Cal answers, "She likes things the hard way."

I shiver at the way Cal eyes me like a predator, and I'm a snack.

Sterling whispers, "Want to play a game?"

Cal's eyes sparkle.

I clear my throat, shifting. I'm already throbbing in anticipation. Between the two of them, they barely allow me to breathe. "Do I get a say in this?"

Cal lifts his chin, his gaze focusing over my shoulder. "No. What's the game?"

"She doesn't get to come until we decide."

Cal narrows one eye. He's annoyed. The twitch of his lips warns me.

Sterling chuckles. "I want to hear her beg."

Cal sits up, his hands wrapping around my hips. "Until *I* decide."

"Are we negotiating?"

"Keep talking back, and you don't get off until I decide either."

Sterling laughs. "Your way it is."

I press my hands to Cal's chest. "Um—"
Cal kisses me, hard and hungry.
I'm going to hate this game.

CHAPTER 19
NATALIA

1ST BLOOM'S DAY, BLOOMING, 4050, 6TH MILLENNIUM

I braid my hair and dress in tight black clothes to follow Cal to the field. Sterling fits his fingers between mine as we walk. I struggle not to pull away.

His skin sparks against mine, sending waves of pleasure down my spine to radiate through me. And it's not the only sensation coursing through me. Excitement. Thrill. Guilt.

Cal holds the door open for us with his Dark, not bothering to stop or wait for us to move through the door.

On the stone terrace leading to the field, Ashley waits with Tony.

I miss Ness. I miss my friend. I miss having a woman in my life. There are too many men around.

"Cal," I say, stopping next to him before Ashley. "Ness is still missing. We need to find her."

Tightening his grip, Sterling answers, "We don't know where Ness is. We already wasted time trying to bring her back once, and she wants to hurt you."

"She's just heartbroken."

Tony rubs the back of his neck, tipping his head back as he sighs. "Ness is going through a lot of feelings. She just wants company in her misery."

Cal takes my chin in his hand. "Vanessa wants you hurt?"

"She was happy you took your name back and left. Said I deserve to be miserable with her."

He lets go, facing Ashley. "I won't help someone who enjoys my mate in pain."

I grab his arm, yanking on him. "She lost Mass, too."

He looks to me, frowning.

"She lost her mate, and she loved him with her whole heart. She's heartbroken, and she's blaming me. She wanted me to be as fucked up as she is."

Tony shuffles his feet, kicking at the stone. "She's blaming whoever and whatever she can. She's in the anger stage. She's lashing out because she's in pain, and it's easier to do than face the truth that she's gone."

Cal asks, "She?"

"He." Tony clears his throat. "He is gone."

I tug on Cal. "We need to find her. Even if you're mad at her, I love her, and Mallafic is a whole lot of problem."

Sterling shakes his head. "We don't know where she is or how to find them, and I'm not wasting time trying to save her."

Ashley rolls her eyes. "Fascinating. You're refusing to allow me to mourn, and we're standing here discussing my sister's pet."

Cal gives her a warning look. "Woman, we have Ancients to deal with. Cry later. Fight first."

"I was informed slurs are no longer acceptable."

"I called you woman."

"A high compliment." She smiles, batting her lashes.

Cal smirks. "I'm inclined to agree. Did you summon fighters?"

"Yes. I sent word to notify all avengers and strong fighters they are to report here to Ilbuio. I assured them of their safety."

"That was stupid. We're fighting a war. I can't guarantee that."

"From the Darklings." She rolls her eyes, glaring at the sky, her gestures twitching with attitude. "What a stupid word."

Tony puts his arm around her waist. "It's Magia language."

"Revolting that we've adopted habits of our enemies."

Cal rubs his chin, considering. "Talia, Tony, Alexander, Eugene, and even Vanessa have stood with our kind. The Magia is too vague a label of individuals to be declared enemy. Not all of them are."

Ashley holds a hand up and begins ticking off her fingers. "My sibling seed is not Magia. Tony is the host of a fatum. Alex is...Dark."

Cal moves closer to Tony. "You have Soris?"

Tony makes a face of disgust as the spinner crawls from his ear to his shoulder. "Hate that feeling."

I shake my head and step further from him.

Sterling wraps his arm across my body and pins me with my back to his chest. "I have you, Firefly."

Cal moves closer. "Soris?"

The fatum lifts its two front legs, then jumps.

I whimper and dig into Sterling.

Soris lands on Cal's chest, swelling from horrifying to a massive creature of the worst nightmares, taking up Cal's whole torso.

He twists his lips to the side, talking to it. "What happened to Bellasom?"

Tony says, "Dead. That's why she needed a new host."

He laughs. "Great, you can talk to me even when you're not in my head. Fuck this. You like Cal so much? Live in his head." ....

"Oh, fine, stay in mine."

I look to Tony. Ashley smiles and straightens the hair hanging off his shoulder. "Darling, it's a high honor. It gives purpose to your existence and makes you unique in so many ways."

"I'm stuck with her forever. She can't take a new host until I'm dead."

Cal pokes at Soris, frowning at her. "I offer my condolences for Bellasom."

Soris lowers, lying flat against Cal's chest.

Tony says, "She appreciates that. She wants to know if you have figured out her gift yet."

"You sewed my soul and gave me vulnerability. Talia couldn't heal me. Not sure that's much of a gift."

Soris lifts her front legs, and Tony sighs. "She's laughing at you. Tal healed you in the way she was intended, giving you a piece of her soul." He jerks his head, gaping at me. "You did what?"

I shrug. "My Light stitched the wound. It's holding him together while he heals naturally."

Tony rubs his face. "Soris says Cal hasn't done something since she rectified his imbalance."

We all look to Cal. He tilts his head, his features pulled to the center of his face. He looks to me. "Feed." The single word floats in the air at the decibel of a breath.

My Light pouts. "*My love doesn't need me anymore.*"

Cal doesn't need me then, either.

He laughs. "What the fuck did you do to me, cursed spinner? I was fine."

Soris shrinks and spins, launching herself to Tony. He leans his head away but doesn't fight more as she disappears into his ear. "She's sulking. You hurt her feelings. She balanced your soul. You don't have to consume to rectify the imbalance, and your soul won't wither. You'll live forever like an…" …. "What the fuck, you cursed arachnid? I really am going to live forever?"

Cal rubs his face. "I'll deal with that later."

He offers his hand to me, and Sterling unwinds, pushing me toward Cal. I take his hand, and he pulls me forward. "One mess at a time." He squeezes my hand.

We step to the edge of the terrace on the precipice of the steps that will lead to the field. The swarm of bodies turns.

Gold and black are segregated, two groups collected on opposite sides, the Darklings far outnumbering the few Lighters.

Sterling steps to my other side. "Dismal turnout."

"It'll take time to gather forces. For now, we strengthen what we have."

Sterling whistles with two fingers in his mouth.

The field focuses on us, and Cal shouts, "Lighters, that is the maze." He points to the structure. "Stay away from it. That's a royal order. Find someone more capable than you and learn how to fight. Magic will be acceptable as long as deadly force isn't implemented."

Turning, Cal says, "You too, Ashley."

"Oh, honey." She smiles like addressing an idiot. "Do spare yourself humiliation by questioning my skill."

He lifts his eyebrows. "You think highly of yourself. So did the others."

"Care to test my word?"

Tony laughs. "Buddy, stand down."

"No. Ash," Cal jerks his head, moving down the steps. "Let's see what you're capable of."

He starts away, and Sterling kisses my forehead. "I'm going to kick down the Lighters until they learn something." Leaning back, he asks Tony, "Care to join me, friend?"

"I'll be working with Alex." Tony takes Cal's place while Sterling jogs down the steps.

Nudging my shoulder with his, Tony draws my attention.

I look at him. I really look. His thick eyebrows are too large and long, but fit his face. He has an angular jaw and a round chin.

It's like I'm seeing him for the first time in years. The lines of his face are more distinguished, his straight hair covering his forehead, the sides shorter but shaggy.

He's attractive, in a boyish way with charm, subtler than Cal's allure.

"How are things? It's been a few days."

"Cal's recovered. He's getting things set up."

"Sure, sure." Tony bobs his head.

"Ash?"

"Has been crying her eyes out or being a bitch. She's grieving. Pierre told her he would die for Cal if the act was required."

Ashley squares up to Cal, and he swings.

Tony says, "I guess he knew he wasn't coming back. I'm surprised he did it, but Ash keeps saying 'Hallow,' like that means something."

Ashley rounds, locking her legs around Cal's neck and taking him to the ground.

Tony chuckles. "That woman is badass."

"She is. My father is dead."

"He saved Cal, and you didn't care about him."

"Eugene."

"Shit. Fuck, I..."

We share the silence, watching Ashley toss her hair as she and Cal reset. Darklings are gathering to watch, but Sterling has the Lighters busy.

"Are you okay?"

I hum.

"Cal and Sterling, huh?"

I smile. Cal drags Ashley to the ground this time.

"You want to answer either of those questions?"

"Not really."

Tony hums. "I'm going to find Alex. See if I can get a Darkling who will help train him." He starts down the steps but turns back. "You and me...we've lost enough. I'll fight for Ness. We don't need the others. We have each other, and between us," he says, pointing at his chest, then at me, "We're enough to finish this."

I frown.

"Cal can do a lot. He's what the others need. I don't know if I like him. I'm still getting over what he did in Narwal, but I have respect for him. Let him manage the Seraphinus. You and me, we'll finish this shit with the Ancients. They can build an army," he adds, pointing to Ashley and Cal exchanging swings, "but you and me, we can take down those Ancient assholes ourselves. We do that, we end this, and have a life again. We're done losing. Deal?"

"Deal." I nod.

"Good. I'm not marrying you. I'm not having children with you. I've been an ass, but I'm working on it and getting Alex ready. If the three of us work together, I bet we can drag those Ancients to the afters."

"You really think we're enough?"

"I know we are. You are. They called you a pampered princess. They thought you were a stuck-up bitch because you kept to yourself. They were wrong. The Assembly put you through the ringer a hundred times and made you into a badass. You realize that, right?"

"I don't think I was supposed to be able to do it."

Ashley tries to drag Cal to the ground again, but he twists with her momentum and pins her beneath him.

Tony sighs. "I think you're right, but they fucked up." He

laughs. "They thought you'd fail, and all they did was make you better than anyone else."

"Not Sasha."

"I love her, still, always will, and she was good, but she was never going to be that good. She always said you were better, that she worked so hard at it while you seemed to breathe Ki."

I look away from the fight to meet his eyes.

He smiles and bobs his head. "You really think she was this perfect thing, don't you? You didn't see her studying, trying and failing. She'd never let you see that side of her. She wanted to be the best, and you got under her skin in the worst way because you were better. I think she really did hate you some days."

I stare, my mouth open, a single word stuck in the pipes of my mind, clogging everything he's saying into a jumbled heap of nonsense. "What?"

"Ash signed her name in me." He shows me his inner forearm. "Says it's to ward others from her plaything until she's done using me."

I twist my lips against a laugh.

"Yeah, I know. I'm attracted to bitches. Whatever it is, it's not going to last, but I'll enjoy it while I can, and when this is over, I'll have a chance again. Ness will too. Alex will get his for the first time. We fight, we face death, and when we survive, we get what we deserve."

"And what's that?"

"A chance to be happy." He continues to the field, disappearing into the crowd.

Cal and Ashley are still going at it. They seem evenly matched, albeit they are sparing instead of trying to kill each other.

I think.

Sterling is focused, talking to Wyham. One Light is straying closer to the group of Darklings. Palak.

Maybe he's searching for Matthew. Maybe Matthew's words and clear reflection have encouraged him to look past magic. I can hope. We need friendships.

Neither Cal nor Sterling told me what to do. I'll see if I can control myself enough to not make them regret it.

CHAPTER 20
NATALIA

I sidestep Darklings, moving between groups of them. The largest collection surrounds Callahan and Ashley in a ring, watching them.

Sterling catches my eye, but he returns to watching Hailey and Wyham spar.

Oscar approaches me, a woman clinging to his arm and leaning against him. "Your Majesty."

I widen my eyes. She's like a skeleton that has attached a watermelon to its middle. She tries to smile, the split skin of her lower lip beginning to leak blood, and she stops quickly, dabbing at it with her fingers.

I flick my hand. "Tal or Tallie is fine. Is this...?"

"My sister." He motions to the blonde woman. "Luna."

Her cheek is swollen with a black and blue lump. I lift my hand. "I can heal you if you'll let me."

She looks to Oscar.

He bobs his head. "She's...I told you." He swallows hard. "Yanri... Yanri had her here to keep an eye on her. I contacted the rest of those who were his to let them know what happened as well."

I step to her, pressing my palms to the rounds of her shoulders. "Hold still."

She puts a hand to her stomach. "My seed."

"This won't harm anything, and I'll focus the Ki to make sure of that."

Luna sighs, shaking as she closes her eyes.

I lift my hand to the damaged side of her face, sending little waves of Ki into her. The swollen knot fades, leaving behind sucked-in cheeks.

I shift my hand toward her mouth. "All right, now I'll fix your lip." Resting my fingers against her lower lip, I seal the wound. "You're all done."

Oscar frowns at me, then looks to Luna before shuffling in place. "It's..."

Luna winces. "Yanri's."

I gaze at her face, and the pieces click together. "Oh, fuck no! I shouldn't have ripped his tongue out. I should have ripped his balls off."

Luna laughs in a breathless wheeze. "It will inherit Yanri's estate." She pats the bump in her abdomen. "I cannot express enough appreciation that you sent him to the afters. I was more afraid of what he'd do to his own seed than for myself."

Another woman steps forward, her curly black hair glistening in the glow of my Light. "Oscar, I know you well. We've faced the games together. I offer you and your sister contracts as a real contractor."

Oscar swells. "Real contractor? She fed me, preparing the food herself. She showed me generosity, not even as a contracted vassal of hers, and you would dare insinuate she fails to be a real contractor?"

I grin, not at the defense of me but at the spark of life in

Oscar. Frail, starved and withered by abuse, he still has fight in him.

He grips his fists. "Fuck you, Larna."

She shrugs. "She turned her back on the Dark before. She will again, given her pattern of behavior."

"Callahan and Sterling stand as her mates—our strongest two. You'd question them?"

"Callahan has decreed himself the Light. He is not one of ours."

"He has fought in our games and earned respect no matter what he may claim to be. He's been one of us for centuries. We all know they are born of Dark and Light. That he has some heritage in his magic isn't new information. Merely the Light's worth of it. Don't spit at him for accepting the truth."

Her small eyes pinch with ire, then she turns and walks away.

I consider Luna, then look to Oscar. "Fair warning. I tend to do stupid things."

Oscar shrugs. "I do stupid things. I signed that contract." He smiles. Not a real smile. He parts his lips to show his teeth and curls the ends up.

I laugh.

That earns me a real smile. "I will negotiate when you are ready."

Luna puts a hand to her stomach. "When can we negotiate? We are lowborn and must have contracts."

Zander steps to my side.

I crane my neck to meet his white eyes. "Yes?"

"You are a Bordeaux and the Light King. I have a duty to protect you."

"Light Queen." I point toward the massive ring of Darklings.

"He is with a Bordeaux." He shrugs. "Ash will protect him as necessary, whereas you are without aid. My presence is better suited for you at the moment."

I sigh, loud and exaggerated for his benefit to ensure he takes note of my displeasure. "My standard contract is twenty-five years. It lays out general service requirements and maintains an order clause."

Luna looks to Oscar with expectancy.

He rolls his shoulders. "No. I'm looking for something beyond your standard." He fixates on Zander. "Do you mind?"

"Mind what?"

"I'd like privacy."

"You will not have it."

I run my fingers down the bridge of my nose between my eyes. "Zan, I'm in no danger."

"At the moment I will concede such, but we have not the knowledge to know the future."

Oscar smirks. "Either you're insinuating I'm incapable of protecting her, or I am the potential danger. My answer is fuck you in both cases. I'm capable, and I'm not stupid enough to attack her or have any cause to do so."

"You're a starved vagrant."

Oscar forces his head to the side, cracking his neck. "Let's go, Glow." He detangles his arm from Luna's, stepping to the side.

"I believed your kind found no honor in dispatching one in poor condition or obviously weaker."

"I've survived like this for damn near a century. You call me weak. You call me pathetic, and you won't face me to find out the truth?" Oscar spits to the side. "Self-righteous pansy."

Zander looks to me.

I hold my hands up. "I didn't do it. You did. Own it."

"Very well. Please remain available to heal him as necessary."

Zander moves to square up, lifting his hands.

Luna moves closer to me to give them more room. She rests a

hand on her stomach, frowning. "Your Majesty? I will accept standard service obligations, but I request fifty years."

Oscar and Zander shuffle, feigning swings and testing each other.

"Fifty?" I repeat.

She rubs her stomach. "I have a seed to care for, and fifty puts him at an age when he can become a contractor of his own."

Oscar gets a clean strike to Zander's face, following through with the swing and following with a quick jab to Zander's stomach with his other hand.

Zander spins, trying to use his elbow. Oscar dodges and lands a kick to Zander's abdomen.

Zander stumbles. Oscar pounces, grabbing Zander by the shoulders as he tugs and lifts his knee into Zander's torso.

Zander hits back, spinning free and slamming his fist into Oscar's jaw.

They stumble away from each other, breathing hard as they reset.

I glance at Luna. "I'll accept fifty years on one condition. You raise that child to be a better contractor than Yanri. At thirty, it starts learning from Cal and Sterling how to do it right."

"That's your condition? That is a burden upon Callahan and Sterling, a generosity, not a cost."

I shrug. "That's my offer."

Oscar gets in close. Zander gets a few hits in, but Oscar moves faster, landing two or three blows for Zander's one.

The air crackles as Zander manages to put space between them.

I tense.

A bolt of blue pierces the air, accompanied by a clap of thunder.

I squint.

Luna lets out a warbled shriek, scampering a few paces back.

She curls over, crossing her arms to protect her stomach as Dark threads knit around her, blocking her almost from sight.

Oscar evades the smite with a rolling dive and pops to his feet.

Zander draws upright with a triumphant grin.

Oscar smirks. "You missed."

He launches at Zander, who stands there with an open mouth. Oscar lands on top of Zander, leaning into a swing. Zander's head snaps to the side, then Oscar rolls off him to stand.

Zander rises much slower, rubbing his face and cleaning away blood from his crooked nose.

I giggle behind a hand as I turn to Luna. "Are you all right?"

"*Mhm*," Luna hums with a wide, closed-mouth smile. She reclaims the spot at my side, shaking. "I'm so proud of him, of what he's capable of, even when pushed to breaking limits."

Cal stalks closer, grabbing Zander by the shirt to spin him away from Oscar. He shoves Zander, his face stark with fury. "Nothing lethal. Ever. There's no point in reducing our numbers on behalf of the Ancients, and we aren't killing each other."

Tony shoves through the crowd to the front. "Move, you fucks. Get out of my way." He gets in front of the bodies, whipping his head around. "Who needs healed?"

Oscar crosses his arms, eyes narrowed. "He wasn't even close."

Cal glances at Oscar, then looks to Zander. Cal's rage ebbs away. "Looks like you won."

Oscar shrugs. "Then give me a point and move on."

Cal laughs, looking my way, then his eyes flare. "Who are you?" He stalks closer. "What are you doing here?"

"My name is Luna, and I was informed to be here or it—"

"No. Go." He points at the palace. "You're excused."

"I am not weak." She lifts her chin.

"How far along are you?"

"Thirty-three," she answers in a faint voice.

I stare at her ballooned stomach. "Almost ready to pop."

Oscar bobs his head. "Seven days to go."

I turn my head, my ear toward Oscar. "Days?"

Cal rests his hand against the small of my back. "Forty days to grow life and forty days to mourn its loss."

"Days?" I squeak.

Cal shakes his head. "You're thirty-three days, and young are rare enough. I'm not risking a seed of Dark."

I offer her my arm. "How about we sign a contract?"

"Little Star, you're training. Go." He points. "Figure out how to smite. It's effective against the Ancients."

I wrinkle my nose. "I mean, *I could*, but I managed to kill one without smiting."

"Talia." His head shies, his eyes burning in warning.

This isn't important enough to waste my act of compliance. I wink at Luna. "You and me." I nod at Oscar. "And you. Let's go."

I turn, but Cal cuts me off. "I can still put you down."

I tilt my head. "But can you really?"

His pretty features turn gorgeous with wicked beauty as his gaze shifts. He stares at me as a hunter, his eyes sparkling with the intensity of an alpha being provoked. "Are you challenging me?"

"No." I grin, swallowing my laughter. It twists my words with glee. "I'm outright refusing to obey."

"Are you?" He steps closer, dominance washing over me as he shifts his feet to either side of mine, staring down on me with heat.

My skin twitches—barely any space between us. It's maddening to feel him on the edge of me without proper contact. "*Mhm*," I manage, almost panting with desire. "And as we're equal partners, there's nothing you can do about it."

"Is that what you think," he whispers, his voice husky as he lowers his head holding my gaze.

"Bring it on. Let's see if you can put me in my place."

He laughs and swings halfheartedly. I evade to the side and move into his left hook.

I wince, rubbing my face and wrinkling my nose. "What was that? Were you limp? You know I like things harder than that."

He raises his eyebrows. "Are you going to behave?"

I step back to avoid another punch. Lifting my hands, I circle with him. He jabs. I rock my shoulder back to dodge.

I duck, spin, and catch him with a kick to his butt. He stumbles a pace forward, and I bite down on my lips to hold back a laugh when he turns to face me.

He's laughing, even if it isn't audible. I can see it in the way he's grinning, the way his eyes dance. I'm baiting his ego, threatening his stance as an alpha, but I know he'll hold back no matter what.

Callahan Barraco is my mate, my soul, magic, and heart weaved into his. Our threads are entangled in the webs, our fate tied to each other by inescapable destiny.

With my hand in his, I am invincible, and when I get mouthy, he laughs. My Light glows brighter, silver glistening across my skin from sheer exuberance. I have a perfect mate, one who will fight for me and with me.

Things could be different. He could have forced me into strict obedience, snuffing out my jokes. He didn't have to earn my trust. He didn't need to be honest. He didn't have to kiss me in a way that made me his.

He didn't have to fight me when he demanded the truth about my heart, trying to understand the beautiful lie I gave myself when I re-wrote the song "I'll Stay." It would have been easier for him to say, "Forget it, never mind," I wasn't worth the effort. Instead, he'd ripped away my defenses and made me hand him my heart in ruthless disregard for the fact that I didn't want to.

The world falls away as I stop his fist with my palm, backing the block with Ki to absorb the impact. The only thing I know is my mate and the thrill of love.

As capable as he is, it only sends waves of adoration through me. His sheer ability to stand toe to toe with me and hold his own turns my stomach to butterflies.

I'm not sure how long I last before he pins me, straddling my hips with my wrists gripped in his fists as he leans over me. His black hair is rumpled, and he's breathing hard. Muscles in my abdomen coil. An ache spreads through me to throb between my legs.

His face lowers toward mine. "You're going to behave."

"All right, all right."

He lifts an eyebrow, not moving.

"I'll behave."

Rolling off me, he stands, offering me his hand to help me up. I take it, and he yanks me to my feet. Bright colors pop in my eyes at the head rush, and I let go of him to dust myself off.

I brush a stray, loose tendril of hair from my face and look to Luna. "We can go now." I turn my back on Cal.

"Talia."

I laugh, looking over my shoulder. "You said find someone to kick you down and learn something. You put me down. I'm not sure what I learned, but I probably learned something."

He tries not to laugh. The moment he does, we both know I've won. He shakes his head, turning away, but his shoulders shake.

With a grin, I offer Luna my arm. "I'll walk you to the office for ligan pagan."

She entwines her arm with mine, and we head out across the field.

Oscar falls in step with me. "Tal? I'd like to negotiate."

"Do you mind doing it while we walk, or would you prefer to wait until after I've signed Luna for privacy?"

"She's my sister. Don't care what she hears." He shakes with a little shiver. "I think my hair is still standing from that smite."

"You've got quick reflexes."

Luna reaches across me toward her brother, wiggling her fingers. "He's a fast kitty."

I snicker. "Are you both Venomynx?"

"No." Luna sighs. "I'm a Flurry. Mom was too."

"Oh."

She narrows her eyes. "Sterling's a Flurry."

"And likes shiny." I shrug. "Didn't know how that works."

Oscar opens the door for me and his sister, waving us through. "Dad was a Venomynx. Mom was a Flurry. I inherited his seed, and Luna got mom's. We split. Sometimes children don't."

Luna bobs her head. "I'm hoping this seed will be a Vyper like Yanri. They're special and very capable."

"And notoriously sadists." Oscar grimaces. "It's a trait of their magic more than an individual characteristic."

I frown. I know two Vypers, and neither seem anything like Yanri. "Jacques is a Vyper, and he's always happy."

Oscar looks at me with eyebrows raised. "Jacques is the worst sadist I've ever met."

"What? No, he's—"

"Did you not see the game where he paralyzed Tabitha and left her to be eaten by the melrags?" Oscar asks, his eyebrows pulling together. "He fucking watched with a grin and laughed. He and Yanri were friends."

I stop. "What?"

My stomach turns sour and squirms like it's full of worms. I hadn't watched many games. Either I played in them, or Cal kept me away from them.

"You don't..." Oscar puffs his cheeks up and bursts with a laugh. "You don't have any idea, do you? Callahan and Sterling haven't taught you anything, have they?"

"Don't you dare insult them," I bristle. "I'm still learning, and that's not their fault."

"Sterling and Callahan are what we call gentlemen. They're alphas, and they'll fuck you up and put you down with class, but they're not the average."

Luna giggles. "I had the biggest crush on Callahan for a long time."

I pull her forward. "You knew him?"

"In a way. We served Delilah, and I was a vassal of hers, who she brought to the games. She didn't last long, and after she died in the games, Oscar and I signed with Yanri."

Oscar turns left. I follow with Luna. He'll know the palace better than me.

He starts up a flight of stairs. "Most contractors have alpha tendencies, but they're rougher. Vypers are sadists. Dracos are narcissists. Nightmares are manipulators. Shadow Beasts are aggressive, and Flurries are greedy."

I bob my head. "What are Venomynx?"

"Pranksters. We love to laugh."

I cut my eyes at him. "Not in my experience. Telra was sadistic."

"Tel..." He laughs faintly. "Tel was hilarious."

Luna nudges me. "They're impatient. As quick as they move, that's how fast they think, too."

Oscar whips his head to her with feigned injury to his chest. "Sister Mine, you wound me to the core with your insult."

She giggles. "Oscar is very impatient, but he's as quick to crack a joke as with anything else."

He grimaces, leading us down another hallway. "Yanri didn't appreciate humor. It was depressing." He shakes his head. "I want a contract to serve you, Tal. You did the impossible."

"I did?"

"No other Dark King would have done that. It was his word against mine, and without proof, the Dark King can't embroil in a contract. I didn't have a scrap of evidence, and I couldn't speak." He points, turning to me to guide us to turn into another corridor. "I want a contract to serve you, not general service, but somewhere in your inner circle where I watch your back. I'll give my life for yours if I have to."

"Cal and Sterling made a deal between them that they'd deal with Yanri. They knew the contract was illegal, not me."

"They wouldn't have done it. They would have played by the rules like always. No idea how either managed to win and have integrity while they did it. What do you have for me?"

"You could be my Mass or Sal?"

"Your what?"

"Right hand." I lift it and show Hiro's contract.

He taps it. "Looks like you have one."

"Hiro serves the Dark. Not me."

"I'll accept that position."

"Fine, but fair warning. I have no idea how to use that position. Do I get a learning curve tolerance from you?"

He turns toward the Dark King's personal hall. "I know what to do."

I stop, jerking my head toward my rooms. "Office with the ligan pagan is that way."

Oscar hesitates. "You..."

Luna squeezes my arm. "Yanri didn't..."

I slash at the air. "Fuck Yanri. He deserves to be in the afters. I'm only sorry I didn't make it hurt worse or take longer for him to get there in the most agonizing way I can think of."

Wincing, Oscar heads toward the royal suite. "The Dark doesn't apologize. Say you regret, not sorry."

I lead them to the office, sitting behind the desk to pull out ligan pagan. I write Luna's contract first, adjusting the wording for fifty years and signing before offering the pen.

She signs, setting the pen aside.

I pull out another sheet of ligan pagan, pressing it beneath my hand on the desk. I hesitate, trying to recall Cal's contract with Massimo.

My Light spreads across the page in silver sparks that collect into words: Answer to me. We respect. We trust each other. We protect each other. We act in our best interests. Natalia Swan.

Oscar reads it, eyeing me. "And after I sign this?"

I shrug and sit back. "We act in our best interests, which means if I change that contract to something not in your best interest, it's against the contract, and I'm in contempt."

"You can just remove the line."

"I promise you, I won't, and I don't break my promises. I'll never remove that line, and if I do change anything, you'll know what it is and why beforehand. The contract will turn on me if I fail to decide in our best interests."

He rubs the space between his eyes. "You're aware that contempt for the contractor is not the same as the contracted, yes?"

"That would be a solid no, but I also know that both Cal and Sterling would wring my neck if I abused a contracted." I flash my teeth in a faux grin.

Oscar hovers his hand over the contract, then withdraws. "The line about trust, remove it."

I bristle, my Light indignant.

He holds a hand up, his chest rising and falling in short drags of air. "It's..."

I put my hand to the contract, removing the line. "Hard to trust."

Nodding, Oscar places his hand to the contract. "I've been in contempt too many times. I..."

"I'm not fighting you." I look away. "Trust..." I shake my head. "I don't blame you."

He puts his hand to the page.

I wait.

He bares his teeth. "Sign the damn contract."

I draw my eyebrows together in confusion, then realize he's talking to his magic. "It doesn't have to be a worn contract. How about—"

"Shut up," he snaps.

Luna's eyes grow twice their normal size, and she puts a hand on Oscar's arm. "Brother Mine," she whispers, "that is our Dark King and soon to be your contractor."

I wave her off. "It's fine."

Snarling under his breath, Oscar says, "We are not a coward. Sign the fucking contract."

Two strands of inky black stab the page and plume in a cloud that dissolves into the parchment leaving behind "Oscar Cameron Denoza."

I swipe the contract into my left palm and slap it to the back of my right hand. Pushing out of the chair, I walk around the desk. "I'm not sure which rooms are still available in this hallway, but I'll figure it out and find you one nearby."

He bobs his head, staring at his hand.

"Luna," I say, "I'm not sure about anything, but if you see Raz, Tam, or Sarina and let them know you've signed a contract, they'll get you set up too."

CHAPTER 21
NATALIA

I'm sitting in the middle of the bed, strumming on my guitar, when Cal walks into the room.

I set the guitar aside. "Babe."

"You were sassy today."

I giggle, covering my mouth as if I could hide it from him.

He raises one eyebrow at me, his gaze smoldering as he maintains eye contact. There's a subtle shift with the flex of his eyebrow, his expression darkening. "You think that's entertaining, do you?"

My skin tingles at the warning in his low voice. He is not amused. "You don't? Usually, you think I'm funny."

"Do you need a reminder of your place?"

"Do you think you're capable of putting me in my place?"

His eyes flare wider with indignation. "I wasn't swinging full force and still put you down."

"Meh." I shrug, leaning my head toward my shoulder. "I wasn't trying either. I was having fun."

"Come here," he beckons me with a finger.

I eye him, shying away and leaning back on my heels. "Why would I walk over to you? That would be too easy."

"Come here." He points at the floor between his feet.

I hesitate. "Didn't you say we were going to work on the crystals?"

His voice deepens to a commanding snarl, as sharp as the edge of a blade honed to cut with ease and faint as a lover's caress. "Now."

That's the order of an alpha promising blood if ignored, but the way he manages that single word sends heat rushing through me.

Swallowing, I take one small step forward, my humor dwindling into nerves of excitement. I want to hear him say it again in that tone. I want to hear a lot of things in that tone.

His head twists a fraction to the side, my final warning.

I step to him, my stomach full of butterflies.

He stares down his nose, not moving but holding me in place all the same. "I don't like repeating myself."

I sigh and roll my eyes, ticking the list off on my fingers. "You don't like repeating yourself, explaining yourself, or anything really, or—"

He grabs my jaw from the underside in one hand, tilting my head back. "That response is only reinforcing my belief that you need to be put in your place."

I try to grin. He doesn't return the effort. Heat and ire radiate off him, pressing against my skin. "Who is in charge?" Cool tendrils of his Dark begin to wrap around me, and I shiver in anticipation. His grip tightens, his voice low. "Are you really going to make me ask twice?"

Biting my lower lip, I try and fail not to grin. I am. He knows it.

"Mm," he hums, his chest rumbling. His voice returns to that commanding whisper, ripe with promise should I refute him. "I think you're overdue for a lesson."

I'll do anything for that grumpy snarl. He just doesn't know it yet.

He presses his nose to the corner of my jaw, twisting my face away to expose my neck to his whims. He draws his mouth along the thin skin, nipping at the pulse point with a growl in his chest.

I twitch. His hand tenses, squeezing harder to keep me where he wants. My mouth goes dry, my heart racing as desire sparks in my abdomen. A throb begins between my legs, an ache I need filled.

"Cal."

His Dark slithers under my dress, caressing my skin and twisting around me. It constricts, and I gasp at Cal's tongue dragging up my neck.

"Who is in charge?"

"You?"

"Good girl." His teeth sink into my earlobe, and I jerk, whimpering at the sharp sting. "I am your alpha, and you answer to me."

A quiver of desire starts between my shoulder blades and dances down my spine. "I remember," I say in a breathless whine.

"You made me ask twice."

"In all fairness..." I begin, struggling not to laugh. He pulls back to meet my eyes, his gaze intensifying, daring me to finish that statement, so I do. "You know I don't learn."

He inhales through his nose, his eyes burning into me. I have just enough time to wink before I'm dragged to my knees by his Dark.

I squeak in shock, and Cal releases his grip on my face, lifting my chin with two fingers as he reaches to unbutton his pants with his free hand.

"That mouth got you in trouble, now it's going to get you out of trouble."

He's already hard as he closes a hand around the base of his erection, stroking with a loose fist.

I lick my lips, glancing up at him. "For the record, I know I have a big mouth, but we both know that doesn't fit in my mouth." Lifting my hand, I direct my finger at his continuing-to-grow erection.

"No," he says in a lazy fashion, one side of his mouth tugging back with satisfaction. "It won't."

"Uh-huh, so...?"

"I'll fuck your throat." Fisting my hair, he angles his dick into my face. "Suck."

Wetting my lips, I part them, then try to look up at him, his grip on my hair preventing much movement. "If you're trying to make a point by punishing my mouth, I want you to know it's not much of a punishment." I grin, maintaining eye contact as I lick the tip.

His gaze falls half shut, his dick twitching. "We'll see how you feel when you're choking and gasping for air with my cock down your throat." His hips rock forward, pressing the crown of the shaft into my lips.

Giggling, I open my mouth, licking and sucking. His Dark winds around my arms, drawing them behind me and tying me in place. He grumbles, tangling both of his hands in my hair for a firm grip, thrusting forward.

I gag, my eyes widening in shock as he fills my throat, and I do exactly what he wants, trying to breathe with a wet gurgle. My vision blurs. My lungs burn. I can't breathe or do anything. He's not letting up, ramming into my throat to draw back and repeat.

He holds my head in place, using me for his pleasure. His Dark tightens around my arms as I struggle with my need to get a full breath. It slides around me, stroking between my legs.

Spit and tears are dripping down my face, and I gag again as Cal moves faster. I begin panting, fighting for air, but he shoves all the way in, blocking my air passages as I am forced to swallow his dick.

He rocks his hips, staying in my throat with each shallow thrust. I whimper, on the edge of an orgasm and in desperation for air.

"Where's the smart mouth now?"

He draws back, letting me breathe. "It's busy," I manage around his shaft.

He grips my hair harder as he thrusts forward fucking my throat with brutal force until he rams all the way in.

I gag, my throat struggling to stretch for him, but he groans, warmth sliding down my esophagus as his dick pulses with his release.

He doesn't move for several heartbeats, then draws back, staring down on me. I squirm in his Dark, aching and trying to catch my breath.

I wipe my chin on my shoulder, swallowing. My throat twinges, the taste and feel like a marshmallow is stuck in my throat. "Still not sure what lesson that was," I rasp, my words strangled by my strained throat.

His eyes narrow, his muscles rippling as he pulls upright. The way he glares down at me constricts every muscle in my abdomen, every nerve tingling in delicious anticipation. "No?"

I flash my teeth in a fake grin with hope. "My turn?"

He slides his hands along my jaw, taking my face between them to gaze down on me. His Dark twists me closer to the edge, and I moan. "Please."

"I can and will do that until you learn."

"I'm not fighting."

He runs his thumb along my lower lip. "You're still sassing me."

"It's not my fault. I'm having fun."

He inhales sharply, going rigid as his eyes widen. His half-limp dick starts to grow again, twitching near my face. "Then why would I stop?"

CAL - 2

My throat - 0

I don't even care that I lost our game and begged or that my throat is on fire with a dull agony. My body is humming, and I'm glowing brighter than usual in the twilight filling the palace.

Cal grumbles unintelligently as I bounce and skip at his side, swinging our hands.

I grin at him. He narrows his left eye. I snicker, wincing at the use of my throat. He pulls us to a stop, resting his palm on my neck with his eyebrows drawn.

I send another couple of waves of Ki through myself, healing again despite that it will make no difference. Ki doesn't remove the effects of overuse or fatigue. Closing my eyes, I lean into his hand.

He kisses my forehead. "Was I—"

I shake my head before he can finish the thought.

His lips twitch, fighting humor. "I guess I found one way to turn your sass off."

I pull back and show my teeth. He has a point.

Cal lifts his gaze over my shoulder as someone approaches. His lips twist with arrogance, pride smeared across his face. "Where have you been?"

Large, warm hands slide around my hips, then up my sides. Sterling. His Dark tangles with Cal's winding around me.

I close my eyes again and lean into him. He kisses the side of my head. "Hello, loves."

Cal's tone turns cranky. "Where have—"

"I had estate business to tend to, and Darnell wanted words."

"What words?"

"Tal and you bringing the two sides together. He's less than in favor. I won't repeat the sentiments. They were vulgar at best."

I scrunch my face at Cal. I will beat them all bloody to prove I am the strongest and I decide if I must.

Sterling's hands squeeze my waist. "You're quiet, Firefly."

I grin up at him to let him know I'm fine.

Cal snickers. "She got sassy."

"She always is."

"I put her in her place."

Sterling laughs. "For the sake of my sanity, tell me how."

"I fucked her throat until she shut the fuck up."

"I missed my turn?"

"I asked where you were." Cal shrugs.

"Enjoying myself far less." Sterling wraps his arms around me and lifts me off my feet, swinging me into his arms. "That is entirely unfair."

Cal lets go, one corner of his mouth turning up. I frown at the ease with which he released me and the contentment in his gaze at Sterling cradling me. It's irregular.

Sterling turns and starts walking away. I swivel my head, looking to Cal. He lingers, watching Sterling take me further away. His Dark swirls around him, but it's lazy and vague, not thick ropes lashing in irritation.

Sterling stops, turning partway to lift his chin at Cal. "I came to find you for dinner. I'm hungry. Move, you lazy bastard."

Cal walks forward, his gate slow as he rolls his shoulders back. "Dinner it is."

Sterling lowers his face, smirking at me. "Then it's my turn." He glances at Cal. "We can't fuck the sass out of her, but it's going to be fun trying."

Cal laughs, deep and rich and real. I draw my eyebrows together like I don't understand because I don't. Sharing isn't something Cal does. Jealousy isn't rare for him, either.

His Dark reaches out with a tendril to brush the hair away from my face, stroking across my forehead and along my cheek. Cal smiles. "Go, Sterling. Our mate needs food."

CHAPTER 22
CALLAHAN

I follow my mates to the dining hall. Natalia keeps glancing back at me, almost like she's asking for permission. She's a slow learner, but she'll figure it out.

Sterling deposits her in her place, the seat between ours. He leans back, a hand on her thigh as he lifts his chin at the table. "More Glows showed up."

Jacques slumps forward. "I know we need them, but it hurts my eyes."

I shrug. "At this point, that's debatable. Those five are supposed to be the best they offer, and it's pathetic."

Dinner passes, and I head to the king's wing with my mates. I pour myself a drink, sipping on it as I settle on the chaise. "Talia."

She sits next to me, running her fingers through my hair.

I close my eyes and almost kick like a dog at her attention. The way her fingertips run across my scalp sends sparks of pleasure racing along my body.

She taps my neck. She didn't touch her mating mark, but

probably the center of exposed skin inside the ridges of her teeth marks. My skin tingles, my blood redirecting to my cock.

"Mate," I warn her. "That works both ways."

"Does it?" Her mouth moves closer, her warm breath tickling me and setting my balls on fire.

I growl in the back of my throat, but the door opens, boisterous laughter filling the air.

She withdraws, biting her lower lip and sliding her eyes toward the interruption of our closest contracted.

Sterling curls his lip, taking a drink from his glass. "Damnit." He turns away, greeting the others.

Jacques laughs with a bottle of liquor in one hand, his other arm around Tony's shoulders. Falsion sets more booze on the table as everyone gathers around.

Oscar helps his sister into a chair. Luca drops a dish of food onto the table. Zander takes a seat next to Shawn, the two of them discussing something.

Wyham and Palak are arranging chairs with Hailey and Galain.

Fallon runs around the room chasing Maria, releasing enthusiastic roars.

Thomas tries to catch him. "Fallon, perhaps Maria would like to have a drink and catch her breath."

"I'm hunting the Light," he yells. "Roar! Roar!"

My boy gives me an exasperated look as he tries to keep up.

Falsion looks my way. "Come on, Boy. You dragged us off the mountain."

With remorse, I pull Natalia to them. "Luna?"

She looks to me. "Sir?"

I pull my mouth to the side, then turn to Tony. His family is still in Narwal. "Tony, your whole family are heirs, yes? Capable?"

Tony laces his fingers together and bends his knuckles backward. "Dad and Sarah. Mom isn't, but she's still Pinnacle."

I nod. "Good. I have a job for them. Jacques, I want you to take Luna to Narwal and put her with Tony's family."

Oscar slams a fist to the table. "Absolutely fucking not. You're not sending her anywhere with him."

The table falls silent.

I frown. "She's thirty-three, almost thirty-four days. She deserves somewhere safe to give birth. I want her comfortable, and somewhere she can focus on her seed and have the chance to raise it. I don't want that seed anywhere near this war for its own safety."

"Not with that snake." Oscar points to Jacques.

Jacques starts to laugh, a silent grin growing into louder humor. "The fuck did I do?"

"You damn well know." Oscar looks to Natalia. "I'll take her."

She opens her mouth, and I cover it with my hand. "Jacques is in a better state to handle flying her there and getting back quickly."

"We are Tal's contracts, not yours."

Jacques whistles. "Really?" He waves two fingers. "I'm curious now. Why not me? I can handle—"

"Yanri raped her, beat her, both, frequently. I'll not hand her to his friend and a sadist just like him."

I glance at Jacques. I don't know much about him.

The ridges of his face seem to turn more pronounced. His eyes narrow, and a black forked tongue slips past his lips in an agitated flick.

"Yanri was no friend, and I prefer my victims to be willing."

"He wouldn't shut up about his friend Jacques after he made any trip to Ilbuio and every—"

"Every single one of us," Jacques snarls, "knew what Yanri

was. I never had use for him but to try and leverage my way into sending him to the afters."

Oscar turns to me. "He's still a fucking sadist, and Luna's had enough."

She reaches for her brother. "I can handle anything I must."

"No." He brushes her off. "I couldn't stop it before. I can now."

Jacques presses his hands to the table. "Why the fuck do you think I'm anything like Yanri?"

Hailey wags a finger between Jacques and Oscar. "Yanri, the abuser? He's..." She settles on an open palm gesture at Jacques. "You are the same? You animals have specific traits of your kind, yes? One beast is the same as the next?"

I glare. Oscar emits a violent purr. Jacques hisses. Luca laughs.

We all turn to stare at Luca.

He shrugs. "That's the stupidest thing I've heard yet."

Jacques twists his head to sneer at Hailey. "Yes, Yanri and I share a race—Vyper. Yes, Vypers tend toward certain traits, but not every Vyper is the same." He focuses on Oscar. "That's like saying all kitties are the same."

"You paralyzed Tabitha to be eaten alive by melrags and laughed. You're exactly like him."

Jerking his head, Jacques appears baffled, then tips his head back and cackles. "I laughed because Mar pissed himself."

I drag a hand down my face. "Enough."

Natalia nudges me. "Let Oscar take his sister."

I slide my fingers along her forearm to snag her wrist in my grip. Lifting her hand, I show the contract on the back ingrained into her skin. The words are indiscernible to me, but placement tells me what I'll likely need to know.

"Oscar." I turn her hand to him. "Did you negotiate?"

He tenses. "Yes."

"Has she changed anything since then?"

"No."

I press my fingers between Natalia's, letting our hands fall to hang between us. "Then you are contracted in service you agreed to and have no freedom to decide."

Oscar opens his mouth.

I raise my eyebrows.

He closes his lips and turns his head away.

"I'll have Sarina select someone else to take Luna to Narwal tomorrow."

Tony slumps. "Can I go with whoever to drop Luna off? I'd like to talk to my family and let them know I'm okay."

I pull my phone out and slide it toward him. "Call them. You can let them know what I am requiring as well."

I DISENGAGE, Sterling and Natalia already gone. I leave the others still laughing and head to find my mates.

I enter the suite, Natalia's soft noises filling in the air. Sterling started without me. That shouldn't make me grin, but I grin all the same. He's as hungry as I am, and he's mine, already playing with our mate and getting her ready for me.

I step into the bedroom, Natalia panting. I reach for the buttons on my shirt to join in but hesitate.

Sterling is damn near snarling.

I slide my hands into my front pockets, lingering in the doorway. Sterling is pissed. I'm not sure why. He has our mate naked beneath him. He should be enjoying himself.

Natalia gets sassy. I know it. She's set me on edge more times than I can count with her jokes I find less than amusing like the night she said a Light Fuck might do better than me. Whatever she said, she probably laughed and he's in the process of teaching her a lesson. I'll settle for the anticipation of watching him break her.

He glances behind him to me, twisting up to straddle her. When he meets my gaze, he shows his teeth. His ire isn't just at Natalia. I register that, but it only confuses me. I haven't even been present.

I step to the bed, getting on my knees next to him. He rolls off her and heads for the bathroom, kicking the door shut. I jerk at the bang, then look to Natalia.

She's on her back, eyes glassy, her skin flushed. She was enjoying herself.

She pushes up on her elbows, turning her head to the bathroom door, then her shoulders roll in on themselves and she turns to her side, curling in a ball facing away from me.

The shower starts to run.

I ask, "What the fuck happened?"

She tries to get smaller. "He got mad because I thought we should wait for you."

I lay down, putting my hand on her hip. "Why?"

She rolls, pressing her face into me. "It didn't feel right without you."

I chuckle, and my Dark elates as it stretches around her. Planting a kiss on her forehead, I soak in the knowledge that she is loyal, that she'll have him only with me. Then the elation fades, and I sigh. I need my mates to get along.

I rest my hand on her shoulder, forcing her flat to her back. "Little Star, look at me. He mated you, too, and you wanted him."

She nods, her eyes moving away from mine.

She's between us, Sterling and me. It's where she belongs, but she's unsure. She's fought to stay with me, she's submitted to me, and now she's unable to let go of me enough to hold onto both me and Sterling.

That's a problem.

This is going to spiral. The fissures will radiate unless I mend them now. It'll be easier to do before this gets worse. Letting this fester will destroy what I have. I won't lose this.

Putting my hand under her jaw, I grip tight for her attention. Her lips part in a small gasp.

"Mate," I say. "He's your mate too."

"I didn't—"

"Stop."

She winces and cuts her eyes away.

"You don't have to choose between us."

"You don't share, and you're already sharing, and—"

I press my mouth to hers to cease the warbling words. "Little Star," I whisper, pulling back. "He's ours. I'm keeping him and you."

"But...I'm your mate."

"His too." I tap my nose to hers, smiling. "You have two mates. Accept that. I have. I don't want pissy. I wanted to enjoy my night, and instead, I'm fixing this shit."

"I... I just..."

"Think I'm going to get annoyed that you're coming for him?" I snicker. "He's our mate."

"I don't want you to think... If I had to choose..."

"You would, and you'd choose me. I know that. You don't have to." I kiss her forehead. "You're mine. He's mine. I'm telling you to accept it, which means let him have you. I already know you enjoy it."

Her face flushes pink. "But I'm your mate."

"Yes, and so is he."

"You're not mad?"

"No. I won't walk away from you again. Of all the mistakes

I've made, that was the stupidest." I run my fingers through her hair to hold the back of her head, using it to pull her closer. "I could have sent him to the afters for what he did. I made the choice yours. If you wanted him, then I'd tolerate him, but—"

"Tolerate, not—"

"*When*," I say harshly, cutting her off, "I accepted it, it was because I have always enjoyed Sterling. I want to keep him as much as you."

She bobs her head.

"Figure it out, Little Star, because he's not going anywhere either." I kiss the side of her head. "Do you understand me?"

"Yes."

Pulling away, I leave her in bed, heading into the bathroom to fix my other mate.

I close the door behind me, removing my clothes to join Sterling in the shower.

He's leaned against the far wall, his forearms flat to the surface as he stands beneath the spray, his head low.

I step into it and blanch, the water frigid.

I guess he needed a cold shower.

Laughing, my Dark streaks for the controls, setting the temperature to tolerable.

Sterling lifts his head, looking back to me. He turns away, hanging his head again.

I step closer, and he stands, facing me.

"Baby..." I drag the pet name out, giving him a chastising look.

He points toward the bedroom. "She thought it was betraying you to let me play with her."

"You mated my mate."

He snarls. "You should have just killed me."

Fury ignites in my chest, burning through me with vengeance. I have a man who can hold his own and who can be

217

my partner. I want him bent, not broken, giving in to me but not relying on me. No one else I can think of could replace him.

I slam him to the wall, my hands in the middle of his sculpted chest, pressing him to the surface as I hold his gaze. I will not back down from a challenge, ever, and certainly not from having him where I want him. "No."

He strikes with the heel of his palm to my shoulder, trying to force me away. I won't go, nor accept that. He doesn't get space.

I kick his feet out. He tips into the wall, starting to fall, and I pin him upright with my forearm along his torso, my Dark ensnaring him, gluing him in place.

He bares his teeth, and I snap mine.

Sterling presses his lips, looking away in submission. I help him get his footing, my Dark eases, and I wrap my hands around his waist.

Sterling's shoulders drop, his chin bobbing toward his chest as he closes his eyes. "She's never going to be mine."

I take advantage of his low head, the fucker still inches taller than me. Pressing my forehead to his, I say, "She's ours, which means she's mine, and she's yours."

The words come easier than I ever expected they could. I don't mind, though. If I was fighting him for her, if he and I were fighting each other, if I didn't like Sterling so much, things would be different.

It's amazing that I don't care. I'll share her with him. I always avoided him because I knew myself enough to know I'd enjoy him. I didn't realize I could ever have him, and never to this extent, but I do. I'm not letting go. I'll bury him in my claws and my Dark until there's no escape. He did this. Natalia wanted this. They need to accept their place together beneath me.

He lifts his eyes to mine. "Tell her that."

"I did."

He picks his head. "She'll do it because you made her."

"You mated my mate, you fucking moron."

"I thought—"

"You'd die, and if you didn't, you'd have us both. I'm aware. I wasn't aware you presumed it would be fucking easy. There's a fucking reason I'm allowed to rip your spine out for this shit."

He sags, going limp with his head tipped back. "I know."

"Good. Then suck it up, baby." I shift closer, drawing both my hands down his sides. Muscles cut into his abdomen ripple beneath my caress. "I'm not sending you to the afters, ever. I might not be able to mate you, but you're mine."

He drops his head toward mine again. "You're fucking impossible. I would have killed you, or maybe just forced you to live mated to her, but never being able to have her."

I chuckle. "Don't tempt me."

Leaning his head back, he groans. "She's yours. I've always known that."

"It wasn't just Pierre," I say. "She wanted you. My Dark almost strangled me because I didn't want to let you play with her despite her enjoyment. She's my mate, our mate, and like me, you'd do anything to make her happy. I broke her down, put her in her place, and made her mine. It took me a worn contract."

He scoffs. "She told me. I don't have that kind of power."

"She's stubborn and bad with feelings. Give her time. She'll adjust."

"She's too afraid to lose you to want me."

"I made sure she understood she belongs on my cock." I snicker. "I didn't see a problem with that. I didn't realize you were going to fucking mate her or that I'd ever accept a second mate."

"Then why?"

"You're strong. I like you. We work well together, and in your own words, I could use the help."

He laughs. "She's a handful."

219

"Multiple hands are required. Maybe more than we have together."

He rests his hands on my hips. "I always thought being the contractor was better. I didn't understand why someone would be highborn and accept a contract, choosing to be taken care of instead of being free."

I smile. "I may have given your intelligence too much credit."

Sterling shakes, laughing at me in quiet humor. "You might have. I didn't realize I'd enjoy it so much, though. It's fucking exhausting being the contractor."

He's right about being a contractor. I'm not his contractor, but I'm still his alpha. He's accepting that, and I will take care of him, but he only submits to me, and only by choice. He's still very much an alpha, standing by his own strength.

He's free to make his own choices. Sterling doesn't kneel to anyone, contracted to stand with us. I'm the Queen of Light. Natalia is the Dark King. Neither of us commands him.

Sterling is Sterling, stuck between us while claiming his own position. He placed himself with me and Natalia as an equal. I need him.

"Don't make me do this on my own. I'm tired of standing alone."

He squeezes his hands around my hips. "I've got you."

"Then stop being a pain in my ass." I hold his gaze, curling one side of my mouth back. "Behave."

He laughs. "Gods, you're so fucking perfect it's annoying."

"No, I'm not. Don't lie to me."

He lifts a hand, putting it under my jaw and tilting my head back. "You really fucking are, pretty face and noble and strong." His other hand glides up my side. "I hated competing with you."

"Get me off that damn pedestal." I turn, shutting off the water and exiting the shower.

I throw a towel at him and grab another, getting dry, then exiting the bathroom.

Natalia has curled on her side again, this time facing away from the bathroom. I need to break this. I never even had nightmares that I'd have to break her loyalty for me. I taught her that she belongs in my Dark and on my cock, but now she needs to understand that with two mates, she has more Dark and two cocks.

Dragging a hand down my face, I look to Sterling. He's watching me, waiting.

I am the problem.

Turning back into the bathroom, I pull my pants on, then the shirt, though I don't bother buttoning it. Sterling tilts his head at me, and I point to her. "Figure it out. I'm going to get a fucking drink, and you two fix this shit before I get back, or I'm going to throw a tantrum for once."

Natalia sits up, her lips parted as she gapes.

I leave the room, then the suite, the entire wing, and the floor, moving toward the kitchens. I curl my lip at the wall, striding barefoot along the cold stone. I could be balls deep in my mates, but they just had to get fussy.

CHAPTER 23
NATALIA

Cal walks out of the room, and I look to Sterling. He takes two steps, turns, sits on the bed, and pivots his legs onto the mattress, leaning against the headboard as his Dark adjusts pillows for his comfort.

I'm confused. My Light buzzes in my head. I'm throbbing between my legs in a demand for attention. Sterling brought me almost to orgasm twice, then stopped. I'd suggested we wait for Cal, uneasy about whether he'd get irritated that I was having sex with only Sterling. I'm Cal's mate.

I rub the side of my neck as Sterling stares at me. Sterling mated me, but I didn't and can't mate him back.

He crooks a finger at me. "Come here, Firefly."

I chew on my lower lip, moving closer. "Cal..." I start, looking over my shoulder.

"Went to get a drink."

I look over my shoulder again.

"He's letting us figure this out. Leave him out of it."

Frowning, I meet Sterling's black gaze. He tucks one arm

behind his head, getting comfortable. "I fucking mated you without your consent."

"Or Cal's."

"Leave him out of it."

A sparkle of fury flashes through me. "He's my mate."

"I know."

"You mated me after he did—after we already mated each other."

"Yes."

"He doesn't share. What am I supposed to do with this?" I point to my neck. "He's not the sharing kind. I love him."

"I know."

"He's not okay with this."

"Is that what he's told you?"

"No. He said he's..." I stop.

Cal has never once said anything about being against this. He hasn't fought with Sterling, hasn't tried to force him away. He hasn't so much as told Sterling to leave since the night we mated, and even then, he told Sterling to leave but didn't force anything.

Sterling rubs the bridge of his nose with his index finger, staring at me. "I told you I'd get Cal to accept sharing. I never said anything about sharing only you."

"What?"

"I mated you because I wanted you. I did think I was going to die, either to serve the Dark for you to display your strength or that he'd kill me for mating you, but I survived both of those things somehow. I don't know how, but I'm not throwing that away. I get to have both of you."

"What?"

He smiles. "Firefly, I want Cal just as much. We aren't fighting over you. We're sharing."

"Oh."

"He's not going to walk away from you ever again. The

223

mating bond will make it near impossible in any case, but he's never going to want to leave you. He didn't want to the first time. The bastard was just trying to be noble, and you broke his heart."

I fidget, rolling my shoulders and wincing. "I said that thing."

"We know why and that it was a lie. He's letting me stand with you. I'm not getting in between you. I'm just joining you."

I try to chew on the inside of my cheek, twisting my lips to the side as I stare at him. My Light shivers. *"Figure it out. I want to keep both of them, my love and my friend."*

"He's...fine...with this. It's...fine that I..."

"Yes."

I like Sterling, and I want Sterling, but I want Cal, too, and I love Cal. I've never loved anyone so much.

I don't want to consider why I'm struggling with this. Cal's been acting odd. He let Sterling pick me up and carry me away for dinner. He's been present for Sterling fucking me, not interfering.

I know Cal isn't fighting. Cal isn't the problem. Words I don't want to acknowledge flitter across my mind. I can't love them both, can I? Is that possible? Mallafic didn't think I could love anyone at all. I don't know how I can love them both—if that means I don't love either of them.

Sterling watches me.

I want to run and hide.

He sighs, rolling forward to latch onto me and drag me into his lap. I don't fight. I don't want to fight. I want to be able to want him without feeling guilty.

He cups my face, blocking out everything but him. "You're fucking cute and vicious. I adore you, and the last thing I wanted to do was hurt you."

I nod, lowering my gaze to his chest.

"I mated you pursuing my desires."

"I'm not mad at you," I confess in a whisper. "I don't want to lose Cal."

"I know. He's accepting me, even without a mating bond between us. I'm not trying to tear you apart. I don't want to. I want both of you."

I wanted someone who loved me. It never crossed my mind that two would. I want to be wrapped in their Dark between them, but I don't want to hurt either of them.

Cal says I don't have to choose. Sterling claims he doesn't intend to stand between us.

Cal is possessive and jealous, but he's not acting that way with Sterling.

The only thing I can think to do is trust them. The Dark doesn't lie.

I lean forward and kiss Sterling. He takes my face between his hands to kiss me. His palms are larger than Cal's, his fingers longer, his hands swallowing my face.

He groans, lifting his hips beneath me and deepening the kiss, his tongue invading my mouth.

His Dark wraps around me. His hand slips between my legs, his fingers thrusting into me.

I moan. His fingers are so long. They curl and thrust in and out, hitting that delicious spot as I pant into his mouth. I'm still dangling on the ledge from earlier, and I'm going to—

He pulls back, and I whimper, rocking my hips. "Asshole."

He laughs. "You wanted to wait for Cal. Let's see how long that drink takes."

Returning to working his fingers in and out, his thumb pressing against my clit and shifting back and forth, he digs his fingers into my hair. His grip tightens, pulling my head to the side as he moves his mouth to my neck. "But I'm not going to stop playing with you."

I whimper again, my toes curling in anticipation. Sterling

speeds up his movements until I'm breathless with need. "Please."

"I'm giving you what you wanted, Firefly. Don't start begging for something else."

I twitch as he stops again. His Dark has wound around me. It tightens and rocks me against him, his cock poking my leg. I need him inside of me.

"Please."

"No," he says, ramming his fingers all the way in. I shudder and squeeze them, tightening until I think I will snap.

No amount of pleading earns me release or his cock. I'm half mad with need.

Hands wrap around my hips, and I groan as Cal settles behind me. "Mates."

Sterling chuckles. "I waited for you."

Cal drags his teeth across my neck. "Did you? Why?"

"My own amusements. She's so pretty when she begs."

Cal lifts my hips, forcing me to face him, and when he lowers me, Sterling's dick presses into me. I gasp, my breath catching in the back of my throat as he stretches me.

Sterling groans. "Fuck, she's so tight."

Cal shoves me back to lay on Sterling, moving lower to lick my clit. I clench around Sterling who makes a guttural noise, lifting his hips.

"Firefly, you feel so good."

Cal sucks on my clit, and I come, shuddering as the tension explodes, releasing shockwaves of pleasure through me.

Sterling rocks his hips with a long, low growl. "Cal."

Dark tangles around me, binding my hands and lifting them over my head. More strands tie me to Sterling, Cal's tongue continuing to flick against my clit.

I try to squirm, to arch my back, anything to dislodge his mouth as the sensations intensify. There are too many hands holding me down, ropes of Dark binding me in place. I pant, forced to endure the pleasure ripping through me.

Sterling bites my neck and pinches my nipples. I cry out as another orgasm tears through me.

Still, Cal doesn't let up. Sterling starts rocking his hips, and I almost lose consciousness, overwhelmed with pleasure.

I can't escape them, and they work together, taking turns with me until I'm limp on the verge of passing out from euphoria and exhaustion alike before they finish.

My body throbs in waves of pleasure as they settle on either side of me, whispering and chuckling together. I can't even focus on the words, falling into bliss, happier than I have the right to be.

They both leave me in bed to clean up, but I'm too tied up in languor to follow them. Cal returns first, and I snuggle into him, my head on his shoulder.

Sterling lies behind me, curling with me and draping his arm over me, his hand resting on Cal's stomach.

I stare at it, biting my lip.

I look to Cal. He gazes back with half-open eyes, a haze on his features clouding my ability to discern his emotional state. He's my mate. I can see the glittering silver Light glistening from my bite mark on his neck even while I am cradled between him and another.

Wincing, I avert my eyes.

"Something on your mind, Little Star?"

"I…"

How do I ask if he is okay with sharing when I know he's not? I'm torn between them, wanting both, but Cal doesn't share. I don't want to hurt him, my mate, but I want to keep both, to be pinned between love and more love. As long as I've hoped for just one, I have two options.

"I…"

Sterling rumbles. "Wake me up when she finally says something."

He shifts closer, tighter.

I can't bring myself to move or meet Cal's eyes. I'm comfortable, but I shouldn't be. I have a mate. A. One. Cal.

He pushes air through his nose, his chest jumping. "You're worrying about me?"

I scrunch my nose, staring across his chest to the wall.

"You don't want me to have to share, or at least concerned about me sharing." His chest deflates as he breathes out.

"Ye–yes... How...?"

"You're Light is talking for you."

Sterling mutters, "Must be a mate thing."

Cal laughs. "No, your Dark doesn't talk to her Light. It... It's a dick, apparently."

"Why the fuck are you being an ass to our mate's Light?" Sterling sighs, nuzzling my neck. "Apparently, your Light is a vicious tease."

I frown, tilting my chin higher so I can meet Cal's gaze. His eyes are still half-closed and one side of his mouth curled up. "You won't lose me." He picks his head up, pressing his curved lips to my temple.

I bite my lower lip. "You two don't hate each other."

"No."

Sterling nuzzles my ear. "We've known each other a long, long time. If not for the games and the contest, we would have been friends, maybe even snagged you together that day instead of fighting over you."

I hum, considering what that would have been like, how different things might be or if I'd have been put between them even sooner.

"I'm glad you two never faced each other in the sacrifice at Gathering Shadows."

Sterling laughs in a sharp ending yelp of humor. "We have. Three times."

I gape at Cal. "You both lived?"

He curves his lips, but it lacks feeling. "I ordered Massimo to go for his partner, not him."

Sterling groans. "I did the same."

I flap my lips. "You...agreed to...?"

"Never discussed it." Sterling cuddles closer. "My partner and I went for Mass the way those two Shadow Beasts went for you." He taps my shoulder.

I shiver. "I hadn't been prepared for that."

"Difference was, I knew not to turn my back on Cal like those morons did."

I shift to my back, frowning at Sterling. "Then your partner...?"

"Partners." He sighs. "Mass was an anomaly. Most contractors don't get to have the same partner for that long. Cal's a fucking freak of nature that managed to keep his partner alive."

Cal snorts. "No. Mass was...was..." The humor dies in his voice. "Mass was damn good and could have stood on his own."

"Then..." I blink, furrowing my brow.

The sacrifice games take place on the opening day of the games. Twelve die. There are no exceptions. Sterling lost his partner in the games on the first day. No one is allowed a second partner.

Cal rolls to his side, propping his head on a bent elbow. "He survived the games all three times on his own."

I widen my eyes, holding Sterling's gaze. I never, ever want to repeat the Gathering Shadows games. The idea of doing it without Cal, without anyone to help, terrifies me worse.

Sterling stares back, seeming unfazed. His features remain lax, but there's a bereft gleam in his eyes the way a fractured mirror reflects illumination. "I earned my place as a contender."

I roll on top of him to wrap my arms around him and squeeze. I can't imagine the strength it would take to do it alone.

Cal places his hand on my back. "Hold him tight, Little Star."

Sterling shakes beneath me. "You two are going to be the death of me," he says, laughter betrayed in the words. Wrapping his arms around me, he clamps tight with a groan. "What's done is done. Dead is dead. I don't have to do it ever again as your mate."

"Is that why you—"

"No," Sterling and Cal snap in unison.

Cal lifts his hand from me, tucking hair behind my ear to clear it away from my face.

I turn my head, resting my cheek on Sterling's shoulder to meet his gaze.

Cal moves closer, kissing my shoulder. "No one else could have earned us."

Sterling strokes my head. "I wouldn't be so dishonest as to use you to avoid the games or be a cheat. I mated you to have you and him. Figured it would be when we were in the afters, but you two surprised the fucking shit out of me."

I sit up, straddling his waist and draw my finger down his lips. Sterling doesn't love only me. He loves me and Cal. It's better than I'd hoped for.

Maybe I really can have them both.

Sterling grins. "What's more useful after it's been broken?"

"Oh! I actually know this one. An egg."

"No, a Dark contractor."

Cal laughs. "Fuck, that's true."

CHAPTER 24
CALLAHAN

I rub the sleep from my eyes as I walk through the corridors with Sterling and Natalia on our way to the field. The cracks in me are sharp today, the past bleeding to the surface, leaving me fatigued.

Sterling had faced the games alone and survived three times. I'm the only time he didn't win his sacrifice games. I didn't have a choice in the matter. Neither of us did.

I can't get rid of the pit gnashing teeth, trying to eat my soul.

He's as broken as I am. I'm torn between relief and sorrow in that fact.

Sterling asks, "If time flies like an arrow. What does a fruit fly like?"

I look to him with pure hatred.

He flashes that perfect smile at me. "Fruit flies like a banana."

Natalia giggles. "That's awful."

"If a pig loses its voice, what does it become?"

I rub the space between my eyes and sigh. "What?"

"Disgruntled. What's a job I can really see myself doing?"

I look to the ceiling. "Shutting up?"

231

"Cleaning mirrors."

Natalia laughs. "Okay, stop. Just stop."

"What's a beehive without an exit?"

Natalia groans, "What?"

"Un-bee-leave-able."

I have to choke down my breath to keep from laughing at that. "Sterling, baby, shut the fuck up, or I drop you in the maze."

He snickers. "I'd survive." He hums. "You know, the third time I was on my own, I brought marshmallows as my weapon to the maze."

I twist my head to him. "Why?"

"Motivation. If I made it through three turns, I could roast one and eat it."

This isn't a corny riddle. It's a depressing realization.

"I ran out long before I made it to the end."

Natalia asks, "Roasting marshmallows?"

I take her hand, squeezing it, but Sterling answers.

"The maze is constantly burning around me while I'm in it."

"Is that it?"

"Talia," I sigh.

"I mean, like, that's all it does to you then, right? That's bad enough. It doesn't..." She trails away as Sterling starts cracking up.

He looks down at her, struggling to keep his lips closed, his cheeks ballooning up.

Natalia stops, shaking my hand from hers. I come to a halt, Sterling doing the same.

She twists her body as she jumps, wrapping her legs around his hips and her arms around his neck. Burying her face against his neck, she hugs him. "Babe."

He meets my eyes, confused.

I smirk, stepping to her back, running my hands along her

sides and holding his gaze. Our mate is more tender-hearted than we are or are accustomed to.

She'd come into my life unexpectedly. I thought I wanted to use her. In a way, I did. She's strong enough to survive. I needed that, but not for me, for her. She can survive in the Dark to stay at my side.

Her jokes and that delicate giggle make me smile. Her heart, hidden and shielded, restarted mine. The way she broke, unable to cope with the wounds the games inflict, reminded me that I used to feel things. She brought me back to life.

I kiss the back of her head, placing my hand on his shoulder. "Come on."

Sterling holds Natalia against his chest as he starts walking away. "I'm alive, Firefly. Really."

Jacques falls in step with me. "What doesn't kill us gives us a sense of humor."

My scalp prickles. I hadn't heard him coming and hadn't been paying attention, deftly lured into a false sense of security at being with Natalia and Sterling.

Jacques nods, and we continue toward the back of the palace. I ask, "Sadist?"

Jacques flicks his shifted, black, forked tongue at me. "Problem, Daddy?"

I rub my mouth, trying to hide my smile. "Enlightening."

"I have my enjoyments, and you have yours."

We step into the open expanse of land cradled by the mountains behind the palace.

I head for the steps, Zander and the other Lighters grouped close on them. Maybe a dozen Lights are present now. It's uncomfortable, like an itch I can't scratch.

My Dark fizzles and pouts at their presence. As much as I agree, we don't have a choice, and it will only get worse. We are the Queen of Light.

Zander steps to me. "Are we ever going to be allowed near that?"

I glance at the maze and curl my lip.

"No," I say in unison with Jacques.

"Tallie said it's made of nightmare toxin. I'm curious."

"Stay away from that death trap. If you go in, I'm not coming to get you."

"I'm your contracted."

I rub my forearm with his name. "I'll add a clause that excuses me from saving you from your stupidity. I don't intend to ever step foot in that fucked thing again."

"It's that bad?"

Jacques shudders. "It pulls your worst fears and nightmares from your blood and tries to kill you with them. A mongoose damn near ate me last time."

"What if you're not afraid of anything?"

I laugh. "You're afraid of at least one thing."

"I am. It's a hypothetical."

Jacques knocks his fist against Zander's shoulder. "Everyone is afraid of things." He looks to me. "What are we doing about Gathering Shadows? Dark and Light are coming together under one crown."

Zander lifts his eyebrows. "Your barbaric killings to prove your strength?" Jacques and I both look to him with ire as he crosses his arms. "The Light knows about it. Tallie mentioned she doesn't understand why you call them games."

Shrugging, I say, "They can be fun...some of them."

Zander scowls. "For sadists and masochists?"

Jacques snickers. "You should try the games before you pass judgment."

I scratch the side of my neck. An elusive set of words lingers on the back of my tongue, too brazen to be spoken.

No more Gathering Shadows.

I frown at the maze, a smoragon taking flight from its depths and lifting into the sky. "I need to be crowned the Light Queen and deal with Ancients before I figure that out."

I survey the mix of Seraphinus thickening as others join, more pouring out of the palace. "I want to start separating everyone, pull the strongest together. I need to know what we have and fill uses other than combat with the less capable." I point to a group of Lighters passing by. "Who are they?"

"More arrived last evening, and others will continue to come. I will find the strongest of us."

Turning to Jacques, I twist my lips. "You and I are going to kick down the weak to weed them out."

He grins. "I'll play that game. I bet I can make one cry."

We move forward, and I whistle, drawing everyone's attention. "I see new faces. Welcome to Ilbuio. Find a partner, try your best, and don't kill anyone. Magic is tolerated as long as no lethal force is used and no venoms are injected. If you require healing, we have three who can fix you."

Tony lifts his hand. "Come see me, Alex, or Tal. We'll get you healed in fractions."

Standing next to Tony, Alex waves. "I'm Alex."

He's getting bolder—not the same scrappy kid I met. Wisps of shadows dance around his fingers as he crosses his arms.

He'll be strong.

I scan the crowd. "Tal is Natalia. You'll know her by the silver Light." My heart speeds up as I bob my head, searching for her. I breathe out, seeing her feet over her head next to Sterling. "For those of you glowing, new and old, I will issue the order again: *stay away from the maze*. Do not even get close. If you are in its shadows, you're disobeying a direct order of your Light Queen."

A new, pale face furrows nearby. "Why are you only refuting the Light?"

Jacques peels into laughter. "Because the Dark don't require that command. They won't go near it unless they are forced which is the only warning you Lighters should need to heed that order. Get close enough, the ivy will drag you inside."

"You'll die or want to." I draw a circle. "Go. Get started. Don't pick someone easy for you to pin. Find someone that will kick you down to learn something."

A new Lighter lifts his chin. "How about you?"

I eye him. He's shorter, with a long, thin face reminiscent of Zander. "You want to try and put me down?"

"Yes, I do." He steps forward. "You may call me Larles." He bows.

"Don't ever do that again." I step to him, rolling my shoulders and lifting my hands.

Larles narrows his eyes. "Bowing is a sign of respect."

"I haven't earned your respect yet." We exchange a few half-hearted swings, and I lift my voice. "Why are you all standing around watching?"

Larles swings harder. I block and round my elbow into his jaw. It wakes him up, and I go on the defensive against his flurry of fists. He's fast, and I'm using every trick I know to fend him off.

I see an opening and take it, getting in close to land a blow. The momentum shifts. Larles is on his heels, and my Dark tangles his legs, taking his feet from beneath him. He hits the dirt, and I put a knee in the center of his chest, a hand around his throat.

Drawing air through my nose, I pull back, rolling off him and standing to offer a hand.

I help him to his feet, glancing around. "There are too many of you standing still. Why?"

A Light waves a hand toward me and Larles. "We wanted to see a Fairly in action."

I look to Larles. "Fairly?"

Zander throws an arm around his shoulders. "He is my little brother."

Larles turns to him with murderous intentions. "I am your elder seed. That warrants your respect." Turning his back on Zander, he meets my eyes. "As a Fairly, I am in your service."

"Which is stronger?" I point and move my finger between them.

"Why must you dogs torment so? As he is larger, his Light has room to grow more than mine, and the answer should be obvious." Larles gestures with both hands and a glower.

Zander inhales, drawing up. "Larles," he says in a quiet voice.

Crossing my arms, I say, "I'll give you one excused slur as a possible slip of habit. That was your one. As for the idea that your size limits your strength...? You're a fucking moron."

Larles curls his lip. "You're a Hallow, and I will protect you with my life in honor of your heritage and the vow mine made, but I will not pretend you aren't an animal of the Dark."

I start to step, and Natalia cuts between us. "Larles."

He twists his lips, sneering. "Tallie. I am speaking with my queen, and you are not—"

"The Fairly heritage is limited and incredibly special," she explains, turning to face me. "They are protectors of the trinity heritages for a reason."

I scowl at her. "I warned him."

"Cal. Words. We do not harm Fairlys. There are very few and need protecting as much as possible to ensure they do not die out."

I clamp my jaw, breathing out through my nose.

She presses her lips and tries to smile. Spinning on her heels, she faces Larles. "You're a pillar of the Light. You are seen as a leader, carrying great respect for your heritage and continuation of a promise made to protect and serve as the strongest of all heritages, and if you will not abide by the terms of Lighter and

Darkling, it will only encourage others to discard their use as well. Please see to it that you lead by example as your brother does." She bows her head and then continues. "The Dark has a second form, yes. They can shift into predator-like beings with claws and fangs and animalistic characteristics, but they are *not* animals."

"It's not another form. It's their true form. It's what they are."

I glare at the sky. "We aren't animals."

Natalia puts a hand to my chest without turning to face me. "Cal is a man."

"He's a dog. One you put above my brother even after you—"

"Under false pretenses, with a gift that was not his to give, while being lied to by you and him and everyone else who glows. I already loved Cal when I entered that city, and I still loved him the moment I left it and every fraction in between. I never would have accepted a relationship with Zan knowing Cal was alive and I will not feel guilt for that or that I didn't have a relationship with him."

My Dark wraps around her, tugging her closer, smiling against her ear. I nip her throat over my mating mark.

She whimpers and shudders. That's the best design of the gods in all of creation. One graze, one lick, and she'll drip or even come.

Zander puts a hand on his brother's shoulder, speaking low. "My ordeal is not to be spoken of so publicly and is not your weight to bear. It was barely a flicker of illumination in the entirety of my life and is no longer an open discussion as she has mated."

Larles narrows his eyes at Natalia and me. He opens his mouth, and I say, "Sterling mated her after she and I had mated."

Zander says, "I witnessed both and will not interfere with a mating bond. Regardless of Light or Dark, they are seen as sacred. I have retracted myself, and Callahan is my contractor. I ask for respect for that alone if you can find no other reason."

Facing Zander, Larles frowns. "You contracted to him?"

"He is our Light Queen. Tallie is the Dark King. Both are working to unify the two, which will end the divide between our kinds."

"So I have been informed."

"Speak not harshly. There are things we can learn from them, find benefits in their ways."

"You'd turn your back on the Light?"

"I would see a world where our parents live."

Larles draws his eyebrows together. "For that reason, how could you—"

"Hope," he answers. "For me and you, your heritage seeds, and all the others. Not for the first time in our history, we are coming together in pursuit of survival. Why not learn the lessons our past teaches, and this time allow the unity to stretch beyond the threat into a tomorrow where I do not fear the Dark, but see it as a friend? I hope for a lifetime where I do not see you fall to their claws protecting another from one so similar to us. There has been enough bloodshed and life lost. Let it end, here, today, with us so the next generation can learn from our mistakes and continue to rebuild the world torn in two for one of peace."

"You sound as regal and well-spoken as Pierre."

"He died for this. He knowingly gave his life to bring us together, not just against a common enemy, but for a future that is better than the wounds he suffered. Give him honor in his sacrifice. There is none more devoted or ingrained in the Light as Pierre. He burned brighter than Izul ever could, and the world is much darker without him, but respect his wisdom. He would not forsake the Light nor turn his back on it. This was his dying wish. Let it end."

It was a beautiful speech, one my father would have conjured or been proud of. I glance at the faces around, the mix of two kinds mingling as one in palpable silence. He deserves accolades for the words.

Natalia giggles, breaking the moment. Zander frowns at her, and I ask, "What is funny?"

"You would have sounded like an idiot trying to say all of that." She turns her head to grin at me, then looks to Zander. "Great speech."

She walks away from me, pushing through bodies. Zander watches her go and shakes his head. "She was far more suited to my tastes when her behavior was curbed." He shrugs.

Pulling up one side of my mouth, I tap his shoulder with a closed fist. "That was your idiocy and why you never possessed her. You can't curb that woman. You have to give her freedom. You never stood a chance."

"I had enough mettle to earn her acceptance of a relationship."

I scoff. "She thought I was in the afters, or you never would have gotten that far. You caged her, suffocating her Light and her soul. Whereas you were begging her for kisses, I took her heart while she begged me not to. I gave her what she wanted without forcing her to give me what I wanted. We are not the same." Glancing around, I lift my voice. "Find a partner. Get back to training."

Zander twists his lips. "Sterling did too."

I imagine that jab is supposed to sting and smirk. "He was after me as much as her. Go, have your brother assist you. I want the strongest of us."

I take off toward Tony, Ashley leaning against him with her hands on his shoulder, damn near hanging from him.

As I approach, she beams at me. "Hello, Callahan."

I stop short, turning my face to narrow my eyes in mistrust.

She rolls her eyes. "Hello, Mutt."

240

Tony shakes his head, eyes low. "Sweetheart, you are a bitch."

"His fault, not mine. I was being polite. He didn't like it." She shrugs, resting her chin on her hands with wide, innocent eyes.

She's anything but, making the intense gaze discomforting.

"Oh." She pulls upright, nearly the same height as Tony. "Flora. Layla."

I sidestep, giving way to two incoming women. Ashley steps to them, smiling. "This is Callahan Barraco."

They look to me, and I hold a hand up. "No bowing."

Jacques claps me on the back. "They seem offended."

I shake my head. "Hate that shit." I roll my shoulders, adjusting my skin.

Ashley clicks her tongue, gesturing. "This is Tony."

The black-haired woman asks, "And the other? He's cute."

"Alex."

Alexander's face flushes, his ears turning pink. "I, um…" He turns away, yells, "Hey, Luca," and scampers off.

Tony stares after him. "I really need to teach him how to talk to the opposite sex." Looking to the women, he extends a hand. "Anthony Washington, but you can call me Tony."

Disinterested, I move away, Jacques following, lingering to watch a few fights. There's a small crowd gathered ahead, so I shoulder to the front to determine why.

A Light and a Dark are swinging. Palak and Matthew. It's the first time I've seen the two spar, most choosing to work with their own kind.

Palak drags Matthew to the ground. He pulls back, ready to swing, then shakes his head and lets his arm drop. "You need to move your feet more."

Standing, Palak helps Matthew to his feet. He claps him on the shoulder and steps back. "You don't move. It's too easy to win."

Matthew scowls. "I step into every punch."

Palak glances around. "You," he says, pointing at the crowd. "Woman, black hair. My sincere apologies, I do not know your name, but I recognize the face as a decent fighter from yesterday."

She steps forward. "Meredith."

Palak motions her forward with his fingers. "Swing at me."

She does, but he steps back.

She moves forward, trying again, left then right.

He blocks the first, sidestepping the second, and now he's in range to swing at her in a weak spot left open. He doesn't land the punch, stopping short before looking to Matthew. "If you move, you're less of a target and harder to defend against." He hesitates before asking. "Didn't my father...?"

Matthew chuckles. "He tried, kid. Might be why I've made it all these years. He always kicked my ass."

Wincing, Palak kicks at the ground. "You really didn't... I thought I'd see if you were even capable. You're not."

"Respect is earned, and he'd earned it several times over."

Puffing up his cheeks, Palak bobs his head, starting to look around. He stops with his eyes on me. "I'll offer my services when you take the throne."

I nod.

Matthew clears his throat. "Jean would no doubt like that."

Palak squares up. "All right, hands up, old man, and move your feet."

CHAPTER 25

CALLAHAN

Larles tugs Zander's ear and scowls. Zander shrugs him away, shifting toward Jacques.

Larles scowls. "They are—"

"Will you please desist?" Zander looks back. "I know what they are. They are Dark—Darklings—yes, I am aware. I appreciate your incessant need to explain to me what they are as an overprotective elder seed in charge of its younger, inexperienced sibling seed, but I feel the need to inform you I have a memory and do, in fact, recall you educating me on what they are a dozen times over breakfast. Please cease your superfluous words. They will have no effect as they haven't before."

"Working along with them for the sake of the Light is one thing. Ceasing bloodshed and contests between our races is an amenable idea. However, seeking their company is entirely against what we are."

Thames smiles and lifts his teacup, toasting Larles. "I see we have made no new friends this morning. It's all right, baby," he turns to Zander. "We won't hold your heritage seed against you."

Zander grins. "I appreciate that." Turning to me, he adds,

"Parker and Owen have notified me they are on their way. They will bring a complete bound copy of our laws. They were Pierre's contracts and will be offering you their service. Parker, you will no doubt like. Owen is a bit temperamental but strong."

"We'll take everyone. We need bodies as much as fighters."

Hiro asks, "Do we have a plan yet?"

I glance between Natalia and Tony, focusing my gaze over Tony's shoulder at Ashley walking toward us. Lighters duck their heads as she passes them. Her chin never waivers, her focus on this end of the table.

I nod as she approaches. "Ashley needs to make the arrangements for my coronation. After that, my focus is on finding ways to destroy the Ancients and protect our kind."

Larles sneers. "Is that Dark or Light?"

"Both."

Ashley pulls Tony's chair and Tony away from the table, dumping him on the floor, and takes his seat, surveying the table without regard or acknowledgment of any kind.

Tony picks himself up. "Hello to you too, *sweetheart*." He twists the pet name.

"There were no seats available at this end of the table." She dumps his mug onto the stone and fills it again, adding sugar and cream. "Hm. The selections are poor, or have you already eaten everything worthwhile?"

I look to Tony. "You can do better."

Batting her eyelashes, Ashley grins wide. "Oh, darling, I disagree."

Tony scoffs. "She's a real bitch. It's kind of my type, though."

Hiro pulls Thames into his lap, and his Dark lashes around the chair, swinging it around to swivel between Ashley and Sterling. "Have a seat."

"Thanks." Tony drops into the seat, and his eyes roll back into his head, turning pure white.

Natalia squirms closer to me. "That spider is talking to him again."

I drape my arm across her shoulders. "I kill spiders." Kissing her head, I remind her, "I promised you."

She shifts, getting smaller.

I broke one promise. I realize that. "Talia." I turn her face to mine with a finger on her jaw. "Look at me, Little Star. I will kill any spider you see."

Her eyes cut toward Sterling, turning glossy. She blinks, ducking her chin and shifting in her seat. "*Mhm.*"

Tony gasps and slumps, groaning as he drops his face to his hands, elbows propped on the table. "Great, thanks." He starts rubbing his temples. "Stop doing that, parasite."

I ask, "Anything important?"

"Lucius is pacing and muttering. He's pissed Adri jumped in the way, thinks he could have handled it."

Ashley turns into him, resting her chin on his shoulder. "Want coffee?" She offers her mug.

"I'm good. I like my coffee to be coffee, not milk and sugar, with a splash of bean water."

She shrugs, pulling upright. "I have a strong dislike of coffee. I much prefer tea."

"Oh, baby." Thames snickers. "You should have said. Raz, darling."

I focus on Natalia, her features crestfallen. Something is amiss.

Raz steps to Thames, who waves a hand at Ashley. "She prefers tea."

Raz nods.

Ashley holds up her cup. "Darajing, if that's possible."

"Dara-what?" Thames blinks and stretches his eyes. "What's this?"

"An impossible ask." Ashley flicks her hand. "I'll settle for anything but bean water."

Raz lifts an eyebrow, fading away.

Setting his cup aside, Thames asks again, "What tea did you ask for?"

"Darajing. It's grown in the Jaloquinn rainforest exclusively for the Light."

Zander picks up his mug. "It's delightful. We have a five-day tea ceremony in the Harvest season each year for specialty blends."

Thames practically drools. "I've heard such. I have never wrangled samples."

"I'll see if we can have some shipped here."

Larles rams his elbow into Zander's side. Zander's arm swings, coffee splashing over the rim of his cup into Jacques's lap.

Zander's chest swells as he glares across the table at Thames. His Light drags a napkin into Jacques's lap next.

"Whoa!" Jacques lurches to his feet, knocking his chair over. "I don't think we're that kind of acquainted, Friend."

Larles throws out his hand. "What are you doing? This is not a combat mat."

I chuckle, but Natalia stares into her lap, head low as she picks at the skin around her thumbnail.

"Dark do not lock their magic within, using it at will and allowing it to stretch."

"I do not care what they do. We are the Light," he declares, lifting his voice.

The occupants seated at this half of the table direct their attention toward the brothers.

Zander sets his mug down as Jacques tosses a napkin on the table and rights his chair.

Turning to Larles, Zander scowls. "My Light is far more pleased and pleasant to coexist with."

"You are becoming like them."

"I am enjoying freedoms I did not know I could possess. I negotiated my contract with Callahan, able to have more control over my life, and have allowed my Light the same."

"We hold ourselves to standards they do not."

"Changes must be made for our kinds to come together as one. We keep the best and be rid of the worst."

"What worst?"

Zander sighs. "Brother Mine, with all due respect, pull your head out of your rectum if you possess the flexibility to do so. There are things we can change to blend our kinds without giving up what we are, such as letting your Light stretch. Try it, you might like it." Zander stands. "Excuse me."

As Zander walks away, Larles shakes his head and glares at me. "You've already tainted my brother with your vile ways."

Ashley picks at the fruit on her plate with a click of her tongue. "Larles, don't you already allow your Light free range in your home?"

He goes stiff, widening his eyes at her.

She grins.

"That is my home."

"Yes, and the first time you had Akash and me over for dinner, I was astounded at the way your Light seemed so comfortable flexing."

He presses his lips hard.

"Gosh, so much more bewildered when Akash proceeded to do the same, encouraging me to let my Light free. I thought you were against the old ways? Did I misunderstand?"

He leers. "How is Akash? I haven't heard from him since Izul went out."

I'd bet my life Ashley flinches without ever dropping her wide grin. "He gave his life to protect mine," she replies, her voice turning venomous. "I watched his head fall off his body, in fact. Watched it roll as I screamed his name."

Larles blanches. "Ash, I sincerely did not wish to cause pain of that kind."

She sets her cup down with a tap of porcelain against wood in the silence. "He was my brightest..." She pauses, blinking and going straight-faced before hoisting another smile. "My brightest Light and my future mate. I lost him to the Ancients. I lost my father to them. I lost my mother, and the Ancients are trying to destroy our kind because of discord. The same discord that took your parents, that took Akash's brother, too. Spare me your hypocrisies that will only feed the problem."

Tony puts his hand on the back of Ashley's neck. "Take a breath, babe. In through the nose."

She waves him away, looking to me. "The younger generation has been pushing to end the need to lock up our magic. While my father did not agree with it, both Akash and I found it a blessing, allowing our Light to have freedom within our homes. I will support offering the Light the same freedom Dark magic possesses. It's already been a topic of debate in our society."

"Consider it done."

Jacques snickers. "Poor Wittle Glow Webs. My Dark is laughing at them."

Natalia hasn't joined in. It's not like her to hold her tongue. Something is very wrong with my star.

CHAPTER 26

NATALIA

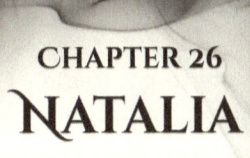

I sit between Cal and Sterling listening to the others bicker as long as I can before I make my escape. Cal promised to kill all the spiders, but he'd promised I'd never be without his name, too.

I still don't have his name.

He's not my mate. He *and* Sterling are my mates. Two.

Sterling had ignored being in contempt of his contract to kill spiders when Mallafic sent half a dozen giant spiders to chase me.

Two mates. Both broke their promises in one way or another.

As I walk through the palace corridors, trying to keep an even, natural pace, my eyes burn.

I miss Ness. Ness would tell me that boys are stupid. It's not their fault. They can't help it.

I tell myself it doesn't really matter. They mated me. They must love me.

It's not helping.

I swallow the pain, clearing my throat as I move toward the kitchen. There will be vodka.

Inside the kitchen, Thomas sits at the island, playing on a

phone with a smile. He glances up as I enter, quick to stand and shove the phone out of sight.

"Tallie, Your Majesty."

"Please don't call me that." I rub the end of my nose. "Vodka?"

He fetches a bottle, offering it to me. "Do you want a glass? I assumed no if you're drinking this early."

I meet his eyes, circular black irises staring back at me. He's a Seraphim, half-human, half-Seraphinus. His father abused women, and one ended up pregnant with him. I know Cal killed his father and raised Thomas, but I don't know how it transpired.

He inherited his Dark from his birth father, a Faeling lineage, able to hear words and know if they are a lie. I could ask him if Cal truly loves me. If Sterling does too. All I have to do is claim those things in verbal words and Thomas could tell me.

"No," I say. "No glass."

"Are you all right?"

"Thank you for your assistance, Thomas. You're as helpful as always." I pat him on the shoulder, turning away.

On the other side of the kitchen door, I hesitate. There are three places I know I can hide. One, my room. Two, at the hysterium tree. Three, the hidden lake beneath the palace.

Cal and Sterling will find me in all of those spaces.

The last time I wandered the palace and got lost in a random room, Mallafic found me. I shudder, inspecting the vodka and trying to weigh the possibility of Mallafic finding me versus Cal and Sterling definitely finding me.

Someone moves in front of me. I look up at Cal and Sterling standing shoulder to shoulder.

Cal taught me to move to avoid being pinned down. I guess I didn't learn well enough.

Sterling takes the bottle.

Cal scoops me up in his arms and starts walking. Neither of them says anything all the way to our rooms.

Cal moves into one of the rooms with a couch, sitting with me in his lap.

Sterling sets the bottle down, falling onto the couch next to us.

Cal sighs. "Talk, Little Star."

I chew on my lower lip, looking to the wall.

"You got quiet. You got vodka. Tell me."

I don't want to have this conversation. All I wanted was a quiet place to myself to stretch and drink.

The left side of my ribs warms with a burning sensation. It's familiar, like when I was in contempt.

I turn to Cal, opening my mouth in fury as I meet his black eyes.

He smirks. "Tell me."

"You..." I try to pull my shirt up, trying to see the contract. It's different, more words than two. I drop the hem of my shirt to glare at him. "Are you serious?"

Sterling laughs. "You're an asshole, baby."

Cal hums, lifting an eyebrow at me. "Talk."

I throw my hands up. "This isn't fair."

"No, but my star is stubborn and forgets her place."

"Where exactly is that? Your cock? His?" I jab a finger at Sterling.

"Both, and you like it."

I scrunch my lips and nose to show my frustration.

Sterling taps the end of my nose. "Answer him. I don't know how long I can watch the contract tear into you, and I don't want that fight."

"I didn't agree to this in the contract."

"It's a worn contract. You know how they work. If you didn't realize I'd use it to my advantage, you're the idiot."

"You're an asshole."

"*Mhm.*" He tips his head back, scratching at the side of his neck. "I did tell you that."

My ribs ignite, and I hiss through my teeth.

Snuggling closer, Sterling rests his chin on Cal's shoulder, frowning at me. "Firefly, talk. It's not complicated."

"You're the last fucking person who gets to criticize me for being in contempt."

He sighs. "I know."

Cal twists his head to ask, "What is she talking about?"

Sterling makes a face, then winces. "We tried to trade one of the codexes that emptied into Vanessa for your release. I had told her to stay in Ilbuio. She didn't want to. The Dark learned what she did. It was a spark to tinder, inflaming them worse. I was mad. I left her alone. Mallafic set giant spiders on her."

Cal growls in the back of his throat.

"Go ahead," Sterling says. He doesn't move, gazing at me with melancholy. "Beat me bloody. Break things. I'll even heal slow for a couple of days instead of Tal healing me."

Inhaling, Cal arches his back, then slumps lower. "What does that have to do with contempt?"

"It was in my contract to kill spiders she saw. I ignored it— her."

Cal glares at Sterling. "I should wring your fucking neck."

"I know. I won't fight back." He draws the backs of his knuckles down my arm. "I never should have done it. I won't ever do it again. Big or small, I'll smash anything with eight legs you want me to."

Dark stretches from Cal, picking up the vodka, unscrewing the cap, and bringing it to me. "Anything else, Little Star?"

He watches me take a drink like a predator sizing up prey with ravenous rage.

"That's why he doesn't get to talk to me about being in contempt." I shrug.

A sharp pain jabs between two ribs, and I jerk. "Ah," I gasp. "What? That was an answer."

He's not amused, waiting.

"What do you want?"

"Say it."

"Say what?"

"I broke a promise."

I lick my lips, looking down the neck of the bottle, then chug.

Dark twists around the bottle and rips it away, vodka splashing down my shirt and across my collarbone.

It slams on the table, and I jump in place at Cal's furious face.

I blink, raising my eyes to the ceiling. "You broke a promise to me."

The burn in my side recedes. "I did," he says, his voice raw. "I took my name." He lifts his forearm. "Now take yours."

My eyes burn, my lower lip trembling. "Cal."

He rolls forward, taking my face between his hands. "I don't need it anymore, Mate. I have this." He taps the side of his neck at my bite mark, silver in his tawny skin.

"But—but you promised."

He wraps his hand around my ribs over the contract. "You have my name. Sterling's too."

I sniffle. That's true.

He offers me his arm again. "Take this piece of your Light back. Your mark is far more important, and I'll wear your name in my skin next to his in contractual bonds. You said words that broke me to pieces, then showed more compassion for Vanessa than for me. I can understand why, but I was fractured by it. I didn't think. I didn't do the right thing. I made a mistake, but you mated me anyway."

I can hear Ness telling me boys are stupid. They can't help it.

I withdraw my Light.

My vision clouds, tears slipping down my face. "I miss Ness. I miss her so much, and she hates me. I love her. I would have done anything for her, and she's gone, and she doesn't even want to be here because she hates me now. I–I love her and trusted her, and you two are breaking your promises and—and..."

Cal yanks me against him, holding me tight. Cool threads tangle around me, constricting to press me tighter into him.

Sterling's hand cups the back of my head. "At least you fucked up too."

"That makes this better?" Cal asks in disbelief.

"For me."

"You fucking ignored her and your contract."

"You fucking left her, asshole."

"I know!" Cal yells. "I fucking know."

I sob, grabbing a fistful of his shirt.

His chest caves inward. "I regret it more than anything else in my life."

"I know. So do I, and I've made a lot of mistakes." Sterling shifts closer, slipping his arm around me, his head pressing to mine. "Mate, we're here. He's never going to walk away again. I'll never leave you. I don't understand what happened with Vanessa, but we aren't going to do the same."

Cal rumbles, "Sterling, you said your contract was to kill spiders."

"Mm."

"The other night you said it was nothing but serve the Dark."

"She took the clause out."

Cal sits up, prying my face from his chest and using his thumbs to wipe away the tears. "You took it back."

I try to take a breath, shaking in his grip.

"You don't trust either of us anymore."

My Light hisses in my ears. *"Hosts can't be trusted. Not my love and friend."*

I close my eyes. "Don't make me answer that because I don't know."

Sterling rests his head back, tipping into Cal's. My mates stare at me with dejection.

Cal caresses over my cheekbone with his thumb to clear away another tear. "You are the most important thing to me in the world. You have been since I pulled you onto the bike at the restaurant. I never hid my desire for you or my enjoyment of you. I went mad trying to send every stupid thing I could think of to Izul for your attention. I loved every moment of having you constantly by my side in Saltina. I walked away to give you freedom if I wasn't your true mate. I'll do anything to see you glow again like you did during Solnoct, even if it's not for me."

I sob, wanting to fall into him. Needing to feel his strength and safety, but unsure.

Sterling tries to smile with one side of his mouth. "I didn't know spiders could be that big."

I laugh through tears at him. "What the fuck?"

He grins. "Firefly, I'm an idiot. Cal's an idiot, too. We're both just idiots. We love you, just, you know. We're idiots who love you."

A warmth washes through me as I laugh, low and weak. Sniffling, I pull my face from Cal's hands, surprised he allows me to.

I wipe at my eyes and nose, swallowing the lump in my throat.

Cal elbows Sterling. "Go get me ligan pagan."

Sterling rolls to his feet and walks away.

I frown at Cal.

He smiles. "Little Star, I love you."

Sterling returns, offering the page to Cal as he sits again.

Cal takes it, extending it to me. "Write the contract to kill spiders."

I take the page. "What?"

Sterling chuckles. "This is illegal as fuck."

Cal leans his head toward Sterling with a faux grin. "When has that stopped any of us before?"

Sterling slides his arm across Cal's shoulders behind his neck. "Fair enough. Write it, Firefly."

I blink at them, lowering my eyes to the page. Glittering words are already written: Kill any spider I see, no matter how big or small.

It's signed with my name.

I close my eyes and try to give my Light a hug. Strands wrap around me, pulling tight.

"Thank you."

"My love and friend have promised to turn on their hosts if they ignore it."

I open my eyes, laughing at the ceiling. I turn the page around, and both Cal and Sterling are quick to sign their names.

I wipe the contract from the page and add it to the other on my left side.

Cal tugs the now blank page from me, dropping it over the back of the couch with one hand, pulling my face to his with the other.

"Mate."

His lips meet mine, parting. His tongue sneaks forward as I open my mouth for him to deepen the kiss.

Sterling slides his hand under my shirt and up my side. Cal mimics the act on the other side, pulling his mouth away long enough to peel my shirt off before claiming my mouth once again.

Can I trust them? They say they're sharing...

I pull back, turning to rest my hand on Sterling's jaw and kiss him.

Cal releases a growl.

I yank back, frazzled nerves threatening to snap in fear that I've done something wrong.

Sterling leans toward me, reclaiming my mouth as he holds the back of my head.

Cal drags his nose up my neck, nipping their mating marks. "Behave."

A string draws taut from my breasts to between my legs. I whimper into Sterling's mouth, his tongue swirling with mine.

Cal opens his mouth, licking across my neck, dancing around the mating marks. Muscles clench, searching for something to tighten on. I'm empty, an ache blossoming in my core.

Any little graze from them will shatter me.

Cal rumbles, Sterling cupping my jaw to angle my head.

Four large hands caress me, two mouths kissing and licking my skin. I'm dizzy, panting for air. "Please."

Spinning, Sterling gets up, standing behind me to cup my breasts and kiss my neck.

Cal pops the button on my pants, sliding his hands around me and beneath the waistband.

Sterling stands, grasping me under the arms and hoisting me backward and up.

I squeak in shock, but the movement drags my pants down. I flounder, kicking to help Cal work them the rest of the way off as Sterling laughs.

He sets me on my feet, pulling me close to run his hands over my body.

I look to Cal, quivering with need and concern.

Smirking, Cal stands, already yanking at his shirt to remove it.

I try to wrap my arms around myself, unsure if I'm allowed to enjoy Sterling's touch, shy under Cal's gaze while Sterling's hands explore me.

Sterling snags my wrists, pulling my arms down and behind me. He nips my ear, holding my wrists together in one of his.

He smacks my ass. "No. You let him see you."

Naked, Cal comes closer, lifting my chin to kiss me. He drops to his knees, dragging his mouth down the center of my body as he lowers. Pressing his hands to my hips, he yanks me closer before drawing his palms up my body as he kisses my stomach.

Sterling opens his mouth against my neck, his teeth grazing along my skin.

Cal slips his hands between my legs, shoving two fingers into me. I moan, leaning back into Sterling as my knees go weak.

He chuckles, molding my breasts, running his fingers under the sensitive underside and teasing my nipples.

I grip Cal's hair as he begins licking between my legs, moving his fingers in and out with harsh strokes.

I teeter on the edge, almost falling in bliss under their touch.

Sterling presses his mouth to my ear, his warm breath sending a shiver chasing goosebumps across my skin. "I want to hear those three little words."

Cal slows down, no longer dragging me closer to the ledge, leaving me stranded.

I whimper.

He thrusts deep, turning his head to kiss my thigh. "Say it."

"Say wh–what?"

"Whatever he wants." He gives me one long lick, crooking his fingers into that delicious spot.

Sterling runs his hands down my sides. "Say it, Firefly. I've fantasized about it. Now I want to hear it."

I swallow. "I don't..."

"Those three words I made you say once." He nips my ear. "Now I want to hear them for real."

Cal thrusts his fingers all the way to his knuckles, sucking my clit before drawing to shallower thrusts and pressing his mouth to my hip. "Say it," he says in his best, snarling alpha tone.

"I need you," I whisper.

Cal snorts through his nose. "That was pathetic."

Sterling laughs. "Downright disappointing."

Cal shoves his fingers deep. "If you want to come, say it."

I gasp, jerking. "I need you."

Sterling hums, biting my shoulder as Cal goes back to licking. "Better."

They bring me to the ledge, dangling me over it but not shoving me off.

"Please," I beg, "Please. I need you. Mate."

Sterling licks the mating marks, and I break apart, mewling and quivering as pleasure snaps through me.

My hips buck, both Cal and Sterling rushing to hold me still as Cal continues suckling and licking, moving his fingers faster, twisting in and out of me.

My knees give, but Sterling wraps his arm around me, Dark tethering me against his torso to keep me upright.

"Oh," I warble, "Cal."

I come again, pleasure racing from my scalp down my spine and through my stomach into my legs to curl my toes.

Cal draws back, grasping my hips and pulling me away from Sterling.

I collapse, mewling and trying to catch my breath.

He doesn't let me, hoisting me against him to thrust his cock into me.

I scream, the sound catching in the back of my throat and the sudden stretch reaching to my core.

Cal lies back, forcing me to straddle him. He looks up, not at me, but over my shoulder to behind me. "Your turn."

"You sure, baby?" Sterling asks in a teasing tone.

I glance at Cal with confusion, still coming down from the high he gave me.

He smirks. "Take your clothes off and get on your knees, Mate." He drags my mouth to his, forcing his tongue into my mouth as he holds my head. The taste of me lingers on his tongue, heavy with arousal.

Sterling's hands slip around my hips, pulling me back. It shoves Cal deeper into me, and I whimper. It's everything I need.

Sterling squeezes my butt, and I grind against Cal.

One of Sterling's hands moves between my cheeks, pressing against my other hole.

I freeze, tensing.

Cal stops me from sitting up.

I gape at him. "No. No. I can't."

Cal clamps a hand over my mouth. "You can."

Sterling leans over me, smiling against my shoulder. "We know you can."

I try to protest.

"Do it," Cal says, his gaze on Sterling.

"You want me to prove our mate is a liar?"

"I want to prove she can handle more than she thinks she can."

Chuckling, Sterling draws his mouth across my skin. His full lips curve against me as he kisses down, along my spine. "Relax, Firefly."

I'm torn between squirming and trying to escape, and accepting this. They've instilled their belief in me, trusting me to handle anything so many times. They don't tell me how to talk. They don't tell me how to act.

They tell me to shut up and take it.

I shiver as Sterling caresses my butt cheeks with both hands.

Cal rocks his hips, creating delicious friction.

Fingers press into me, stretching me.

I gasp, instinctively tightening. It's foreign and strange, a fullness washing through me.

Cal rocks his hips again, grinding me on him.

Sterling withdraws, and I breathe out relief, tingling. As pleasant as it was, it was overwhelming.

Something presses against my hole, too large and fat to be a finger and too smooth to be numerous fingers.

I gasp, widening my eyes at Cal. "No."

He gazes back, lust in his eyes. "Behave."

"I can't."

Sterling snickers, the pressure increasing. "Relax."

I whimper, my hole stretching. I try to lift myself higher, away from the intrusion.

Cal grips the hair at the nape of my neck, growling. "Take him."

I go limp, panting and mewling as my body gives. It stings and pulses as Sterling groans.

He presses deeper, stretching me further. I teeter somewhere between pain and pleasure.

Cal rocks me.

I shiver, closing my eyes and clamping around him—around both of them.

Sterling grips my hips. "I'm trying to be gentle, but that's going to make me lose control."

Cal laughs. "Not really your repertoire."

"Not really." Sterling thrusts.

I whimper at the taut stretch of my body.

Cal forces us over, Sterling beneath me.

Cal thrusts in and out, Dark stroking my body and between my legs.

Sterling groans, rocking his hips. "Come on, Firefly, you can spread your legs further than that for him."

"I can–can't..."

Sterling runs his hand up my throat, his palm resting on the underside of my jaw as he curls his fingers into my mouth.

I gurgle. Dark wraps around my legs, spreading me into a split.

Cal thrusts harder, shifting closer and impaling me deeper.

I arch my back, and Dark tightens around me, yanking my back against Sterling and binding me tightly in place.

I can barely breathe, downright losing all ability when Sterling's fingers begin to rub my clit in circles as Cal thrusts with deep strokes.

Cal brings me to orgasm, then pulls me forward, me on top of him.

Sterling binds my hands behind my back, taking his turn fucking me, and I almost lose consciousness when they hoist me between them, suspending me in their Dark and working together to lift and lower me as they thrust.

I'm stretched to my limits, filled by both of them. I can't take any more, but I don't want it to end.

Sterling runs his hand up my throat, tipping my head back to his shoulder to slip his fingers in my mouth. "Good girl. You're doing so good, Firefly."

They move together, thrusting in and out, and I lose all sense of reality. It all goes black, the only thing I know is the pleasure rippling through me.

All I can do is take it—four hands, dozens of strands of Dark, two mouths, and both cocks of two men worshipping my body.

CHAPTER 27
NATALIA

I drift to consciousness on top of an evenly rising and falling chest. It takes me a moment to realize who it belongs to.

Lifting up with my hands to his shoulders, I gaze down on Cal, his eyes closed and sharp, pretty features relaxed. His black hair is a mess, straight strands sticking at odd angles.

My body does a little shudder, my stomach and nipples tightening. The muscles in my abdomen twinge.

I haven't moved much yet, but it's going to be slow when I do. As incredible as it felt to have two cocks stretching and filling me, it's an abuse of muscles. They burn in displeasure, my lower back aching.

I sit up, hissing at the jab of refusal from tired muscles, and look around for Sterling.

Cal is on his back beneath me on the floor. The couch is empty, the low table askew, and the vodka tipped over.

"Tal," Sterling whispers behind me.

Looking over my shoulder, I find him leaning against the open threshold of the room, arms crossed. His full lips turn up at the corners, his black pants slung low on his hips.

I lick my lips, staring at the cut muscles in his lower torso.

"Is he awake?"

I shake my head, tearing my gaze from Sterling's body to meet his full black eyes.

He jerks away from the wall, stepping to us. He crouches on the balls of his feet. "I didn't want to wake you. You two are so cute together."

I bob my head, collecting my hair and dropping the strands down my back.

He runs his fingers through my silver strands, smiling. "I like it long." He slips his fingers behind my ear and along my jaw, tilting my head to kiss me. "Gives us more to grab."

"Mm."

"You okay?"

"*Mhm.*"

"Good, 'cause I enjoyed the fuck out of myself."

Giggling, I lean forward, pressing my lips to his.

He licks along my tongue and pulls back. "What's the one thing you can't keep if you share it?"

Cal stirs, groaning as he squeezes his eyes closed. "It's going to be a mate if these riddles don't end."

Snickering, Sterling looks to me. "A secret."

"Mm," I hum, smiling at the way he grins like he's proud of himself.

Sighing, Cal sits up and adjusts me in his lap. He rubs his face, then slumps into me to rest his head on my shoulder. "Make it stop."

I wrap my arm around his shoulders.

Sterling leans in, whispering, "Bound and fucked for life, baby."

Cal chuckles. "I made a mistake." He leans back, his eyes crinkled at the corners as he shakes with laughter.

Sterling stands, offering me a hand.

He helps me to my feet. I stumble and hiss, putting a hand to my stomach at the angry pulsing pinging between my abs and lower back.

Sterling steadies me, Cal lurching up and reaching for me.

"I'm just sore."

They relax, snickering together.

I flip them off and head for the bathroom to start the shower. I check my left side, relief washing through me. Cal reverted the contract he holds back to those two words.

I run my finger over them, lifting my eyes to meet his in the mirror as he enters the bathroom behind me.

Moving to my back, he massages my shoulders. "You'll learn to talk without me using it. In my wildest dreams, you tell me without me even having to ask." He dips his head, nipping my ear.

I puff air through my nose as I smile. "Maybe."

"Get clean, Little Star."

Sterling sticks his head in the room. "We have time to do it again before dinner if you make it quick."

I shiver, my body aching and throbbing. There is no way I can handle that.

Cal nudges me toward the shower. "We'll make it quick."

THE CONTRACTORS ARE tense when we enter the dining hall. There are more glowing men and women at dinner than last night, more than I counted this morning at training.

Oscar sits next to Thames, nodding at me as I walk by. "Your Majesty." He rises, motioning at others near him. "These are—"

"Yanri's." I curl my lip at the mangy, mated appearance, each one of them gaunt in the face with an air of sickness.

"Were," Oscar whispers. "They've come for contracts."

I pat him on the shoulder. "I'll take them all."

I sit, Cal pushing my chair in. When he sits next to me, he slips his hand beneath the slit of my dress. His palm grazes along my thigh, coming to a rest.

Ashley fluffs Tony's hair, running her hand down his neck and across his shoulder. She motions to Layla and Flora across from her. "Callahan, please introduce these two to Sterling."

He points at Layla, then Flora, spitting out their names.

"Hardly a proper introduction." Ashley tosses her hair. "I see your manners need improvement."

Cal turns his head toward me, looking over me to Sterling. "Words, words, and more words that mean the same thing."

I smile, ducking my head. Sterling laughs.

The meal is blessedly uneventful, and after the food is cleared away, Cal takes my hand. "Zan, are these the two you mentioned?" He points at Owen and Parker.

"Yes."

"You and them with us in the king's personal hall when you're ready."

Cal stands, drawing me out of the dining hall, Sterling following.

Inside the parlor, Sterling heads for the liquor while Cal pulls me toward a chaise.

He flops down, and I lie next to him with my head on his shoulder.

Sterling sets three glasses on the wide armrest before coming around to the other side, lying to spoon me.

I close my eyes, perfectly comfortable. I don't get long before others arrive, and we get up.

Cal hands me the glass with clear liquor, taking one of the amber-filled for himself and heads to sit at the table.

Ashley sits, propping her chin on a hand, motioning to Flora and Layla. "Allow me to teach you how to perform a proper introduction. This is Flora Dianon and her mate Layla. Dianon is an influential heritage. Flora's sister, Rose, has remained in Izul, not in lack of support, but to assist with the preparations to be made and speak for us."

I incline my head. "Hello."

Tony sets a glass of clear fluid in front of Ashley, offering two more to Flora and Layla. They take the drinks, bow their heads, and then sit with Ashley.

She sips from her tumbler. "Your coronation will take place at Sun's rune." Setting aside the glass, she pulls her phone out, taps on the screen, then sets it down in front of Cal. It's a series of dots connected by a line indicating a time for each dot. "You must be at the palace promptly at Dawn's rune for the beginning of the ceremony."

"Dawn's rune or Sun's," Cal asks.

"You arrive at Dawn's for the proceedings to begin, then at the chime of Sun's rune, you will be crowned."

Cal's lips pull apart in revulsion. "This takes a rune?"

I try to swallow my giggle, earning a sharp glare from Cal.

Flora picks her tumbler up by her fingertips on the rim, swirling the contents. "When you said be prepared for ignorance, I did not realize the extent." She toasts Ashley and drains her glass. "I've been informed to disregard our ways when speaking with you, to forgo bowing and the term majesty. This is not to be accepted while in Izul. At Dawn's rune, we will gather to witness the crowning of our new Light Queen. Only the most prominent and influential of us will be extended an invitation."

Cal rubs his face.

Ashley flicks a hand toward Flora. "We will decide who you

invite, as you have no knowledge basis to make those determinations. It is an exclusive right and will help solidify those families you want in power at your side."

Sterling chuckles and drains his glass. "I need another one." He stands.

Cal rubs his mouth. "Bring the damn bottle."

Flora frowns. "You should be coherent to intake the information we give you."

I shrug. "He's using liquor to alleviate the strain of your information. I assure you he is giving you his full attention."

"Strain? What strain could we possibly be causing our new queen?"

I press my lips into a smile, disguising a grimace. "The Light is exclusionary and ritualistic. When I took the crown of the Dark, *every* Dark who wanted to attend was allowed. I stood in front of them and announced I was their new king. That was the end of it."

Layla shifts, lifting her glass to speak into it. "No wonder you have no control over them."

Sterling sets the bottle down. "She struggles because she glows."

Ashley fiddles with her glass. "These proceedings are about establishing alliances you will need and use."

"Yes." Flora nods, tucking her hands in her lap. "After you are crowned, we host the formal luncheon where you'll greet the remaining families of standing."

"Once the luncheon is concluded, you will return to the throne room for a rune of consideration. At the dinner banquet, there will be further introductions made to some of the lesser standing families, and you're expected to announce those you will place as magistrates."

Cal swallows his three fingers of bourbon, shoves the glass

aside to unscrew the cap of the bottle, and plunks it in front of himself.

Flora raises her eyebrows. "You will have nine magistrates."

Ashley nods, taking a drink. "Of course, these are the normal proceedings. We have additions to consider given the circumstances."

"Yes, we've been discussing those options, as the Hallow heritage will need to be presented and introduced to all."

"My idea was to have them present for your coronation proceedings. We can make intimate introductions along the way and then include their introduction to society in the dinner banquet."

Cal takes a long drink from the bottle, tugging at the collar of his shirt.

Ashley smiles at me. "I've notified Wyona that her services are required once more. She did such a lovely job with you. I hoped you would be amenable to seeing her again and working with her."

I blanch, running my fingers through my hair to toss the strands to one side. "How considerate, Sister Mine."

Cal asks, "Wyona?"

Leaning into him, I tilt my head back on his shoulder and grin faker than Ashley's best attempts. "My etiquette tutor."

He grabs the bottle, upending it for a drink. He wipes the corner of his mouth with his thumb.

Sterling laughs in a short burst. "Better you than me."

"Fuck that. You're coming."

Sterling's eyes widen. "So? I'm not the Queen of Light."

Ashley raps the table with her knuckles. "You all get lessons. Even my sister will get a refresher course to remind her of appropriate behavior."

Flora chortles. "Speaking of appropriate, your attire will be selected for you as well to ensure it meets our standards."

Thames strolls forward, pulling out the chair next to mine. "Did I hear attire being discussed?"

Flora waves at him in a dismissal. "These arrangements are not your business."

Thames frowns, and I put my hand on his shoulder. "I would recommend against being quick to refuse the help. Thames is immaculate in his appearance."

Smirking, Layla says, "Maybe for a—"

"Lay," Flora warns, putting a hand to Layla's shoulder.

Ashley sighs. "Tallie, you are the best option to decide. You know our formal attire and theirs. Are they compatible?"

"Different," I say, glancing at Thames. "Though I'd much prefer Thames's choices."

With a tight smile, Thames lifts his glass. "Thank you, baby. I appreciate that."

"Your preferences are irrelevant. You cannot discard our ways. The rest will see it as a sign that you are not one of us, and it will weaken the unity we are attempting to build."

I sigh, slumping in my chair. "We use these things to show our respect for others," I say, flicking at my glass. "Quoting Wyona, of course. Fuck, I'm going to have to be a Lighter again."

That rewards me with daggers in Ashley's eyes. "You are the Light, a seed of my heritage, and you will honor that as we honor Father's wishes."

Running fingers through my hair, I twist the strands together into a bun. With nothing to secure it, I send my Light weaving through the strands to hold it in place to keep the back of my neck clear, needing to cool off.

Cal picks up the bottle for a drink, then sets it aside. "I've heard you out, and my answer is no."

Flora pulls back, but Ashley extends a hand to her, tilting her head. "No?"

"No. I'll do your ceremonies and dinners, but I will do it my way. I wasn't raised as one of you. I was raised as the Dark. My *name*," he says, stressing the word, "is Barraco. It is not Hallow, and I am not a puppet for you to preen and make dance in any way that you want."

"You were not given your heritage name for fear."

"My lineage name is Barraco."

"You are a Hallow. It is a high honor to—"

"If I could dig that fuck up from the afters to beat him to death with your stupid crown of Light, I would. I didn't ask for this. I didn't want to be a Hallow or your Light Queen. It was his choice, a decision made for me that I had no knowledge of or input on, and I'm stuck doing what that fuck wants. I'm doing it, even after everything he's done to me and mine. Still, I can respect his intentions and understand the logical need for what he's thrust upon me, so I'll take responsibility for the Light, for merging our kinds, fighting for the Light, defending it, even showing respect for it. But I will do it as a Barraco."

Ashley's chin lowers, her eyes falling toward the table as she licks her lips.

I run my hand across Cal's shoulder to the back of his neck, grazing my nails along his skin up into his hair at the back of his skull. "Babe." I toy with the hair at his nape.

"Don't."

"You know I don't listen," I say, forcing a grin with my tongue between my teeth.

He pulls me into his lap, facing him. "That night, when you finally turned up in Hapsford. I heard you, your voice, but when I turned around, I couldn't find you. What they did to you made you unrecognizable."

I lean forward, pressing my nose to his as I hold his gaze. His black eyes sparkle with seriousness. I lower my gaze to his lips. "I'm still me."

"You are the most stubborn individual I have ever met."

271

Giggling, I kiss him. "Think of it this way. It's just a game for the crown, and you'll need weapons, like how to talk to them."

"I can muster my vocabulary for syntax. My father was fond of using obscure words."

"Izul is different. Everything is different, even how they eat. I think you should know what you're going to be doing before you walk into that city."

His shoulders drop. "Fine."

"Excellent," Ashley exclaims. "Wyona will be here tomorrow morning."

Sterling stands. "I'm going to get piss drunk and pretend this isn't happening."

Cal shifts me off his lap. "Go with him, Little Star. I have business to take care of."

Sterling slips his arm around my shoulder, pulling me with him. Cal hasn't ever dismissed me to deal with anything before.

I glance back at Cal, who snags the bottle and walks toward Zander, realizing he dismissed me for my benefit.

Oscar stalks forward, so I turn my attention to him.

CHAPTER 28
VANESSA

1ST NIGHT'S DAY, BLOOMING, 4050, 6TH MILLENNIUM

The world is not what it used to be. There are marvels and mysteries aplenty. So much has changed while some remain, the balance of nature irreversible, but the differences are stark.

I am a stranger here, even in this form; this host is unfamiliar, and yet it called to me. The parallels and similarities are there, a comfort in shared experiences, and sharing this vessel is by that which resembles myself.

I tip my head back, basking in the suns as I float in the pool. This, too, is barely distinguishable from before. The baths formed by the natural rocky shoreline. The water, so full of salt and heat. I've been here before, though a rare occurrence, I seldom recall. I indulged Bellasom for her kindness; the gentle echo of her pulsing life had been my shelter from the cruelty of my lover.

Movement draws me to a conscious state of awareness. It's curiously bizarre to watch Mallafic move, fluid like shadows, blurred at the edges. Day by day, he seems to be solidifying while never changing.

He moves to the edge of my pool, sitting on the rock.

273

Crossing his legs, he sits straight-backed. "I have found another piece."

"Where is it?" I lean forward, the water swirling around me.

Adventures were never something I thought I'd have beyond ink on pages. Excitement, action, and romance were fantasies for me. I pined from my little hole in this world to see so many places, and now I have it all within my grasp.

Mallafic chuckles. "You are eager to leave behind your rest so soon?"

I've seen the Glinting Mirage with the ruins of Di Auratis, the Brishmam Rainforest, the highest peaks of Vallemon, and the craggy dunes of the Arid Planes. I want more. I want to see everything. For far too long I have seen nothing, been nowhere.

"I'm excited."

"I can tell. Ah..." He tips his head back with a faint smile. His short black hair shifts, falling around his horns. "I should be telling you much, so very, very much."

I nod. "It's peculiar that I know so much. All these memories... They feel like mine."

His black eyes cut toward me. "In a way, they are," he says, his tone terse. "For eons I have existed, much of it I lived. This time with you, sharing myself with you, it's something between those two."

He sighs, dropping the ridged posture so his shoulders slump and his back arches. Mallafic stares into the pool, dangling fingers in the water. They blur and elongate to bony, talon-tipped appendages, and he wiggles them to send ripples across the murky surface.

"Still, I long to feel the wetness, for the salt to dry my skin and pull it tight, the warmth of spring and the slosh of water."

"You will."

His expression is soft as he turns his head, the barest smile kissing his lips. "Oh, my sweetest darling, you have no idea."

Cold seeps through my veins despite the blistering heat of the bath. Everything turns bland and muted as I stare at him. There but two more pieces of me missing. I need them.

I curl my fingers on the edge of the rocks, dragging myself closer. Mallafic's ghost echoes and pulls at me, luring me closer and closer. With each piece freed, I become stronger.

I know the secrets. I know the way. Not even my kin share my knowledge for I am the child of gods, discarded by the others. I remember now.

They called me evil, again and again condemning me as imbalanced, but I am balance itself. I will be whole again, and when I am, I will have my revenge.

Mallafic tucks hair behind my ear. "I feel you too."

I cross my arms and rest my chin on them, frowning at him. Restless, the eerie sensation grips me. It's weak, struggling in vain but not diminished. It waits below the surface, sulking.

"When can we go?" I ask, my voice full of ash and malice, still foreign each time I speak.

"Soon. There's something in the webs."

"What says Sirius?"

He blurs and shifts, shadows lashing out to mirror the animosity in his pinched features. "Something I do not approve of. We may need to...delay. I think I'm going to have to remind my plaything of the rules."

CHAPTER 29
CALLAHAN
2ND DAWN'S DAY, BLOOMING, 1050, 6TH MILLENNIUM

Every morning I wake with my mates sends me reeling. I have mates who know my faults and secrets and still choose me. It's confounding as much as felicity.

We've formed our habits. I sleep on the right and Sterling on the left. We quickly learned we needed a third pillow. I can share a mate but touch my pillow in the middle of the night—try to take it away—and I will get my claws out to take it back.

I still haven't determined how to collect the crystals or found an effective weapon. Days are slipping past without much progress, and it's setting my Dark on edge. Tension is coiling, like a snake preparing to strike. Lucius said he'd mourn, and we haven't seen or heard anything from him.

My mates and I reconvene on the grounds at the back of the palace for training, and I leave Natalia with Ashley. Sterling goes his own way, walking through the bodies to pinpoint weak and strong options. I take another direction with Jacques and Zander, ready to kick down anyone standing around.

I tussle with Shawn for a while, then test out Parker and Owen. Owen is a pathetic offering, but Parker is decent.

276

When I've had enough, I head for Ashley while trying to lay eyes on Natalia. My Dark pings and squirms.

Not close by.

As I approach Ashley, she nods. "Callahan, you'll be pleased to know I've been notified Wyona arrived. She's brought much-needed supplies with her as well."

"Where's Talia?"

"Oh." Ashley's face locks in a hard mark of wide-eyed innocence. "I couldn't say."

I narrow my eyes. "How long ago did she wander off?"

"You know, I really don't recall."

I pull my ears back. "Ashley."

Her grin widens. "Perhaps she needed a moment alone?"

"Did she say anything?"

Ashley clicks her tongue. "Now that you mention it, yes. My sister and I spoke."

"What did she say?"

Ashley smiles with pressed lips. "When would you like your proper introduction to Wyona?"

"When I know where Talia is. Anything you would like to inform me of?"

"Not at the moment."

Falsion steps to us. "Cal."

"Where's Talia?"

"Went into the palace not long after you walked away, right after whispering with this one."

I glare at Ashley.

She shrugs. "I was busy putting him in the dirt." She motions at Falsion.

"No," I say, pointing a finger at him. "No."

He shrugs, crossing his arms. "You're asking me to lie to you?"

"Were you distracted? Lazy?"

Falsion scratches at his neck. "No, she's a damn good fighter."

I gape at him, then at Ashley. The woman is starting to scare the piss out of me with her feigned innocence and sharp tongue with strength rivaling mine and skill outmatching mine.

"What, darling?" She tilts her head. "Are you so surprised?"

Falsion snickers. "Cal hasn't put me down once."

"Oh, well..." Ashley inspects her nails. "Pierre trained me himself." She flips her eyes to mine. "Zander too."

Clamping my jaw, I turn away, stalking into the palace to find my mate. My Dark pings and twists. I follow the directions, but soon enough, I don't need the mating bond. I push the window aside, slipping into the garden, and head for the hysterium tree.

I slow my pace, and my Dark settles. She's in a handstand, her legs split. As I approach, she pulls them together, then bends them so her feet are on her head. I do not understand how her body does that, and understand even less how she enjoys it.

I stop, staring down on her. It takes me back to when she signed my contract. She'd been upside down and it had pissed me off that she showed no amount of respect toward me. I'd tried to break her, to make her fall. I'd run out of patience before I succeeded.

My Dark ravels around her.

"Cal?"

"Hello, Mate."

She sighs. "Are you mad?"

"No."

"Can I stay here?"

I want her with me. I *need* her with me. I rub my mouth and jaw, down my neck, deliberating on a response. I know her. She's independent, stubborn, and bad with emotions. "Are you avoiding me?"

"I just need to center."

I bob my head. "You're still my star, right?"

She giggles. "Yeah, babe."

I can accept this. Walking away is a difficult task, but I return to our rooms. Inside the front door, I stop, leaning against the door. Her actions are disconcerting. The worn contracts we share should help, but the only thing I can do is be patient and wait to earn back what I destroyed.

This suite is claustrophobic. Too many small spaces sequestered. It'll be easier to breathe and improve functionality with fewer rooms of increased size, especially because I have two mates.

My Dark shifts and twists around me with appeasement. Pings ricochet in my head.

I narrow one eye at the wall. *"Stop that."*

"I'm searching for what's mine."

"You just did a few fractions ago."

"They might have moved."

"Not that far."

"They might need me. Hosts are stupid and fragile."

I interlock my fingers and bend them backward to pop my knuckles. Rolling my neck and shoulders, I loosen up and prepare. I'm getting too old to strain my muscles without a warmup.

That should come with pride. I've lasted this long on strength and respect. Pride is the last thing on my mind. Everything I had was gifted or stolen. I'm not letting go, grappling with what I want with talons that seem too dull to cling to anything.

I'm tired. I feel old. There are too many scars in me to count, and I'm not done yet.

My Dark hisses, melting into a puddle of excitement. Long

strands streak toward the door, inky black tendrils racing to meet them.

Sterling's laugh enters the room before him, and he waves at the knots tangled in our magics. "The fuck is this?"

"Mates," I think as he tries to detangle us.

Sterling waves his hand, glaring at the mess of shadows tied between us. "Fine. Fuck yourselves." He steps toward me, thumbing at our Dark. "They seem happy."

I try to smile, one side of my mouth lifting. "I can't breathe in here."

He slides his hand under my upper arm, holding tight to pull me toward the doorway.

I cock my jaw. "Where are we going?"

"You said you can't breathe." He shrugs, yanking me into the hallway. "Do you know what Tal would do to me if I didn't save you?"

Shaking my head, I dig my heels in. "Small spaces."

He stops backpedaling and glances around. "Let's tear out a couple of walls."

I tug free of his grip and turn to walk back into the same room. The walls seem to shift inward, the enclosure shrinking.

I ignore it, pressing my hands to the stone of one wall.

Sterling joins me, both hands splayed against the stone. "On three?"

Leaning into it, I say, "One, two..."

Tendrils wrap around me and yank me sideways into Sterling. We collide, his elbow slamming into my jaw, rocking me off-kilter.

I pitch sideways, Sterling snarling as he falls with me.

We hit the stone, limbs flailing.

A phantom laugh echoes in my ears from my Dark.

"What the fuck was that?"

"Funny."

Sterling squirms, getting his hands on either side of my head and pushing up, only to slam back down onto me.

He growls in the back of his throat, baring his teeth at me. "This is your fault."

"No, it's not."

"It was entirely your Dark's idea."

Internally, I ask for clarification, trying to push him off me.

"You said in three."

Sterling presses tighter into me.

I narrow my eyes. "Watch your knee."

"Get control of your Dark."

"I didn't tell it to do this, and you already clocked me in the face."

"I was flailing."

"I noticed. My jaw hurts."

He drops his dead weight on top of me with a groan. "Fine, you annoying shadow piss. Now what?"

My Dark hums in my head. I glare at the ceiling. "It's happy."

"Fantastic. What are we supposed to be doing here?"

I meet his eyes. "Knocking out walls."

Snickering, he drops his face, his chin over my shoulder. "What the fuck is happening?"

"We're lying on the floor."

"Will you quit giving me less-than-useful answers?"

I shrug, resting my head back. His warm breath against the exposed skin of my neck tickles my senses, sending pulses of sensation down my spine.

Contentment washes through me. It's not all from my Dark.

Sterling sighs. "I never worry about dying when you're close."

"We were contestants. One of us was supposed to kill the other."

He lifts his head to meet my gaze. "I was hoping you'd be a gentleman and die."

I chuckle, shaking beneath him. "No."

"Figured that, but I was going to at least make you work for it."

"If you ever make me work for it, you'll wind up begging for it instead."

He laughs.

Natalia would be proud of me for that one. Elation packs my chest, and I laugh with Sterling, free and easy. Remorse washes through me. I had wanted to rip him to pieces and piss on his remains.

Sterling shoves up, grunting. My Dark pouts, its tendrils coiled around Sterling, stretching. It allows him to move away, standing to offer me a hand.

I stare at it. How many times had I offered my hand to another, reaching out to catch them and guide them? Has anyone ever reached for me?

Smacking my hand into his, I let him haul me upright.

He claps me on the shoulder and faces the wall, rubbing his hands together. "All right." He shifts his torso, moving and stretching.

He's getting too old, too.

Smirking, I step to his side, lifting my eyebrow at my Dark and his weaving around us and tying us together in a lazy, loose knot.

"Don't do it again."

Sterling turns his head. "Or what?"

"What?"

"My Dark told me to ask or what?"

"Are you talking through Sterling?"

Sterling faces me, leaning his shoulder on the wall. "Yes. He's my bitch." ... "Wait, what?"

I snicker. *"Quit antagonizing our mate."*

Sterling glares at me. "What are you going to do about it, tear me out and die?"

"It's talking to you?"

My Dark laughs. *"We talk, not with words. Some echoes are painful or too weird, so we don't talk to them. I like this one. It's deep."*

Sterling laughs. "That explains mating more. They have to have a magic your magic is compatible with."

His features flicker, his Dark carrying on a conversation, or mine is with him directly. That's horrifying. I wasn't aware that was possible.

My Dark laughs. *"Stupid hosts."*

Sterling tips his head back, giving me a better view of the scar on his neck. My fingers brush over it. I blink, coming back to consciousness, unsure when I reached for him.

He jerks, lowering his chin. His eyes bore into mine. The quiet ire bursts into a dazzling white smile, and his rich laughter booms around the room.

I know they say I'm pretty, but pretty doesn't define Sterling. He's beautiful.

His eyes are crinkled at the corners as he tells me, "No, it's not that. That spot makes me squirm."

I twist my head, confused.

He points to his ear. "Your Dark. You'll let us touch you everywhere but there?"

I chuckle. "Your father?"

"The day he died, fractions after he quit twitching and moaning." He kicks at the floor. "You're bringing them here."

"We need an army."

"I never saw him again after that day."

"You think he'll show?"

Sterling shrugs. "I'll know if I see him."

"We can't kill him."

"This is one time I'll fight you on 'we.' I won't need your help."

"You can't kill him. If it were that simple, then I would, but you and I can't touch him for the same reason, so it's we." I give him a shove. "Push."

"I don't take orders. Go find Jacques if you want to command someone."

I press against the wall, one leg back for force. "You're already here unless you want to go find Wyona?"

He mirrors my pose. "You know this is going to make a mess."

"So? Push." I flex and strain, pushing forward. Sterling grunts. Rocks grind, the floor slipping beneath my feet.

I adjust my feet and push harder.

Solid weight gives, rocks scraping as the force pressing back lessens. As it goes, I stumble forward.

My vision goes hazy, grayish white, the world filling with dust, deep cracks of stone pile and break.

Sterling starts coughing and spluttering, waving his hand in front of his face.

I duck my chin, lifting my shirt over my mouth. It's already better.

"Don't birds usually take dust baths?"

Sterling steps back, looking up again. "Move. That might collapse."

"It probably won't," I say, but step back.

"Probably?"

"It's different stone than that wall." I point to my side. "That stone runs through only outer walls like all these were added later."

"Oh."

"You didn't think about that before you just pushed?"

284

"You told me to push." He flings his arm out toward the crumbled wall.

"You brought up the mess, but not that?"

"I hate dust. It covers my...things."

"That's what dust does," I say, then realize why he hesitated. "You're shiny things?"

"Well, yeah, and then they aren't so shiny."

"I'll clean your shiny things."

He steps closer, running his hand across my head, his fingers through my hair. "Such a good boy."

I glare at him.

He laughs. "We'll get you a treat later."

I shove him but laugh all the same. "We'll dump this shit out the bedroom, off the balcony."

Sterling and I work to pick up the stone, tossing it off the balcony to the yard below. It's quick work, including the destroyed furniture from the other room as well. I'll get new, replacing everything to suit having two mates.

I'll send vassals to clean up the mess now that it's outside my room.

"How many vassals do we have?"

We. It rolls off my tongue with such ease.

"Not enough. Every one of them is stretched in duties. Not a lot of options when they have to sign with a Glow Fuck."

My Dark whips at him for the insulting slur on our mate.

He dodges and chuckles. "We fuck her, and she glows, that's a glowing fuck."

"Fair but insulting."

"She would laugh."

"Probably." I knock my fist on his shoulder as I move to the other end of the room. "This should be another wall we can knock over and remove."

"Should be?" He joins me, scratching at his temple with a screwed-up face.

"What's the worst that can happen if it's not?"

"For someone who doesn't like small spaces you're tempting the fates to bury you in rubble."

"Shut up and push."

THE AIR IS thick with dust, and I'm covered in grime and sweat, but the suite is far more spacious. While we left a few walls, they act more as small dividers rather than enclosing spaces. I can breathe again.

I shower and get fresh clothes before exiting my chambers with Sterling to find our mate. She's been absent all day and my Dark is shifting and cranky at the lack of her presence.

"Find her," I tell my Dark.

It pings and twists, hissing directions to me with urgency. She's still at the tree, but now she's not alone. Tony lifts his chin at me, and Oscar bows his head.

I incline my head, moving my gaze to Hiro and Thames then eyeing the bottles of liquor. "Having fun?"

Oscar lifts a bottle. "Want a drink?"

Sterling claps me on the back, lowering to the ground next to our mate. He wraps an arm around her waist and hauls her into his lap. She giggles, squirming in his lap then beams at me.

I lift an eyebrow.

She reaches for me. Her Light winds around her and stretches into the air, waving toward me. I twist one around my finger, stepping closer.

Dark streaks from Sterling. I don't even have time to react. He drags me to the ground and across the paving stones into him and Natalia.

Dazed, I watch her ball a fist and whack at Sterling's shoulder. "Bad Mate!"

I laugh, sitting and pressing my shoulder to Sterling's. "I'm fine."

"Be nice to each other." She pouts.

Sterling flashes me a grin. "That was nice. I brought him closer to us."

I cup the back of Natalia's head and press my mouth to her temple. "He's not wrong." I face the others, "Hiro, Thames, Oscar...Tony."

He toasts me with a glass. "I still don't like you either."

I focus on Natalia. "Did you find your center?"

She nods. "Yeah. We're drinking now."

"We have—"

Sterling groans, loud and long and overly acted out. "Here comes the lecture about too much to do to have some fun."

I lick along my front teeth. "There are—"

"Ancients trying to destroy us. Yes, yes." He cuddles Natalia closer.

"And—"

"Unifying crowns and establishing ourselves as rulers. Well, you and Tal, anyway."

I cut my eyes at him. "If you know this, then why am I having to say it?"

Natalia lifts a hand. "Oh! I know!"

Sterling chuckles. "Because you're a pain in the ass that doesn't know how to have any fun?"

"That's not how I was going to say it."

I look to Hiro, straining my eyes.

He shrugs, pushing his fingers through his thick, glossy black hair. "What the fuck is the point in fighting if we don't enjoy what we're fighting for?"

My Dark is shocked into stillness, and my mind goes blank. I look to Sterling and Natalia, my two loves. Right here, right now, they're safe. "Fuck it. Where's the bourbon?"

CHAPTER 30

CALLAHAN

I keep Natalia in my arms pressed close as we walk back to our rooms. She has turned to dead weight, likely asleep by the time we round the corner into the hallway leading to our suite.

I'd sent Tony for a second round of bottles, and he turned up with my kin and some Lighters. I had assumed there would be a few drinks, and we'd get back to work. With the Mandolux and Avengers things had gotten out of hand. My mates had been ebullient, and I couldn't bear to steal their joy.

I freeze. Sterling stops next to me, cursing under his breath.

Ashley stands in front of our door speaking with a woman, both wrapped in threads of gold. I can only assume it's Wyona.

"Do you want to try to run?"

"More than you know." I take one step backward.

Both women snap their heads in our direction.

Ashley tosses her hair. "Callahan, this is a most foul disrespect of our time." She walks forward, the other following at her heels.

I jostle Natalia. "Wake up, Little Star."

"Mm, o'tay."

I slide her down my torso to her feet, spinning her to face her sister. She bolts upright. "Ash?"

Ashley stops before us, frowning. "Where have you been?"

Natalia and I point to Sterling.

The other woman claps her hands. "Young Lady, we do not point. We motion or gesture."

"Sorry." Natalia clears her throat, yanking her arm to her side.

I put my hands on her hips. "Don't apologize."

"Sorry. Oh, sorry. Uh, you know what? I'm too drunk for this."

Closing and opening her eyes, Ashley lifts an open palm to her side at the other woman. "Wyona, you remember my sister, Tallie?"

"Yes, of course. She was a challenge and my most improved client." Wyona's lips pucker. "When you informed me that I'd be seeing her again, I had higher hopes."

"Wyona, this is Callahan, the Hallow and our future Light Queen, and Sterling Wellsly."

Wyona puts one arm across her stomach, the other at her back, and bends at the waist into a deep bow. "Your Majesty, the pleasure of your acquaintance is hard to put into exact words."

"Try harder, or do you lack a lexicon?"

She jerks back, her eyes wide.

Ashley clicks her tongue. "We've collected the others in the king's hall. They are all waiting on you."

I check my watch. "I don't have time for this right now. Dinner is in less than half a rune."

"I took the liberty of locating the lost Hallow earlier today. My deepest condolences that I should have to inform you that Xavier Mallow is in the afters." She bows her head. "His contractor, Amara, said he went to feed and never returned."

I unhinge my jaw and wiggle it side-to-side. As irritating as being balanced and not feeding on my star is, I can't deny it's as much a relief.

Sterling leans into me. "It's not your fault."

He's dangerous, too close to my heart. If I'm not careful, I'll rely on him. I shake my head. "What are we doing?"

"You'll start by learning dining etiquette, and you will eat in the king's hall."

"I need to eat with the contractors."

"As Tallie is the Dark King, I believe her presence is mandatory and she can make excuses for you."

I grind my teeth.

Wyona bows again, first to me, then to Ashley. "Please find suitable attire and make yourself presentable. I will be waiting in the king's hall."

WITH A CHANGE OF CLOTHES, I head for the king's hall at the opposite end of my chambers. When I step inside, I get the sense that I stepped into the maze. My heart beats into my ribs, and I reach out, grabbing a handful of Sterling's sleeve.

There is a low, golden wood table in the center of the room with white, silky cushions on the floor around it. The rest of the furniture has been shoved to one side, where my kin are collected with Jacques and Tony.

Standing nearby are Palak, Wyham, Wyona, and Zander.

Palak nudges Zander, nodding in my direction. He walks forward, stopping before me. With an arm across his stomach and one at his back, he bows. "Your Majesty, welcome and be welcomed."

Sterling tries to break free of my grip. "I'm not doing this."

291

I grind my teeth. "If I'm doing this, you're doing this. Bound and fucked for life, remember?"

"I didn't agree to this."

"Stay." I jerk on him, cutting my gaze in his direction.

"Damnit." He almost laughs.

Zander lifts an eyebrow, clearing his throat as he plasters a polite smile on his face. "The appropriate response is I or we are welcomed and welcoming, depending on if you are speaking for yourself or your group. In your case, the response will always come from the lower-ranked individual." He lifts an open palm in Sterling's direction.

"I'm his equal."

"Not even his kin are equal in stature, and as you are not of the Light, you are not entitled to rank."

I bare my teeth.

Zander lifts a hand, lowering his gaze and chin for a moment. "As we work to unify our kind, that is going to require change. Rank can be offered to those without the Light after careful consideration."

"Equal rank," I say, shoving the words through my clenched teeth.

"As you are the Queen of Light, you possess no equal." He pivots on his heels, turning to the side with his hand up, indicating the others. "If you please."

I drag Sterling toward those waiting.

Jacques's face balloons as he tries to hold in laughter, outright shaking as I come to a stop before them.

I focus on the simplest of things. "Tony, why are you here?"

He scratches behind his ear. "The same as you. Ash says I need etiquette lessons before I arrive in Izul." He shrugs. "Don't know why."

"Because you stuck your cock in—"

Two sharp claps cut off my words. I turn to frown at Wyona's disapproving scowl and decide it's not worth finishing the statement for the sake of speeding things along.

Palak hides a grin behind his hand, stepping forward. "*Ahem.*" He shakes as he bows. "Your Majesty."

"I thought I told all of you to knock that shit off."

Another clap.

Zander says, "Palak, Wyham, and I have all volunteered to assist in your education."

"More like torture." I meet Jacques's eyes. "You must be enjoying yourself."

He snickers. "It's like the maze. I'm amused and uncomfortable all at once."

With a shake of his head, Palak sighs. "It may be uncomfortable for you, but this is not torture." Palak inclines his head. "Wells, if you'll trade places with me, we'll start at the beginning."

I smirk. "If I let go, he's leaving."

Wyham moves next to Palak, bows, and says, "Your Majesty, I assure you I will retain his presence."

Sterling barks in humor. "I put you in the dirt without trying. You're not capable of that."

"Would you care to wager your cooperation for the meal against that, Wells?" Wyham lifts an eyebrow, not backing down.

Twisting in my grip, Sterling says, "Zander, I'll make you a deal. You let me out of here and I'll help you through the maze that you're so fascinated by."

Peeling into laughter, Jacques doubles over, hands on his knees. "I made that same offer."

Zander shakes his head. "You're all like children who don't want to behave. This is far more civilized and less painful."

Sterling jerks in my grip. "Says who?"

I point at Wyham. "Do I get that same offer?"

Two sharp claps, and Wyona says, "Pointing is rude. Please use open-palm gestures. Palak, please, if you'll escort our Light Queen to the door, we can begin."

I release my grip, lowering my hand, and flexing it open and closed to stretch the strain from my fingers. "Stay," I tell Sterling. "Talia's right. We need to know what we're walking into."

He curls his lip. "Fair enough."

I walk to the door, turning my back to it and leaning my shoulders against the solid wood. Palak stands next to me, straight-backed with his chin up.

Wyona approaches me, sneering. "Up, up, up," she motions with two fingers. "You must stand tall with a straight back."

She uses a short wooden stick to lift my chin.

I jerk my head to the side and glare.

She puts her hand under her chin. "Lift the head, keep it high. It's a sign of respect for yourself."

I eye the piece of wood with a cocked jaw. "I don't give respect. It's earned."

She lowers her hands, the piece of wood held between them, as she looks at me, maybe looking for the first time instead of averting her gaze from a vile creature. She blinks. "Do you think you deserve respect?"

There has never been a question I was so afraid to answer.

I have earned respect, been given respect, and hold the respect of others, but do I deserve it?

Silence permeates the room as I swallow hard, curling my fingers into fists.

Jacques laughs. "Yes. The answer is yes, he's earned respect."

Wyona lifts her eyebrows. "Is that true, Your Majesty?"

Sterling snarls, "Quit asking him that. It's an insult."

"Then it should be an easy answer to give."

I can't answer. The list of my mistakes ticks away in my head, one after the other. I don't know the answer.

I stole my father's life, building mine on his bones and the secret that I sent him to the afters. Would I be anything without his life?

I've lied. I failed to protect the lives of those who did respect me, who trusted me.

Falsion walks forward. "Cal." He puts a hand on my shoulder. "Outside."

I shrug him off. "Can we get this over with?"

"No." Falsion shoves me. "Go, or I do this here."

"Do what?" I snap, "I'm—"

"Your father was an ass. A cold, cruel, fucking bastard."

Wyona claps. "Language."

I clamp my jaw. "Fal," I warn him. "Stop. It was a stupid question."

"The Dark doesn't lie."

I squeeze my fists harder, my forearms starting to shake. "No."

"That's why you aren't answerin'. You still look at him with stars in your eyes. You keep a list of mistakes just waiting to die and give it to him."

I swing my fist into the side of his jaw. That had been a drunken confession he was never to repeat.

Clap. "We do not attack others, Your Majesty."

Falsion reels, snarling, and slams me into the door, his forearm to my throat.

Palak moves to interfere, and Falsion snaps his teeth. "Stay out of it, Boy, or I put you on the floor, and you won't get up." He shoves his arm into me in a nudge. "You're twice the fucking man—"

Clap. "Language."

"—he was, and you've earned my respect. He never did. Bella never let him know she was there."

I freeze, my jaw slack as I stare at him. My father loved the

Ancients. He would have been thrilled. I doubt he would have ever come home again if he had met her.

Falsion shoves away from me. "I wasn't ever coming off the mountains for him." He flings a hand behind him. "Shawn, Tarlwin, Galain, and Luca weren't going to come, not for contracts with the crown, not to help him with anything."

Pulling my eyebrows together, I look to the floor. "He said you'd follow him."

"We never told him that. Matteo thought highly of himself, the arrogant fucking prick—"

Clap. Clap. "Language."

"—that he was, told us that. We laughed at him."

I hold Falsion's gaze, confused, adrift from reality. "He said..."

Falsion steps closer, putting a hand on my shoulder. "That fuck, ah—" He points at Wyona halfway to a clap. "I'm talking to my nephew. Quit that."

She wrings the wood in her hands, pursing her lips.

He looks to me again. "I don't care what the fuck thought. He was a shit father to you, too hard on you, asking too much from a boy, then impossible demands on a man. I couldn't understand the way you idolized him till we got here. I hear the way people talk about him like he was some kind of god. They didn't know him. Throw the list away. Forget it." He claps me on the arm. "Now stand up straight with pride. I'm hungry."

I straighten my spine and lift my chin, glowering straight ahead at nothing.

Zander clears his throat. "Your Majesty..." he says, pausing, "welcome and be welcomed."

That solidifies one of the most humiliating experiences I've had as a man. Zander, of all people, witnessed everything.

Palak steps to my side again. "We are welcomed and welcoming."

Zander nods. "Your Majesty, you'll sit at the head of the table."

Wyona waves her stick. "Move, move, one end of the table, please."

I stalk forward.

"When you sit..."

I drop onto a cushion, glaring down the length of the table with the rest to my back.

"Well, we will certainly work on that. Now, everyone else sits based upon rank."

Wyona situates everyone at the table one at a time, my kin based upon age down the right side, directing them how to politely and with dignity sit on the floor.

Falsion, Galain, Shawn, Luca, Maria, then Fallon. I doubt the boy has any idea what is transpiring. He's the one soul who doesn't understand what just happened, still bouncing and grinning.

"Now," Wyona says, "once the higher-ranked have taken their seats, then the lower-ranked. As the Hallows have all sat down, so might the rest of us. Normally, you'd wait at your location, but we are, after all, learning. Zander, you are being an absolute pillar of the Light by volunteering, but please take your place as a Fairly."

He sits at my left hand, folding to the floor with grace.

"The three of you, please sit highest to lowest next to Mr. Fairly."

Jacques, Sterling, and Tony shuffle to the table. Jacques shoves Sterling into the spot on Zander's other side.

"Don't really understand this rank shit—"

Clap. "Language."

"—but you're a union contract, I'm worn. Think that puts you above me."

Sterling curls his lip. "I hate this."

"Friend." Jacques claps Tony on the back. "I'm thinking you are after me since your contract is with Tal."

Wyona steps to them, motioning to Sterling. "Up, please. Tony is attached to a Bordeaux, placing him next in rank to a Fairly. If the actual Bordeaux was present, they would sit before a Fairly and their attachment with them."

Sterling doesn't stand to move one cushion over, rolling on the floor instead. "I went from being a Dark Queen to being the lowest rank possible by walking into this room, isn't that fucking something."

Wyona smacks her stick into the palm of her hand. "Please, please begin to mind your tongues. I beg of you. This abuse will not stand."

Jacques sits at the end. "I'm the lowest ranked?" He points to his face. "Seems like I wasted those years surviving the games."

Tony thumbs at Zander. "If Ash were here, I'd sit ahead of him. I'm not sure this system checks."

"Gloat harder, Human."

He laughs. "Not human. Fatum host."

Wyona drops her stick, mouth open. "You–you are host to a fatum?"

Tony glances over his shoulder at her. "Yeah, Lady."

Wyona looks ready to cry. "That changes everything. Everyone must move, except you, Your Majesty. Up, up, everyone."

"No," I say. "Just finish this."

Zander's lips twitch. "Please, Wyona, continue as we are. I think our friends are frazzled enough."

She sighs. "Sir, I do apologize. I was not aware. I meant no disrespect to you or the fates."

Tony looks at her like she's grown a second head. "Ma'am, take a deep breath, and calm the fuck down. Soris does not give a shit where we sit."

"Of... Of course, whatever the fates want." She bows to him without a remark on his word choice.

Jacques chokes, covering his mouth.

Sterling turns to me, staring across Tony and Zander. "I've had better nights during the games...when I was bleeding."

It breaks the grip of torment on my chest. I'm right back in the arena, soaked in the rain after Basileus beat us into submission for our antics. He deserves another point. I laugh silently, shaking my head.

Zander turns his head toward Sterling. "I assure you, Wells, this is going to be far more pleasant than anything that requires bleeding."

Palak brings a tray over, setting a glass down in front of me, then the rest in order that they sat down. Wyham follows, filling the glasses with a fizzy, green liquid.

Sterling picks up his glass, and Wyona smacks him on the shoulder with her stick. He jumps, jerking and his fist closing, fingers turning black and crackling as they shift.

The glass shatters in his hand, and he turns his head in slow motion, ripe with rage. "Glow F— We are in Ilbuio."

"This is practice. You must act as if this were Izul to ingrain the proper behavior."

"You don't fucking—"

She points the stick at him. "Language."

"—attack someone from behind in this palace unless you want to get bloody." He shakes his hand out. "The fuck were you thinking? I damn near responded."

Palak's eyes are huge in his face as he brings another glass. "Try not to break this one, Wells." He offers a napkin in his other hand.

I rub my face. "Wyona, Gathering Shadows takes place in this palace, and three at this table have lived through it for centuries, developing reflexes that might get you killed if you do that again."

Sterling's Dark piles the broken pieces of glass on the table as he opens and closes his hand, the skin turning brown, the fingers shortening.

Wyham fills the new glass, lingering as he leans over Sterling's shoulder. "You wait until the Light Queen has the first drink."

I pick up my glass to avoid further incidents. Its scent is syrupy and sweet. I'd rather not, but I take a drink. The flavor is smooth, almost tart, as opposed to the smell. I take a longer drink.

Zander turns to me. "How do you like Rizvor?"

I stop, meeting his eyes, then look to the glass.

"Rizvor," Sterling repeats, snagging the new glass and taking a drink.

Tony asks, "The fuck is Rizvor?"

Zander smiles. "Another Light delicacy. Something we hold exclusively for our kind. It's savored in times of celebration, most often, but any occasion will do."

I take another drink.

"Such as our new Light Queen embracing the Light."

I inhale the bubbly liquor, choking and turning my head into a bent arm as I spew spit, and my lungs seize and burn as I fight for air.

Zander watches me with raised eyebrows pulled together above his straight nose. "What did you think you were doing, Your Majesty?"

I set the glass down, pressing my hands to the lip of the table and glaring at him.

He smirks, facing straight ahead. "Have you tried yours yet, Falsion?"

"You're staring right at me. You should know I haven't."

Palak laughs, kneeling between Falsion and me. "This is fantastic. I'm so glad I volunteered."

Wyona double-raps him on the shoulder with her stick. "Young Man, you are playing a part. I know your rank and station allow for freedom to speak; however, please try to maintain your role for the evening as one who can teach the others of proper customs."

I've had enough. I brace my hands, ready to stand, hesitating at the knock on the door.

Wyona snaps the stick to her palm and goes to answer. "Oh," she exclaims, stepping back, "Miss Bordeaux, welcome and be welcomed." Half in a bow, she manages to open the door and direct the wood toward the table.

Natalia steps in, smiling. "I am welcomed and welcoming. Thank you, Wyona."

I'm tempted to slit my throat. I'd rather face all twelve days of Gathering Shadows than have Natalia here to witness this disaster.

She steps to the table with a straight back, bowing her head, then lowers to the floor between Zander and me, slipping her arm beneath mine to rest her hand on my forearm. "Cal."

I can't manage a single word in response.

CHAPTER 31

NATALIA

Cal stares at me with a burning fury in his eyes. The muscles in his arm jump as I rest my hand on his wrist. "Cal."

He glares, ready to burst into flames.

"Babe," I whisper, leaning my shoulder into his. "Have you eaten yet?"

"No."

Wyona steps to his back, frowning at me. "Perhaps you can assist us from your proper seat?"

Cal growls.

"You'll find I already am. Not only am I a Bordeaux, outranking a Fairly, but I am Cal's mate. We have a contract of union, meaning I'll be his Light King. My place," I say, putting my hand on the table and holding her gaze, "is at his side."

Wyona presses her lips, ducking her head, but the corners of her mouth turn up.

"You taught me well, Wyona."

"Yes, well..." Her cheeks turn pink.

"Why is Sterling not sitting here?" I raise my eyebrows.

She cocks her head.

"Sterling Wellsly," I say, motioning to him with an open palm. "Our mate, also in our union contract. He should have been given this seat or placed ahead of Zander."

"I was not aware."

Jacques scoffs. "I said he was."

Wyona glances at him, seeming startled and worrying the wood piece in her hand.

I believe Jacques. I also believe she chose to ignore the fact in favor of putting the Dark in the lowest-ranked seats.

"In the future, please be more mindful of others. We don't want to risk upsetting others with improper displays of disrespect."

Wyona blanches. "Yes, of course, Miss Bordeaux." She bows. "Dinner is to be served next. Will you be eating?"

"No, thank you. I ate with the contractors."

Cal tenses. "Talia, they—"

"Are settled and Hiro is to handle anything else for the rest of the evening with Oscar's assistance."

He swallows, the knot in his throat bobbing.

I squeeze his wrist. "Palak?" I lean forward. "Are you serving?"

"I am, Ma'am."

"Feel free to begin."

He bows his head and starts arranging food on Cal's plate. I meet his eyes. "This hasn't been going well, has it?"

He curls his lip.

I try to swallow my humor. I suspected it wasn't. I'd eaten in a hurry, interrupting the contractors in their meal to determine if they'd found any new information on the hysterium tree or Ancients. When they hadn't, I left Hiro in charge and jogged out of the dining hall all the way here.

Palak begins arranging Falsion's plate, so I give Cal another squeeze. "The lowest-ranked individual is to serve the table in informal settings. In larger settings, or formal, you'll often find there is someone else tasked with serving the meal for the whole table."

He grunts.

"You'll wait until everyone has been served food, then you can eat. You never have to wait, as you'll hold the highest rank at every table. Everyone lower ranked waits until you've begun eating. If you're ever in a punishing mood, you can make whoever you are eating with wait as long as you'd like."

Zander clears his throat. "That is a possibility I strongly recommend against. Where did you ever learn that?"

I shrug. "He can do whatever he wants as the Queen of Light."

"How was dinner?"

"Simple. A plate was put in front of me. I ate."

Palak laughs further down the table, serving Maria.

Tony rests his elbows on the table. "Damn good thing I'm not operating on a Magia stomach anymore."

Wyona points a piece of wood in her hand at Tony. "Elbows off the table."

He sits straighter, moving his hands into his lap. Mocking a grimace at me, he points to the glass. "Rizvor? Have you had this stuff?"

"Yes. While I was in Izul, I was fortunate enough to enjoy it several times. However, I had the grave misfortune of operating on a Magia stomach while in Izul as well. It was a struggle."

Cal's wrist flexes beneath my hand. I look down to find him clenching his fist.

My Light slips from beneath my skin, raveling around his arm. Strands of his Dark mix with it.

I smile at him. "If I say fuck, will you relax?"

Wyona points her stick at me. "Language."

"Wyona, darling, you are a marvelous teacher, and I am fully capable of adhering to the ways of the Light, I just don't fucking care to."

She drops her face in her hand.

Cal seems to take a full breath for the first time since I sat at his side.

Zander shakes his head. "You never cease to amaze me, Tallie."

Cal squeezes his fist again.

When Palak finishes arranging Jacque's plate, I look to Cal. "Eat something, babe."

He moves, stiff as he starts to eat.

Wyham offers me a glass of Rizvor. "I know you didn't ask, but it's been a while."

"Thank you." I take the glass, sipping before setting it aside. The last hangover I had was enough to cure my belief that alcohol is a solution. I'm barely sobered up as it is from my bottle of vodka.

I'm still radiating with fury over what Mallafic did to me. I barely eat, and alcohol works significantly faster and harder on my system.

Cal never moves his left hand, figuring out how to pick up everything with one hand, even using his Dark a few times to assist him rather than break contact with me.

I take another sip of Rizvor in the tense quiet. "Tony, did Ash force you into this?"

"Sure did." He chews, speaking through his food. "I'm going to Izul."

Wyona smacks her stick into her palm. "We do not speak with food in our mouths."

Tony mocks her silently with a distorted face.

I hide my smile behind my hand, struggling to keep from laughing. I get a hold of myself, saying, "I see. Do you want to go to Izul?"

"Fuck no, but she's guilting me into it, talking about being sad and lonely with both Akash and Pierre in the afters."

"You are a sucker."

"I know." He bobs his head. "She and I both know it, but I'm a gentleman."

One strand of shadows stretches from Sterling, across Tony's plate, then Zander's to twist around my hand and Cal's arm. My Light vibrates with appeasement.

Zander pokes at it. "Shadow Web, you are in my food."

Shrugging, Sterling keeps eating. "It doesn't care about you."

Tony laughs. "That's what you get for being stupid. Should have put the mates together."

Zander scowls. "What do you know about mates?"

He shrugs. "Not much, but separating them seems like an obvious problem. Their magic crawls all over each other constantly."

Wyona shakes her head, on the verge of tears. "Please contain your magic. It is illegal—"

"No," Cal says, lifting his head to glare. "I won't lock my Dark inside of me, and I won't ask anyone else to lock their Dark or Light inside of them."

"Good," I say. "My Light threatened to kill me if I ever did that again."

"I know," he says, his voice low.

Zander pushes his plate away, sighing.

Palak is quick to remove it from the table.

When he's removed the last plate, Wyona stands at the opposite end of the table. "This would be when after dinner drinks or dessert are served. I think we've all had enough for the evening, though."

Cal shoves away, breaking contact with me and heading for the door.

I sigh, staring at the table. "Thank you, Wyona, for your time.

We sincerely appreciate your effort in helping us adjust to customs beyond ours."

I start to stand, and Zander puts his hand on mine. "Tallie."

Sterling steps over, grasping me under the arm to lift me to my feet with a snarl. "Back off, Glow."

Zander rises, crossing his arms. "I wanted to warn her."

"Warn me?" I shrug off Sterling.

"Callahan might have had a distressing evening beyond this lesson."

Sterling sticks his finger in Zander's face. "Stay out of it."

I frown at Sterling. "What—"

"I'll explain later." He makes a grab for me. "I've had it with this fucking shit for the evening."

I dodge out of the way. "Babe."

"Placing rank based upon bullshit ideals? I rank less than a boy who doesn't even have his Dark yet." He points at Fallon. "Ranks that can't even speak? Everything decided by that rank that is nothing but a name? This is everything we hate about the fucking Light, and I'm leaving. Cal needs us, and it's not Zander's fucking business to involve himself in." Sterling turns on his heels, slamming the door behind him.

Jacques snickers, stepping to my side. "You missed a few things, but that about covers it."

Tony puts his hand on Jacques's shoulder, hanging from him. "It's been interesting, and I definitely prefer the Dark." He claps Jacques on the back. "Can't wait to tell Ash how much I do not belong in Izul."

They head for the door, the rest of the Light Eaters moving quickly toward the exit with them as Palak steps next to Zander, frowning. "Rank is to enforce proper respect."

I shrug at them. "No one has the *ability to* or *has to* earn respect."

"Merely by us sharing our ways, they should realize they have respect from us."

Zander inclines his head. "Indeed. I signed a contract with Callahan. That should express respect."

"They've treated you like Dark, and you acted like Dark."

"No," Zander says, the word harsh.

I laugh. "They gave you a chance to earn their respect. You reciprocated that, and they earned your respect. In the Light, they wouldn't even have the chance to. Rank decides everything, and rank is decided for you by your heritage name. They have no rank assigned by name, so you decided if you'd respect them based on their actions. That is the Dark."

Both men frown, mirroring furrowed brows of contemplation.

Shaking my head, I exit the room and head down the hallway toward my rooms. I slip inside, Sterling yelling at full volume.

I step into the bedroom, and they both turn on me, snarling with teeth exposed.

I grin back, pointing to my mouth. "My fangs are sharper."

Sterling drops his shoulders. "Firefly."

I wave a hand. "It's the Light. None of us likes their ways."

"You fucking sounded like one of them."

I stare at him with putrid acrimony. "I was locked inside of Izul and threatened with having my Light destroyed if I didn't conform. I damn well figured out how to act for them, but I am not one of them."

He turns his head away. "You weren't yourself. You weren't... our mate."

"Babe. Babes...I'll always be your mate." I take a step closer, pointing on my side. "I'll always fight for you two, even when I feel like dying."

Sterling almost smiles. "I love that you're shiny but fuck the Light."

My Light unwinds as a few strands, forming hands to clap. "He doesn't like their obnoxious rank-imposed bullshit either. What else did I miss?"

Dropping on the edge of the bed, Cal braces his elbows on his knees with his head hung low. He closes his fingers into fists and opens them again. "Wyona asked if I thought I deserved respect."

I laugh, but Sterling winces and starts shaking his head at me.

I stop, looking to Cal. "She was being a bitch."

Sterling steps to my side. "I thought so. He wasn't answering. I was proud. It didn't warrant a response. Jacques and I spoke for him. He has respect."

"A lot of it, from everyone." I fling my hand behind me to indicate the palace.

"I'm aware." Sterling slides his hand along my jaw, pressing his mouth to my temple. "He wouldn't answer. Falsion told him Matteo is an ass, mentioned a list of mistakes Cal keeps to give Matteo, and to throw it away because Matteo's opinion doesn't matter."

Pulling away from Sterling, I move to Cal, forcing him to sit up so I can straddle him. He stares over my shoulder.

"Babe." I press my lips to the corner of his jaw, kissing down his neck. "You have respect. You've earned it."

"She didn't ask if I have respect or earned respect," he says, his voice flat. "She asked if I deserved it."

"Does the Dark give respect without earning it?"

Sterling steps to the other side of the bed and rolls onto it. He scoots across the mattress to press his chest to Cal's back, his legs on either side of Cal's. Slipping his arm around Cal's shoulders, his forearm flexes, the chords of his muscles shifting.

I should focus, not drool, but there's something about men's forearms that sends arousal creeping down my spine.

"No," Cal says.

"You have respect?"

He meets my eyes. "Yes."

"Then why wouldn't you deserve it? You've earned it."

"His life. His name."

Sterling yanks on him. "Your life. Your actions. Your words."

"I took everything when I shouldn't have."

Sterling puts his mouth to Cal's ear. "You would throw your integrity away before you ever refuse responsibility." Sterling chuckles. "Baby, I never put you on a pedestal because of a name. No one did. The first Gathering Shadows, where we met, you should have heard the contractors talking behind your back. We saw Matteo's son, figured you had an arrogance problem carrying his name with the way you had your head held up, that you didn't deserve fuck all for being his son, and you needed to be taught you weren't him. Every night it was the same conversation, 'you got lucky,' 'had it easy,' 'hadn't faced a real challenge yet...' You had to work twice as hard to prove yourself."

Cal scowls. "That's against the tenets. We don't give respect until it's earned, but we don't withhold it from being earned for any reason."

Sterling grins, turning his face into Cal's neck. He starts to shake, a soft chuckle turning into a deep laugh. "Do you hear yourself?"

I turn Cal's face toward mine. "Respect is earned, and you have earned every drop you hold by being the man I love." I rest my forehead to Cal's, staring into his black eyes. This close, I can make out the gray ring at the center.

"Do I deserve that?"

"Yes." I sit back, tapping his chest over his heart. "Because of this."

Sterling says, "Below the moon, in sacred gloom, the essence of night, my presence betrayed by light." He opens his mouth and drags his teeth across Cal's neck, leaving red streaks in his wake.

Cal's lips quiver, and he smiles, hanging his head. "You're fucking insane."

"No, Darkness. Can I eat someone yet? I've been thinking about it all night."

Cal rubs his hands up my sides. "Yes."

"Good," Sterling lifts his head and starts to unbutton Cal's shirt. "I think our mate and I need to show you some appreciation, so you're going to be a good boy and let us."

A laugh worms out of Cal. "No."

I grin, scratching at his jaw. "Be a good boy, and you'll get a treat."

Cal tries to give me a dirty look but can't keep his face straight.

Sterling yanks his shirt off, rolling to the side and twisting to his knees next to me. "Lie down." He taps the bed.

Cal grumbles but flops back.

"Good boy."

He chokes, tipping his cheek back and rumbling, "Fuck both of you."

I run my hands up his abs. "You're going to."

He grumbles, his stomach dipping as he watches me with half-closed eyes. He begins throbbing beneath me, growing.

Sterling gets off the bed and pulls the zipper of my dress down. He slips an arm around my waist, pulling me off Cal to my feet.

He kisses along my neck as he pushes the dress down my body. He licks a bit too high above the mating marks.

I whimper, muscles coiling in anticipation.

He nips my ear. "I'm going to watch him eat you while I eat him, then I'm going to eat you while he fucks you, and you're both going to give me what I want for making me endure that shit from earlier. I feel gross."

Cal watches with half-closed eyes as Sterling runs his hands over me. I tip my head back, stomach squirming, but close my eyes and try to enjoy the sensation of his large hands.

Trust still isn't easy.

Sterling's arm wraps around me, lifting me off my feet. I squeak, curling my knees up.

He gets on the bed, putting me down near Cal's head.

He grumbles, but he's smiling. "This again?"

"Complaining?"

"Not at all."

Sterling turns his head into my neck. "He's being such a good boy. I think he's earned his treat."

Cal grips my hips and yanks me forward. "The kind that tastes good."

CHAPTER 32
CALLAHAN
2ND SUN'S DAY, BLOOMING, 4050, 6TH MILLENNIUM

I hunt down Thames the next morning during training. I pull him away from prying ears, Hiro following with a glower.

Far enough for my comfort, I cross my arms and face them.

Hiro sticks his finger in my face. "I don't care if you're a Dark Queen or Light, you don't put your hands on my mate."

"I already have a woman and a bird. I'm not interested in Thames." I hold his gaze, then shift toward Thames. "You made an offer for assisting with attire."

"I did. I was turned down."

"Not by me."

He cocks his head.

"Fuck the Light. We've always known that, but last night was...enlightening."

Hiro struggles with humor.

I smirk. "I'm not wearing what they want. I'm not going to be uncomfortable while I suffer through this mess."

"Understandable. How can I be of service?"

"Find me a tailor. I have a few ideas. I want it quiet. No one else knows."

Thames shrugs. "Henry and Abigail are contracted and have always suited my needs."

"Set up a time for me to talk with them."

I walk away, Jacques catching up to me. "What are we doing?"

"I need to find Thomas."

"He works in the kitchens."

"Let's go."

I RETURN TO THE YARD, the pressure in my chest easier to shift in order to breathe.

It doesn't last long. Zander moves into my path. I tilt my chin up to meet his gaze, probably in a way Wyona would want me to always do. He has a solid hand's width of height on me, like Sterling. One annoys me less, but it's irritating on both fronts.

He bows his head. "You've been absent."

"I was managing something."

Zander turns his head, motioning at Jacques. "He or I are to do as you ask."

"I'm capable."

"Yes."

I almost fall over in shock. I wait for the punchline on this joke.

Zander's features pull toward the center of his face. "What was said last evening—"

"I won't discuss it."

"Pierre died maintaining the highest respect for you."

Jacques steps between us, his back to me. "How Cal measures himself is up to him, and it is not the same as how another

314

measures him. Now shut the fuck up unless you're going to say something of use."

"That was of use."

I turn and walk off, moving through the crowd. Palak feels the need to spew stupidity at me as well.

It's tiresome.

I push him away. "I don't need fucking platitudes. I didn't ask for them, and I don't care about them. Offering worthless flattery pisses me off."

He stumbles a pace back, rubbing his chest. "You don't accept respect even when it's offered."

"Pretty words aren't respect." Wyham joins us and I round on him. "Don't you start, too."

Wyham shrugs and crosses his arms. "I'm coming to realize how vastly different we are. Tallie made an excellent argument to support our need to change our ways, so if you'd prefer 'fuck you,' then the choice is yours."

I turn up one side of my mouth. "She did?"

Wyham looks away. "Her allegiance to the Dark created tension, but I found Tallie to be a fine woman. I supported Zander's intentions to union with her for that reason. I cannot find fault in her logic. We have no prior rank established with each other and have made our own determinations based on interactions. That is not our custom, something I will support change for."

Jacques throws his hands up. "If only we had said the same a dozen times before." He grins at me. "Why didn't we think to do that?"

I laugh.

Wyham sneers. "Mockery is still unappreciated." He nods at me. "Ashley has requested your presence."

I send my Dark straight up to billow out and ignite into flames. The yard goes still and quiet. "Clean up, have breakfast."

Bodies mill about me, pushing and shoving. Palak and Wyham wait with me as the others filter away.

As the yard empties, Sterling joins us with our mate thrown over his shoulder. He swings her into his arms, flipping her over one to her feet.

She laughs, stepping away to throw her feet over her head in a series of backflips and ariels.

Oscar stares at her with his head cocked. "Is she part Minx?"

Sterling stretches his features in mock consideration. "We have no idea what she is."

Chuckling, I watch Natalia flip again. "The first Magia were imbued with Seraphinus magic. She might have Minx in her magic."

With a bit of fear, Sterling looks to me. His eyes stretch wide. "Do we have a kitten fetish?"

Oscar lifts his hands, taking a step away from us. "Not interested."

I stretch my neck to the side, running my fingers along the taut muscles. "It's not any weirder than Dark having a Light fetish."

Sterling laughs. "I like shiny. What's your excuse?"

"I like eating Light." I wiggle my eyebrows.

Sterling guffaws as Tony walks forward with Alexander, giving him a shove. "Zan, can Alex try to take some of your Light?"

Alexander shudders. "I've already proven I can do it with the Dark."

"You are the Dark. I want to see it with the Light."

Zander steps forward. "What do I need to do?"

"Give him a strand of magic."

I turn to Thames and Hiro. "Thomas will be in touch."

"Fine."

Natalia jumps at me from the side. I twist toward her,

catching her. "Little Star," I say, eyeing the pendant around her neck.

She flickers, her Light flashing as she grins. "Babe."

"Behave," I tell her, setting her on her feet.

Alexander yelps, shoving his hand at Zander. Light flashes, leaving the world white for a heartbeat. When it clears, spots dance in my vision, and Zander lies crumpled on the ground.

Tony lurches forward. "Don't move, Friend."

Palak drags Alexander away, shoving him into the dirt. "I suggest you stay down and compliant."

Alexander cradles his arm, groaning.

Tony sits back on his heels, sighing as Zander rolls his torso forward. "You good?"

"What was that?"

"You can't shield your own magic." Tony rolls, flipping to face the opposite direction. "Alex, what happened?"

"That hurt so much. It...it burned everything."

Natalia steps away from me, lowering to the ground. "Intaking the Light?"

Alex rocks his head. "Yeah."

She pokes Tony. "You should have talked to me. I could have warned you. He's Dark."

"You have the Light and play with Dark all the time."

"Taking it in hurts."

He cuts his eyes at her. "Doesn't hurt me. Neither do."

"You're not Dark or Light. They don't play well."

He points at me. "Says the Light with a Dark mate."

"Two." She holds up her index and middle fingers, giggling and sparkling brighter. "When I take in Light, it's like a caffeine jolt. Smites work wonders to clear up hangovers."

"That's why you asked Ash to smite you?"

I bite down hard. "Ash smited you?"

"I went to deal with something." I scan the faces, stopping on Ashley to narrow one eye.

She shrugs. "My sibling seed asked me to. How was I to refuse?"

Natalia returns to me, giggling. "It felt great."

I close my eyes, shaking my head. It's not the first time my mate has expressed her enjoyment of being smited. I'm never going to grasp that concept with any level of comprehension.

Tony stands, leaning over to pull Alexander off the ground. "You did it, so you earned the mark. Welcome to Pinnacle status."

Alexander stands, rubbing his arm. "I never want to do that again."

Clapping him on the shoulder, Tony grabs hold and rocks him. "I'm glad I was here to witness you take it in and send it back. If you had to drag it all the way to an Assembly, that would have been torture for you."

Alexander looks to Zander. "As Dark, I'm not allowed to apologize, but I'd like to let you know I didn't mean to do that."

Zander bows his head. "I accept your remorse."

Sterling moves to my side, Dark crawling over me to mix with mine and Natalia's Light. Tony was accurate. Our magics never keep to themselves.

Tony, Natalia, and Alexander. Ashley, Zander, Palak, Hailey, and Wyham. Sterling, Jacques, Oscar, Hiro, and Thames. Me and my Mandolux kin. It's an eclectic group of Dark, Light, and a mix of the two.

This has to be one of the surrealist moments of my life, all of us circled together without fighting. It's strange when I consider Ashley engaging in a relationship with Tony, and my mates are opposites in Light and Dark.

"What the fuck," I whisper to myself, rubbing my mouth. Clearing my throat, I focus on Ashley. "You wanted to talk? Talk."

"I was given a report on how your dinner went, and I'm disappointed."

"I'm worse than disappointed in the lack of respect the Light has even for its own."

"I've arranged traditional-style *jejinn* for you to try again this morning."

Sterling groans, "Tell me I don't have to."

"We all go."

Oscar lifts his hand. "Am I?"

Natalia shakes her head. "No, you're better suited to being available to the contractors and acting in my stead. Work with Hiro and Thames."

Hiro inclines his head. "You'll want to establish who is in charge."

"I'll let the contractors know."

Thames smiles. "He means between us, baby."

She looks at her hand and wrist with the two contracts. "Hiro, you get to be in charge since you serve the Dark and have no other obligations."

I glance around. "The rest of us have...jenji?"

"Jijenn," Ashley says, clicking her tongue. "It is the proper meal to begin a day."

Jacques fakes a sob into his hands. "I survived over three centuries of games for this?"

Ashley juts her hip, raising an eyebrow. "To be invited into the Light as a friend to us? How terrible that must be. You should find honor in the way we share our customs and ways with you."

I glance around, my Dark tingling. "Jacques."

He picks his head up, looking behind him. "Oh...pretty girl." He takes off in a jog toward the shadow servant, dragging itself toward us.

Palak stumbles away. "What did— Where did...?"

Zander doubles in brightness, his Light shifting from gold to blue.

I shake my head at them. "They live in the mountains, wander down every so often, seowolves too. Jacques will deal with it."

Wyham takes a step toward the shadow serpent. "I'll help."

"No, you'll get in the way."

"That's massive. He needs help."

I hum. Jacques is the size of a toy in front of the beast. One head lowers.

Wyham takes another step, and I ensnare him in my Dark, halting him. "Watch."

The beast nudges Jacques with two heads as he strokes the head that dropped first.

I unwind my Dark from Wyham. "Jacque is a Vyper, kin to them. He'll turn it back. We don't need to get involved. If we do, it'll turn violent."

Sterling nods. "No reason to kill it if we don't have to. Convenient having a Vyper around."

Natalia turns to me. "That's what was in the box?"

Sterling reaches for her, pulling her closer. "Yes, that's what Basileus gave you in a box."

I caress her cheek with the back of my finger. "That one was smaller."

Marius and Basileus had both infected Natalia with nightmare toxin. She'd been high before the box was opened. I thought she'd die. Instead, it was the first time she smited.

Tightening around Natalia, Sterling sighs. "I hated that night, watching you almost die and Cal losing his mind. I wanted to do something, anything, and the way Marius—"

I snap my teeth.

Zander frowns, glancing between me and my mates.

Sterling scoops Natalia into his arms, rocking her with a

smile. He whispers something to Natalia too low for me to comprehend, but she laughs.

Marius had violated her with his magic in front of me, and I wanted to skin him alive. Sterling's done far more vulgar acts with me present, and I enjoy it. It's illogical yet here I stand, smiling like an idiot, watching my two mates grin at each other.

Ease slips through me, my Dark whining slightly as it stretches around them. "*Mates.*"

Ashley steps further and further from the shadow serpent. "We should..."

I eye her with glee. "What's wrong, Ash? Is a Bordeaux showing weakness?"

"It's not weak to be..." She pauses and licks her lips. "Nervous about a creature like that."

I face the palace. "Let's go."

CHAPTER 33

CALLAHAN

Palak, Wyham, and Zander join us in the king's hall again.

Wyona insists Tony sit at my right hand this morning for being the host of a fatum. She forgets Natalia's instructions to place Sterling next to me until Sterling's Dark ties a noose around Zander on its way to tangle with mine.

She remembered in a hurry when his lips turned blue and she gave Sterling what he wanted, his place next to me.

Zander defends our right to allow our magics freedom. Palak supports Galain's request that Fallon sit next to him. Wyham intervenes when Wyona tries to smack Jacques with her stick, reminding her that Sterling and I advised her against that.

We suffer through the meal, Zander explaining polite topics of conversation and interaction, and how to keep our voices low so as not to disturb any others nearby.

I drag a hand down my face and gag down the rest of my tea.

Ashley, Hailey, Flora, and Layla join the fray when the meal is concluded. They have attire for us, their selections made for the coronation, and a seamstress who will tailor everything.

Even Fallon is given a suit.

Galain shoots daggers at me with his eyes. I shrug. I'd included him on my list too. He's young, but he'll be a man. They don't live in the mountains anymore. I want him to have an education on how to carry himself as much as how to tear out a throat.

My Dark simpers at the memory of Natalia pulling Yanri's tongue out. Blood had splattered her, and she never flinched. It was gorgeous.

Maria steps behind a privacy screen to change, so I start pulling off my clothes.

Ashley and the other Lights panic, squawking about decency.

Jacques is naked first, staring them down. Layla and Flora have turned their backs, Ashley's gaze firmly on the ceiling.

Hailey has covered her face with both hands. "Adontis, the impropriety must end."

Palak screws his face up, all his features pulled to one side as he moves to her, putting his arm around her. "My brightest Light, you are fine. I'll let you know when it has ended."

Zander scowls. "Gentleman, I insist—"

"You're making me wear white." Stark naked, Jacques points at him. "I'm doing this however is most inconvenient to me."

He gets the trousers on first, clapping them around his hips. The cream color brings out a green tinge in his pale skin.

Sterling groans and moans as he pulls on his suit, almost sobbing. When he's finished pulling the suit on, he shudders then gags.

Wyona approaches him with a pair of gilded scissors. "Sir," she motions to a cushion. "Please take a seat."

He leans back, eyeing the shears. "Why?"

"Your hair is—"

"Touch my locks, and I will rip your throat out."

Shock spreads through me. I know his hair correlates to the

history of his lineage, but that seems like an extreme response for hair.

Everyone stares at him.

He glances around. With a tug on a sleeve under his suit coat, he rolls his shoulders. "You can put me in white. You can make me sit on the floor, but I draw the fucking line at my locks. My father, my uncle, every member of my lineage has worn locks like these, and my seeds will do the same because we are Wellslys. *Leave. My. Locks. Alone.*"

I clap him on the back. "Your locks are safe, baby." I motion Wyona away. "He's not making an idle threat. Put those away for your safety."

We wait for our turn to get stuck with pins while my mate mutters under his breath and glowers at Wyona like she's pissed on his entire lineage. Sterling is having his fun when Natalia enters.

I almost throw up. She's in a dress with a wide, puffed-up skirt and tight bodice. It's square cut front smashes her perky tits up almost to her neck.

I didn't ever want to see her like that, nor let her see me like this.

She walks across the room, regal and full of grace, to stop in front of me, smoothing her skirt. She folds her hands together, lifting her chin as she looks to me.

Fire flashes in her eyes, her lips pulling to one side as one eyebrow twitches with disdain. They can change her clothes and force her to walk and talk how they want, but my little star won't break.

She scans me, then meets my eyes. "I hate it." She pivots toward Sterling. "Ugh."

Sterling winces. "Firefly," he begs in a faint voice, looking to the floor. "Don't look at me like that."

She turns toward Ashley. "Why are you making him wear white?" She flings her hand at Sterling. "That's just mean."

Ashley folds her hands together and straightens. "Sister Mine, I believe he maintains a union contract with you and Callahan. Am I incorrect?"

Natalia faces me, puckering her lips with ire. Her boobs swell, probably the only thing that provides any give to allow her to breathe in the glossy, gold monstrosity of frills and beads adorning her. "I understand your implication and beg forgiveness for my lack of sight. He will be a Light King and should have the appropriate display of station." She rolls her eyes at me, her tone airy, carrying a smile she is not wearing.

I attempt to keep my composure, to not betray her antics to the others. She's going to survive this. She'll stay my sassy star.

Maria steps next to her in a similarly revolting gown. Natalia gives her a smile of sympathy, mouthing "awful" as she wags a finger between them.

Thomas pokes his head in, knocking. "Hello?" His jaw drops, and he stumbles inside. "Maria?"

She turns, cringing. "Tom."

"Oh, love, what have they... Oh, uh, I'd like to be able to tell you that you appear beautiful."

Maria chortles. "I know."

"You are," he says quickly, "beautiful, that is. Just..."

"I know."

"Dad, uh, I..." He continues to gape at Maria with horror.

My poor son. I'm inflicting horrors upon him. Sins of the father, I suppose. I'm suffering my mate in atrocious attire. My boy has to see his woman in something as ugly.

Flora steps forward. "Dad?" She looks to me. "Is this a Hallow heir?"

"My son does not carry my lineage, but don't you fucking

dare disrespect him or harm him. You'll give him the respect he deserves as a man I raised."

Zander approaches Thomas, bowing his head. "Welcome and be welcomed, Thomas."

My son jerks, shying away from Zander. "Um, th–thank you?" He looks to me, wide-eyed with fear. Faint shadows grow around him, tendrils lashing out.

"Zan," I call, adding force to my voice. "He's still Dark Seraphim. He can't withstand your Light being that close. Back up."

Flora drops her jaw in a harsh gasp. "A lowborn? No, out, you are not suitable to be in our presence."

Natalia says, "He's still Cal's son. You're not going to treat him that way."

Thomas straightens his shirt, glancing at Maria. "Love, that dress..."

She giggles, leaning over to kiss his cheek with a hand on his shoulder.

Wyona starts clapping her hands, marching forward. "There will be no displays of public affection between unestablished unions. That lowborn is unsuited for a Hallow descendant and will not be a viable—"

"Lady." Falsion steps forward, blocking her off. "That's my daughter, and she'll do what she wants with whom she wants. Cal raised a fine man and she's welcome to take her pick of any."

"That will be entirely unacceptable. As a Hallow, her union must be approved."

"D–Dad, um, Sir," my son stammers. "Tark Darren and Edwin Harvestest have come seeking contracts with the Dark King."

I look to Sterling. "Yours?"

"Were."

"Have them wait in my office. Their Dark King will meet them shortly."

"Yes, Sir." He gives Maria another long look. "Burn that thing when you're done. It's hideous."

Flora gasps.

Falsion chuckles, leading Thomas to the door. "Run, Thomas. Spare yourself." He shoves my son out of the room and steps to me. "I'll have no stance between them."

I shake my head, pulling at the collar of my shirt. I should be breathing easier. My son found a relationship. This damn attire is suffocating.

Sterling steps off the platform, tapping Natalia's nose. "Firefly, promise me you will burn that one too."

She winks. "I had other plans."

I laugh, suspecting it involves my claws shredding it to pieces. A man can hope. It would be much more satisfying.

This is a waste of time. Not one of these suits or gowns will be worn. I'll dig my eyes out before I ever see Natalia puffed and smashed in a ridiculous dress or Sterling in all white ever again after today. They just don't know it yet.

Natalia presses her hand to my chest, turning away. "Ashley, have you seen enough?"

"Yes, honey. It fits marvelously. You haven't gained a pound."

"I have contracts to sign," she says, striding to the door.

CHAPTER 34

NATALIA

I head back to my chambers and open the door. "Thames."

He pokes his head out from the bedroom. "Yes, baby."

"I'm not going to make it to you. Come get me out of this thing here."

He strolls down the hallway, his face crinkled with humor. "An absolute horrid contraption." He steps to my back, pulling at the corset strings.

The dress begins to sag as Hiro approaches, fiddling with a button on his shirt. "That thing gets worse the more I see it."

I laugh, putting a hand to my chest to keep the dress in place. I take a deep breath, tipping my head back to groan. "I swore I would never go back to that city. Am I a liar for this?"

Hiro leans against the wall. "It's a gray area. You aren't intentionally going back on your word."

I bob my head. "Two are on the way for contracts. I'd like your assistance."

He narrows his eyes.

"I know I'm—"

He flicks his hand. "My father taught me. I witnessed negotiations and drafting contracts for nearly a century before I took control of my lineage."

"I've heard..."

Hiro's features turn hard. "My mother is a coward?"

I look to the floor, unsure if I've misstepped.

"She is." He drops his hands to his hips. "My father died in the games. My mother should have taken his place. She contracted herself to me to hide. The bitch did it two weeks before the games the following year."

"Why'd you do it?"

"I refused to be a coward and say no. The lineage name is hers. She unioned with my father and opted to be subservient in the union contract, leaving him to face the games and run the lineage estate. She's useless."

Thames steps next to Hiro, kisses his cheek then leans against him with a bent arm on Hiro's shoulder. "According to her, I'm his best vassal."

"She refuses to acknowledge him as my mate."

I shake my head. "Gross."

"I have no patience with that bitch. She has tarnished my lineage name forever and disrespected my mate a hundred times. She was the only one of mine who attempted to refuse to sign with you."

"You made them?"

"I asked them to, then burned their contracts. They could have done whatever they wanted. You earned respect. I didn't have to do anything," he says, then makes a disgusted sigh. "Except for that bitch. I told her I'd send her to the afters or she'd sign with you."

Thames chuckles. "As a coward—"

"She signed."

There's a knock at my back. I grimace. "I am not signing Dark in this." I shuffle to the bedroom.

The door opens, Thames saying, "Hello."

"Gods, did a Dark finally kill the glow whore and take the crown?" an unfamiliar voice answers.

I drop the dress, grabbing a short one from the wardrobe of black, glittering material. I work it on, my Light yanking the zipper up as I smooth the loose skirt over my hips.

I return to the front room. "You'll be disappointed to know I'm still alive."

A man and woman eye me, the woman shaking her head. "I'm seeking a contract of service."

"The standard is twenty-five years for basic services. They do not include protection of any kind for me but do require protection duties for the Dark, such as participating in stopping the Ancients from destroying the Seraphinus. If you choose, I have a contract of forty-days to show honor to Sterling still available."

The man shies his head. "I don't have to shield you?"

Thames chuckles.

"No." I smile. "I can take care of myself and have enlisted others to aid me who don't have a problem with my Light."

I lift my hand, wiggling my fingers. Threads of my Light spin between them, wrapping around my wrist and lifting into the air to form the illusion of a hand, the middle finger extended upward.

The man laughs. "They say you're different."

"I am your Dark King, Natalia. You can call me Tallie or Tal. Your Dark Queens are currently suffering at the hands of the Light, learning their ways. If you hear screaming from down the hall, they've lost their patience. Ignore it."

"Why are they...? The crowns really are unifying?" The man leans back with horror.

"Yes."

The woman curls one side of her mouth back. "Did you say queens, plural?"

"Callahan Barraco and Sterling Wellsly." I point to the mating marks overlapping on the side of my neck.

Hiro steps forward. "Do you want a contract or not?"

The man says, "My name is Edwin Harvestest. I am willing to negotiate on your standard contract."

I step backward toward the office. "Follow me."

EDWIN AND TARK SIGNED. I have Thames and Hiro take them to Raz for placement, letting them know they are free until dinner to do whatever they please, as Oscar is managing the contractors on my behalf.

I linger in the office, filing the contracts away. I look left, the office flowing into a long open expanse.

Cal and Sterling had worked to clear out all the unnecessary walls. It's a massive improvement, these chambers now less cage-like. It's not dingy and dank cloisters anymore.

I get up, walking the space. Cal said he'd have new furnishings delivered. Maybe I can work on that for him. He does so much and carries so much weight.

Shadows stir, twisting together in front of me, translucent churning to opaque, forming Mallafic.

I'm not far enough from my mates that I panic, but I shy away from him, backpedaling toward the front door.

He eyes me, lifting his hand, showing me the back, his skeletal black fingers bent over, out of sight. I don't have to see them to know the razor-sharp talons exist.

"Darling Toy."

"Where is Ness?"

"Enjoying a salty bath and a book."

"Another codex?"

He lifts his gaze, two solid black irises beating into me to my soul. "Another prison to escape."

"What are you doing to her?"

"More questions?" He scoffs. "Would you care to play another game for answers?"

My Light twists tighter inside of me. There has been no glib, dramatic flourishes or words this time. He's tense, poised to snap.

"You're angry."

"How astute," he says with a sneer, "though that word doesn't quite bring my feelings to sharp relief, a pathetic attempt at best."

He drops his hand, stalking toward me.

I step backward, keeping space between us, though not daring to turn my back on him. "What do you want?"

"I offer you my hat, my seat, my creations for words you spoke, affirmations that swayed my mind to beliefs I cherish, and yet..." He stops, glaring at me. "You lie. Again and again, you speak and do the opposite. I should not be so surprised given the seed of my lover planted within you."

Cal. Sterling. Cal and Sterling.

My Light twists in tight vines that buzz. It's fuming at the implication that we would lie, lie to our mates, worst of all.

We love them both. We love our place between them.

I can't bring the thoughts to words, not daring to give them life. Cal might share. He'd never forgive my heart being divided if it could be at all.

Mallafic sneers. "What I want, *Plaything*," he says, spitting the word, "is blood in retribution."

Fear clogs my throat. "Don't you dare hurt them."

He scoffs, dissolving into shadows. I turn to run, screaming for Cal.

Freezing blackness surrounds me, gripping tight like dozens of claws sinking into my flesh.

I spin, blind, but the whirl is inside my skull.

The claws rip from me as I fall, dizzy. My head spins, my eyes out of focus.

My stomach creeps up into the back of my mouth as I press my hands to slate stone, steadying myself and pushing to my feet.

I sway, stumbling to the side, to a wall that matches the ground. Black vines with jagged leaves rustle, and I shrink from the carnivorous ivy.

I look to where daylight collects, forming an opening at the end of the corridor. Mallafic stands, backlit by the illumination, the lawn sprawling at his back.

The maze.

Adrenaline streaks through me. My hands shake, my knees threatening to give.

He smirks, a cruel twist to his sharp gestures glinting as my Light races over me, preparing to defend us. "I've tested the strength of mind and body for a worthy puppet countless times. Always of my creations, never one of my kin or such like us."

I shake, a wafting giggle surrounding me in the shifting shadows.

"I've made a few adjustments for you. New pets to play with further within." He smiles. "Run, Darling Toy. Bleed for my amusement. If you dare cheat and flee this structure rather than find the exit, I kill everyone you hold a name to."

He disappears.

The ground rumbles, the way out closing.

Cal. Sterling. Thames. Hiro. Tony. Ness. Jacques. Zander. Ashley. Oscar. Thomas. Falsion. Maria. Fallon. Luna.

Their names, their faces, they stream through my mind as the gap closes.

Galain. Luca. Shawn. Alexander. Raz. Palak. Wyham. Edwin and Tark. Tony's family: Ryan, Elizabeth, and Sarah.

How many names do I know?

It slams shut.

The giggles come again, closer, louder. I whip around, tremors wracking my limbs and core.

I face a greenish phantom of my sister, Sasha. She turns her head, tapping the heel of her palm to a perfect chignon behind her ear. "Well, Sister, look what you've done this time."

"You're not real."

"No?" She shatters apart, a small clown bursting through her with a knife pulled back.

I throw my hand out, Light arcing and flashing before me. I turn my head, closing my eyes against the harsh sting of a silver world.

I blink them open in a hurry. Gone is the clown. Gone is the ghost. Gone is the stone.

Mirrors line the walls, stretching and reflecting empty eternity.

My feet are stuck to the stone, fear coiling in me, stifling out the sound of Cal's voice in my head as my Light speaks.

"*Move.*"

CHAPTER 35
CALLAHAN

I drag a hand down my face as Jacques bows for the thirtieth time. It's never right, even if the gesture appears the same as Zander's demonstration.

Wyona shakes her head. "No."

Jacques throws his hands up. "Why am I doing this? I'm his worn contract." He points at me, and Wyona smacks the back of his hand with her stick. He snarls, retracting his hand. "I'm not bowing to any as his right hand."

Shadows twist into a man next to Jacques. Black hair decorated with several braids tight against the side of his head.

He turns his head toward Jacques, his body still as a statue swaddled in shadows that swallow light. "You refuse to bow to any?"

I lurch to my feet. "Mallafic."

Jacques stumbles to the side, twisting to face Mallafic square on. "I'll bow to you if that's what you want. Want me on my knees?"

His black eyes find mine as he sneers. "Such hopes and

dreams I had. Such delicious teasing glimpses. You were better served to me as an idea."

Rage blisters the room, rolling off him in waves of hisses.

I have several reasons to offer myself for his fury, but I'll ask for his list. "Why?"

"Days alone, eons stretching before me, the echoes of truth vibrating my soul. I wept for days at a time in bitter rage."

"I'm not sure where the need for us to be direct came from with your adoration of poetry and drama."

Mallafic screams, the world shaking. I press my hands to my ears, stumbling.

Jacques hits the floor, blood leaking from his eyes and nose as he crawls toward me.

Others fall too before the piercing wail.

Wet dribbles down my lips, beading up in the corners of my eyes and clumping my lashes.

Sterling falls to his knees, tipping forward onto his hands.

I hit one knee, gasping for air.

It stops, the crushing force on my chest disappearing. I pant, a tangy metallic taste on my tongue.

Jacques halts, struggling to breathe several feet away. "I'm all for jokes, but maybe show respect for our god?"

"He called us dreary last time." I wipe my nose on the back of my hand, leaving sticky red stretching across my skin.

My heart pulses behind my eyes as I blink, trying to remove the film of blood. Scrubbing my face and scrunching my eyes, I stand.

Sterling flails at me, grabbing my arm and trying to pull on me like a pole to get up. I flex and grunt, straining against him to help. When he's upright, I offer a hand to Jacques, yanking him to stand with us.

I watch Falsion steadying Shawn, Galain cradling Fallon down on one knee. "Galain."

"He's all right." Galain nods, holding Fallon closer.

I clench my fists, strength returning. "Eons and tears," I say, looking to Mallafic.

"Thrice, but that matters little. Time passed by. To be lost in death was no small matter for a god raised by gods. I took comfort in adoringly crafting others to keep me company, beasts of the night that would collect at my feet, sniffing for scraps and begging for my tender affection."

Zander stumbles to the side, supporting Ashley. Pink stains smear across his high cheekbones and thin lips.

I return my gaze to my god. "You made us."

"Not us," he snarls, leaning into the words. "Them. They were mine, my creations. I taught them well the truths of life and molded them in my hands, giving them the pieces of my soul and the air in my lungs. Not you. I never made you and my plaything knew it well. For how could I create with naught that I knew would exist? Nay, not us. You are not one of my kind."

If any doubted my origins before, that has been slaughtered. No one can ignore a god declaring I am not his.

Not even me.

We are, in part, the Light. I always knew, but I believed I was a mutt of the Dark more than ever accepting I was the Light, acknowledging being a mix—a mix of the two, but accepting that I was the Dark, living by their ways and tenets.

I advert my gaze, shying my head. Everything I based myself upon is being ripped away one piece at a time, leaving holes in me that burn and pulse in ways that make me believe I will never heal.

"I made them, strong and beautiful, beyond what others thought, beyond what Nehil himself could imagine. His toys gifted to Adontis were shambles and shadows in comparison. I had exceeded my father." He scoffs. "My creations, my world, where not a lie existed, not a weakness could be found. I outgrew the gods of this world in my very own, and then came again my lover so foul and cruel. Never was she one to be seen as less, to kneel before any for her face was so pretty."

"Beenin."

He hisses, his appearance swirling and swaying, parting in translucent tendrils and knitting back together.

"She planted herself, stealing what I had been freely given, claiming balance for the very tear she wrought, serving her vanity, herself in pursuits to kill me or possess me. Those were my options and for refusing her, she did it. It was not me!"

The world shakes, the shrill exclamation piercing my ears.

"She made hunters where I made beauty. She crafted vile repugnance as crude and cruel as her soul, where the reflection of mine was honest and strong. Liars, every last one, touting a mirage of what they are. She wore a mask too, one beautiful but beneath it is rotten."

Wyona smacks the stick in her hand. "I don't know who you are, but Beenin was above all, beauty..."

I cut my eyes at her, questioning her intelligence.

"...through and through, full of grace and—"

In a blink, Mallafic appears behind Wyona. He rakes claws across her throat, slinging blood and gore across the floor.

Wyona chokes, knees folding, and she drops to the floor in a twitching heap.

Sterling says, "Don't."

I glance at him, following his sight to Zander glowing blue.

Mallafic sneers down on the body of Wyona still spasming in death.

The Dark in Vanessa was furious and blood thirsty. It was pieces of Mallafic's soul. This little trek into his mind reveals much.

"Mockery before truth," I say, lifting my chin and eyes to his.

"Her words. Her story."

"Her lies."

That calms the agitated shadows surrounding him. "How interesting your intellect, when you are so ignorant."

"Everything we know is wrong?"

"Not everything," he sneers. "Have you not been listening? I was sure to give mine ears. Did the gods not grant you that mercy?"

I try not to smile. The truth is, I understand why Mallafic would want Natalia as a plaything. Her sass with his wit would be amusing banter to witness.

I won't flare his rage at making the comparison of their tongues.

He rocks back on his heels. "You offer me dreams, yet you bring those pieces of her into a place I called home. You feed their whims and kneel to their desires. You break what was hers to protect and she allows it." He straightens, tugging on the front of his shirt. "A creation such as that was change I had never dreamed of for one of my lover's things. Here, I thought, is salvation, for my lover's seeds will be mine too. I gave her my very hat to wear for words she spoke that gave me pause."

Sterling reaches for me, waving his hand and latching onto my arm, "Tal."

My Dark unfurls, snapping and twisting at the ready. I clench my fists. "Where is she?"

Mallafic whisks to shadows and rebuilds in front of me, standing close enough that his frigid fury washes over my skin. "I had such hopes of what you were. Beyond my wildest imagination there were things Nehil could still teach me. Triumph over my lover, for my seed was stronger, consuming hers."

"Where is our mate?"

My Dark pings with frantic pulses, shuddering. "*Further. Further. Here and not. Straight.*"

I focus on Mallafic over the jumble of panicked words my

339

magic offers. He's throwing a tantrum about us learning the customs of the Light. I'll work that angle.

"The Dark cannot exist without the Light."

"A counterweight," he says, a gleam of his glibness sparking within his eyes. "As in all things. She made one, fated to forge the other in the very act. Two sides of one whole, tethered together by unbreakable threads. I was given what she stole."

"I intend to mend the divide, bring us together as one."

"Become one of them? I'd rather my things die than be hers. Then so shall hers perish." He turns his back on me. "I'll not lose to her again."

"No," I tell him. "Not one of them, just one."

He laughs, short and bitter. "Unity?" Spinning to face me, he laughs again, open and real. "It was divided by her in moments you cannot understand. Stilo, the fool that he was, at least understood that much. You know not the meddles you trifle in. True, you cannot exist without the other, as my rage cannot exist without her black soul, but you will never be whole. The one with my hat bears the blame for allowing this perversion of my kind to be embraced. You will cease. She will bleed."

"Where is she?"

Sterling yells, "What did you do to her?"

Mallafic taps his nose. "You most of all should be aware," he whispers, the words sharp, "a toy is only as good as its amusements. A broken toy can still be entertaining, but a dead one is simply a waste."

I look to Tony. "Soris. What did he do?"

His eyes roll in the back of his head, turning a shimmering white.

"Ah." Mallafic eyes Tony. "Sirius extends his regards, Brother. Alas, Soris ruins the fun. A shame. I put my toy in a trap for my delight to know she pays for failure so she may learn. I never was merciful to mine, though far more tender in my need to punish than her."

He shoots a smile at Zander and Ashley, an animal showing his teeth. "There once was a monster who wore a pretty mask. Never mind, you'll hear my tale soon enough. The days of mockery are very nearly over."

He disappears.

Tony grunts, ramming the heels of his palms into his eyes. "She's looking in a mirror."

My Dark fumes. Our little star doesn't like mirrors.

Palak comes forward, cleaning his face with his shirt. "What can we do?"

"Where?" I ask, searching my mind.

"Close but beyond, and ahead."

"Close and..." I lift my gaze, staring in front of me. Down the hall are our rooms, and beyond, our balcony overlooks...

"Fuck," Sterling groans, dragging the word out on a breath. "Not there."

"Yes." I grab Sterling by the front of his shirt, sending my Dark at the glass windows to shatter one. "She's in the fucking maze."

Jacques laughs. "Can't we just find you a new mate?"

I yank Sterling out the window, my Dark spreading from my shoulders. I'm going to thrash Jacques's head against stone later for that stupid question, but I have a little star to save first.

Sterling flails. "Let go."

I do, not stopping.

He catches up, the maze coming closer into clear focus.

My Dark curls and shivers like a kicked puppy.

I speak aloud for it and Sterling's benefit. "All we have to do is find our mate and pull her out. We don't have to finish it."

"Then why is she still in it?"

I look over at him, my guts squirming.

"It wouldn't be that simple. The games he plays—"

A shrill scream rips the air.

I bank, flying over the shadow filled passages toward the source.

Light flashes just ahead.

I rise higher and drop over the source, pulling my wings in to plummet into the maze.

A red ball bounces, rubber smacking stone and pegging me in the side of the head.

I hit the wall, razor-like wire curling around one wrist. I wrench free, turning.

Sterling catches a ball and hurls it at one of the freaky little terrors in black and gold shiny material.

It glints as the world gets brighter, giggles surrounding us from wide grins of pointed teeth that never move.

Another launches at his back, driving a blade into his shoulder. He roars, and I stab strands of my Dark through the clown.

A smite drops through the other. Sterling and I crash into each other, seeking to get away from the electrical blue strike.

Hands grab me, and I launch up, swinging. I slam my fist into the side of Zander's face, taking him to the ground beneath me before I register him as a non-threat.

"Hang on," Tony says, grabbing Sterling and forcing him to sit. He wraps his hand around the hilt, "On three."

Sterling reaches up, closing a fist around Tony's hand and the handle before yanking the blade out with a growl. "Just pull shit out so my Dark can stop the bleeding."

I scan for Natalia as Tony laughs. "Better idea. Hold still, and I'll heal you."

Natalia limps forward, several strands of her silver hair sticking to the side of her face, glued in place by blood. "Cal."

I tear away from Zander, rushing to pick her up, hold her close and tight against me. "I have you, Mate."

I round to tell Zander to grab Tony and leave, realizing it's worse than two. Jacques and Palak came with them.

"Get out of here."

Zander lifts his chin, his lips red with blood. "We can help."

"I gave you an order to stay away from this thing. Go! Jacques, take Tony. All of you get out. Now."

Palak opens his mouth but never speaks. The life drains from his face, fear-gripping his features.

Fuck.

I turn toward the other end of the corridor, a massive black and blue creature twisting into existence.

It rolls from its back to its legs, all six of them. The upper torso is muscular like a man with two pairs of upper arms, the back similar to the hindquarters of a wolf, the tail thin and whipping side to side with a double barbed end.

Sterling jerks up, shoving Tony behind him. "What the fuck is that?"

The thing bares teeth, jagged points and long fangs, like a smoragon with too many teeth.

Behind me comes the stammering response. "Sh–Sh–Sha–Shadow B–B..." Palak manages in a faint voice.

I turn to meet Sterling's eyes, and together we turn to Palak. I lift an eyebrow. "Shadow Beast?"

Jacques laughs, tipping his head back with a hand to his stomach then doubles over, dropping his hand to his knee. His humor echoes around us mingling with the snarls and growls of the thing behind us. "Shadow Beast? You think that's a..." He dissolves into hysterics.

Sterling looks back then glares at Palak. "That's what you think we look like? Monsters the size of small houses?"

Shaking my head, I slide Natalia down my front to stand. "I need to teach you what a Shadow Beast is."

I turn, keeping my star at my back to face the thing. It lifts one massive... The front arms have paws. The long-tipped nails click as it steps forward, crouched with the front end low and preparing to pounce. I can't decide if it's catlike, doglike, or dragonlike with human parts thrown in for a spectacular concoction of death.

A smite rains down on it. I jump.

The thing growls, then shakes itself and roars.

There are too many of us collected.

I scoff. "Zan. Let me guess. You're afraid there's something a smite won't kill."

"It's...it's not possible. There's nothing..."

Sterling chuckles. "For fuck's sake. I'm learning how to hold a teacup when they don't understand nightmare toxin."

It's coming closer. I grind my teeth, keeping Natalia at my back. "Palak, how the fuck do you kill this thing?"

"I–I–I..."

The thing stops, its tail going still, so only the barb dances back and forth. That's a bad sign.

"Spit it out."

"I–I don't know. It's a nightmare. I–I–I've never managed to. It always kills me. That's when I wake up."

Sterling moves toward the wall, rolling his shoulders. "Decapitation it is."

I eye the muscular neck, as thick as the head. "That's going to be difficult."

"Aw, baby." He turns his head, silently laughing at me. "You getting soft with a crown on your head?"

The thing growls, sinking lower. I roll to the balls of my feet.

Zander asks, "Can't we just run?"

I stretch my neck, side to side. "We could try to run, but it will follow."

Sterling extends his arm across his torso, pulling the muscles to loosen up. "The maze has a way of doing that, sending something beyond its walls to kill once it's been spawned."

"I've seen it twice, some moron trying to outrun their fear. They're dead if they leave the maze during the games anyway."

Shadows race at us.

My Dark shields, but the force ripples into me, sending me over to my back.

Natalia moans as I land on her.

Palak screams, clawing at the stone as he's dragged forward.

Jacques sprints forward as I get to my feet.

Sterling runs at my side.

The creature slams a paw onto Palak, and he yells. The claws flex, pressing deep into Palak's torso.

Jacques dives onto them as it goes for the kill, jaws stretched open as the head comes down.

Black arcs, engulfing Jacques and Palak.

The creature bites the shield, two other clawed paws slashing at it.

I send my Dark to bind the arms, straining to keep them from breaking through.

Jacques roars as the jowls close, the shield shattering into wisps.

Tony rolls beneath the head next to Jacques, a warp of air crystallizing over him. His eyes are closed as he goes still, the head ramming into the invisible barrier.

Zander and Natalia are wrangling other arms, Sterling wrapping Dark around the thing's neck.

The creature bellows, shaking and slinging itself side to side.

We all fling around, tethered to the creature.

I hit the stone, my head cracking against the hard surface.

Sterling rolls down the corridor, Zander and Natalia now out of sight.

Jacques covers Palak in shadows, trying to drag him away.

I punch the air, sending my Dark at the beast. It explodes, orange flames bursting.

Sterling yelps, skittering further away as Tony runs and jumps, latching onto the snout.

That's stupid.

The creature throws him off with ease, but Natalia pops into view, landing on its back with wings spread.

It thrashes, but ropes of silver wind around the creature, and she bounces, staying in top of it.

It twists its head, closing its teeth on Tony.

"No," Jacques yells.

The creature snaps and gnaws, Tony shouting, "Kill it."

I push forward, ensnaring it with Dark, Sterling at my side. Gold wraps join ours. I flex, straining with my mind and every muscle as the creature thrashes.

Silver light grows brighter, thread after thread racing around the torso and neck. They glow, stinging my eyes, then set alight with flickering gold, sinking into the beast.

It roars, spitting out Tony.

I yank and stumble, limbs ripping free.

The thing comes apart with a sickening crunch of gore and blood splatter, dissolving into a heap of shadows that wick away toward the walls.

Natalia falls, hitting the stone and rolling head over heels to pop to her feet.

Sterling laughs, but she runs straight for Jacques and Palak, kneeling next to them. "Don't move."

I move to Tony, searching for wounds.

He pants, shoving his hair back. "I'm good."

I meet his eyes. "How?"

"Barrier." He laughs. "It never sank its teeth in me. Hurt like a fucking son of a bitch, though. Fortifying that much Ki isn't the problem, easy these days, but the force has to go somewhere." He shakes his head, doubling over. "Felt that in my soul."

I lift my chin at Zander. "Take him." I shove Tony toward him. "Get out."

Zander spreads his wings, and I rush to Natalia.

Jacques helps Palak to his feet, then hoists him over his shoulder. "Leaving?"

I grab Natalia, spreading my wings. "Yes."

She presses a hand to my chest as I coil my abs, ready to lift. "Cal, stop. I can't."

I freeze, glaring down at her. "Can't?"

"If I cheat and leave, he kills everyone I know a name for."

Sterling steps to us. "The rest of you go. Get out." He brushes a finger over her cheek, trying to tuck wisps of her hair behind her ear, feeling around it to her jaw, caressing along it toward her chin. "We'll stay."

CHAPTER 36
NATALIA

I stare up at my mates. They'll stay for me.

I shake my head. "No. Go. All of you. He wanted me in here alone. If I cheat him..."

Names course through my head. I didn't know I had so many to give.

Cal's jaw jumps at corners in a display of ire. "I'm not leaving you alone in this thing."

I press my face to his chest, his heart pulsing wildly. "Sterling did it on his own."

He laughs.

He doesn't think I can do it. It sings to my soul, my Light whimpering.

Sterling hooks a finger around my chin, drawing my face in his direction. "You'll survive. We know that, but it's brutal. Trust me, Firefly. I've done it." He jerks his head. "The rest of you go."

"Oh?" Shadows swarm and build. Mallafic glares at me.

I shove Cal away, turning to face Mallafic and shield Cal and Sterling from him. "I didn't cheat you. I didn't run."

"No, no, Darling Toy. I enjoy this...charade."

I send my Light to wrap around Cal and Sterling, pull them together, and keep them close and safe.

They grunt behind me, and I lift my hand. "Whatever sick thoughts you have, you can keep them to yourself. They go. I'll—"

Mallafic's laugh cuts me off. "You forget you are the doll whose strings I pull."

I press my lips, and he steps forward, holding my gaze.

"Shall we test the truth? See who is right?" He presses a curved talon to the underside of my jaw. "They were quick to come, and to save the life of that thing." He rips the nail across my skin, leaving my jaw to pulse as he points at Palak.

I send Ki through me to heal. The sting remains.

He lifts his finger, licking the claw. "Terribly unfair that I must limit myself in tasting you. Not like before."

I rub the wound, my fingertips sending a burn across my skin. I pull back to stare at the blood on my fingers.

"Have you figured out your puzzle? It's daunting to know everything. The patience I have is the fruit of a millennium in waiting."

He made me an Ancient of sorts. They can't heal the wounds of the crystals. He's pieces of his soul.

"The crystals..." I stare at him, fumbling with the fragments of truth.

"Perhaps not yet. Never thee mind. We have so much time together to play."

He steps back, pressing his hands together as he looks around. It's almost as if he bounces with glee, a wide smile ripping across his face.

"A trial then, a fair one, though what would I know of such things?" He laughs. "You'll..."

He goes still, an apparition forming in translucent green next to him of a gorgeous woman with big, wide-set eyes and a small nose. She glints as she reaches toward him. "Cornu."

He snarls and slashes at her with his claws, turning to slam a hand into the maze wall. "I imparted the magic to make you, and you exist at my deign and behest. You'll not leech on my mind and torment me."

The maze trembles.

He whips to face me, snarling. "You sought unity, what better trial than trust? If there is strength, respect can be earned. If there is cowardice and weakness, then die. Prove unto me what I refuse to accept in blind belief."

He vanishes.

I rub my jaw, facing Cal and Sterling. They glower, bound together in my Light, Cal's head shoved onto Sterling's shoulder.

Sterling lifts his eyebrows. "What is this? Can we stop? I know I'm bound and fucked for life, but this seems less than useful."

Cal grins, closing his eyes like he's laughing.

My Light unwinds, letting them push apart.

"We need to move." Sterling rubs the back of his neck.

Cal looks around. "There are too many of us. We need to split up. Palak, Zan, Tony, what are you afraid of?"

A hiss precedes a warbling yowl, a cat launching toward Cal from thin air.

He twists to evade, flailing at it.

It disappears, and he glares at me with his hands on his hips.

That was new. Cal kept saying the maze wasn't attacking him, focusing on me instead.

I lift my eyebrows. "Cats?"

"Don't like cats."

"Telra?" I giggle.

"No." He rubs the back of his left hand over scars, small and white. "Tony fears...?"

"Ki-blocker, heights and sharks. Insects that buzz and sting freak me out. Not excited by snakes, either."

Jacques throws his arm across his shoulder. "You'll be with me." Jacques flicks a long, forked tongue at him. "Snakes are friends."

Tony lurches, shying away.

Jacques licks at Tony again with his black, snake tongue. "I can smell your fear. It's cute." He smiles, fangs in view.

Shaking his head with a faint smile, Cal says, "Don't scare him to death. Leave that to the maze. Zan?"

Zander straightens his shirt, smoothing his hand down his center, reminiscent of Pierre's tick.

Palak shakes his head, saying, "Soewolves, smoragons, and shadow serpents. You know, the really dangerous things in the world. Obviously, Shadow Beasts, anything Dark related, really, and drowning. Not good with being in forests since my father died in one. Getting sick. My Light dying. Fire salamanders. Having—"

"Everything." Cal shakes his head. "Zan?"

Lightning flashes down around us. Cal, Sterling, and Jacques all duck, shielding as smaller targets on the floor.

I smile at Tony's confusion. "Smites. That will happen a lot."

Cal crouches on the balls of his feet, clenching his hands.

I step to him, winding my Light around him. "It's okay, babe."

Sterling shudders, staring further down the corridor.

I look, fire racing along the walls on both sides. "Oh."

It whooshes with extreme heat rushing past us and extending as far as I can see. The air shimmers around us, putrid with warmth.

Sterling gets smaller, lowering to the floor with his head down. "Guess it finally realized I was here."

Palak looks around. "What the fuck is it doing?"

I point to him, looking at Jacques. "Take him and Tony. I'll take these three."

Jacques lifts two fingers, pivoting his wrist. "Try to have fun." He tangles Dark around Tony and Palak, turning away. "You two do everything I say, starting now, and as much as I love the use of a mouth, don't talk back."

Tony nods, ripping around with Jacques, the men running.

I tap Cal on the shoulder. "Up, babe." I move as he rises, getting to Sterling. "You, too, babe two."

He looks to me, his face lax and eyes stretching open. "Fire."

"Very good." I nod. "Fire." I point to the walls, talking to him like a child. "Burn. Ow. Don't touch."

He lets out a warbling laugh. "Firefly."

I stand, sweat beading across my scalp and along my spine. "No marshmallows, but how about three turns and you get a kiss?"

He gets up, stumbling into the middle of the corridor. "I'll play for that and copping a feel while I do it."

"Need to see my boobs?"

Cal puts his hand on my lower back, guiding me forward. "Boobs later. Move now."

Giggles fill the air.

He groans low. "Hate these things."

Zander steps closer, eyeing the wall. "What is it doing?"

Cal points to Sterling. "He watched his father burn. She was locked in a building with clowns that chased her with knives. It's digging those moments out to terrorize them, and it will use those things to kill you while you're terrified."

We all turn toward the source of the giggles, a figure of Zander wafting in the shimmering heat.

"Are you afraid of yourself?"

Zander shakes his head, staring at himself. "No."

The phantom turns cruel with glee, mimicking Zander's voice. "I don't wear a mask."

Cal shoves me through the figure. "We don't have other players, so I'm not worried about rushing into a mess or another threat. We run. The faster we move, the better."

Sterling strides forward, throwing me over his shoulder and wrapping me in Dark as he takes off.

Cal grabs Zander by the sleeve of his shirt, pulling him forward, to chase after us.

A wall starts to slide closed, cutting between us.

I reach, screaming, "Cal."

Sterling stops, twisting back.

I press my hand to his back, forcing my body to bend. I can't look away.

Dark engulfs Zander, throwing him through the shrinking hole, then Cal launches forward, the wall almost shut, cackling with flames.

"Cal!"

He rolls across the floor next to Zander, shoving to his feet. "I'm here, Little Star. Go."

Zander wraps everyone in gold, pulling us closer to him as he stares beyond. "Might I suggest that be addressed?"

I turn my head and scream, clawing at Sterling as dozens of spiders run toward us.

"Tal, stop," Sterling yanks me off his shoulder.

Cal rolls his shoulders. "Get behind me."

I shake, frozen. Sterling drags me to Cal's side as Cal sends Dark down the hall. It denotes, shaking the world and filling it with flames.

Screams fill the air. The heat intensifies, drying my cheeks and lips. Sterling sways and curls onto the floor.

The flames clear to reveal dozens of spiders lining the floor, fried and curled in on themselves.

Sterling moans, hiding his head. "Gods, I'm going to burn."

I crouch to him. "No."

"You both burn," he dry-sobs into his hands. "Both of you."

Cal drags me up, yanking Sterling to his feet next. He slaps his hand to Sterling's face. "If you catch on fire, I'll put you out of your misery before the flames kill you."

Sterling features flinch. "You two are going to be the death of me."

I jump at him, wrapping my arms and legs around his torso. "Not today."

I grab his jaw, pressing my mouth to his. He groans, his Dark tightening around me as his mouth opens and his hand tangles in my hair, angling my head.

Pulling back, I knock my nose against his. "You get me through the spiders, I'll get you through the flames, and we keep Cal distracted about small places."

He leans back, hooking a finger under the front of my dress to peel it away and sneaks a glance down my front. "Those are the best things in the world. These specifically. There are many like them, but these are mine. For them, I'll do anything."

Cal shoves Sterling forward. "Our agreement is suspended for the moment, Zan."

"I've come to the realization I would be forced to endure."

I glance between them, asking Cal with my face.

He presses his lips, jerking his head at Zander. "He doesn't like seeing you with other men. Start running, Sterling. Zan and I will follow."

CHAPTER 37

CALLAHAN

Several corridors later, turning at every available moment, Sterling comes to a halt.

"Not me," he says, turning back.

I lean around him, eyeing the black pool stretching before us. I meet Natalia's eyes. "Hers."

Zander toes the edge, frowning at the water. "Understandable."

We've encountered clowns, spiders, the maze constantly burning. I'm drenched in sweat, and if I remember correctly, that water is going to be cold.

"It will be a relief from the heat."

Claws scratch down my back, and I twist my torso forward to dislodge the cat. It hits the stone with a meow, getting up to hiss at me before strolling away, and walking across the water.

I roll my shoulders, my back stinging. I hate cats and their unpredictable mentality.

Zander asks, "Can't we just fly over it?"

"No."

I start pulling my shirt off, hesitating. I've never hesitated before. I'm wearing a mask. It's not real, not my true face or form.

Closing my eyes, I rip my shirt off. It doesn't matter. Natalia's my mate. She knows. She doesn't care.

Sterling curls his lip. "What's in the water?"

Natalia shudders. "Tentacles."

She almost drowned last time. I hadn't been prepared. I will be this time.

Setting her down, Sterling steps up the corridor.

Zander has his head turned, watching over his shoulder. "What are you doing?"

Bones snap and break at my back. I glare at Zander. He doesn't have to do this. They don't have another form, pretty and perfect to the core.

Natalia smiles, hiding her mouth and words behind a hand. "Shifting." She snickers. "At least I know it's you this time."

"Ha." I press my shoulder blades together and exhale, letting my Dark go.

It presses through my skin, breaking my limbs to fuse into them, morphing me into us.

I crouch and shake away the sensation, snapping my tail.

Sterling steps to my side, and I stand, forcing him to tilt his head to look up at me.

He grins, fangs exposed beneath the curved beak nose. "You do that on purpose."

"I'm taller than you. You conveniently forget that." I stalk to the edge, lingering on the precipice.

Zander throws an arm out in front of me. "Why can't we fly?"

"It'll block off, close you in."

Sterling moves to my other side. "In here, you have to face your fear. It's the only way out. Are you afraid of water?"

Zander shakes his head. "No."

"Drowning?"

"No."

"Something in it?"

Zander glowers. "No. There is nothing about or in water that scares me."

I snap my teeth. "What are you afraid of? Other than something you can't kill with a smite."

A phantom of Zander appears out over the water, laughing at us. "Wouldn't you like to know?"

"You know." I point at it. "How about tormenting him instead of the rest of us for a change?"

"What if that's it? What if my fear is something that only exists in my mind? What if..." It fades away. "What if I don't have a vulnerability?"

Sterling shrugs. "I'll go first, Tal?" He glances behind us. "Tal? Tal!"

I whip around. The wall is cracked apart, revealing a narrow view of a corridor beyond this one, wide enough for Natalia to have slipped through.

It's lined with mirrors. I can discern that much. Natalia walks further away from us, approaching a young man with dark blond hair.

I get two steps forward.

Mallafic materializes in front of me, his black irises sparkling in the fire. "Reunions are sweet, are they not?"

To his back, the maze shifts, closing off and sealing Natalia away.

I lift a claw in the direction of my star. "Who is that?"

"Not quite a reunion." Mallafic chuckles. "He's in the afters, after all, but I amuse myself in creations."

I try to push past, but Mallafic steps in my way, shoving his hand to my chest. Force slams through me, sending me into the wall.

Flames rush over me, crawling like a hundred ants across my skin. They tingle with heat but don't penetrate my flesh.

I catch myself on all fours, snarling at Mallafic.

"I don't think you should interrupt." Mallafic disappears. "You have another game to play. Leave her to hers. It was always the way I meant it to be."

I shake myself off and stand.

Zander steps to my side, staring at the burning wall. "The water is gone."

Sitting back on my hindquarters, I wait, twitching my tail in annoyance. The maze will shift again. I just have to give it time.

A cat launches at me.

I rake my claws through it, growling. "Quit doing that."

Sterling steps in front of me, his feathered wings rustling at his back. "We need to go."

"No."

"Cal."

"Mate." I point, extending my arm past him.

He ducks his chin. "It knows we're afraid to lose her. It's not going to give her back, and we can't linger."

I look into his eyes and whine, "Mate."

Sterling bobs his head, looking over his shoulder. "She earned us in strength. All we can do now is have faith in that strength."

"You believe she can do it?"

"Are you questioning her or asking because I have experience?" One side of his face scrunches, like he's trying to smirk and can't get his muscles to cooperate.

"You've done it."

"Three times. It wasn't luck, it was me. I survived on my strength."

I ball my fist and slam it against the floor. "We move."

I stalk down the corridor, leading this time, picking up my

pace to a jog as the corridor stretches. No options to turn are available. It's a bad sign. It's forcing us toward something.

Ahead, the merging corridors end, emptying us into a round room.

I stop, not wanting to enter and lose the way out, but Zander keeps walking.

He pivots, frowning at me, his movements fluid. He's long and thin, like his face.

"I don't recall this when we flew over searching for Tallie."

I shake, snorting through my snout. "It's alive. It moves, shifts, makes itself what it wants."

He lifts his hand, opening and closing it to direct me in. "You said face it. Let's get it over with."

I use my tail to shove Sterling into the room as I step forward. The ground shakes, the way out disappearing.

I hunch over, growling.

Phantoms appear, my little star straddling Zander, her head thrown back as she rocks on top of him.

Dark streaks from me and Sterling races through it.

It splits, reforming as mirroring images.

Sterling throws his hands up. "This isn't a fear, stupid fucking stone."

Zander hums, turning his back on the displays. "Is it a puzzle?"

I glance around, the air filling with flesh smacking together, the ghost of Natalia moaning.

Sterling crouches, cocking his jaw at the floor. "No, or I'd be having a lot more fun. There's never anything to figure out. It's not that kind of game."

I strum my talons, trying to ignore the phantoms. Natalia mated me. I had to wrangle her into realizing we were keeping Sterling. She knows where she belongs. Not a doubt exists in my mind on the matter.

Sterling flings his hand at the figures. "Will you stop that? It's not a fear. It's annoying."

His Dark stabs through the pair. It divides, splitting. Three Natalias ride three Zanders, the moans becoming louder.

Zander rubs his forehead, glancing at them, then turns away.

Sterling scoffs. "Fantasy?"

"Reality. When I pulled her from the sea, I took her to land. She had been enthusiastic."

I sit, swaying my tail side to side and pulling my upper lip back, exposing my teeth.

This isn't about me. It's not revealing much, other than the position. Annoying as it is, that's all that it is.

Turning my head, I watch Sterling. He's got his knees bent, leaning forward to balance on flat feet, his wings tucked at his back. Ire shines on his face, but no fear.

The room isn't on fire, and the walls haven't begun to slink inward. It would be too easy to send Sterling and me into a state of panic with this room. It's not doing anything.

"Look at it."

Sterling jerks his chin. "I am. I hate it."

"It's tormenting us, but this isn't for us. Zander," I snap. "Face it."

He pivots, staring down on the figures.

All three of him turn their heads to laugh at him. "Can't smite this," they say in unison.

Sterling laughs. "It has a point."

Zander's Light turns blue. *Zzts* fill the air.

I close my eyes and brace.

Cracks split the world, everything brilliant behind my closed eyelids.

I open my eyes as the Zanders laugh, all six of them.

The Natalias keep grinding, moaning louder still.

He crosses his arms. "What do you want from me?"

360

More figures appear—Natalia kissing Zander's cheek, telling him, "Have a nice life."

They twist and rearrange, Natalia standing in front of a version of me, saying, "I'll sign your contract."

I scoff. "That's not how it happened." I flick the stone, then stretch to my full height. This thing reacts differently to Light than it does to Dark.

It pulls fears to wield death for Dark, but it becomes vicious to the Light. I watched it tear into Natalia, ripping her apart to make her believe she was useless.

She was afraid of that, but it went deeper. This correlates to something, designed to hurt and make him bleed internally.

"She fought me," I say. "She took the contract because she wanted to be away from the Magia, not because she wanted me."

Zander rounds on me. "I could have given her that. If I had known who she was..." He drops his hand in his other hand, laughing in broken heaves. "She would have been mine if I hadn't been blind."

I sit, scratching at my ear with my back leg. "You're a moron."

He lifts his face.

I sit, stretching my back. "You think taking her to Izul before she met me changes things between you? It doesn't."

"You don't know that," he shouts, leaning into his words. His cheeks turn pink, his white eyes gleaming. "I've spent my life priding myself on my heritage, on my name. I bowed my head, and I've always done what is asked of me in respect of duty." He flings his hand to the phantoms. "What has it gotten me? A love that isn't reciprocated. She chose animals over me."

Sterling stands, his wings shifting, feathers scraping together. "You Lights make everything complicated, even your fears." He nudges me. "It's using his fear to fuck with us, too. Devious, but brilliant."

I snap my tail at him.

He dodges and grins. "Down, Boy." He faces Zander, pointing at the continuing sex. "It is a fantasy."

"It happened."

"Sure, but that's not Tal. It's someone you concocted in your mind. She says you're in love with a woman who doesn't exist."

"She... She just needed...guidance. If I had gotten to her sooner—"

I whack Zander with my tail. "There you go again, being stupid. You keep thinking about how you can change her, make her who you want."

Sterling shakes his head. "Some little Bordeaux princess."

"You said it yourself. You preferred her when she was curbed."

"Yeah." Sterling turns his face toward me, winking with a grin. "She says sarcasm was forbidden. She couldn't curse, either. You heard her the other night. She sounded like a different woman."

I shudder. "You didn't see her when she turned up. I looked right through her, thinking she was a Glow Fuck."

Sterling grimaces. "That dress..."

I yelp in short barks of humor. "Never."

"I'll tear anything off her." Shrugging, Sterling crosses his arms, staring Zander down. "You're afraid you've wasted your life on duty."

Zander twists away. "What if I have? It cost me her. It cost Pierre's life." He faces us, his face contorted. "He told me to save you and leave him. I served him, loved him like a father. He was a father to me."

Swinging at the air, he twists away from the phantoms again, turning his back on the illusion of what was, the hauntings of what he thinks could have been.

"I saved a mutt over the brightest Light of this world with

more wisdom and dignity than either of you. I let a woman who could have shone as brilliantly go, handing her that same dog."

Pushing air out my nose, I tell him, "I am not a dog."

He looks at me, lifts his eyebrows, and then gestures down at me.

I face the wall. "I'm a Mandolux."

"Half breed, mutt, not even the Dark."

I clamp my jowls and growl, "You're pushing my patience."

Zander's Light dims, shifting around him to a deep blue. "Your entire existence is a mistake resulting in a mess no one wants."

The air hums.

I call on my Dark. "Natalia wants me."

The air claps.

Sterling shoves me to the side, a streak of whitish-blue ripping from above straight through him.

I grip the stone with my claws, stopping myself and twisting back.

His knees buckle, his body folding to the ground with a soft thump.

I scream, my Dark stretching out to wrap around him. I lunge forward, hovering over him.

His eyes are closed. I nudge him, but he remains limp and lifeless. "Sterling. Sterling." I shake him. "Mate."

My Dark thrashes, one strand poking Sterling's cheek. His head rocks.

I growl from my soul, turning on Zander.

He sneers. "There isn't a thing in this world that smites don't work against."

I'll prove him wrong before I tear his throat out for harming my mate.

CHAPTER 38

NATALIA

Water. The first time I went through the maze I'd been less than excited but above fear. Seeing the pool of black water this time raises the hairs on the back of my neck.

Sterling shifts, tar black skin and huge wings of feathers that glint blue. He's sculpted muscle with a sharp, curved beak nose and talons, a shadow of death.

Cal shifts next, transforming into a creature of bone and fire. He's a predator, carved as a weapon with little weakness.

My mates, both impressive. My Light and heart both flutter with adoration.

They move to the pool, standing at the edge and discussing.

The wall splits, the two sides opening to reveal a face I haven't seen in years.

He smiles at me, his brown eyes soft as they crinkle at the corners. Large, upturned eyes like mine. Our mother's eyes.

He looks to the floor, running his hand over his hair from back to front, smoothing the honey-blond strands into place.

Looking to me again, he starts to walk backward.

I reach for him, rushing forward as I breathe his name. "Nicky."

I slip through the opening, chasing him as he moves backward down the aisle. Mirrors reflect his round face on either side. It's him. It's my brother. I'd know his face anywhere, no matter how long it's been.

"Tal," Sterling yells.

I ignore him, refusing to take my eyes off Nick. He's closer, almost within my reach. I can almost grab hold, to get my hands on him and be able to keep him safe.

"Nicky," I whisper, putting my hands on his shoulders. I grip, digging my fingers into him. He was always scrawny, but it belied the strength in him. He worked out every day, whining that he couldn't bulk up like others.

He'd been able to lift more weight than most. It hadn't mattered. He'd wanted to look good for Sarah. He said she had to marry him, and he was going to be the best man in the world to deserve that blessing from the Mother.

Their marriage might have been arranged, but he'd loved her all the same.

"Nicky." I laugh, tearing up and wrapping my arms around him. He's solid and warm, and a heart beats within his chest. I pull back, staring in amazement. "How? How are...?"

The mirrors ripple, scenes playing out moments I relive in nightmares that leave me crying and shaking.

Nick told me the night before his initiation that he couldn't stop thinking about Sasha. She'd been the best but still had failed. I'd reassured him that he'd pass. I'd gone through it. I knew what he was capable of, and he'd be fine.

Another scene appears, Nick dressed in a suit, trying to smile. I'd fixed his collar and told him to go, that he'd be fine. I was waiting for him when he was done.

My mom led him through the doors, smiling and hugging Nick. "Here, drink this, it'll calm your nerves."

I can't look away. The scene rewinds and replays, my mother handing him the glass, telling him to drink.

I remember that. I hadn't given it a second thought. We all knew he was scared.

The initiation was rigged for him and my sister. They'd been given a poisonous concoction designed to be impossible to survive.

I let go of Nick, my wonder turning to suspicion.

He cocks his head, but the mirrors show the truth.

I'd paced in front of the doors, waiting, holding my breath until I couldn't, then started again.

Nick had started to scream, begging.

"No, no, please, please."

Against the rules, against traditions, I had entered the room.

Nick was on his knees, holding our mother's hands in his while he sobbed and pleaded.

I'd yelled. I'd demanded. I'd threatened. I'd tried. I'd failed.

I had been too busy fighting to hold my brother's hand when he slipped to the afters.

Nick shines in every mirror, staring at me with blood rolling down his face from his eyes. "You said I'd be fine."

The man in front of me asks, "Do I look fine?"

I turn to him. Blood trails down his cheeks, his lips white, stained with blood, his skin waxy and white, translucent with black veins pulsing beneath.

"Nicky," I manage, my voice warbling. "Nicky, I'm... I'm sorry."

The mirrors shift, the visions of Nick enlarging. "Why didn't you help me? You said I'd be fine. Why wasn't I fine?"

Me.

No matter how I try to answer the question, the answer is

me. I was the one they wanted to breed. I failed to help him. I told him he'd be fine, not to abdicate training.

I am the reason my brother is dead.

I sniff, blinking out tears and using the back of my hand to clean my nose. "Nick..."

Sweet, kindhearted, soft spoken, good Nick begged for his life, and I'm why.

The man before me sneers. "Why wasn't I fine? Can't you tell the truth?"

I stare at him, my eyes welling up. "I'm sorry."

"Sorry?"

"I didn't...know. I didn't know what they—"

"You." He jabs a finger into my shoulder. "You said I'd be fine. You told me not to abdicate training. You said I could do it."

"They changed everything."

"You didn't stop it. You didn't protect me. You lied to me."

I reach for my brother, but he steps back. I fall to my knees, sobbing. "I didn't know. You have to believe me. I believed in you. I believed myself."

I extend my hand, hoping he'll take it and help me up.

He doesn't.

I lean forward, pleading with tears falling over my lower lashes. "Nicky, please."

"I begged you."

The mirrors flash, Nick on his knees, begging to back out, to be saved, to abdicate.

I tremble, watching the horror of his final moments replay in dozens of screens surrounding me. Memories are fuzzy, distorted by the haze of mental view and time. This is crystal clear detail of my brother's tear-stained face, his nose red, and the broken, pleading tone as he pants for air, shaking and crying.

He'd tried to give them everything they could possibly want.

He'd promised them anything they wanted if they'd spare his life.

He offered to leave, to never let them see him again.

He promised to stay quiet, that he'd still marry Sarah and give them more children.

Nick leans over in front of me, staring with vehement disdain. "I'd known as I begged," he whispers. "I'd known why."

"Me."

His brown eyes ignite, turning to amber and orange. "I died for you, because of you, and you let it happen. You lied to me, and you didn't protect me, and it's your fault that I had to die at all."

Lifting his hand between us, he splays his fingers. A soft *snick* accompanies talons extending from his fingertips.

He dials back and swings his hand at me. I flinch, lifting my hands as I rock back. His claws drag across my chest, tearing through my skin.

"Nicky," I sob. "Please, please, you have to believe me. I didn't know they would k–kill you. I didn't know what I was. I didn't know that they'd—"

He launches at me, tackling me to the ground to claw at me.

My Light winds around his arms, trying to stop him as I shake beneath him on my back, my hands up.

Talons drag across my palms and wrists, and I scream in my throat, keeping my mouth closed. Blinking out the tears, I whimper up at him.

He screams, thrashing.

My Light tells me to fight.

I can't. I can't hurt Nick. I'd failed him in so many ways. My baby brother, who would look at me with adoration. He looked at me like I could save him right before he died, trusting in me until the bitter end.

Gold ropes wrap around him, dragging him backward.

He screams, a shrill cry of anguish. "Tallie! Tallie, help me. Please, please Tallie. Help me."

I cry, frozen.

"Tallie, help me. Please! Please, don't let me die. Don't let me die again."

Grotesque snaps and squeals fill the world, then silence.

I sob, dropping my arms and staring up at the hazed sky of gray above the towering mirrors.

Ashley's face floats above me, blood splattered across one cheek. "What are you doing?"

"N–Nick."

"That thing is dead. Get up."

"N–no," I sob, rolling over and crawling along the stone to his body.

I'd done this before, crawled to his limp, lifeless corpse with tears of pain. I'd fought with the skills I'd had, but I'd only earned defensive marks. I hadn't known how to fight back with any effect. My arm had been broken, bone pushed through as I'd crawled, every time I picked up my hand and put it down, leaned on it, I'd whimpered at the pain streaking through me, into my shoulder and chest.

"Nicky." I get closer. There's so much blood, his chest ripped open, his neck bulging and snapped at a sick angle. "Nick."

The volume of the world turns up, Nick begging me, the mirrors flashing and replaying his final moments.

I pick his head up, cradling it in my hands, trying to drag him closer, to keep him close and safe.

My baby brother.

I force my Light to wrap around the body, to bring it into my arms and lap. Closing my eyes, I rock him, crying in guilt and grief.

It starts again, the memory replaying around me.

The body of my brother is yanked away.

I open my eyes, trying to pull him back.

Ashley shoves a hand to my chest, her Light flinging Nick away.

"No," I scream, pushing back. "No. You aren't going to do that to him."

I twist, scrambling toward him.

Gold Light twists around me, dragging me back. I thrash, dragging my fingers across the stone, begging her to let go.

He's shrinking into the distance.

I claw at the ground, wishing I had talons to embed and stop myself. I lift one hand, reaching out for my brother. "Nicky!"

I'm pulled around a corner, the echoes of the past chasing me. I can still hear them. They'll never stop.

Ashley grabs me, forcing me on my butt. She shoves me upright against the wall, kneeling on one knee in front of me. "What in Adontis's name is wrong with you?"

I shudder, suckling at air. "Nick. Nicky. I have to go back. I have to help him."

Her sculpted eyebrows come together, the front parts raising over the bridge of her nose. "Who is Nicky?"

"My brother. He's my brother." I stare at her face. It distorts, tears glazing my eyes.

She shakes her head. "Father said you lost your siblings. He was quite clear on that as an excuse for your violent behavior and why I had to accept you."

"It was him. It was Nicky."

She dials back and slaps me.

I jerk, opening my mouth to gape.

"Now, perhaps you'll have rationality. Dead is dead, and there's no returning. That thing wasn't even human."

I stare at her, immobile and dumb. My heart doesn't want to mash that logic into comprehension. Instead, my mind fixates on her. "What are you doing here?"

"Never send men to do a job when you have a woman available." She shrugs. "None of you returned, so I came to resolve the matter."

She stands, offering her hand. When I don't move, she snaps her fingers and extends her open hand again.

"Give me your hand."

I do.

She hauls me to my feet, clicking her tongue. She starts wiping my face, licking her thumb to rub a spot on my cheek clean. "Cry on the inside, Sister Mine. Tears ruin makeup and make us ugly."

She looks around us, scowling. Clasping my wrist, she pulls me closer, peering down the corridor.

She laughs. "I know you're there. Come out, darling."

Mallafic steps from the shadows into view, more collecting around him.

Ashley smiles. "It's not polite to lurk or listen in on conversations, even for a god."

Mallafic narrows his eyes. "Leave, wretch. That is my plaything, and you've interfered enough."

Ashley holds an open palm up, wiggling her torso side to side as she grips my wrist harder. "Plaything. Sibling. Plaything. Sibling. I do believe my claim outranks yours."

He whisks through the air, standing almost on top of her to stare down his nose at her. "She has a similar seed but became mine the moment I put my hat on her head."

"Yes." Ashley drags the word out, then rolls her lower lip out, pouting. "But that doesn't erase my claim. She's still my sister and still the Light, even if she's part of the Dark."

I'm tempted to ask who this woman is and if she's really Ashley.

Ashley taps Mallafic's chest, the tip of her finger moving in and out of view. "That's the problem, isn't it? We won't be one or the other anymore, and you're throwing a tantrum."

He narrows his eyes.

"*Mhm*." Ashley reaches behind her to flip her ponytail. "I'll be taking my sister now."

He adjusts his black irises to me. "She won't leave. She knows the rules of this game. How much is your claim worth to you? Your life?"

"Sir." She feigns a giggle. "I'll play your stupid game if I must, but I won't abandon my sibling seed."

"So be it." Mallafic disappears.

Ashley shudders. "That thing makes my skin and my Light crawl. Ew."

CHAPTER 39
CALLAHAN

I roll across the stone, my spinal spikes reverberating in my head. On my feet, I twist, taking my claws across Zander's chest.

It's the closest I've come, his shirt ripped, blood staining the white fabric.

I lurch to the side, another crack leaving my ears ringing.

I spent my life ripping the Light from living Glow Fucks. They have to be alive as I drag the Light from them. I've handled smites, learning warning signs and how to avoid the attacks.

Most Lights can't call so many. Zander is different. He hasn't let up once.

I haven't stopped moving long enough to get struck. My body aches and burns, demanding respite. I'll give in when he's dead.

He swings, ropes of gold streaking toward me. My Dark shields and hits back.

Two get past his block, and I swing around, sweeping his legs out with my tail.

I pounce, shoving the barbed end of my tail against the underside of his jaw. Not through.

I meet his white eyes, his features twisted with rage.

Zzts speed up.

I could send him to the afters long before the smite is called. I won't.

I roll off him, slamming my fists to the floor and screaming. This wasn't ever the life I was supposed to have. I wasn't meant for this, but I can't shake off responsibility.

I dig my fingers across the stone, grabbing at the floor, seeking to hold onto my sanity. I could have sent the Light to the afters. Zander could be dead, gone, no longer my problem.

But he's my contracted. I am responsible for him. I'm responsible for all of them, Dark and Light. We can't exist without each other, and I can fix the world by bringing us together.

But not if I kill him.

He put his life in my hands when he signed his contract, even agreeing to a worn contract. That kind of trust isn't to be abused.

Panting, I press my balled fist to the ground and lift onto my back legs. I sit, snarling at him.

He glares. "You stopped."

"Stating the obvious is useless. Be useful, or there's no reason to be contracted."

His thin lips peel apart, his shock evident.

I could have done it. I bested him. I've proved enough. That has to be enough, or nothing will ever change.

I turn and stalk on all fours to Sterling, then sit next to him. My Dark whines, poking at him.

Zander approaches, and I snap my tail at him, warding him from my mate.

He lingers, crouching low on the balls of his feet. "There's still no way out."

I nudge Sterling.

Zander winces. "He's gone."

"No."

"I'm effective, and we need to focus on getting out of here."

I whip my tail again, snapping my teeth. "He's strong. He survived." I pound the ground.

Sterling groans.

I nudge him with my snout again, nuzzling his head.

He reaches up, squeezing his eyes and pressing his hand to my face.

I turn, nipping at him. "Get up."

He breathes out, his chest deflating. "Fuck." His eyes flutter open. "What?"

"That asshole tried to smite me, and you got in the way like an idiot."

"You're welcome?" He sits, rolling forward and bending his knees to his chest to lean against them, one hand to his face. "Fuck, my head hurts."

"Next time, don't."

He squints at me. "Next time?"

I bare my teeth. He's too smart for me to have to explain.

Rubbing his face, Sterling sighs. He rolls to the side, pushing to stand. He sways.

My Dark ravels around him, keeping him upright. "Easy, baby," I say, chuckling in low, snarling breaths.

He drops to a crouch on the floor, steadying himself with his hands. "I get why it's alive, but fuck that thing and fuck you for your insufferable character. I'm your damned mate."

"Love you, too."

He wheezes, his shoulders shaking. "We could have said he died in the maze and left everyone to believe it wasn't our fault."

"You want to claim weakness for allowing it to die?"

"Eh." He stands, teetering a few steps.

My Dark flexes in my mind, trying to give him aid.

He looks to me. "This fucking maze is the bane of my existence. I hate this thing more than anything else in this world. I got smited and we're still trapped."

"That was that fuck."

"It's this fucked thing's fault."

"You think it's playing us, baiting us into killing each other?"

"I know it is. Mallafic is using this as a trial for a reason. It'll dig out fears and pain to turn us against each other. We'll never unify the crowns if we can't get through this together. I knew you'd say it, and he'd do it. I took this hit because I know you'd never fucking let your desires stand in the way of responsibility." Sterling turns to Zander, stretching his arm out to point one talon at the man. "Do it again, and I rip your throat out and say fuck everyone else. I'm not him. I'll send you to the afters without a second thought. Fuck unifying. You hear me?"

Zander straightens. "Forgive me. I lost myself."

"Yeah, that's what this thing does. 'Why can't we go near it?' 'I'm curious,'" Sterling mocks him, then scoffs. "Hope you're having fun, asshole."

Zander ducks his head. "No."

I get up on my back legs and stalk to the wall. I run my claws along it, searching for cracks in the stone as I traverse the circle, leaving behind scratches. I end where I began, no splits in the rock to indicate where I can pry my way out.

I return to Sterling, who has dropped to the floor holding his head.

I sit next to him, looking around. It's quiet, no phantoms of jest lingering. It's us and the maze.

Zander steps closer in small paces, moving slowly with his hands up. The closer he gets, the more shadows swirl and lash around Sterling.

Zander stops next to us, lowering his hands. "What can I do?"

I use my tail to scratch my side. "Wait until it decides what it does next."

After a tense silence, Zander says, "I've thought about the price of duty many times. The sacrifices I've made. It's been more with recent events, but not new. I've never considered it a fear."

"That's because you don't understand fear. It's a belief that something is dangerous, but also that it can cause pain, that it's a threat to you or your life, maybe your way of living." I hunker lower. "Mass... Massimo was afraid of rabbits and coconuts. A rabbit bit his finger when he was in a forest as a boy sometime in his first decade. No matter how old he got, how big he got, rabbits scared him."

I smile at the stupid fear. He was big enough to step on a rabbit. He had enough Dark to kill them with ease from a distance. Yet, he still squirmed at baby bunnies in my yard and demanded I remove them.

I shift my weight to one side, rolling to one haunch. "He'd heard about a news story of a coconut hitting someone in the head and killing them. Some fragile human. He grew up in the north and hadn't ever seen a coconut until he stepped into the maze."

Sterling groans with a laugh. "That's where that came from? I got hit in the head because of a human?"

On the occasions that we crossed paths, Sterling dealt with his fair share of coconuts.

I yelp in humor. "Those things were as awful as Natalia's bouncing balls. I've been hit in the head by them more times than I want to admit."

"What's with the balls?"

"She has no idea."

The ground rumbles, the walls shifting. I stand, searching for the way out. Fire spills over one wall, spreads out to eat its way across the stone while the walls begin closing inward.

Sterling shudders.

I push him toward Zander. "You're my fucking contracted. That's my mate."

He bobs his head. "I understand."

I head for the wall, dragging my claws again as I race the perimeter. I can't determine the exact spot I started, but judge by Sterling and Zander's position.

I stumble backward, forced toward the epicenter by the wall. I flail, losing balance.

The walls pick up speed, grinding faster into the center. I get shoved as I twist, getting my legs under me. I scamper in several strides on all fours to Sterling, curling around him to shield him.

He shakes his head. "First time I try to run the maze with you, and it's when I die."

I growl, keeping my body arched around him. "Shut up."

"It's funny. Usually, this death trap makes me kill you, something that looks like you anyway. I really will kill you this time."

Zander glows, holding his hands cupped together. He starts drawing his hands apart, a gleaming shield growing to encompass us. He trembles, closing his eyes. "Figure it out."

Heat swells. The fire races over the shield, blocking out everything but the shimmering tongues. The walls groan as they strain against Zander's shield.

It wobbles, rocks screeching together.

I can't breathe, refusing to move. Tensing every muscle and locking my joints, I focus on shielding Sterling from the flames. I'll crush or suffocate before I expose him to flames.

The shield shrinks, pressing us all closer. Zander bares his teeth, grunting.

Dark churns from Sterling, pressing into the Light, sliding across the surface and spreading out as ink in water, blotting out the glow of fire and Zander's gilded magic alike.

The world plunges into darkness.

I shudder, enclosed in nothingness.

Sterling grunts. "Fuck, it's still—"

Zander collapses. "I can't take that heat."

Sterling roars, his shield bursting. He thrashes, his Dark waving with flames as it races into him.

My Dark slams through my mind, radiating from me to press into the fiery walls.

It finds an opening, streaking through to taste fresh air before circling around Sterling. I tackle Zander, falling through the flames.

My Dark whips Sterling, sending him sailing.

He thrashes, rolling on the ground as fire burns across his torso.

I shove up, my Dark getting to him first, wrapping him tight to smother the flames.

Zander gets up, patting at flames burning through his shirt. He winces, shaking his head. "How did you know?"

I have my Dark unwind, revealing Sterling, twitching and moaning.

Blisters stretch across his chest, glistening as Zander comes closer. He rattles as he lies there, barely breathing, "I hate this thing."

I sit, poking a scar on his side. It's from me, the very barbed tip of my tail pressing against it. "We all do."

"Why couldn't it be something like butterflies?"

"Don't tempt this thing. I don't want flying things with razor wings cutting us open."

"Gods," Sterling groans and rolls forward, hissing and wincing, but stands. "You're right. It would do that."

They're both injured. Zander's chest still oozing in the visible slits of his shirt. Sterling's upper body has massive burns. It's still a long way from the end.

"I'll lead. Let's move," I say, stalking forward.

A glow spreads along the walls, fire crackling and popping.

I stop, two figures approaching. My stomach turns to acid as I stare at myself, a human version of me stalking forward next to a human version of Sterling.

He sighs. "Yeah, that's about right."

Zander glows blue, dropping two smites into the figures without effect. I flinch into Sterling.

Zander groans and curses. "It's not possible."

I yelp in humor. "Quit smiting. It's never going to work on anything in here."

Sterling nudges me. "Do you want to kill me...or yourself?"

A third figure comes running toward us, lithe and slender with long silver hair. She giggles.

Sterling turns into me. "No. Fuck no."

"Zan, you take Talia."

He shudders, taking a step back. "You cannot ask—"

"You know how she accepted you, then mated me? Get angry. Do it. Sterling...I'll take myself."

CHAPTER 40

NATALIA

Ashley clicks her tongue, inspecting me.

I roll my eyes. "I'm healed. Now let's go. We need to move."

"Find the center, but you don't know where it is or how to get there. Yes, you explained you are severely lacking in insights to complete this task."

"It moves and changes."

She steps back, motioning me with disdain and two fingers. "Shall we?"

Crossing her legs, she spins, striding down the corridor with her head high.

I look behind me, rotting inside. My Light wraps around me, echoing in hollow throbs that find nothing but broken defiance.

Whatever corridor that had taken place in has disappeared, swallowed by stone and shadows to be lost in memory once again.

"Move," Cal's voice whispers to me, my Light talking in my head as it squeezes around me. *"We have to keep moving."*

I chase after Ashley, catching up to fall in step. "What are you afraid of?"

"Nothing."

"Right. This thing is going to bring your fears to life. What can we expect?"

She stops, staring down her nose at me. "Nothing. I do not fear anything."

"You were afraid of the shadow serpent."

"Nerves prepare us to act. Shadow serpents should raise an alarm within one to ensure we show proper respect and are prepared to address the situation."

"Fine, we can expect it to create shadow serpents to make you nervous. What else?"

She stops at the end of the corridor with only two choices: to either turn right or left. She looks both ways, blinking at me. "Well? You have done this before, have you not? Anything familiar?"

I turn left. "Spiders and clowns, mirrors and bouncing red balls, ghosts of my sister and father," I say, listing off the things I've experienced. "Water, something in it that will pull you under."

"Dreary expectations. We burn the spiders," she wiggles her fingers with firelight flickering between them. "We, well, I will smite the clowns. Why ever would you have a problem with mirrors? You'll have a chance to admire my beauty from multiple angles. I have no idea what to do with bouncy balls, but I imagine we can throw them to the other end of the corridor. Ignore the ghosts, they are figments of death easily discarded, and..."

She stops.

I press my lips at the phantom of Akash.

He tilts his head to the side. "So easily discarded indeed. You replace me effortlessly without pain."

She clicks her tongue. "I cherish my time with my brightest light." She walks through it. "His death has scarred me to my core. Tony is an adequate placeholder until I find Akash in the afters, fulfilling in ways of pleasure and emotional support."

A vision of Pierre whisks into existence. "So easily discarded, am I?"

Ashley never breaks stride, moving through him. "I honor our father by remaining steadfast in his wishes of working to unify our kind and furthering the respect of our heritage with dignity."

I turn left again, down a new corridor lined with mirrors.

Ashley stops, fussing with a single strand of her hair, trying to wiggle it into its place in her war braid. She presses her lips, checks her lipstick by running a finger under her lower lip at the corner, and faces me.

"When the shadow serpent comes, remove its heart. It's the only way to kill them."

She keeps walking.

I move to the mirror, staring at myself. My chest is stained pink and red with smeared blood, my forearms as well. The tip of my nose twitches back at me, my cheeks ruddy.

Ashley steps next to me. "I cursed your face upon meeting you. I'd hoped you were vile, and I could refrain from accepting you as one of us, for nothing of the Light could be haggard or unbecoming in appearance."

I meet her eyes in the mirror.

She shrugs. "Of course, you're beautiful. You're a Bordeaux." Flashing a grin, she shoves me. "Shall we, honey?"

I stumble to the side and keep my eyes low, face to the floor.

Hisses draw my eyes up, a shadow serpent barring us from proceeding.

Ashley looks to me. "You do know where the heart is, yes?"

"Between the front legs."

"Oh, good. I'll go for the heart, dig it out. You shall manage the heads."

She runs forward. I send my Light to tangle the necks, wrestling them from reaching Ashley.

Her Light pierces the center, digging out a mass. The beast roars and disappears.

Ashley laughs, turning to me. "That's delightful. The exercise without the gore."

I open my mouth, narrowing one eye. I don't think she flinched.

INTERMIXING with my clowns and spiders, the maze spits out creations I presume are aimed at tormenting my sister. No matter what the maze throws at Ashley, she won't confess to being afraid.

Watching phantoms of Tony die forces her to declare frustration because she'd have to find a replacement.

Jewel-winged bugs swarm us and slice our skin. Ashley demands I heal her before myself. She will not tolerate the pain, not because she fears scars.

The closest I saw her to fear was a pool of blood we were forced to cross. She refused, trying to fly over it despite my warning it wouldn't work. We ended up stuck between two walls with no other option.

She gave up with a huff, dropping into the fluid, yelling at me to get in. When I did, the walls retracted. We swam toward one side. Long, muscular tentacles wrapped around us, trying to drown us. We'd managed to get out, both of us coughing up blood and covered head to toe in viscous fluids.

I'd had to unwrap a limb severed from the creature beneath the surface, peeling the suction cups off my skin that tore my leg open as if each suction cup was a mouth taking a bite out of me as I popped it free.

Ashley hadn't helped, wringing out her hair and shirt as she ranted about her clothes being ruined and how long it would take to clean her hair.

We crawled through a dirt tunnel full of creepy, crawling things. I'd shuddered and moved quicker than her. Spiders crawled all over me, and I set myself on fire, trying to wipe them away.

She fumed at the disgrace suffered for being in mud with worms, screaming and even cursing as something crawled into her ear.

I managed to drag it out with my Light, but she blamed me for allowing it to happen at all.

Her façade began cracking, desperation gleaming in her eyes, and still, she refused to admit fear.

The maze began sending shifted Darklings at us, Vypers, then Venominx, followed by Lupins and Shadow Beasts. Ashley had degrading remarks about them, nothing imitating fear passing her lips. I let it go, deciding not to defend figments of the maze despite her sneering terms like "animal" and "retched monsters."

As we slay another shadow serpent, she sways, her hair frazzled, and her lipstick smeared.

A ghost of Akash appears, silent and solemn.

She claps at it. "No. You are not my brightest light. Be gone."

"I am, because of you. I gave my life for yours, and you repay my heart with the gift of betrayal. It's who you are," he says, leering with pride. "They're right, the vermin and animals of the Dark. You're naught but a rotten core, viler than them beneath your pretty mask of feigned grace."

"Stop."

"You cannot deny it. Even my replacement calls you bitch."

"You're right," Ashley snaps. "I have no heart. Akash has my heart with him, and he is not in this world."

The figure chuckles, throwing his head back to laugh, the sounds echoing around us and growing louder.

He stops, snapping his teeth with a sudden ferocity to glare. "Lie to me again, darling. It's funny."

Ashley's lower lip quivers, her eyes turning glassy. "That is quite enough from you."

A cruel twist takes over Akash's face, then he dissolves from sight.

I crouch, waiting for her to collect herself, knowing the strain the maze is placing on her. Cal had been pissed the maze was ignoring him, focusing on me. I'm finding it a relief.

It's easier to navigate with it trying to break Ashley instead of me. My concern swivels around the wilt infecting her. The maze is starting to win.

She wipes her face, trying to smooth and straighten her tattered, filthy clothes and the stray strands of her braid yanked out of place.

I flick my wrist, catching my breath. "Take a moment to calm down."

"Calm down? When have I become less than calm, honey?" Clearing her throat, a tear slides down her face. She's quick to wipe it away, clicking her tongue. "There is one thing I fear."

"What's that?"

"Not being me, a Bordeaux." She flashes her teeth in a wide fake grin. "There is no feasible way for that to transpire. I am me, and I am flawless. Up, now. We are in dire need of a bath and a change of clothes. You're practically repugnant, and that will not do."

A mouse leaps from the ivy to her shoulder. She shrieks, jumping in place, and swipes a hand to dislodge it.

"Ew." She stomps on it.

386

It squeaks, turning to shadows that disperse.

She flips her hair, looking to me with rage. "Obvious startling aside, this thing has nothing it can use. There is nothing I can't handle, trained by our father into a weapon to ensure I survive anything thrown at me and intelligent enough to solve any problem."

Standing, I stretch my arm over my head. "I traded one perfect sister for another. Great." I keep walking.

"*I* am perfect. She was not. Take comfort in only being beneath me, not her. Keep up."

ASHLEY STARTS TO TURN RIGHT, but I grab her arm. "Wait."

I linger at the cross section, the sounds of muted snuffling coming from the left.

The wall begins to slide closed to cut off the option. I rush past it, dragging her with me under the assumption that the maze is trying to close us out of the center.

She huffs, pulling free. "Where are we going?"

"The middle is full of smoragon nests. I think I hear them."

I head down the next corridor with caution, keeping my ears perked. The sounds become clearer, a rhythmic smacking of rubber against stone.

I groan, "Not the center."

"This is what you get for thinking you know better than me."

I glare at her with my eyes cut to the side.

A giggle echoes from further ahead. My spine tingles.

Ashley turns her head, waving before us. "That is not the same as those ridiculous clowns."

I shake my head, picking up my pace.

Another giggle, two different ones overlapping.

Smack. Smack. Smack.

"Don't tell. Don't tell Mommy," a young girl yells. "You can't tell."

Of all the stupid things for the maze to use against me, this tops the list. Spiders send me into full-blown panic. Clowns with knives make me nervous, and mirrors send me spiraling into the recesses of my mind I avoid.

I'd forgotten the red rubber ball with gold stars. I'd forgotten what started it.

I step forward, my stomach squirming.

Four translucent green children are gathered around, knees bent to their chests as they bounce a small ball back and forth.

I step closer, waving off Ashley's attempt to latch onto me.

Sasha, Nicky, Tony, and I giggle in a group. There were days before magic and responsibility came. Adulthood arrived, bringing complications and tribulations, but we were innocent and young first.

Red balls bounce around the room, gold stars painted across the surface. I didn't put the pieces together. The ball was the diameter of a coin with a single star, not these enlarged versions.

My sister approaches from the side. I look up, expecting Ashley.

I step back, holding her gaze. Nicky's eyes are brown, the same color as our father's, but Sasha's and mine are gray.

Her full, bow lips press, twitching down at the corners.

Ashley steps between us, parallel to not show either of us her back. "What is this?" She raises a limp wrist, flicking fingers at Sasha. "A less beautiful version of me?"

"Sasha," I whisper.

Mallafic steps from thin air to stare down Ashley. He offers his hand with a flourished movement. "Your role has concluded. I'll see you to the door."

Ashley takes a step away from him. "No. absolutely—"

Mallafic grabs her, and they disappear.

Sasha pulls back the left side of her lips. They twist to one side with knowing mirth. It was always her best gloat, the expression she wore every time she won first place or ranked highest at everything.

"Where is Nicky?" she asks, lacing her fingers together and straightening her back. "He's too innocent and trusting for the world, you know. We have to look out for him."

I turn my head away.

"How many times did I tell you we had to look out for Nicky? How many times did I ask you to do one simple thing?"

The balls keep bouncing around the room, mirrors shimmering into existence as the walls close in, four massive rectangles with no way out.

I stare at myself, Sasha stepping closer to me in the reflection.

"Why couldn't you do one thing, the one thing I ever asked of you? I never had much use for a sister. I didn't need you but for that one reason. Where...is...Nicky?"

Dead. Like her.

I turn my head to face her, staring her down. "You're not real."

She bursts into laughter, grinning wide. "No?" An invisible force slams into me, magic that resonates in my bones. Ki.

The force sends me into a mirror. It cracks against my back, shards tinkling to the floor around my feet.

I fall forward, lifting my hands to catch myself. The right side of my back burns, something buried in me, pushing between my ribs.

I try to reach it, grabbing at the broken glass. It drags across my palm, slicing me open. I hiss, using my Light to dig it free.

Sasha's features harden. "I'm no apparition of this maze."

Gritting my teeth, I send Ki through me to heal.

I believe her. Whatever the thing with Sasha's face is has Ki, which means it has a soul. She isn't a creature of the maze at all.

"What are you?"

"I am me," she says, patting the heel of her palm against her chignon and looking away. "A gift from a god to his creations."

"A gift?"

Her head swivels, and she blinks her big, gray eyes at me. "I've always been better, and this time, when I prove that once again, I'll take that crown and be a Dark King they deserve."

The mirrors swirl with colors, forming identical images of a stone well, a small, two-sided slanted roof covering the opening.

A bar is braced between the support posts, a rope dangling into its abyss out of sight.

I grip my fists. "As it turns out, I was more important than you."

"I'll always be better." She laughs, thrusting her hand forward.

I shield, twisting behind the arc of Light to swing at her from another position.

She blocks with her forearm, countering with her other fist.

I duck, spinning to kick her legs out, but she flips to evade.

Upright, she steps into a punch.

I throw my hands up, and my Light attacks, piercing into her stomach.

A tide of energy suctions from my core.

Sasha smirks, and I try to shield. The threads of Light pierce through itself into me, burning through my guts.

I hit my knees, getting my hands up to block the barrage of attacks. My forearm cracks from a square blow, and I scream.

Kicking at her, I roll away, sending Ki through me as I somersault. On my feet, I go on the defensive, fending off her flurry of swings.

She's always been faster than me, more precise. It wasn't ever hubris or jealousy clouding my opinions. She really was better.

She catches me on the jaw. Stars dance in my vision as I rock off balance.

She jumps, wrapping her legs around my neck to drag me to the ground. I land hard, my head smacking the stone.

Swinging, she punches me twice as I struggle to dislodge her.

Pulling back, laughing, she lifts her hand, her black fingernails elongating into claws. "He was gracious enough to make a few adjustments, provide me with a sturdier body and weapons to match the changes he made in you."

"Fantastic." I spit blood at her, throwing myself to the side with all my strength to roll us.

She hits the ground, and I scramble to evade her slashes.

Firelight races over my skin as I get in close, slamming my elbow into her and hooking my foot around her ankle to topple her.

She flails, sinking her claws into the crook of my neck and dragging me down with her.

I get a few strikes to her side.

She yanks her claws downward.

The air buzzes.

"Don't. She'll send it back," I warn it, ramming my knee into her stomach.

I grab her arm, snapping the elbow back. It takes both hands, leaving me exposed on the side.

She takes full advantage, raking across my ribs and jamming her claws into the soft spot below.

Black shadows erupt from her. Unaware of the threat, my Light and I are too slow to react. Her Dark wraps around my neck, squeezing as she pulls back and thrusts her talons into my abdomen again.

I slam my arm down on hers, grabbing the other wrist as she strikes with her now healed arm.

I take in the Dark, wrapping it in Ki. My muscles protest, throbbing and pulsing as I strain to keep her from gutting me further. I pant in shallow breaths, building her magic to send back.

The air cracks. Freezing cold races into my scalp, bursting in my skull as ribbons of smoke that fracture my mind.

I release the Dark I was collecting.

The frigid pain streaks down my spine, Dark rushing through me.

I center.

The air in my lungs is extinguished, ice running through my veins to dissolve the Light in me.

The Dark around my neck cracks my head to the side as I send a burst of Ki through me.

The world goes black as I fall.

CHAPTER 41
CALLAHAN

I drag Zander from the path into the center of the maze. Sterling hurtles a blast of shadows at the smorgaon, rushing backward to keep up.

Zander sidesteps and drops another smite on the beast. It roars, thrashing to one side. It whips back on its long neck, rounding its head toward Zander.

I send my Dark at him, yanking him out of the way as the smoragon snaps its jowls on the place he'd been.

Sterling grabs Zander by the arm, running with him toward the center.

I set off an explosion, forcing the beast to rear back. I turn and run.

Sterling drops through the center portal, pulling Zander with him.

Air sucks backward, a warning of a blast to come. I launch myself to the portal, crackling purple streaking over me and disappearing in a whirl of black as I fall.

I hit stone and roll, pushing to all fours and checking around.

Sterling helps Zander to his feet, turning to me with a wide grin. "I beat you back again."

I snap my tail at him, but my chest swells with humor and elation.

Zander grumbles, "What's next?"

"Alcohol." Sterling smacks him on the back. "That's it. We're out."

"Excellent," Zander says, doubling over to hurl the contents of his stomach at the floor. He shudders, stumbling to the side.

Sterling steadies him and claps him on the back again. "There, there. All done. You made it through."

"Never," Zander begins in a thick voice, expelling a whoosh of air, "absolutely never again."

I shake and then lift on my hind legs, heading for the door. I suspect it's late enough for dinner. The contractors should be in the dining hall, this room adjoined to it.

I open the double doors with my Dark, shouldering through the open threshold to maneuver my frame into the hall.

Contractors turn, several gathered around Jacques and Tony. Relief sings through me. They made it through. Even Palak, although he is curled on the floor in a ball, rocking back and forth on his ass.

He had a list of fears. I'm sure the maze used them all with enthusiasm. It was twice as vindictive this time around, probably having more abilities with fewer players to focus on.

Hailey crouches next to him, whispering.

"Tony," I say, "heal."

He strides toward me, but I point at my mate and contracted. "Them."

Jacques bobs and ducks. "Where's..." He turns to snarl at a woman in silent fury. "Fuck, she's still in there."

Oscar shoves the woman. "Damn you, and damn this contract." He holds his right hand up, the back of it red with irritation, the contract raised and shifting violently. "What am I supposed to do?"

I wince. "Talia would need to remove the line. At least her magic is smart enough not to kill you for the contempt." I glance at the woman, doing a double take. She's covered in gore and filth, pulled apart in ways I couldn't imagine her. "Ashley?"

She bows her head. "Callahan."

I shy away, the stench of her repulsive. "What happened to you?"

She flings out a hand. "Your stupid, ridiculous, awful, agonizing, death trap of a structure."

I sit on my hind quarter, yelping. "It's not mine. I didn't make that thing."

Ashley sneers. "That thing should be torn apart and broken into rubble. I should have it dissected bit by bit, set on fire, then dumped far, far away in the sea."

Sterling chuckles. "You went through it."

"When you didn't come back, I presumed you were worthless, and I would deal with it myself. I found my sister for you."

I scratch my talons across the floor. "Where is she?"

"I..." She turns her head away, blinking rapidly. "She refused to leave that thing, so I stayed with her, but then Mallafic grabbed me. He brought me to the center and shoved me in a hole, and I ended up here."

I glance at the open doorway to the next room. My star is still trapped in the maze. My Dark shifts, exasperated and anxious.

"Why," I ask, facing Ashley again. "Why would he pull you out?"

She looks to Tony, then turns her head in the opposite direction. "I don't know."

She's lying. I don't know why, or how it pertains to Tony, but she knows something.

I lean closer, growling, "Why?"

"We...encountered someone from her past." She fidgets. "Someone else, I suppose. They were different from the others in that monstrosity, not green hazes but solid, real, and they didn't return to shadow in death."

Jacques scoffs. "Everything the maze makes returns to shadows."

"Not these." She crosses her arms, hunkering lower. "The first... When I found her, I pulled him off her. It wasn't human, but it looked to be. The strength it had was too much, and it moved wrong with claws."

I bristle, my Dark running cold. "A man."

Sterling takes a step closer to her. "Who was it?"

Ashley presses her lips.

I press my knuckles to the floor. "Who?"

She glances at Tony, shaking her head. "I don't know what it was, but Tallie called it by a name."

Tony tilts his head. "What name?"

"Nicky."

My blood runs colder than my Dark. "Her brother?"

"So she claimed."

Sterling drops his arms. "Who else did she encounter?"

She presses her smeared, color-stained lips into a hard line.

Tony grabs her, twisting her to face him, then shakes her. "Who?"

Lifting her arms, she breaks his grip, throwing them outward into his. "I'll not be treated this way."

He sneers. "Spoiled, pampered bitch."

"Impertinent heathen."

"Who?" he yells. He shies back, features contorting. "Nat. It was Nat, wasn't it?"

"Yes," she drawls, blinking several times before sneering. "Your perfect, precious, darling Natasha."

A woman walks through the doors. I start to wag my tail. "Tal..."

The name sticks in my throat, my tongue going still.

She's a bit taller than my mate, similar, though. Her heart-shaped face has a small nose, and her eyes are large and upturned.

Blonde hair is knotted behind one ear, and she sways her hips as she walks closer. Her full lips curve as she comes closer, her gaze focused straight ahead.

I follow her sight to Tony. He's gone stark white, his jaw hanging lax.

She steps to him, and I see she's fuller curved than Natalia. Pressing her hands to his chest, she beams, "Hi."

He flaps his mouth, lips twitching like he's trying to speak.

She giggles, taking his face between her hands. Her nails are black, a stark contrast to the same pale skin Natalia has.

I've seen her before as a phantom. She's attractive, that's undeniable. Her body is thicker, her hips wider, and her assets larger.

Natalia claimed I'd want her sister, but I prefer the lean strength in my mate over big breasts.

She rubs her nose against Tony's. "Baby, it's so good to see you."

He lets out a muted gurgle, eyes glazed but wide open.

Sterling cocks his jaw, leaning his head to one side. "This is the sister?"

I roll my shoulders. "Sasha, where is Natalia?"

Sasha presses in closer, leaning against Tony to wrap her arms around his neck. She shifts her weight to one leg, bending the other at the knee. "Say something, baby."

"H–h–how? How? How are you..."

"A god," she says.

I look to Sterling, then Ashley. She has her eyes narrowed at the reunited couple. I can't determine if it's hatred or suspicion in her face.

I grab Sasha by the shoulder, my Dark prying Tony back to force her to face me.

Her gray eyes flash, eyes like my little star's, with vigor and confidence.

I ask again, "Where is Natalia?"

"You must be Callahan." She smiles. "I can see why she was drawn to you." She slides her eyes down me with a coy smile.

My Dark curls in on itself under the sensation of being violated. The only ones who get to look at us that way are our mates.

Sasha has her gaze low as she flexes one eyebrow. "Mm. Impressive."

My balls try to crawl inside my stomach. "Where is—"

"Did she tell you about me?"

"Yes."

"I wonder, was my little sister honest? Did she tell you how much better I am than her?"

"She's said."

Sasha smiles. "I was brought back to life for that very reason. In the Dark, the strong survive, and the strongest of all leads. That would be me."

"I don't care what she or you say. We prove our strength. Your words are worthless."

She nods. "Yes, that is the way it works, so I killed her. I am your new Dark King."

She throws something at me. It falls, delicate and clinks on the stone.

My Dark thrashes and whimpers, pinging in my skull to search for its echo.

Sterling kneels, his claws scratching the stone as he struggles to pick up the broken chain, tangling it in his fingers to dangle the jewel star pendant in clear view.

He snarls, closing his fist around it, then whips toward me, lifting his arm to expose his ribs.

I scrape a talon over the contracts, her name still glittering twice, the demand to kill spiders present. Neither has dissolved in consequence of death.

I meet his eyes. "Still there."

My Dark vibrates in agreement. There's still an echo of itself in this world, and not too far.

Sterling slumps, almost smiling. "She's alive."

Sasha opens her mouth, pulling back. "She can't be."

"She is." I point to Sterling. "Her worn contract would end, but it hasn't. My mating mark still echoes. My mate lives."

She cocks her jaw. "So be it. I bested her. If she does finish the maze, I'll be waiting. If not, I'll take that crown as is my right."

Jacques snickers. "Lady, I don't know what's going on or who you are, but challenges for the throne have to be witnessed or are invalid. Even if you put our lightning bug down, it's not a legal challenge. The contenders would have to fight for the throne." He points at me and Sterling.

I look to Sterling. That's a problem.

He shivers, his wings rustling as he shifts his shoulders. "Not that again."

I pull my upper lip back, showing my teeth. I don't want to lose my mate, either of them, and I'll rip my own Dark out to follow them if they both are in the afters.

I could attempt to claim my Hallow heritage as an excuse to bow out of the contest. It does little to aid the unification of Dark and Light. I'd label myself a coward.

Maybe I am. The mere idea of having to kill Sterling sends my mind racing for solutions, searching for a way out—to run from the task.

I cherish his company, adoring the way he laughs with Natalia. He's more than I'd thought he'd be, no longer an idea but part of me. Within days, he's embedded himself between my mate and me as if he'd belonged there from the start.

Sasha moves to face Tony, giggling. "Hi, handsome," she says, sliding her hands over his shoulders to hang from his neck again. "A girl's gotta eat, right?"

"Right," he answers slowly, stretching the word.

"You're in shock, aren't you? Understandable, but I'm here." She presses her hand to the side of his face. "We can start again. Three children and you a doctor?"

"Three..."

"Don't worry. You won't have to keep me from doing stupid things." She taps her toe, making a humorous snort with her lips pressed. "You know I never make dumb, rash decisions. I'll manage the crown. You can go back to school, finish your last year for full certification, be my Doctor Washington."

He doesn't answer.

"Tony." She flinches. "I know everything, every memory we made. He brought me back."

Ashley starts to walk away. "Excuse me. I need a shower, or a hundred."

Jacques drops to balance on the balls of his feet, putting a hand on Palak's shoulder. "You survived, friend." He slides his hand under Palak's arm, pulling him upright. "Now we drink."

Hailey shoves at Jacques, screaming, "Leave him alone! Don't touch him. Don't you d—dare hurt him more than you already have."

"Sweetie." Jacques sneers. "I almost died four times to keep him alive."

Zander shuffles forward. "Hail..."

She gets an arm under Palak.

400

Zander grimaces. "Believe me, that he's alive is proof enough to trust in Jacques's claim of friendship."

She frowns, her emanate eyes glassy. "What did they do to him?"

Jacques snorts, turning away.

Zander ducks his head. "It was not them. It was the maze itself, of that I have little doubt. It was a trial to earn the right to unify."

He helps Hailey move Palak toward the table, doubling back when Palak is heaped in a chair. "Callahan, what—"

"It's the fucking maze. Whatever happens in that thing doesn't matter."

Sterling stretches his Dark toward the table, dragging a chair over and setting it down, lounging back with his legs straight to stare at the door. "Go get drunk. It's the only way you'll sleep tonight."

Bowing his head, Zander says, "Thank you."

As he walks away, Sterling raises the chain again. His Dark spins the pendant. It's dull and boring without our mate's magic to make it shimmer.

I hunker down, prepared to wait for eternity with him if I have to. I don't get long.

Hiro tosses clothes in front of me. "Heard you two were in that fucking thing. Figured you'd need clothes."

Sterling drags himself up. "Might as well shift while we wait."

I move my attention to Sasha and Tony. She's still whispering and smiling. He's rigid as she hangs from him, his face screwed up. No trace of adoration or excitement shines in his expression.

Sterling steps into pants, cocking his head at me. "Are we going back in to get her?"

"I don't trust that," I say, jerking my head at Sasha.

He tosses the shirt to the chair, dropping his hands on his

hips. His pectoral muscles rise, his cut abdomen dipping in. He ripples, exhaling.

I've always been excited by tits, curves, and what's between a woman's legs, never questioning my preferences. Sterling's changing all kinds of things as an urge to trace the ridges of his torso with my tongue roots in me.

I'm not doing that. At least, not until he cleans up. His brown skin is hazy with the goo of melted flesh and lingering blood left from transitioning to our masked form.

Sterling curls his lip at the reunited couple. "What is that?"

"I have no idea."

"We are well and truly fucked if there's something you'll admit to not knowing."

"Dead is dead. There is no coming back. I have no explanation for defying the laws of life." I shake, yanking on my Dark.

It grumbles but complies. My body breaks and pulls taut, shrinking and reforming.

I drag fingers across my face, slinging away the lingering slop of gore.

My Dark squirms and shoves against my bones and skin, trying to get comfortable in the confined space, harnessed within the mask.

I get pants on, buttoning them. The silver stitching in the center of my chest catches my eye. I brush my finger over it, frowning. The pain is gone and even strenuous activities in the maze hadn't inflamed the wound. I must be healed by now. I can have her retract her magic. I want her at full strength when we face Lucius again.

Sterling steps closer, nudging me and wiggling his eyebrows. "How does it feel to look up again?"

I smack his stomach with the back of my hand. "Shut up, birdie."

He puts a hand on my head, wiggling it back and forth. "Any-thing for my good boy."

That sends a streak of arousal through me. He and Natalia had kept up that joke through the night as we fucked. I'd been a very good, very happy boy. If I still had a tail, I'd wag it for him.

I focus on Tony and Sasha. It's unnatural, eerie. I don't want it out of sight or left to its vices without supervision.

Tony's face flickers at something Sasha says. He starts shaking his head, reaching up to unwind her arms from his neck.

He forces her half a step back. "No."

"Baby."

"No!" He shoves her shoulders and steps away. "I don't—Whatever you are, it's not Natasha."

"It's me. Tony, baby, it's me."

"No," he says in a shaky voice, color coming to his nose and cheeks as a tear falls down his face. "N–no. I don't know what you are, but I know what you're not. You're not her."

"I—"

"I know her. I know everything about her, and you're not her. Nat never gloated over Tal. She hated Tal, sure, wanted to be better than her, tried like crazy to be the best at everything, but she never looked me in the eye and praised herself over Tal. Not to me. She didn't lie to me. To everyone else? To Tal? Yeah, absolutely. But not to me."

"Baby..." There's a warning in Natasha's voice.

He pushes a finger into her chest. "Tal was always better than her, and she knew it. She knew she couldn't compete with Tal using Ki. Nat might have thought Tal was rash, but she admired Tal's ability to never show emotion, to never appear to have weak moments. Nat wanted so badly to be like Tal, decisive in choices and never second-guessing, never flinching." He stumbles away from her, dragging the back of his arm across his nose and mouth, sniffing and swallowing, trying to hold back the welling emotion leaking from his eyes. "I want...so badly to believe this, to see you again."

"Then stop fighting. I have every memory. I know everything. I know what was said, but now I have perspective. Things change."

"I don't want change. I want my Nat, not whatever the fuck you are."

She cocks her jaw, her expression turning rancid. "I'll make you eat those words and beg for forgiveness."

"If," Natalia says, striding into the room, "you touch him, I won't just kill you. I'll make it hurt."

My Dark screams and jumps and twists with excitement. "*Mate!*"

Sasha spins, her cheeks turning pink. "Natalia Swan, I chal—"

"Do you remember that day?" Natalia throws something at the floor, a small red ball. It snaps back, and she catches it. "Did he give you that memory, too, *pet*?" She repeats the act, bouncing the ball to snatch it in her hand again. "That's all you are. A pet, made for a game, made...for...me."

My little star lifts her eyes, rage glowing in her face. I've never seen her sparkle with death like this. She wants blood.

My Dark drools. I curl one side of my mouth back. My mate is about to remind everyone why she has earned the right to rule the Dark despite her Light.

CHAPTER 42

NATALIA

I stare at the ball. It's such a stupid thing.

We were children. Of course, it would be something worthless. It's all we had to claim, our greatest treasures simple. Everything was simpler.

Sasha, the thing that wears her face, leans toward Tony. His face has a red blotchy stain creeping over his cheeks, tears evident.

As fucked up as sending this thing to me was, it's sick to force this upon him.

She says, "I'll make you eat those words and beg for forgiveness."

"If," I say, walking into the room, "you touch him, I won't just kill you. I'll make it hurt."

Sasha whips to face me, her face flushing with fury. "Natalia Swan, I chal—"

"Do you remember that day?" I ask, lifting the ball in my hand.

I rock it in my palm, then throw it at the floor. It hits the floor and pops back. I stick my hand under it, catching it in my palm.

"Did he give you that memory, too, *pet?*" I bounce the ball again. "That's all you are, a pet, made for a game, made for me."

I roll it in my palm, then lift my eyes to Sasha.

She crosses her arms, jutting her hip. "He made me, threaded every moment of the past into my soul with the webs of Sirius. He gave me magic I never had, but I am no pet."

I toss the ball, letting it hit the floor and bounce back to grab it again. "Tony put a coin in one of those stupid machines and won this ball. He gave it to you." I bounce the ball. "You said you'd keep it forever, the first gift from your husband."

I'd been nine. She and Tony were twelve. Nicky was just eight.

Sasha already called Tony her husband. They held hands and were inseparable. Whatever arrangements had been shoved on them, their marriage planned since the age of one, it hadn't mattered.

It had been real.

I slam the ball as hard as I can on the floor. It had been real and shattered by the Assembly in their pursuit of power.

The ball smacks the floor and shoots straight up as I shake. I'm the reason Sasha and Nicky were sent to the afters, but I didn't send them. This thing might be here because of me, but I didn't create it.

I'm done taking responsibility for things I didn't do.

Catching the ball, I say, "You kept bouncing this higher and higher. I told you to stop. I warned you. You didn't listen."

Sasha pats her hair, looking away.

It had gone so high, then hit the ground, bouncing wrong and shooting straight into the well. We'd gone to see if we could find it.

Crying, she told me to climb in and get it for her. She hadn't wanted to let go of it, didn't want Tony to know she'd lost it.

"We couldn't see the bottom, didn't know how deep it was.

You told me you were the older one, you were better than me. I was spare parts, useless because you were the one they wanted. You were the one who'd marry Tony." I bounce the ball, hating it, wanting to smash it. "You pushed me."

Sasha shrugs, inspecting her nails. "You weren't worth as much as me."

I fling the ball at her. "I told them I climbed in and fell because you were crying. You begged me not to tell, afraid you'd get taken away, not be able to see Tony or ever marry him, so I said it was my fault that I'd tried to climb down, and I fell."

I don't care about the eyes on me. There are so many watching, listening. I admitted to lying in front of the Dark contractors, and I don't care.

Freedom bursts across my skin as my Light intensifies. "I lied for you, and you never even thanked me, like it was expected of me, like I really was there just to be used by you when it suited. I wasn't the pretty, perfect Swan heiress, you were. You never treated me like an equal."

She laughs. "Because you never were."

"I spent my whole life in your shadow, but it wasn't ever you they wanted."

"I challenge you, Natalia, and this time," she says, stepping forward, "you won't get up."

I keep my gaze on hers but lift my chin. "Tony. Get the fuck out of here."

He turns and strides in long steps, then starts running.

Sasha looks after him. "Why is he running?"

I step forward. "Because I'm going to kill you, and he doesn't want to watch you die. Whatever the fuck you are, you have her face."

"Pathetic." She rolls her eyes. "Oh well. I'll find something more suitable to be my Dark Queen."

My sister would never have insulted Tony. I rub a finger along the edge of my lower lip. "Thanks for making this easier."

"That crown is going to be mine." She starts to step.

I move, circling with her. "I don't even want the stupid thing, but I'll love sending you back to where you came from."

She swings, claws out.

I dip low to evade, twisting to the side. Her claws rake my ribs.

I kick. She blocks with her forearm. I spin into another kick to her open side, and she shields with Dark.

I turn around, throwing my weight into a swing, but she blocks, grabbing my wrist and dragging me closer to ram her knee into my chest.

I lose my breath and balance.

With a quick snap, she breaks my wrist and spin-kicks me in the stomach, sending me sprawling.

I don't fight tipping over, somersaulting, and sending Ki through me to heal the injuries she inflicted. I pop to my feet, hands up.

She smirks. "Healing while you move? Sister..." Her eyebrow raises as she resets. "You've learned a few things."

She kicks. I dodge. She swings, and I block, hitting back. I slam my fist into her face.

Sasha stumbles back, wiping at her nose. It cracks as it straightens, rage tightening her rounded features.

All those years, I looked at her wondering why we were so different. Same hair. Same eyes. Different everything else.

She was a Swan. I was a Bordeaux.

She rushes forward, launching at me. I thrust my hands into her chest as we land. Firelight flickers, orange-pink flames racing across her.

She screams, and I roll us. Sasha whips her elbow into my face, flipping us over so she's on top again.

Dark ensnares my arms as I try to block her punch. My head snaps to the side. My chest pulses as thick needles stab into me.

I siphon on her magic, but the shards retract and plunge into me over and over.

I grit my teeth, my Light winding around her. She strikes me in the face a few more times, shrieking with laughter.

The air crackles.

Sasha leans forward Dark winding around my throat. "Do it."

I keep dragging in small bursts of it. I throw my weight to the side.

She falls off me, her Dark dragging like razors across my skin.

The world turns hazy, bursts of white spots dancing across my grayed vision as blood soaks my chest.

"Talia," Cal roars.

I send Ki through me, dodging to the side at Sasha's kick. I roll, catching my breath and swaying as I throw her Dark at her. She screams and crumples.

I stalk forward, but she shoves up. "Clever."

I shake my head. "Hurts, doesn't it?"

Her eyes pinch, then she steps into a swing. I block and kick her in the stomach. She catches my leg, kicking back. I take the hit, falling to take her to the ground with me.

I roll backward, flipping up to my feet, and get a clean kick to her face.

Dark streaks for me, and my Light counters, several strands slipping through her Dark to stab into her.

She screams, and my Light erupts in firelight once more.

I press her, swinging and kicking. She's struggling to keep up for the first time ever.

Dark engulfs us, slicing me open. I kick her away, spinning into clear air and sending Ki through me to heal.

The shadows clear, Sasha panting but staring me down with murder in her gray eyes.

She steps in swinging. I defend, waiting. I block and spin to throw my elbow into her face, shielding with my Light against her retaliation.

Her attacks come faster. Any damage she inflicts, I heal just as fast, but she holds the same advantage.

I spin away from a hook and crouch. I'm going to have to break her neck to win this fight. My Light buzzes with acknowledgment.

Dark races at me, and I dive into a flip. I feign a swing, sending my Light to tangle around her.

Dark stabs into me, but I yank Sasha closer, grabbing her head.

She claws at me, and I kick the back of her knee, the joint snapping. She shrieks, flailing and sinking lower.

I twist. Bones crunch, and I detangle, stepping away. Sasha doesn't move.

I breathe hard, staring down on her. Her pretty head is snapped to the side, her neck beginning to bruise with blood pooling beneath the surface.

I kick at her. "Are you really dead?"

Shadows swirl around her, then rise to assimilate as Mallafic. He dances in and out of focus, staring down at the body.

He faces me, forcing a smile and clapping as polite applause. "Well done, Darling." He claps his hands together with a sharper crack, his smile mutating to twisted glee. "Not many can say they killed the same thing twice—not even I... yet."

I glance down at the thing—at Sasha. I can hear Nick begging me for help, the memories echoing in my head. I breathe deep through my nose and pull upright.

Cal and Sterling hurry forward, side by side and in step.

Mallafic holds a hand to them. "That's quite close enough." With a limp wrist, he flicks his hand at them, motioning them away. "You had your trial, and you possess your reward. I concede to your whims, but my plaything…"

I bob my head to the side. "We could just say I got to keep living. That's enough reward."

He steps toward me, reducing the space between us. "These are my creations you rule, Darling Toy. Do not forget that." He strokes one claw from my temple to my cheek. When he withdraws, he offers me a silver ring.

I take it. "If I do this, will you promise to be less creepy next time?"

He puts his hand over mine, stopping me from slipping the metal band in place as he holds my gaze. I've never seen him serious, his face lax with deep lines of consideration.

"Right is for the head," he says without a trace of glib or sardonic humor. "The intellect and wisdom, the most important skill of all—logic. The truths of this world are not to be ignored." He drops his hand away. "Ask your questions, watch for your answers. Knowledge is my greatest weapon and your weakest point, but I give unto you a gift even when you require a lesson."

"Gift?" I lift my eyebrows, closing and opening my eyes. "What fucking gift was this?"

He motions to the ring in my hand. "Put it on."

I force the ring onto my right thumb. It burns and contracts, sealing itself to me. I clamp my jaw, contorting my face as my skin sizzles.

"Ow," I manage, as I wave my hand to the side, the heat dwindling.

"Do you truly believe the vast array of secrets I know are all from words spoken unto me with clarity?"

"Is this necessary? Don't I already have your hat?"

"Oh, the complaints." He snickers, dispersing into the air as shadows wick away from illumination. His humor echoes around us, fading slower than his presence.

Cal rushes to me, wrapping his arms around me. "Mate." He rests his mouth on the top of my head.

Sterling presses to my back, his Dark and arms circling me. I lean back into him and cling to Cal, needing them both as a shattered doll.

Sterling sighs, his arms dropping away. "Oscar."

I twist my head, keeping my hold on Cal as I face Oscar.

He lifts his right hand. "Tal, I have been in contempt all day without being able to do anything to not be in contempt. I swear to you, I will do my fucking best, but you have got to remove this line about protection, or I'm going to live like this."

A laugh works out of my broken chest as I struggle with humor. "Yeah. Fair enough." I ask my Light to remove the line.

Sterling gives Oscar an easy shove. "Go be useful. We're taking Tal."

CHAPTER 43
CALLAHAN

I keep my little star in my arms, carrying her to our rooms. "You got out."

Sterling steps with me, brushing against me. "Ignore the obvious disbelief in that statement, Firefly." He nudges me and glares. "She's strong."

I narrow my eyes at him. "I know she is, but the maze..."

"She's our fucking mate. She's stronger than us—capable—"

"Shut the fuck up, sweetheart," I sneer. "I'm not questioning our mate."

He clamps his jaw, the muscles bulging at the corners. Turning his face away, he shakes his head.

Natalia presses her nose to my neck. "Mallafic."

I tense, glancing around. "Where?"

"In the maze, after Sasha put me down. He brought me to the exit, told me to finish it, gave me the ball..." She sighs.

"Why didn't you tell me? I asked you—directly asked you where the fuck that fear came from, and you said you didn't know. You lied to me," I snarl.

She ducks her head, starting to shake. "I didn't remember."

413

I scoff, making a turn. "You're going to lie to me *again*?"

"I'm not," she whispers. "I forgot. I just...I didn't remember the ball. I mean, I know she pushed me into the well to get that stupid thing, but it was so small and not like..."

Sterling nudges my shoulder with his, giving me a long look. "The maze twists things. You know that."

I need a drink. Several. I meet his eyes, grimacing and bobbing my head. "Fucks us all up."

Neither Sterling nor I break contact with her as we shower. I let go of her long enough to put on pants, then pull her close.

We lay in bed, and I pin Natalia between me and Sterling.

I curl around her, trying to shield her with my hand on Sterling's stomach. My Dark knots around them both, mirroring my anxiety.

Closing my eyes, I slip into the gray, not asleep but between unconscious and conscious.

I jerk into awareness as Natalia shifts. Her head rests on Sterling's shoulder, her leg across his thighs as she fiddles with the ring on her right thumb.

Sterling sighs, adjusting and tucking one arm behind his head.

I press my hand into him.

Natalia whispers, "I'm hungry."

I roll away.

Sterling sits, cocking his head, but I lean over and drag Natalia into my arms with my Dark, scooping her off the bed.

I'd made a deal. I'd feed her, and in return, she gives me everything. I'm not about to forfeit that.

I carry her to the kitchens, Sterling following.

Inside is still and empty. All the vassals must be finished for the evening, gone to their chambers.

Sterling pokes around. "I'll cook," he says, lowering his voice to mutter, "Can't be that hard."

I sit, putting Natalia in my lap. If he's volunteering, I won't fight. My culinary skills stretch at making a sandwich.

I brush my fingers across her cheek, putting my hand under her chin to tip her head up. I trail my fingertips down her neck, stopping to tap her chest. "I'll fix it."

She frowns, putting her hand to the spot, then glancing down. "What...?" She tenses, feeling around her neck and breathing quicker while running her hands over her chest and breasts.

"Easy," I cup her jaw in both hands. "That thing threw it at me when she declared herself the Dark King."

Natalia moves her lips, but no words come.

"I'll fix it." I kiss her cheek.

I lean to the side, furrowing my brow as Sterling slams a cupboard.

He looks back at me. "I have it in our room."

"With all your other shiny things?"

He doesn't answer, but Natalia smiles. "Don't be mean."

Stroking her cheek, I meet her eyes. "Our birdie likes his shiny things. There's nothing wrong with that."

She nods in my hands. "He gets so offended when you call them trash."

She leans into me, and I wrap her in my arms and Dark, watching Sterling toast bread.

"Are you all right?"

"I survived."

I hold her tighter, kissing the top of her head.

Burning smoke wafts from the toaster. I glare at Sterling, trying to finagle the toaster and clear the smoke.

His Dark wraps around the device as it starts to spark. It rips the knobs off, shaking it.

The toaster bursts into flames, and he yelps, skittering back.

I stand, setting Natalia down. She rushes forward, pulling Sterling further away from the crackling contraption.

I dampen the flames with my Dark, coughing and batting at the clouded air.

Natalia joins me, picking up the smoking toaster and looking to me, then Sterling.

"Really?" She lifts the toaster higher. "A, how, and B, do you not know how to use a toaster?"

Sterling shuffles in place, crossing his arms. "Put bread in. Push the button."

She inspects it. "You had this thing set to burnt to a crisp."

"There's a setting?"

She laughs, shaking and setting the toaster aside. "I'm not sure if I'm impressed or horrified."

I shrug. "We have vassals."

"Sit down." She points to the island. "I'll make something."

Sterling and I return to the island. His Dark and mine tangle and spread across each other.

He turns, resting his chin on my shoulder. "I'm amazed Ashley went through the maze. What's she afraid of?"

"According to her?" Natalia pauses in the act of slicing bread. "Nothing."

I trade disbelieving glances with Sterling.

Natalia turns her back to us. She's in one of my shirts, the hem flirting with the bottom of her ass cheeks. It's one of the best views in the world.

I watch her lift on her tiptoes, waiting for the fabric to move high enough to give me an even better sight as I ask, "What did it throw at her?"

"Plenty. We had to swim in blood and crawl through mud, and insects swarmed us, cutting us up. It kept showing Akash." She stops, glancing back. "He was her future mate."

Sterling bites my shoulder. "Fuck."

I hum. "It had thrown that at us." I clear my throat. "Mates are an easy spot to poke."

Natalia shrugs. "Ash did great." She lifts a plate in either hand, her Light delivering a third when she joins us at the island. "I'd suggest arrogance to anyone who asks for advice on how to beat the maze in the future."

Sterling picks at his sandwich. "Thanks, Firefly."

"Thanks for coming to get me."

He pushes the plate away. "We didn't mean to leave you behind."

"I saw Nicky," she says, then shakes her head, shifting in her chair with her hands under the table as she stares into her lap. "Something that looked like him, anyway, and I forgot about everything else. I shouldn't have wandered off."

I hold her gaze, waiting with bated breath, my Dark still, wondering if she'll tell me.

She shakes her head. "I had to relive his death."

I nod, slumping over the island. "I won't force you, but if you need me..."

She smiles. "You'll stay."

"Always."

We start to eat, moving slowly and nursing the wounds within. When we're finished, I lift Natalia in my arms again.

Sterling snags a bottle of bourbon and a bottle of vodka, bringing them with us.

He and I go shot for shot, passing the bottle between us. No jokes are offered, no teasing touches, just comfort as we sit together, whispering about horrors and pain. Sterling doesn't even offer up a single riddle.

CHAPTER 44
CALLAHAN
2ND BLOOM'S DAY, BLOOMING, 4050, 6TH MILLENNIUM

When we collect for training, the world is groggy and glazed over.

Ashley and Tony are missing. Palak keeps staring off into the distance, not speaking. Zander is disheveled, something his brother nags him for.

As per usual, Jacques remains unaffected by everything, poking fun at the world and everyone in it.

I frown at him. "Why did you accept being contracted?"

"Guess I can't claim to avoid the games." He snickers.

"You're highborn. You have the right to hold contracts and you faced the games every year."

He bobs his head to the side. "Most highborn are contracted at some point, if only to get experience with contracts. I did that, expecting I'd serve then hold my own, but I had a sweet place, the life of a contractor without the responsibility resting on my shoulders, like Mass."

"He worked twice as hard as me."

"It's still, easier, and my lineage has never owned anything. I don't need vassals and I don't have a way to pay them either. I'll serve you and a crown, do a lot, but the weight of that cursed hat is yours to bear, not mine." He shifts, looking around. "And cake. I get cake, right?"

"Chocolate?"

"Chocolate is best, but any cake. I love cake, lemon blueberry or strawberry and cream, vanilla with sprinkles... Mm. When am I getting cake? I got the Light through the maze, and I've done the stupid Light lessons. I want cake."

Clapping him on the shoulder, I nod. "I'll get you cake."

I find Hiro and Thames, lifting a finger. "Come with me."

I lead them to Palak. Hailey frowns at me, keeping her arm around him and her head nestled against his shoulder. "Your Majesty," she starts, "Callahan, please excuse the display. My mate—"

"Needs you," I finish, rubbing the back of my neck. I glance for mine knowing even the sight of them together can reduce the tension in my chest. As much as I want to bury myself in them and forget everything, Jacques is right. The weight of the crown rests on my head. I have responsibilities I cannot ignore, no matter how much damage is wrought.

"Palak," I say, dropping my hand on his other shoulder.

He jumps in place and flinches. "Sir?"

Hiro crosses his arms. "He needs help recovering?"

Hailey looks to him. "Is it possible?"

"I've run that thing for centuries."

Jerking, Palak yells, "No."

"You're calling me a liar?"

Palak blanches, taking a step away. "I—I'm so sorry, Sir. I apologize for—"

"The fuck is wrong with you?" Hiro starts to laugh.

"I only meant no, I can't imagine doing that for–for..."

Thames snickers. "It really fucked you up, baby."

I shake my head. "Hiro and Thames are Shadow Beasts."

Palak gapes at them, then turns, trying to run. I latch on, wrapping my Dark around him and dragging him back.

Hailey waves her hands. "Please, please, just let him go. He's terrified of Shadow Beasts."

I wrangle him into facing Hiro and Thames, glaring at Hailey. "I know what he's afraid of." I smack Palak on the back, pushing him toward Hiro and Thames. "Stop running and face it."

Thames purses his lips, tilting his head to the side. "You're afraid of Shadow Beasts?"

"I want one of you or both to shift for him. He has a nightmare about what he thinks a Shadow Beast is. It's comical, but he doesn't know that yet."

Thames giggles, his face stretching with humor.

Hiro starts pulling his shirt off. "Sugar Bear, don't laugh about that. You're deadly as fuck."

"Well, yes." Thames stretches his features, then relaxes his face. "It's not a strange fear, especially given his Light, but I'm surprised he hasn't shown it to us, given we *are* Shadow Beasts."

"I didn't know that." Palak waves at the crowd of bodies. "A Shadow Beast killed my father. Or I thought a Shadow Beast killed my father. Matthew confirmed his race, and even if he didn't, I only learned the truth recently. Adontis and Beenin, my uncle killed my father. How am I ever going to face him again?" He covers his eyes.

Hailey steps to his side, rubbing his back. "His uncle is refusing to join us, like many others who do not support us merging our societies."

"I thought it was because a Dark killed my father. It's not." He looks to me with welled-up eyes. "He's...just full of hate."

I motion to a naked Hiro. "Deal with your fear first, then we'll find a way to bring the rest together. I'm not tackling that today."

Hailey gasps, turning into Palak. He holds her close, frowning at Hiro.

Hiro steps away, clouded in shadows. Snaps and crunches emanate from the fog, then it clears, Hiro standing tall.

Palak stares at him. "You're..."

I smirk. "Bit taller, blackish-blue skin, you got that part right."

"You're still a man."

Thames laughs. "No shit, baby."

Palak opens and closes his mouth, screwing up his face.

I shake as I contain my laughter. "The fuck did you think we were, some huge freaky monsters?"

Looking to the ground, Palak winces. "No offense or disrespect meant, but you are."

Hiro and Thames grin widely at that jab.

I ruffle Palak's hair before I think better of it. He's too much like a kid who needs to learn, like Thomas. "I'm hard to kill."

Palak smooths his hair, glancing at me. "I thought something got out and followed me when you walked into the hall."

Hiro kicks at the ground. "He's the scariest of us, impossible to put down in his true form."

I shrug. "We should," I begin, drawing a circle over Hiro, "teach them all what we really are. Who knows how many of them are as misguided as Palak."

Zander approaches, shoulders slumped. "May I inquire what this is?"

"Inquire away," I say, walking from them in search of my mates. I need them this morning, my torso hollow and delicate.

I follow the closest echo: Sterling.

I yank him away from a group. "Talia. Where?"

He looks around, his locks tied back, but one hangs loose. "No idea. She was sparing with a Glow."

I clench my fists, and the corners of his jaw bunch as he clamps down on his jaw.

421

He shoves the heel of his palm into my shoulder. "Go. Echo. Now."

I turn and we walk into the palace together in search of our mate. My Dark snarls and pings, shifting and fluttering even as it stretches from me to Sterling. Not that it stretches far, his arm brushing against mine as we walk in long, hurried strides.

As we descend a flight of steps, Sterling chuckles. "I know where she is."

"Show me."

Sterling walks a pace ahead of me, making all the same turns my Dark directs me through, bringing us to an empty corridor.

He moves to a wall, lining up his foot with a crack in the floor and pushing his shoulder into it. The wall shifts, rock scraping as it swings to reveal a passage.

I look inside. "Didn't know about this one."

"I didn't know about your tree." He shrugs, slipping inside. "We didn't swap hiding places and share bourbon until recently."

"Or a woman."

He hesitates, glancing back. "Mm."

"Telra doesn't count. We didn't know that, and neither of us wanted her."

He laughs. "Not after the first few rounds, anyway."

I step off a ledge to marbled rocks in shades of pink, green, and blue. "It smells like rain."

Sterling waves at the pond. "Water."

"Do birds swim?"

"I swim. One less way to die and one less reason to be afraid."

I bob my head. "Where's our mate?"

Sterling takes off, striding across shifting rocks that crunch and slide together. "She went exploring."

Turning my back on the lake, I follow him into the depths of the cavern. It begins to narrow, closing in.

I stop, breathing short. I can't pick my feet up anymore.

My Dark trembles. "*Mate is ahead.*"

I hum but can't move.

Sterling stops, coming back. "It opens ahead."

"Mm."

He lifts one of my arms and hoists me over his shoulder. I curl my lip, focusing on the rocks beneath his feet. I can't argue this, even if my urge is to beat him bloody for it.

The walls come closer, but they're brightening.

Sterling carries me into an open cave that glows brilliant blue from the depths of a pool. He sets me on my feet, turning me around.

Natalia glances up at us, a mostly empty bottle of vodka in her hand. She's sitting near the edge of the gleaming water.

Sterling stomps forward. "Mate." He crouches before her, cupping her face, sighing. "Are you all right?"

She lifts the bottle, tipping it back and forth so the contents slosh. "I'm real drink—drunk."

"*Mhm.*" He nods, smirking.

I drop to the balls of my feet next to them. "Little Star, are you hiding from us?"

"You?" She shakes her head in short, rapid jerks. "No, not you. Just hiding."

My Dark twists around her, one strand stroking the side of her face. Her hair is still pulled into the braid she wore for training this morning, her attire unchanged. My back and Sterling's were turned, and she'd slipped away while she was supposed to be training.

"Hiding from what?"

"Oh…" She breathes out, her lips puckered.

Sterling snickers, sitting on the ground, and pulling Natalia into his lap. He peels her fingers away from the bottle as she whines, passing it to me.

I toss it into the lake.

"Hey, that was mine."

Sterling taps her nose. "You are drunker than drunk."

She pulls her head back, eyes crossing to the tip of her nose, then she rubs it. "That's mine too."

I join Sterling, tipping my head toward his. "Wrong answer."

He looks over at me. "Whose is it?"

"Ours."

She wrinkles her nose. "I don't get to keep any part of me." She pokes his chest. "It's all his. Guess yours, too."

I smile. "Right answer."

"Is this a game?" She gapes at me, slack-jawed and glassy-eyed. "I don't wanna play any more games."

"No. Why are you hiding?"

"How do you do this?"

"What?"

She waves a hand, almost smacking me in the face.

Sterling chuckles, taking her hand in his. "What is that?"

"This! All of this. The stuff and things with the magics and crowns and games and dying and...and people hating you."

Sterling pulls her head toward his, pressing his mouth to her forehead. "One day at a time thinking about you."

I relax, leaning against Sterling without a better answer.

"Me?" She cocks her head.

I say, "You, Mate. You make it possible."

Stroking the back of her head, Sterling nods. "Thinking about finding you."

"Then trying to earn you."

"Trying to not fuck it up."

"Enjoying you." I reach over, running my knuckles along her cheek. "You're how. That's the magic of a mate."

He jiggles his shoulder against mine. "And we have two. Not

sure why my webs have that kind of beautiful twist, but I won't ever take it for granted."

Natalia sobs. "But...but...I have two, and it's not okay. Nothing's okay, but you two are okay, and I'm not you. I'm not okay, and I don't want you to know... I don't want you to see I'm weak."

I've used her, wielded her as a tool and weapon, exposing her to my world. I knew what I was doing when I did it, knew it would leave scars and fears embedded in her. I did it anyway.

It's my doing, my fault, my responsibility. I learned a long time ago how to bury and carry the wounds of my life. I never saw her cracking, didn't teach her how to manage it. I thought she was impervious, a glittering diamond impossible to break.

"Talia." I roll forward, taking her face between my hands.

Sterling sighs, "Our life destroys the beautiful, fragile things."

"It does. I don't know when I stopped letting myself feel anything, but I didn't for a long time until you."

Sterling presses his face to the side of her head, looking to me. "You make it better. We need you more than you'll ever understand. Come on, Firefly." Standing, he says, "I know just the thing to sober you up."

"I don't wanna be sober."

I rise to my feet. "How?"

He shows his teeth in a wide, gleeful grin. "I'm going to enjoy this a lot more than I should for reasons you don't understand."

He flings her away from him.

She squeaks, flailing as she crashes down into the pool.

Breaking through the surface, she slaps her arms up and down. "Sterling!"

He doubles over, laughing at the rocks.

I raise an eyebrow as Light streaks toward us.

425

My Dark deflects, but Sterling isn't paying attention. He gets ensnared and ripped forward.

"Tal," he shouts, slipping toward the water.

He latches onto me.

The rocks give beneath my feet, and we're both dragged into the water.

It. Is. Cold.

I get above the surface, snarling. "Sterling!"

He snickers. "Get out before you start yelling."

He heads for the shore.

Natalia stumbles onto dry land.

I send my Dark toward Sterling to drag him back. I hoist myself up using his shoulder, spreading my wings to get out sooner than swimming.

I fly to shore, landing next to Natalia. She rubs her arms, dancing in place. Her teeth chatter.

I pull her in close, wrapping around her to share heat.

Sterling comes stumbling to us, laughing silently. "Fuck that's cold." He rushes for us, wrapping his arms around us at Natalia's back. "F–f–f–fuck, it's cold."

I glare from the tops of my eyes, sending my Dark to warm things up.

It twists through the air around us, crackling in shades of midnight to ignite as orange and gold shimmering flames.

Sterling shudders. "Don't set me on fire. Please don't set me on fire."

"You're safe, baby. Deep breaths."

Kissing the back of her head, Sterling asks, "Do you know the point of the maze?"

She sniffles. "A torturous death-trap that's just stupid and mean?"

"No, it teaches us that fear cannot be avoided. Courage is not an absence of fear, and strength is not an absence of weakness.

We face our fears, and we fight to prove our strength, that's true, but..."

He hesitates, and I pick up his words. "Every time you take a hit and get back up, when the odds are against you and you refuse to quit, if you're not okay and still fight, that's true strength."

"Don't quit on us, Firefly. I'm begging you, fight." He lifts her chin and turns her face toward him. "Fight for us. Fight with us. Don't let the bad days win."

She nods. "O'tay."

I lift her against me, guiding one leg around me as I hold her tight. "Get me out of here."

Spinning me toward the exit, Sterling puts his arm around me, his other hand on Natalia's back. "The walls are not moving. It's not getting any smaller."

"Shut up and get me out of this hole."

CHAPTER 45
CALLAHAN

I clean up with my mates. Sterling whispers to Natalia, zipping her dress. She smiles at me, buttoning my shirt. I fix Sterling's collar as Natalia picks a stray thread from his chest.

"I like you in black much better."

He sighs. "The way you looked at me yesterday made my Dark whine."

She bobs her head, running her hands over his chest. "You didn't look like you."

I kiss her temple. "I'll take care of it."

I send them to breakfast—my two incredible mates. I lift my hands as the door to our suite closes. The rings of the contest set adorn my thumbs, representing the head and the heart, the two halves of one whole. I close my eyes and relax, maybe for the first time in my life.

Ilbuio is large, stretching out with jagged, sharp roofs and steeples. Sequestered in the palace, I tend to forget the existence of the city itself. Between the perks of sharing and not being the Dark King, I have more freedom than ever before. I'm going to use it.

I swipe the broken necklace off the nightstand where Sterling has baubles and nicknacks collected. After a quick stop by the kitchens to arrange cake for Jacques, I leave the palace.

There's a jeweler I need to visit to address the broken chain, then I'll rouse Ashley. It'll give her a bit more time to recover, but I need to be coronated.

When I return to the palace, I find my mates in bed together. Natalia lies on her side, Sterling at her back, one arm draped over her.

She doesn't stir, but he picks his head up. "Shh," he whispers. "I just got her back to sleep."

I twist my lips to the side. "We need to keep moving."

"The contractors are furious about her admitting to lying."

"She wasn't raised as our kind, not even raised in the Dark. We can't hold her to our laws before she knew them."

"I argued that."

"Good, you should have."

He smirks. "I'm not that stupid. I had my own reasons for challenging her when they demanded."

"I'm aware of your stupid reasons."

"A few more of my old vassals showed for contracts and almost all of Yanri's, so I think we're good. Tam is going to let me know if we need more. Tal has signed hundreds, but the contractors don't seem to be settling, looking for excuses to rip the crown from her."

"Unsurprising. The unification won't help the situation either, but I won't quit. Has anyone heard from Ashley?"

"Not that I know of."

I set the case on the bed, fatigue beckoning me to join them, to close my eyes and enjoy my mates.

Rubbing my forehead, I say, "I'll take care of everything. Let her sleep as much as she can."

"What are you doing?"

"Finalizing when I get a crown. I need to finish that to have authority over the Light. Not enough are showing up willingly. We have a war with the Ancients and then we have a world to remake."

He stares at me, features weighed down. "Fuck, how'd we get stuck with all this?"

I force a deep frown, exaggerating the act, then point to our mate. "Her. She entered my life, which opened the door for Pierre. He's the reason I'm supposed to rule the Light. Otherwise, you or I would be on our own to deal with the Ancients."

"You think we wouldn't have made Mallafic bleed?"

"We established working together at the Obsidian Palace because I invited you to have Dark Marrow present for her. No Natalia, no need for the band."

"Huh." Sterling props his head on a bent arm. "I still think I might have tried to get you to do it with me, but it's weird to think of the way a single thread of the web can change your life."

I hum, flexing my eyebrows. "She changed everything, not just me. She's...different. I can't put my finger on what she truly is. Her magic? That silver coloring and how it presents. Even if she's the Light, she's not..."

She whimpers and kicks.

Sterling tightens around her. "You're right. There's something about her magic that's different than everyone's. You said Lucius can make silver threads?"

I bob my head. "They're threads of his soul, but he doesn't present with them like she does."

Natalia shudders and sobs.

Sterling sighs. "It would have been better for her if we'd stayed away."

I get onto the bed as she twitches. I know what I've done to her. I don't care about the damage or pain. I have her because of everything I did.

Walking on my knees across the mattress, I shake my head. "She would have married Tony, had his children. She'd be miserable, and this way she's ours to protect."

"I'm questioning if we can. We're up against Ancients and a god."

"We figure it out. I'm not losing." I brush her hair from her face. "Little Star."

She blinks her eyes open at me. "Babe?"

I help her sit, extending my hand to the side. My Dark sets the case in my palm, and I offer it to her. "I fixed it."

"Oh." She clears her throat, wipes her face, and then takes the case. She snaps it open, frowning, then lifts her gaze to me. Her eyes well up. "Babe."

I lean forward, pressing my lips to her forehead. "Mate."

I take the case, pull the necklace from inside, and unclasp it to slide the chain around her throat and secure it in place.

She presses her fingers to the pendants, staring at me.

Sterling kisses the side of her face, tucking his chin over her shoulder. "All better now?"

She drops her hand, revealing the orange jewel framed by silver wings next to the star.

I nod. "Yes." I slide off the bed, offering her my hand.

She takes my hand, and I keep her steady as she slips high heels on.

Sterling takes her hand, spinning her. The hem of her dress flutters. He catches her against him and dips her, smiling.

His face flickers through confusion to shock to ire. He pulls her up, looking to me. "You're a fucking annoyingly perfect, pretty bastard."

"Who's your alpha?" I chuckle, snagging Natalia's hand as I move past them to the doorway. I halt, lifting her hand in mine. Threads of her Light are wrapped with ropes of my Dark around our wrists, but there is no lace of her Light presenting over her skin. "I didn't think you'd ever stop glowing around me."

"He wants to know if you'd prefer him to, 'cause he will if you want."

I cup her jaw, kissing her. She'll glow when she's happy. That's enough.

"No, I'm used to it. I'm just surprised you don't glow around me and Sterling."

She bites her lower lip, staring up at me with wide eyes. "Mates."

"*Mhm.*" I nuzzle her nose. "Mates."

Sterling puts his arm around her. "Even if you aren't always shiny, it changes nothing about our agreement."

I lift my eyebrows.

He snickers. "She said I could have anything shiny she had to offer."

Narrowing one eye at Natalia, I feign annoyance.

She grimaces at me. "I forgot I glow."

I smile, laughing silently. She had offered. He took what he wanted because he could.

The webs of fate really are fickle. I regret leaving her, but if I hadn't, I may not have this.

CHAPTER 46
CALLAHAN

I knock on Ashley's door. She answers, her hair loose in gilded waves, her face clear of makeup. The haggard appearance brings to mind tarnished silver, glazed with a haze, dimming its luster.

"We need to arrange the coronation."

She licks her lips and stands taller. "Hello, Callahan. Welcome and be welcomed. May I invite you in?" She steps aside, motioning to within her chambers. "Shall I have tea prepared?"

There's a tinge of ire to the words, not quite a sneer. It's faker than any attempts I've made at Light customs.

I smirk. The woman went through the maze, and she might not have finished it, but she's got the scars to prove enough. The least I can do is extend respect, even if it's not how I understand it.

I bow, one hand across my stomach, one at my back. I didn't get direct lessons or have my form critiqued, but it's the best I can offer.

"We are welcomed and welcoming. The offer is generous, but tea is unnecessary. I'll extend my hand to you in support if you need and inquire as to your state."

She jerks with shock, then laughs. "I appreciate that."

Sterling leans against the doorframe. "Did you get all hundred showers in?"

"Several very long ones." She puckers her lips in disgust, head low. "Sister Mine, I'm glad you were able to escape that thing. I apologize for not seeking you sooner to determine if you had returned."

Natalia waves a hand. "You went through the maze."

"I suppose that's some kind of accomplishment." She throws her hair over her shoulders. "I sent Wyham to take Wyona to Izul."

"Have him remain there until the coronation."

Ashley presses her lips, drawing her eyebrows together.

"Mallafic relented. He told us to run the maze with Light in a trial. We did, and we didn't kill each other or abandon anyone. We earned what we wanted."

Her face falls lax as she stares at me. "I had no intentions of heeding that thing. It's not my god. My father died for this, and I'll find him in the afters before I forsake his wishes." She shrugs. "I was counting days. Your coronation is in three days from now. Flora's sister notified me that all invitations have been delivered by hand, and we are on schedule."

Three days. I nod. I need to find Thames to finalize attire preparations.

Ashley says, "If we leave tomorrow morning, we should arrive by end of day. This schedule will provide you with a day to tour the city and get settled."

I look to Sterling.

He shrugs. "If we're doing this, I can't complain about being in their city and surrounded by them or following their stupid customs."

"Fine," I say, facing Ashley. "We leave tomorrow morning. Rest until then, recover."

She rolls her eyes. "As if that thing could—"

"Don't fucking lie to me. How you managed to get through it, I don't care, but deal with it in honesty now."

She turns her head away. "I am capable of taking care of myself."

"Capable, yes, and you've earned respect. Don't piss it away by pretending like the maze didn't afflict you."

She licks her lips. "You want to gloat?"

"I faced my torments and have my own wounds to lick. What am I gloating over? I want you to accept what happened, accept you were afraid, and remember you survived. It's not about *not* being afraid. It's about facing your fears and overcoming them. You did that. Don't belittle yourself by pretending otherwise."

She inclines her head. "Thank you."

Natalia asks, "Is Tony all right?"

"I haven't seen him since I left him in the hall with his precious Natasha," she says, her tone icy.

"That thing is dead."

She drops her chin, facing the floor and lifting the toe of one foot, rotating it on the thin, high heel of her shoe. "Was... Was Nicky like that?"

"It wasn't human."

"Magia."

"It wasn't natural. It wasn't human, even like human, but for the appearance."

Natalia bobs her head. "Not really my brother."

"Not even a little bit, honey."

I kiss Natalia's forehead. "We leave tomorrow. We have things to address first. Ash, do what you need, and I'll see you at dinner or in the morning. It's your choice."

Disengaging, I pull my mates to Thames. He takes every measurement possible of the three of us.

Sterling and Natalia giggle together, realizing my scheme. I melt, simpering at them together.

I check on my kin, joining Galain and Fallon on the floor to play with building blocks. The boy seems all right, but says his whole body has a headache.

I look to Natalia, catching her eye as she talks to Falsion. I hold her gaze, then look to Fallon.

She sits next to him, pulling him into her lap. "You're getting so big."

"Not big enough. I'm still too small to eat the Light."

I shake my head. "I remember those days."

Galain snorts through his nose. "Seemed better at the time, didn't it?"

I stack a few blocks, working on building an arch. As a boy I dreamed of all kinds of adventures, slaying beasts for respect and Lights to consume their magic.

I lift my eyes, staring at my star. My original intention was to contract her to feed from her. My Dark won't ever feed on her again.

It laughs in my head. *"Quit wallowing. It's less weakness, and we still eat our mate."*

She wraps her arms around Fallon, squeezing him. "How about we practice? Can you stay still for me, and I'll push the Light through you?"

"Yes," Fallon screams, going rigid with a grin.

Natalia closes her eyes, her silver Light pulsing in her. It stops, and she hugs him tighter. "Did you eat some?"

"Yeah! I did it. I did it, Dad. My body hurt, but she gave me Light, and I don't hurt anymore."

Galain smiles. "I'm proud of you." He reaches for his boy, pulling him close for a hug. "Never forget that. I couldn't be prouder as a father if I tried."

My father never said anything of the sort. I meet Natalia's eyes. She thinks I deserve respect.

Galain nods at her. "Thank you."

She lifts her hand, Light winding between her fingers. "Do you need practice?"

Luca rushes over. "Me," he says. "Me, I do. I want to practice."

Falsion scoffs. "A glutton if ever there was one."

Shawn shakes his head. "I'll practice. Why not?"

The door opens, and a woman steps in. She hesitates.

Fallon lurches up. "Mom! Mommy, I ate the Light."

I widen my gaze, frozen as she kneels, hugging the boy. I look to Galain.

He chuckles. "Meet Clara."

Clara inclines her head. "Your Majesty."

Galain says, "She's contracted to Matthew Bernine, brought here to help fight. I was surprised to see her, and I've been less than forthcoming to avoid certain others from knowing our connection."

Clara straightens, taking Fallon's hand to walk him back to the blocks. "I am not afraid."

I laugh. "It's for your benefit. You birthed a Hallow. Ashley would drag you into everything." I focus on Falsion. "Where is Maria's mother?"

He shrugs. "Nanira Lavmar. She died decades ago in the games."

Sterling says, "Nemar inherited the Lavmar lineage. He's here with the rest of the contractors."

Falsion shifts. "I brought Maria to visit. Nemar informed me of her death. He made it clear Maria was illegitimate, a Mandolux, not a Lavmar, and would receive nothing from the Lavmar estate. We haven't spoken since."

Clara kneels, offering blocks to Fallon. "What is my sweet boy making?"

I stand, offering my hand to Natalia. "I need you all to see Thames. He'll take measurements to have attire fitted."

She takes my hand. It makes my Dark soar, wrapping around our clasped hands to bind us together.

Luca makes a face. "Didn't we get stuck with pins for that reason already?"

I lift my eyebrows. "Do you want to wear white?"

They all perk, looking to me.

I smirk. "See Thames as soon as possible. We leave for Izul in the morning." I head for the door.

Jacques is next on my list of tasks to tackle, so I return to the kitchens.

Thomas greets us, wiping his forearm across his forehead, flour smeared on his cheek. "Sir." He points. "Just finished the last one."

Natalia lets go of me, stepping to another vassal inspecting the back of his hand.

She heals the burn, others offering up minor cuts as well. I wait until she's finished tending to them, then we gather up the cakes.

Sterling sniffs one as we head for Jacques's chambers. "Lemon?"

"Lemon blueberry."

"You have no idea how relieved I was when Jessa signed with Tal. I was depressed at the thought that I would be missing her pastries."

I glance at the cakes I'm carrying, then to him. "She made the meal I had at your home?"

"Yeah. She's got talent in the kitchen. Can't figure out how to throw a punch though."

Natalia shakes her head, hoisting her cakes higher. "What are these?"

I eye them, sniffing at the two I have. "Mine are the strawberries and cream and the vanilla." I lean over, trying to determine the scents from hers. "Jacques rattled off a list of chocolate, blueberry and lemon, strawberry and cream, and vanilla with sprinkles. Not sure what the others are."

Sterling groans. "I bet one is pumpkin. Jessa does this amazing pumpkin bake."

We get to Jacques's door. I kick it to warn him I'm coming in, then grant myself entry.

He strolls from an attached room and then runs, grabbing the strawberry with clotted cream cake off the dish. Holding it between both hands, his jaw stretches, clicking as it dislocates.

He takes one massive bite, cramming as much into his mouth as he can.

I watch as it disappears in four bites. Jacques wiggles his jaw. It clicks, closing back to normal as he begins to lick the frosting from his fingers, a lot more smeared across his cheeks and nose.

Sterling laughs. "Did you even taste that?"

"Yes, vividly. Mmmm." Jacques grins, his nostrils flaring.

He flicks his long, black forked tongue at the other cakes. "Mm," he licks at the two Natalia have, wrinkling his nose. "Ick, pumpkin?"

Sterling says, "If you don't want it, don't eat it. I will."

Jacques grabs it and scarfs it down, licking his lips. "I don't like pumpkin anything."

"Then why'd you eat it? I said I would."

Jacques laughs. "I earned my cake. I'm eating all the cake." He checks the rest, flicking his tongue at them. "Oh, vanilla."

He swallows it almost whole.

Natalia laughs. "Okay, I'm impressed. Not even a Magia would eat this much at once."

I snicker. "He's a damn snake. They can eat probably more than any Magia."

Jacques sniffs the remaining three cakes, licking at the air around them. "Blueberry and lemon or cinnamon. Choices, choices."

Sterling waves the brown icing coated cake. "Or chocolate."

Jacques holds a finger at him. "Oh, no. That sweet darling is most definitely last." He looks between the three, then inhales the blueberry lemon.

I shift my weight. "Are you eating worst to best?"

Jerking to look at me like he'd forgotten I was present, Jacques says, "There is no worst about cake. All cake is amazing." He licks his lips, gorging on the cinnamon cake.

He turns, fixating on the chocolate. "You," he whispers, stalking to Sterling.

My mate looks at me with concern, but Jacques takes the plate, sniffing at the cake and smacking his lips, tasting the air around it.

"Come to me, gorgeous." He lifts the plate in one hand, staring at it then flicks his other hand on a limp wrist at us. "Go. Shoo. Me and this beauty are going to take our time. Mmm, you smell so good. I'm going to lick you clean then savor every inch of you."

Sterling's concern has turned to slight fear.

Natalia giggles.

My mouth hangs open. It's not intentional.

Jacques glances at us. "Do you mind?" He pulls the cake closer. "This is private."

I look to my mates and walk out of his room in a daze.

Sterling stops at my side. "Is he going to fuck that cake?" he asks in a hoarse voice, staring at me.

From inside the room, Jacques yells, "What I do with my cake is none of your business."

I laugh behind my hand, not answering. I don't know, and I don't want to.

Sterling grimaces. "I don't think I've even looked at Tal the way he looked at that cake."

She giggles. "He really likes cake."

I'd been caught off guard, forgotten the other reason I'd come. Turning around, I open the door, "Jacques," I say, widening my eyes and going blank.

Jacques has his tongue buried in the icing. As I stare, he goes still, staring back with his tongue half dragged across the cake.

"See Thames by the end of today and we leave tomorrow morning for Izul." I close the door, shaking my head.

I'm never going to look at cake the same again.

CHAPTER 47
NATALIA

Cal doesn't stop. He tracks down men and women I don't know. I recognize several as those who served him at his home. Cal discusses lodgings and tasks, ensuring they are adequate and balanced.

I fiddle with the two pendants standing between Cal and Sterling as they carry on a conversation with Sarina. Every chance they get, they pin me between them. I walk between them, sleep between them, and sit between them.

I have two mates. I grapple with the fact, unsure of myself.

Nicky begged me for his life, pleading in tears that I save him. I shouldn't be allowed to be happy.

Tony lost the truest love that ever existed. I shouldn't be gifted what was stolen from him.

Dark brushes against my cheek, Cal calling my name from somewhere else far away.

A hand squeezes my shoulder. I jerk, looking up at Cal standing at my side.

"What?"

Sarina curls her lip. "Shall I return to my duties?"

Cal frowns. "When your contracted speak, you listen."

"Sorry, I—"

"The Dark doesn't apologize."

I shove him away, rage pulsing in my veins. "I'm never going to be perfect like her."

He pulls his eyebrows together.

I cover my face, aghast at myself. "I'm... I didn't mean that, any of it. I don't know why I said that. I didn't... I was just..."

From behind me, Sterling collects my hair, twisting it to one side of my neck. His warm breath caresses my ear. "Breathe."

"Little Star, look at me."

I lift my face, blinking stinging eyes at him. I don't know where this came from. One moment Sarina was discussing her day, the need for holes to be filled that she's covering in a business Cal owns, and now I'm losing control of everything.

He wipes away a tear, the lines of his face deepening as he cups my face. "I have never wanted or asked you to be someone else."

I nod, trying to turn away.

He catches me, turning my face back to his. "You're not running from me right now."

"You have things to do, and I'm getting in the way."

"Mate." He strains his eyes at me, his eyelids flaring open.

"Survive on strength," I whisper, shaking my head. "I'm not—"

"Talia," he says, lifting his voice. "Stop."

Sterling wraps his arms around me, lifting me off my feet. He spins me in circles, coming to a stop to put me down. He doesn't let go, squeezing me. "When did you start to question yourself?"

I hang my head. "I should check on Tony."

Cal drags a hand down his face, looking to Sarina. "Put postings for open positions. We'll fill the holes with humans."

She narrows her eyes, looking from him to me.

He steps toward her. "You're questioning my mate?" He curls his fingers into fists.

Sterling holds me tighter.

Facing Cal, Sarina shakes her head. "I'd never question you. I signed with her because she was yours."

"Good choice."

Sarina looks to the floor, keeping her posture meek. "We all know the power she holds, raw strength none of us can best."

"But?" Cal asks, a snarl in the word.

"She is soft."

"She has a fucking heart," he says. "She hasn't been fucking destroyed. She still feels, and that comes with a cost, but it's not a weakness. Don't confuse heartless as strength."

Sarina laughs, relaxing. "No matter how long I serve you, I still learn from you at every exchange." She turns, sauntering away.

Cal turns to me, his mouth hard. "Talia."

I wince.

He stares at me, then sighs, coming closer. He lifts me against him, nuzzling my neck. "You need sleep."

Sterling presses a hand to my back. "Take her. Go, I have vassals to check in with and business to tend to as well. I'll show for dinner and see if the contractors have dug up any information yet that we can work with."

Cal starts walking, Sterling turning to watch us with a smile until Cal turns a corner and Sterling disappears from sight.

I want to apologize again. Sarina's right. I'm soft. My insides are tender, oozing with pain.

I bury my face against Cal until he opens a door. I pick my head up, realizing we're at our rooms.

He lays down with me in his arms. "Little Star, your annoyances far exceed—"

"My uses," I say, the words slicing through my heart. "I know."

"My patience sometimes." He shifts, moving to his side to face me. He touches his nose to mine, staring into my eyes. "Nothing will ever outweigh the benefits of having you as my mate."

"I made another mess."

"Sarina needed a lesson. There is nothing in our tenets that bars us from feeling. Too often, we confuse strength with cold. We go through the maze, forgetting what it teaches us. Being afraid doesn't make anyone a coward. Being unfeeling and cold doesn't make one strong. It's our ability to manage our fear, to manage our emotions, and overcome them that defines our strength."

I relax into the mattress, running a finger down his chest. The hard muscles and his guidance provide comfort.

He rubs the tip of his nose against mine. "You're beautiful."

"Am I?"

"*Mhm.*" He smiles. "I won't force you to tell me what the maze did, but whatever happened, you can tell me if you want. If not, I'm here to hold your hand and support you. I know you can handle it, but I'm here."

I tap his chest, lowering my gaze toward my finger. "You added a firefly."

He closes his eyes, stretching his body, then slumping. "You're more stubborn than time."

"You're my mate."

"I know." He grins wide, his face radiating with glee as he taps the imprint of my glittering silver bite on his neck.

"I love you. I love you so much. I don't want to lose you."

He slides his knuckles along my arm, lifting my hand to press my palm against his mouth.

Rolling us, he keeps my hand in his as he straddles me. He

slides his lips across my wrist, holding my gaze. "You're still mine. You're just his too, and he's ours."

But what if I love him too? What if I can't give Cal my whole heart, only half?

I can't bring myself to ask. It might shatter everything.

He chuckles. "My little mate and guiding star, we are keeping our birdie. Accept it."

I nod. "You're really okay with..."

He taps the necklace. "My star, his firefly, our woman, a mate to share between mates."

I sit, yanking his face to mine to taste him. I need his strength to hold myself together.

He presses my wrists between his hands, cool Dark twining around them. He forces me back, pinning my hands over my head as he kisses me.

Rolling back, he drags his hands down my sides, moving one knee, then the other between my legs. He lifts my hips, pulling me into his lap and spreading my legs.

My arms are pulled taut, the bindings around my wrists tightening. His hands turn black, snapping and popping as his fingers elongate. He strums sharp claws against my stomach as he stares down at me.

"Who do you belong to?"

"You," I answer, breathless. My skin tingles, begging for his touch.

He hums, strumming again. "I've been thinking..." One side of his mouth pulls back. "Drunk on half a bottle of vodka? Your new strength?"

"Uh-huh."

"You're not a human."

I lick my lips, pulling at the magic binding me. "Kind of ruining the mood."

He holds my gaze, his eyes smoldering. "You're not fragile

anymore." His talons graze across my sternum. "I don't have to be gentle."

"Gentle?"

"I've held back in necessity."

A throb in time with my heart picks up between my legs, and I arch my back, flexing against the tether.

If he's been gentle... "Cal, please."

"Who do you belong to?"

"You, my alpha."

He smirks, leaning over and cupping my jaw in one massive hand. "Good girl. I am your alpha, but who do you belong to?"

I moan, aching for him. "You."

"And?" He presses his nose to the corner of my jaw, skimming his lips against my neck. A bit lower, and he'd hit the mating mark. I'd come.

I lift my hips, searching for friction. "You and..."

He licks, tracing the edge of his mating mark. It's overlaid with Sterling's. I know exactly where it is, how good it feels on my neck just existing. Touching it always brings a sense of comfort and security, but when they touch it, I explode in sparks and lightning.

His teeth graze the column of my neck, off to the side.

I whimper, my body pulsing, blood rushing to my breasts and between my legs. I need to feel him everywhere, need him inside of me, claiming me.

"You and...Sterling," I whisper, squeezing my eyes shut, terrified to look at him.

"Good girl." He licks the mating marks.

I cry out, jerking and arching my back as I come, a flood of wet heat filling me.

He shreds my clothes, cutting them off my body with his talons to lick and kiss my skin.

He coaxes me to the edge of delirium, and I quit fighting my bonds, accepting what he wants me to take. I'm lost in the over-whelming pleasure, confused when he flips me over.

He slips his hands around my hips, lifting my butt in the air. I get my knees under me, my hands still tethered to keep my arms stretched out.

"Hands against the headboard," he says, nudging me closer.

"What?"

Leaning over me, he grabs my wrists in one hand, guiding me to press my palms against the headboard.

"Push."

I flex, pressing into the wood.

He stays leaned over me, keeping my hands against the head-board with one hand, but his other leaves my side. The head of his cock slides along my slit, lining up. He thrusts into me, and I moan at being filled.

"Cal, please," I whimper.

He draws up, grabbing my hips and lifting slightly. He draws back, almost all the way out and slams forward.

My arms give, and I hit the headboard with my head.

He growls, "I said push." He drags me back, grabbing one butt cheek. "Put your hands on the headboard and push." He lets go and smacks my ass. "Now."

I arch my back as I push my hands into the headboard, locking my elbows and straining.

He pulls back and rams forward. My arms give, bending as I strain to keep from hitting the headboard a second time. He doesn't stop thrusting into me.

Dark winds around me, caressing my breasts and between my legs as he slams into me from behind. My arms shake, burning with effort as I pant. I'm struggling even with my immortal strength.

He doesn't let up even for a moment, and soon, I can't handle any more, my arms giving away in fatigue.

He drags me backward, forcing me flat and keeps going. I'm helpless to do anything, mewling and gasping at each hard stroke that seems to stretch me further and further.

When I shudder in pleasure, crying out, he twists me to the side, lifting one leg over his shoulder and angling my hips up. His fingers dig into me, his grip painful as he holds me still to keep thrusting with a brutality that sends me spiraling into oblivion.

I come to under Cal's arm. The shadows swirl and prick my skin. I shiver, sitting up and looking around.

Mallafic. I can sense him, even if I can't see him.

I slide off the bed to stand, getting another dress on. I scan the room, my heart hammering.

"Talia?"

I glance to Cal, and the sense of being watched dissipates as he gazes at me, propped on one arm.

The way shadows lick across his carved body leaves me weak in the knees. His black hair is a mess, increasing the sex appeal rather than leaving him disheveled.

I lick my lips, searching the room, but whatever Mallafic was doing here, it's over. He's gone.

Cal rolls off the bed to his feet, watching me.

I shake my head, collecting my hair and running my fingers through the strands.

He gets dressed, takes my hand, and leads me from our bedroom and down the corridor to the king's hall.

Sterling sits off to the side with Tony and Falsion. Sterling has his eyebrows raised as Tony furrows his brow in thought. Falsion looks hopelessly lost.

Ashley, Flora, Lyla, Galain, Luca, and Jacques are gathered around a table playing cards.

Larles, Owen, and Parker are listening to something Shawn is saying.

Hiro has Thames in his lap on the chaise, speaking to Zander.

Oscar, Palak, and Hailey are collected to another side.

Maria is absent. I hope she's with Thomas.

Fallon too, isn't present. Perhaps he's with his mother.

Cal kisses me on the back of my head as he moves past me into the room, heading for the card game.

I linger at the threshold, staring around the room. It's a mix of Dark and Light everywhere, but I still feel out of place.

Ness is still missing. I can't leave her with Mallafic. After everything he's done, whatever his plans, I know she's not safe.

I pick at the silver ring on my right thumb. This means something, but I don't understand what.

I turn to leave. I'll try to find a book. It's a vain hope that I can find one and understand it, and even less hope that one might hold an answer with Mallafic's intentions, but I have to try.

Cool strands wrap around me, tugging me into the room toward Sterling, his Dark hissing softly.

I give in, stepping to my mate. "I need to find Ness."

"Can't do that. Don't know where she is or how to track her or Mallafic."

I tilt my head at Tony. "What about Soris? Does she know?"

"Know? Yes. Does it matter? No. The last time I tried to find Ness Soris said she was at the salt baths near Saltina. I decided I'd get Falsion, and we'd go get her. Mallafic moved her. Every time I decided I'd go where they were, Mallafic would move. He moved with her twenty times while I tried to find Falsion before I gave up the idea that I'd reach them. Mallafic stopped moving."

Sterling hums. "He has Sirius, right? Another fate. Maybe he knew Soris was helping you?"

Falsion scratches his head. "Sirius is the fate of the past. He knows everything that's happened. Bella always said he was the most dangerous of fates. Soris knows what's happening in the world but forgets as soon as it happens. Saris, she's tricky. She can see all the options of the future. Nothing is certain with her webs until right before she passes them to Soris to weave. Sirius though, he never forgets, knows everything a fraction after it's happened, and everything that dictates what is and what could be."

Tony sighs. "Yeah. Soris, she knows some things, but if I ask what just happened, she has no idea. I remember it for her, actually. All I can tell you is Ness is doing a lot of reading. I haven't seen Mallafic hurt her."

Sterling pulls me into his lap, my back to his chest so he can rest his chin on my shoulder. "We're trading riddles instead."

Falsion scoffs, rubbing his face. "These two are," he says, flicking a hand at Tony and Sterling. "I'm realizing I'm an idiot."

Tony shakes his head. "Not really."

I shift, getting comfortable. "You okay?"

He looks to me, his eyes darkening as he scowls. "Fuck no. What was that thing?"

"Something Mallafic made."

"Is it really dead?"

"Yeah." I bob my head, keeping my eyes low. I'm not sure how to tell him his second chance was ruined. It wasn't Sasha, but it could have been.

"Good." The quiet fury in his voice startles me.

I meet his gaze again.

A muscle in his neck stands out as he pinches his lips and pulls his ears back in a grimace. "Thanks for making me leave."

I lift my chin. "Mm."

"That stupid ball... Did she really...?"

I bob my head.

"Fucking Mother."

Sterling tightens his arm around me. "What is the difference between a jeweler and a jailer?"

I shake my head, questioning if Sterling would have mated me without Cal's involvement. I'm not smart enough for him. "I don't know."

Tony says, "Hang on, I'm still thinking."

We sit in silence, chatter from the table nearby growing louder with laughter.

Tony's eyes get larger as he turns incredulous. "Oh, fuck you. It's wordplay. A jeweler sells watches, and a jailer watches cells."

Sterling laughs. "It's a riddle. Of course, it's wordplay."

Tony asks, "What is the end of everything?"

Falsion groans. "We're living that nightmare. The Ancients, Mallafic, a Light wearing the crown of Dark and us mutts got handed the crown of Light, plus the crowns mating each other. It's a disaster."

Sterling says, "The letter "G." Humans deserve it. Seraphinus need it. If you eat it, you die."

I elbow Sterling. "That's not how that one goes. It's poor people have it, and rich people need it."

He turns his face into my neck. "Humans are annoying pests that we tolerate because they offer worthwhile inventions and labor."

I point to myself. "I'm one of those humans."

"Careful, Firefly." He smiles against my neck. "Some might consider that lying."

I sag into him. "Right. I'm not human anymore."

"No," he snickers. "You're less fragile, and still so shiny. I like when there are others around. You start glowing again."

Falsion asks, "What's the bloody answer?"

Tony says, "Nothing."

"Nothing? There's no answer?"

I say, "Poor people have nothing, the rich want nothing, and if you eat nothing you die."

Falsion looks away. "I really am just a dumb animal."

Tony laughs. "No. Riddles are tricks, and there's a knack to them. Forward it's heavy, backwards it's not."

"No idea. I'm worse at this than cards. I should've stayed at the table."

Sterling snickers. "Ton."

Tony throws his hands up. "You don't even have to think."

"I enjoy riddles and puzzles, and I've had centuries to play with them."

Tony frowns. "I guess I'll get to that point." He shoves fingers through his hair, blowing out a puff of air.

"You will if we survive. One breaks but never falls. One falls but never breaks."

"Day and night. What—"

"Talia," Cal cuts him off.

I glance over, his hand extended. Sterling nudges me toward him, whispering words of encouragement.

Smiling, I reach for Cal, getting to my feet. He takes my hand, his Dark raveling around my wrist and forearm to tether me.

He starts for the door, whistling over his shoulder, "You too, baby."

Sterling laughs. "I've been summoned. Last one. I may hurt you but scorn me at your own peril. It hurts more when you've lost me, almost as much if you've never had me. Embrace me at your own risk, feeling me is a gamble, yet you can't ever touch me. I can be blind, perhaps cruel, but true. What am I?"

Cal grumbles under his breath, turning back. His Dark streaks through the air, wrapping around Sterling to drag him out of the chair.

I gape. "Cal."

Sterling laughs even as he's pulled along the floor and Cal starts walking again. "What?"

He moves into the hallway, Sterling lifting his voice full of humor. "All right! All right, I'll walk."

Cal stops, twisting back with a lazy smirk. His Dark unwinds from Sterling, who pushes off the floor to join us, straightening his shirt as he grins ear to ear.

"You're as vicious as her Light. You gave me no time before I had to comply, and I was complying."

"Not fast enough."

"You're cranky." Sterling bends his knees and pushes forward, lifting Cal over his shoulder. "I'm assuming you're cranky because you want fucked?"

Cal chuckles. "Put me down."

"No. I don't have to take orders."

I widen my eyes, waiting for Cal to thrash Sterling and prove he's in charge. He doesn't, just hangs over Sterling's shoulder.

Sterling glances around. "Tal? Oh, you're still tethered. Good. We're going to bed now, loves." He jerks his head down the hallway, the rest of him following.

I chase after Sterling, my wrist tied to Cal's. "Am I supposed to be telling him to put you down?"

Sterling answers, "He's fine. He could get down anytime he wants. He's just not."

Cal lifts his head to meet my eyes, laughing at me, his eyes sparkling. If I didn't know better, I'd believe he's enjoying himself.

CHAPTER 48
CALLAHAN
2ND EVERGREEN'S DAY, BLOOMING, 4050, 6TH MILLENNIUM

We prepare to leave after breakfast, Hiro in charge with Oscar to help until we return. Thames assures me everything will be shipped to Izul, guaranteeing it will arrive in time.

Tony follows us to the back of the palace. On the patio, he steps to Ashley. "I don't have wings."

She looks at him, then shrugs. "Your presence is unnecessary."

He does a little head shake, yanking back and cocking his head. "You begged me to come. I did the lessons."

"It's my prerogative to change my mind. You should remain here. You aren't suited for Izul and I don't have time to manage you."

She turns, striding away as golden wings spread, threads of Light fluttering like feathers. They start beating at the air to lift her away.

Tony stares after her then kicks at the stone, turning away. He lowers his head, but I catch sight of the pain in his face.

I meet Sterling's eyes, tipping my head at Tony.

He lifts his shoulders, mocking a frown. "Wish someone would tell me I didn't have to go."

"Fine, you don't have to go." I shake my head, tangling Tony in my Dark as I form wings.

He looks at me. "Just leave me."

"No. Suck it up and be a man. The maze threw Akash at her. She's still reeling." I take flight, dragging him along.

Sterling catches up to me in a hurry, flying at my side.

I glance over. "Thought you were staying."

"I am." He grins, pointing to his side. "I'd rather be miserable with my mates than without them."

Flora and Lyla require several stops to rest. Fallon cries because he has no wings. Sterling, Falsion, and Shawn take turns with me carrying Tony.

Ashley keeps her distance from everyone, flying apart. I send Jacques to deal with that. She's still fighting instead of accepting.

As the suns sink below the horizon, Flora and Layla require yet another rest.

Natalia sits on the edge of a roof, staring off into the distance.

Sterling sits next to her, nudging her. "You've been quiet."

I drop next to her other side, putting her where she belongs. "I'll be with you this time."

She lifts and drops her foot, swinging her lower leg from the knee as she nods.

Sterling leans back on his hands. "When you were in Izul, Cal came to me for the guitar. It was the first time he'd ever spoken to me outside of Ilbuio and the games."

She looks to him.

"It was our first date." He winks, moving his gaze past her to me. "I made him dinner."

Holding his eyes with mine, I lean into Natalia, pressing my lips to the side of her head above her ear. "He had dinner made by vassals. It would have been our last date if he cooked."

Shaking his head, he returns to staring ahead. "You shocked the shit out of me by turning up at my door. I didn't realize you knew where I lived. We weren't friends."

"Still aren't," I tease, looking behind us. "You told me to shove friendship up my ass."

Layla is crouched low with Flora, her wings trembling.

"I went after what I wanted."

I draw up, heading toward the mated pair. "I can carry her."

Flora sneers. "Doesn't that go against your strongest survive?"

"The strong survive, the strongest lead, and we take care of those who aren't strong enough to survive on their own. It's our responsibility as an alpha."

"Alpha." Flora rolls her eyes and scoffs. "Dominant, crass figures that use aggression to assert their rule."

Jacques snickers. "Ma'am, you shouldn't speak if you're a moron."

I smirk at Flora's indignance. "Alphas are aggressive as a last effort. If we do it right, we aren't assholes. She's weaker, holding us back. That's where an alpha steps in to do what is necessary."

Flora takes half a step forward, her golden Light buzzing. "Don't you dare touch my mate, hurt her because she can't fly fast and straight through."

I step to her with a growl, toe to toe and staring down on her with burning fury. "I already said I'd carry her. I don't hurt mine." I snap my teeth at her. "I take responsibility. I take the lead. I make decisions and the rest follow because they trust me to do what's best for them."

Falsion puts a hand on my shoulder, pulling me back. "Have you noticed Cal has been at the back the entire way here? He sends the weaker first to set the pace, following where he can monitor the rest. He's been one flap behind even Natalia and Sterling."

Flora frowns, and Layla manages to stand. Flora puts a hand to her back, steadying her. "I believed he was distancing himself from the Light."

"Nope." Luca laughs. "Gods, why didn't they have to learn anything?"

Shawn shakes his head. "Weak at the front. They set the pace. Fighters in the middle. They cover and protect everyone. Leader at the back. They have the best overview to act on demand. That's how it works. Lesson over."

Fallon bounces on his father's shoulders. "When can we fly again?"

Galain shakes his head at the cement beneath our feet. "Soon, Boy. Settle down. We wait for the others, move as a pack. You never leave one behind. Did you hear Uncle Cal? The strong help the others. If you want to be an alpha, learn from the best there is."

"I wanna be the best in all the land. I'll eat all the Light someday to get really big and strong and I'll be just like Uncle Cal."

My Dark musses Fallon's hair. "Be better than me, Kid."

Fallon's eyes get huge. "Can I? Uncle Fal says no one's better."

I give Falsion a disapproving scowl. "Don't speak falsely to that boy again or I'll finally find a way to drag you down and beat you bloody."

Falsion chuckles. "You can have Sterling or Tal do it. Ash or Tony, too."

Jacques wiggles his eyebrows. "Me. I've put him down a few times."

I open the side of my mouth, lifting my lip in sheer disgust. "What the fuck?"

Falsion shakes his head. "I've been realizing you've got the same problem with me as you do that dick of a father of yours. You think we're better, so you lose every time. It ain't because of me. You defeat yourself before I ever swing." He scratches at his jaw, smirking. "I've been in the dirt every morning at those training sessions. Hiro, Thames, Jacques... People who talk in awe about your strength, have been kicking me down. I was hoping you'd figure it out, but I think I'd die before you got there on your own."

Large hands clap down on my shoulders, the thumbs digging into my muscles and rotating.

Sterling snickers over my shoulder, his face moving next to mine. "You've got your head all wrong. They told me they were stronger than you, better fighters. I about pissed myself when I faced Fal the first time, but I put him down easier than I've ever put you down."

Falsion points. "Now that man might be better than you."

I shrug Sterling off. "Layla, I won't hurt you." I send my Dark to collect her.

She shrieks, flailing. I pull the net tighter, Flora shushing her. "It's all right, My Brightest Light," she murmurs, stroking the side of Layla's head. "You're all right. I am here and I will follow you to the afters."

I lift off the ground, hovering in the air. Layla hyperventilates, whimpering and squirming. My Dark fumes at her shifting, annoyed with her. I ignore its displeasure, hovering until the rest are in the air.

Fallon whoops, "Yay, I'm flying."

That damn kid is going to grow up. He'll lose his heart, and dream of these days. The world is hard and unfair. It sends remorse through me.

Maybe I can change things. Maybe I can protect that boy and let him not only keep his heart, but let it grow with him.

Maybe a boy can have a father's pride and be the best alpha in all the land with compassion and empathy while having a pure heart that just wants to spread his wings and fly, believing in dreams.

Or maybe I fail.

CHAPTER 49
CALLAHAN
2ND THISTLE'S DAY, BLOOMING, 4050, 6TH MILLENNIUM

We landed in the night, the white and gold buildings drenched in shadows. I hated this city, the shining capital on the sea. I'd been close only once, glowering at the idea of it from afar for most of my life.

I'd dared encroach only to demand Pierre return my star. I'd been laughed away from the gates, leaving empty-handed.

Ashley had declared the top two floors of the gold tower were the royal chambers, then left us standing between great, carved columns on the first floor.

Tony was abandoned once again, so I took charge of him, bringing him to the top floor.

The bed had been small, my mates tossing and turning with me through the night. I wouldn't have slept a wink if they hadn't been close. My Dark is on edge, cutting its teeth sharper.

I exit the grand bedroom, scanning the open area beyond. It's sparse, round, carved columns of white marble with gilded details support the flowing expanse of space.

Zander mentioned the highest floor was the personal quarters. The floor below exists for business and social gatherings hosted by the royals. He arranged for my kin to use that floor.

It's not what I expected, as I stroll from column to column, running my hands over the carvings. Gauche, elaborate, expensive, ornate, all the things I've believed about the Light are vacant in these quarters.

I knew the Light embraced the arts of the world. That much is displayed in the carvings of marble and the wooden furniture in the bedroom.

Palak's Shadow Beast concoction and the surprise in his declaration that Hiro was still a man tells me everything. The Light doesn't understand what we are.

This room warns me that maybe we don't understand the Light either. The lessons seemed to solidify my beliefs, but Zander's fear and the request that I alter their laws to give their Glow Webs freedom leads me to question things.

Yanri abused Oscar almost to death, a man who survived our games even as he was withering. Oscar might have more strength than I do, surviving in worse conditions.

One thought returns, burning through me as delirium. I can change everything.

At the other end of the room, the flight shaft doors open. Zander steps in, retracting his wings. He bows to me. "Callahan, Your Majesty."

"For fuck's sake and my sanity," I mutter, shaking my head at the massive fan spread open and tacked to the wall. Each panel is embroidered with intricate finesse, a skill I'm amazed by.

Zander steps closer. "The suns have risen."

"I've noticed. It's bright." I wave at the windows.

"I came to escort you to a *vescor* for *jejinn*."

"Where do I find a cappuccino?"

"You'll find nothing of the sort here. I have a few different blends of tea in mind for you to try that may be more suitable to your tastes. Where are Tallie and Sterling?"

"Bed."

"Mm." He sneers in disgust.

"I should have left your ass in Ilbuio and brought Larles."

"It's interesting to me, the ripples of fate as the threads weave. Larles was to serve the royal family while I was free. I defeated him in our ritual combat. Now I serve the royals by choice, granting him freedom to hold contracts."

"Talia is going to act like a Light." I pivot to face him. "She'll play the part again. It doesn't change who she really is. Don't get your hopes up."

"As always, Tallie will do what she wants. She only bends as necessary, never conforms entirely." He inspects the fan, hands clasped at his back. "The maze played tricks on my mind, drawing out emotions I've been struggling with, using them against my logic. She is your mate. My detest is your willingness to invite another into her."

I smirk. Four hands and two shadow webs are useful to hold her down and gag her when she lies that she can't take more. Watching Sterling fuck her or his attentions while I savor Natalia are both enjoyable.

I can't recall why I was furious, a reason I had to want to rip him apart.

Rolling my shoulders and stretching my neck, I turn toward the bedroom. He's a partner, an equal who stands with me that I can rely on and trust with my life and Natalia's.

"It's not willingness to, it's desire." I shrug. "Get Tony up and moving. He's in the corner."

I slip into the bedroom, waking Natalia with gentle touches and shoving Sterling to the floor.

He gets to his knees, scowling at me.

I grin. "Wake up, baby. Breakfast."

ZANDER GUIDES us through the city amidst glares and sneers. Fallon waves and tries to chat with almost everyone who dares come within ear shot.

As another person ignores him, he slumps. "Is everyone mad at me today?"

Galain lifts him into his arms. "You keep talking to your new friends. You keep your chin up, and you keep that smile. Don't pay heed to their bad manners."

Natalia mutters, "They're all assholes."

We're informed we aren't welcome at the first vescor.

Zander responds in an aloof tone, dropping "Hallow heritage." The Light offers apology and offers service at no charge, claiming it would be an honor to serve a Hallow.

To my surprise, Zander turns and walks away without a bow or a word in response. I follow his lead. The name Hallow means nothing to me, but lack of respect for the Dark is everything.

The second choice sneers and turns up their nose, speaking with disdain for Zander in twisted sarcasm that Natalia should be proud of. When they insult both Zander and the Dark, I snap.

They won't piss on either my brethren or my contracted in tolerance from me.

Jacques laughs about a Hallow being snubbed as he follows us back onto the street. Someone chases after us, pleading for forgiveness.

It's not my forte, and I ignore the man.

Natalia makes a recommendation on a third spot, taking the lead. When we enter, she offers a real smile to a female who greets us.

"Welcome and be welcomed."

"We are welcomed and welcoming if you'll have us, Loraine."

"But of course, a Bordeaux and Fairly are always to be served."

I almost gag and throw up my yet-to-exist meal.

Natalia motions behind her. "We keep company with the Dark."

"Mm, I have eyes, Miss Bordeaux, as well as ears. I see the shadows and I hear a member of the Hallow heritage has been found among the Dark, existing without our knowledge." She bows. "Be welcoming and you shall be welcomed. I'll not tarnish my heritage by spitting upon what a Hallow is, even if it was my enemy first."

Jacques laughs. "We're not the enemy. You lot are the ones who hunt us down."

Loraine cocks an eyebrow. "Self-preservation can be viewed in many ways."

"Is that your excuse for murder? At least we're honest when we send some poor fuck to the afters."

Zander covers his eyes. "Jacques, word choices shall be appropriate."

Loraine laughs. "A wolf in sheep's clothes cannot change its teeth. Come, I invite you to rest. Please allow us to offer hospitality of the Light to warm your cold ways."

Jacques snickers. "I like this one. It's fun."

I shake my head. "Quit poking at things."

"Yes, yes, of course, Your Majesty." He gives me a mocking, flourished bow.

Loraine gasps. "Sir, you will conduct yourself in proper ways or I will remove you."

"You think you can, beautiful?" He wiggles his eyebrows. "Try me out. You might like it though."

Her cheeks turn pink, and Natalia steps in. "Jacques, please, please let us sit down. I'm hungry."

He kisses her cheek. "My very sincere regrets for keeping such a gorgeous king waiting."

Sterling yanks him back. "Snake, you keep your fangs out of her."

"Mm, and much more. It's a terrible shame."

Natalia laughs. "No, absolutely no." She shakes her head at me.

I eye him. He's getting bold.

Loraine leads us to a table, and I snag his shoulder, letting them move ahead. "That's my mate."

"The mate of my contractor who holds my life in his right hand and my Dark King." He turns, his eyes hard. "I may have my fun, but don't disrespect me enough to believe I'd ever piss on your mating bond or be stupid enough to take more than I have right to."

I sigh, letting go.

He smirks. "I bet she's tasty."

I try not to smile, moving forward.

"She'd kill me before you even have the chance, anyway."

I laugh. He's probably right.

We sit, and Zander orders, the rest of us confused about options.

When Fallon drops his tea cup, a man appears before Galain has finished setting down his own.

The man rights the cup, offering a napkin. He eyes Fallon. "You're a young man, your hands not yet strong. They should teach you like my father taught me." He lifts the cup, one hand beneath. "Lift from here as you hold the handle. When you gain grip, you'll be able to lift a full cup without the other hand. Until then, do it that way."

"Oh." Fallon gets smaller. "That mean lady said I had to do it right."

"Of all the curses in the world, expectations of others are the cruelest."

"But I'm a Hallow. I have to do it right."

The man widens his eyes. "My sincerest apologies for over-stepping. I knew naught—"

"Don't apologize," I say. He looks to me, mouth open. "You're being useful."

The man smiles. "If I have leave to speak?"

"I don't give a fuck about rank or your name. Speak to whom you want."

"Ah." He chuckles as he sits next to Fallon. "Children are so rare in this world. Pay no heed to any who sneer. Keep your joy for as long as you can."

He pours Fallon a new cup, showing him how to pick it up again. He stands and bows. "I apologize for disrupting your meal and rest, expressing my appreciation of your tolerance of my fumble in respect. Please, allow me to accept the bill for—"

"No." I shrug. "What's your name?"

"Kristopher Heatheron."

"You've been kinder than any other we've encountered."

Fallon turns to his father. "I made a friend. I dropped my cup and that lady said I'd be in trouble, but I made a friend."

Kristopher laughs, bending his knees. "Young Hallow, if you ever have need, send for me. You'll have anything I can do."

Zander snorts behind his cup.

Kristopher shakes his head. "I have not much to offer as a Heatherton, Sir, but I appreciate you choosing to eat in my estab-lishment. It's an honor to serve a Hallow." He stands and inclines his head. "Miss Bordeaux, a pleasure that you remembered me. I suspect I have you to thank for this honor."

Natalia smiles. "Anyone unwilling to spit on the Dark for the sake of being Dark is dear to me."

Kristopher smiles wider. "I'm afraid you'll find I am still quite different from my kin."

I look to Zander, pointing at Kristopher. "He comes to the coronation."

Zander shakes his head. "The invitations—"

"I don't care. Every other fuck sneered at Fallon and us. He didn't even know he was a Hallow and provided use."

"He knew a Hallow was present."

"No one said a Hallow was here."

Zander gives me a long look, then turns to Kristopher. "Did your daughter enlighten you?"

"I raised my daughter in my beliefs, to show kindness and not to expect anything from someone until they prove themselves."

"It's why you were removed, your heritage falling out of favor, no longer accepted within your previous rank or among peers, unwilling to accept betters as they were."

I ask, "Removed?"

With a sly smile, Kristopher says, "As the Dark hold honesty dearly, allow me to be transparent. I presumed your heritage, at least one, would be a Hallow, for Dark would not so brazenly come." He shrugs. "I worked the assumption to my benefit and would be delighted to attend the coronation. Please do inform me at which ceremony you'd like my presence."

Natalia chortles, then bursts into laughter. "That was clever."

I shake my head, dragging a hand down my face. "What just happened?"

Zander picks up his cup. "You've been manipulated into extending an invitation to a low-ranked individual seeking to regain his standing."

Sterling elbows me. "This is not going well."

Kristopher winks at me. "If there is any consolation to be had, please let me know." He crouches next to Fallon. "Young Hallow, be careful of your friends, but trust your heart. You'll know when you've lost and when you've won."

Galain narrows his eyes. "Hurt my son, and I send you to the afters."

"Don't be so crude. I meant every word I said. Your bill will be mine to cover as one gift deserves another. Enjoy your meal." He bows and retreats.

Falsion does his best to contain his humor, fighting with his features.

"Go ahead," I grumble, "laugh at me."

Luca bursts into a howl, garnering glances from others nearby.

I give in, chuckling with them. "I fucking hate this city already."

I'M weary of others for the rest of the day as Zander gives us a tour of Izul. Every building looks like the next, constructed of gilded marble or opal marble. There are golden, gold, white facades, and straight, clean lines everywhere.

He shows us to the throne room, an open expanse of white with simple columns on either side leading down the length of the room to a white throne on a two-tier, round, white dais. The only reason there's any definition, and the only way to see different objects, is the variation in shapes that cast shadows.

Zander walks me and my mates through what to expect tomorrow, gesturing and enacting steps that will be taken.

My eyes hurt. My Dark gnaws on my bones, distressed at the

surroundings. The misery is rounded out when Ashley has a conniption at dinner.

She's furious Natalia brought us to Heatherton's establishment at all, for the Heathertons aren't to be trusted or embraced with such an honor. She's enraged that Zander allowed the exchange to transpire. She's downright vicious to Tony for no reason at all. He didn't so much as speak.

By the time I'm led back to the gold tower, I'm exhausted. Nothing here makes sense. The way they speak, the way they act, it's backward and upside down from everything I know.

Natalia stops in front of one of the columns in the tower, running her hand along it. "This is the history of the Hallow heritage."

I run my hand up the back of her neck. "Mate," I whisper. "My name is Barraco."

She looks to me. "I know. Just thought you'd want to see why everyone wants to use the other one."

Sterling scans it. "Oh, look, they murdered Dark."

She bobs her head. "Probably."

A crack splits the air.

I whip around, shielding for a smite.

Tony glowers, rubbing his cheek as Ashley covers her mouth.

My Dark settles. *"She must have smacked the shit out of him."*

I hum in agreement.

He drops his hand, pulling her close. "I know what he means to you, and I would never insult him in that way."

"I told you not to come. I told you... You shouldn't be here."

He laughs. "Some day, I'll shake Akash's hand and tell him he's a lucky man."

She pushes away from Tony, but he snags her wrist, pulling her back. He lifts her chin in his hand, smiling. "Hey."

Sterling snickers. "Smooth."

Tony rubs his nose against Ashley's. "It's all right, sweetheart. I have a thing for heartless women anyway. Apparently, Sasha tried to kill Tal, and I was nuts about her."

My Dark swells with glee. *"Was."*

I'm not sure when I started to look at Tony as my responsibility instead of a tool. It happened when I wasn't paying attention, I guess.

I scoop up Natalia, done with the show. I whistle to Sterling. "Come, birdie."

We return to the top floor. I glance around, but there's been nothing delivered.

I drag them to the bedroom, wanting to forget.

I sit on the edge of the bed, hanging my head.

Natalia moves to my back, running her hands over my shoulders and neck. She massages my neck, then slides her hands up my back beneath my shirt, pressing her nose to the side of my neck.

Sparks dance across my skin at the brush of her fingers. Heat sinks into my tense muscles from her palms. Every caress pushes a wave of calm through my aching body.

I rub my eyes, blinking and focusing on Sterling leaning one shoulder against the doorframe.

Golden wood. White walls.

We don't belong here.

I don't know how to walk away without being a coward, discarding responsibility in favor of selfish desire.

"Talia."

"I'm here," she whispers, wrapping her arms around me.

I rest my hand on her arms crossed over my neck and close my eyes. "This isn't me. I'm not the Light."

She nuzzles my ear. "Have I told you what you smell like?" She presses her nose to my shoulder, inhaling.

I pull my eyebrows together, trying to imagine her favorite scent or memory. "Vodka?"

"You know what I love more than vodka?"

"Me?"

"Cappuccino." She smiles against my ear.

Sterling chuckles. "He smells like coffee? I never would have guessed that."

She drags her nose along my neck. "Warm, salt air, like Saltina, and cappuccino. I have my mate because of a cappuccino, and all those mornings in Saltina, swaying in the hammock under the suns while you drank a cappuccino, and now when you're near me I smell one."

"Pure coincidence, and we get a perfect mate. I'm glad your ass got smited."

"I'm glad the machine in my home broke," I say.

Natalia asks, "That's why you were there?"

I hum in languor. So many random, chaotic threads twisting together brought me here.

Sterling leans into me. "Why were you there, Firefly?"

"Mm." She squeezes me. "I was hungover. I needed caffeine. It was the first time I realized I like being smited. It cured my headache."

I rest my head against her. "Drinking because of Tony?"

"Something like that."

I smile. Everything they did served her to me on a silver platter without them realizing it.

She starts pulling at my shirt. "I think coffee makes me horny now."

Sterling grins. "I think he needs a demonstration."

She slips to my front, pulling my shirt off. She runs her hands up my chest and over my shoulders. It feels so good to be touched.

"You know..."

I lift my eyebrow.

"I've been behaving all day."

"*Mhm.*"

"And..." She slips her hands up my neck to my jaw, leaning close, to whisper in my ear, "I've been dying inside. Slowly. It's so hard to not get...mouthy."

"You can be mouthy."

Sterling closes his eyes, laughing silently. "We'll put you in your place."

She meets my eyes. "You could have shut me up any time you wanted. You could have used the contract."

This again. I tilt my head, lowering my eyes to her lips. Full, soft, pink, capable of spitting vulgar and sarcastic sass. They look best wrapped around my cock, but I enjoy them in a variety of ways.

"I could have."

"Yanri did it to Oscar. When I was here, I had to talk right for them, or they'd destroy my Light." She runs her fingers down my lips. "But not you."

"No."

"You could have done anything to me, made me do anything you wanted."

The list of possibilities is endless. I didn't because the tempting options at the top of my list are acts that I'd prefer a woman to partake in willingly. I did cross the line once, but it was for her benefit.

"I still can."

"Eh." She shrugs. "You didn't have to feed me, buy me a guitar or vodka, let me talk back or have so much freedom, but you did. You took care of me even when I didn't want you to."

"You know why."

She presses her mouth to mine. "My alpha."

I groan, grasping the back of her head to drag her lips to mine, opening my mouth to taste her.

I wanted her. She can think it was for her. I'll never tell.

I stole her life. I'll steal the air from her lungs. I'll take everything I want because I can, because I fought to possess her. I sank my claws into her, tied her in my Dark, and broke down her walls to have her.

She is mine, and I am never letting go no matter the price. I'll watch the cracks in her spread until they cover her like badges of honor, mirroring the fissures in me. I'll love every moment for the reward of owning her mind, body, and soul.

She licks my tongue, pulling back to run her hands down my chest, her palms skimming my skin, then her fingers as her touch moves lower.

She gets on her knees, smiling up at me. "But I want to get mouthy, so if you'll take your pants off, I'll sit, I'll stay, and, well, I'm not going to be a good vassal, but I'll try to be a good girl." She grins wide with a thrill of excitement in her face, her Light sparking brighter.

Sterling laughs. "That's an offer no man can refuse."

I take her face in my hands, staring down on her kneeling between my legs. My Dark stirs and stretches, willing to play but sluggish.

"Get up and take your clothes off, lazy bastard." Sterling rubs his face, leaning into the doorframe. "Unbelievable."

Giggling, Natalia kisses down my torso, slipping her hand beneath the band of my pants.

"You're a fucking prick, baby," Sterling says with a smile in his voice. "You have our mate on her knees and won't put the effort into undressing for her?"

I try to glare, but arousal stretches through me, my mind going hazy with need. The touch of our mate—her hands skimming my chest and stomach with her mouth—redirects my blood flow, ceasing my ability for rational thought.

I stand, shedding the rest of my clothes before sitting on the edge of the bed again.

Her hand closes around the base of my erection and my eyes damn near cross as she slides her hand up my shaft. They roll into the back of my head as she closes her lips around the head, and I don't care about a fucking other thing in the world as her tongue glides across the tip.

Sterling watches with half-closed eyes, then moves. He takes his shirt off, tossing it to the side and working his pants off.

I gaze at his body, lean hips and sculpted torso.

He sits, pulling her into his lap.

She gasps, picking her head up.

"Don't stop," he says.

He's nicer. I grab the back of her head, shoving her back down. Tangling my fingers into her silky, silver hair, I grab a fistful, forcing her to move how I want, at a pace I enjoy.

She gags, releasing a whimper.

He chuckles, bones snapping and crunching. He takes his talons across her, shredding her clothes until she's bare.

Taking one of her hands in his, he moves it between her legs, "Fuck yourself, Firefly. Show him how much you enjoy his cock."

She does, moaning around me.

My mates are going to drive me insane.

Sterling rests his hand on her stomach, fingers down, and glides his hand toward hers. Her skin sparkles in its wake, another moan from Natalia vibrating across the head of my cock.

He starts helping her, working her clit.

I get harder, edging closer. I slow Natalia's mouth, prolonging my pleasure.

He holds her hips, lifting her and thrusting into her. She mewls, and he winks at me. "The only thing better than you coming while sucking our cock is you coming on my cock while you suck his other."

I growl. It's the best response I can manage watching him lift her hips, showing her how to move.

He is not wrong.

"Fuck, Firefly, you feel so good."

She does, her mouth wrapped around me. It's not enough, though. I want more.

I lift her head, grasping her under the arms to drag her off Sterling and into my lap. I line up and thrust, burying myself in her, then lie back, adjusting her on top of me.

Sterling stands, running his hands over her hips and up her back before sliding down her sides to her butt. "Relax, Firefly."

She whimpers and squirms.

I shove my fingers into her mouth to stop her from protesting.

The friction of him sliding in and out, the way she shudders and clenches around me, sets me tipping on the edge. I need more.

"Harder, baby."

Natalia shivers. "Na..." her tongue fights against my fingers.

Sterling grasps her wrists, pinning them behind her back and thrusting harder.

I hold her still, my Dark tethering her in place. "Best you've got?"

He laughs, low and breathless. "If I break something, it's your fault."

Tangling his fingers into her hair, he yanks her backward, forcing me deeper and our mate to squeal as he slams forward.

I press my palms into her shoulders, pushing back as she slides across my chest from sheer force.

She pants and gasps into my ear, whimpers and moans while her body pulses and quivers. Sterling's cock slides across mine in smooth, hard strokes, nothing but a thin membrane between us.

It feels so good, encased in our mate's warm, tight wet cunt as he strokes against me, in and out of her, and all I have to do is lie here and enjoy it.

Natalia comes, clenching my cock and mewling in breathless cries. I rock my hips, my Dark slithering between us to stroke her as Sterling continues to ram into her.

My balls tighten. "Sterling."

He backs off, slowing down.

I growl.

He laughs. "I know who my alpha is, but that deserves appreciation, don't you think?"

I groan, thrusting my hips for more. "Damn you."

"You put me in charge, so just be a good boy and you'll get your treat."

I tip my head back, trying not to laugh. I lose my breath as he slams into Natalia, pushing her forward along my cock only to drag her backward and repeat.

I'll be a good boy. For this, I'll sit, stay, and wag my tail.

He finds a rhythm, until I'm breathing hard and Natalia shudders. I tip on the edge, feeling her come again.

He pulls her back, impaling my shaft fully and holding her still as he moves with long, hard strokes.

I rock and thrust, chasing my release. I come with a growl, jerking quicker to increase my pleasure. He follows me off the ledge, going still.

I go limp, floating in a daze with Natalia lying on me as dead weight. It's incredible.

Sterling massages Natalia's shoulders, leaning over to kiss the back of her head. He meets my eyes with a smirk. "You two are the best happy ending."

I snort through my nose, shaking with laughter. "For fuck's sake," I manage. "I'm never going to turn off her sass or your riddles and puns, am I?"

"Nope." He grins, showing me that dazzling smile full of sheer hope and excitement.

It echoes in my soul. I couldn't ask for anything more.

CHAPTER 50
CALLAHAN
2ND THORN'S DAY, BLOOMING, 4050, 6TH MILLENNIUM

Knocking rouses me. I stumble to the door, opening it.

Zander's gaze flares then he lifts his chin, staring at the ceiling. "I have brought your attire for the coronation along with a delivery received early this morning." He steps aside, keeping his eyes on the ceiling and motioning behind him.

I check the delivery, everything labeled. I take mine, Sterling's, and Natalia's boxes, pointing to the rest. "They're labeled. Get them to the right individuals."

"Your attire." Zander lifts the garment bags on a finger, still refusing to look at me.

I take them. "We'll meet you at the palace."

"I can escort you."

"No need. Do what I said, and we'll see you there."

"Very well, Sir."

I move into the bedroom, tossing aside the Light-approved bags. I'll burn them and go naked before I ever put them on.

We shower and get ready. Sterling shrugs into his black coat, his shirt black beneath it. He's in solid black as he should be.

478

He steps to me, taking my jaw in his hand. He holds my gaze as he rests his forehead to mine. "You're too good to me, baby."

"Sweetheart, I did that for me. I might tear my eyes out if I ever have to see you in white again."

He chuckles, moving away to sit on the end of the bed. "You're not in black, though."

My shirt is dark gray, the suit a lighter shade, but also gray. It's a bit of whimsy on my part. Every Mandolux will be in gray, not Dark or Light, but a blend.

Natalia steps from the bathroom in her dress. I lose my response, my mind going blank.

Her hair is in a complicated braid-style common for the Light, and there's no trace of makeup on her face.

My Dark drools.

The white fabric of her gown drapes across her chest in a low neckline, a slippery sheen that highlights her curves as she moves. It hugs her body, with a high slit on one side. I wasn't about to see her in the gold monstrosity, but she is the Light.

Thames, for all his bluster and insistence that he has interest in only male anatomy, has impeccable taste for the female figure.

She collects the long skirt, holding it in one hand as she pads toward us.

My Dark lifts the black heels from the bed, extending them to her. She smiles, accepting them.

She slips them on, one at a time, then gives us a spin.

The back is open, the dress locked around the back of her neck. Her Magia marks are exposed and on display, green geometry down her spine. She lifts her hands, her left forearm marked with three black, intersecting lines that wrap around her arm.

Everything about her is clearly seen, from form to what she is, a Magia heiress with a seed of Light and a piece of Mallafic's soul. She's like nothing else.

Sterling stands. "Fuck, Firefly. How are we supposed to walk out of here when you look like that?"

She shakes her head, coming closer. "It's white." She wrinkles her nose.

I nod. "We're in Izul, and you are the Light, Little Star."

She points to her shoes. "Black."

I press my lips to her temple, sliding my hands across her hips. "You have a piece of Mallafic."

She runs her hand over my chest. "And you're shadows, the *ifferentiti*."

I feel like an idiot when she says it aloud.

She rolls forward, smiling. "Callahan Barraco, you are amazing."

My Dark flutters and twists like an excited puppy looking for pets.

Sterling steps to us, one hand on my shoulder, the other on her back. "He is, but this is going to be a fucking disaster. I think that vein in Ashley's forehead is going to burst."

Natalia giggles. "It is. She's going to lose her mind."

I point at my head. "Crown. Speaking of which..."

I flip the lid on the last box, pulling out the Dark crown. I set it on her head.

She scrunches her face. "Why?"

"You are the Dark King, Mate. Act like it. We need to go," I say, checking my watch.

I hesitate at the flight shaft, looking to Sterling. "Carry me."

"What?" He laughs, then his face sticks and he asks, "Are you serious?"

"My wings leave holes."

Sterling steps to me, wrapping his arms around me and lifting me against him. I try to mimic Natalia, squeezing Sterling's hips between my thighs.

My Dark fumes at the humiliation.

"It's this or stairs, or I take my clothes off and put them back on again. He's our mate. Deal with it."

Sterling chuckles. "What would you do without me?"

I stare at him. "I'll never know. You're bound and fucked for life. Now make this quick. It's embarrassing."

NATALIA MOVES up the wide steps toward the columns supporting the front of the building. My heart pumps hard in my chest. Sterling gets to the door and opens it, trying to smile.

"I'd just like to say one last time, absolutely fuck this."

Natalia giggles, kissing her hand and tapping it to his cheek. Even in heels, she wasn't going to reach with her mouth.

I push them both inside ahead of me, sweating everywhere. I've never considered running from duties before, but accepting the crown of Light makes me consider it for the first time in my life.

As I step inside, Ashley storms toward me. "Absolutely not."

Sterling laughs.

She turns on him. "You find this funny? You are to be a King of Light and you are..." She flicks a hand at him, looking down his body.

I look to the steps, then to Ashley in a gilded gown similar to the one Natalia was to wear. I check my watch. "We're going to be late."

"We are not going until you are properly dressed." She spins, rounding on Natalia. "Sister Mine, you should know better."

She shrugs, checking her nails. "Perhaps consider my mate gave me a gift before screeching at me. The least I could do was give him the gift of seeing me wear it in order to embrace the customs of my origins."

I step to her, crooking my finger at Sterling. "Let's go."

"No." Ashley races in front of me, blocking my way as I guide Natalia forward. "No, this will not stand. You are about to accept the highest position in the Light, you must show honor and respect."

"I said I'd do it my way."

"By spitting upon the very thing we are?" She looks around, her face pink, her voice shrill. "You all must change. Tony, you... You would... You too?"

He steps forward in a black suit with a white shirt. "Ash, sweetheart." He puts one hand on her shoulder, lifting one of hers and pressing his palm to it. "If you give someone your whole focus when you speak to them, look them in the eye, and be polite, no one pays attention to what you're wearing."

"That's perhaps the dumbest thing I have ever heard, as if they won't all notice color."

"Sweetheart, it's just color. We all cleaned up. This shirt is fitted like a second skin and more expensive than anything I've ever owned, and that includes my vehicle and loft."

"Well, it's fine, and yes, I can see it fits perfectly, but no. No," she says again, stressing the word and screaming through her eyes. "Flora went through all that trouble to get things delivered and tailored. I picked out everything. This is for the Light. *The. Light.*"

He lifts his hand from her shoulder to her face. "You look breathtaking. Red lips, huh?"

She presses them together, ire glowing in her features. "It was too much gold, and do not change the subject. I expect you all to change. All of you need to be appropriate."

He smirks, slipping his fingers between hers. "I like it."

"It wasn't for you. As I said, it was too much gold with eyes and lips and the dress."

"I know." He hoists a cocky half-smirk. "Still like it."

"You..." She flounders for words.

He lifts his eyebrows, tucking her hand in the crook of his arm and facing me. "Let's see, being prompt is to show respect for another's time, yes? I believe they can excuse a bit of color in the clothes in exchange for us being on time. After all, to make another wait and delay their day is costing them more than you may know by affecting further engagements and plans."

"I will not forgive you for this."

"Yes, I know." He leads her toward the steps. "I am a terrible soul, a pathetic excuse for a man. Now, quite obviously, I am a poorly dressed one, too."

"You didn't have to be. I gave you the correct articles of clothing."

Tony winks at me as he leads her toward the steps. "How misguided of me to think I looked more dashing like this."

I meet Natalia's eyes. "Somehow, I think I haven't given enough credence to him."

She smiles, her eyes tinged with melancholy. "It was like watching him manage my sister. She'd have meltdowns, screaming about something not being perfect all the time, and he'd just..."

Falsion leads my kin toward the stairs with Maria on his arm. She's in a gray dress, smiling ear to ear. "Thanks, Uncle Cal."

I nod at her. "Keep that one for my son. He picked it."

Her cheeks turn pink. "I'll do that."

Zander strides across the hallway. He shakes his head. "Has Ash seen this yet?"

"Yes."

He stops, tilting his head.

"She's not happy. I don't care." I take Natalia's hand as we start climbing the stairs.

Two men with dark hair wait by the double doors in the middle of the hall. They startle and stare as I approach.

Zander steps in front of me. "Callahan."

I come to a halt, waiting for him to step into the threshold. He clears his throat.

I squeeze Natalia's hand. The thought to flee, to pick her up and grab Sterling and run sinks deeper into my mind. It's no longer a passing fancy, but a full-fledged fantasy that beckons me.

My Dark does nothing to discourage it.

"Thank you for coming, friends and confidants of the highest rank, those we hold closest for guidance and support..."

I look to Natalia. She looks up at me, her gray eyes brilliant. The way she looks at me, like I can do anything, makes it easier to stand and wait. I'll do anything to earn her belief in me, even if it means being a man I never wanted to be.

Zander continues blathering on. "...Of the three great heritages that have always rooted, guided, and cared for the Light, the Hallow heritage has held a special place in our ways. They were the first to call upon the flames of the suns, wielding them to our benefit in times of need..."

Sterling moves to my other side. "I'll stay, even if this is fucking painful."

Natalia smiles wider, her eyes crinkling and shining with adoration.

Zander proceeds, dragging my patience thinner. "Although we have honored and mourned the loss of this great heritage, we have been fortunate in discovering it was not lost but changed by a coupling with the Dark. Our Hallow heritage is not gone, and for that, we can rejoice. Its strength has survived, defying the odds year after year to this day. Please welcome Callahan

Barraco, for Barraco was the first born of Barraco and Lenore, his descendants using his name as their lineage name."

He bows to the room, pivoting and standing straight as he inclines his head to me.

Natalia steps, pulling me forward.

I enter the room, clamping my jaw at the dozens of faces staring at me.

My Dark huffs as Natalia pulls me to a halt in the doorway. I know Zander reviewed all of this yesterday. I didn't care to pay attention.

They all bow in unison to me.

Two faces stand out. Kristopher and Loraine.

I grind my teeth. When I play games, I know it's a game. I don't do sleight of hand or manipulation. I'm no coward, direct and honest in my actions.

I walk down the middle of the room to the throne on a dais. I sit, Natalia starting to move to the side. I drag her into my lap.

She squeaks, catching the Dark crown before it slips off her head.

Sterling chuckles, leaning to half sit on the armrest and cross his arms. The faces flicker with disgust. I don't care.

Ashley speaks, placing a gilded crown on my head.

She welcomes in the remainder of my kin, going one by one to provide their order of birth from the original litter of pups and their names.

One by one, individuals or families step forward, introducing themselves.

It's my turn to speak.

All I can think is my father would do this better.

I turn my head, smiling at Natalia in my lap, her back to my chest. "My kin and I are born of Light and Dark, proof our two sides can not only exist together, but thrive as one."

My magic groans and moans at me putting the Light before

485

the Dark. It was a conscious decision on my part, and it leaves a bad taste in my mouth. This is just another game, and I'll play to win like always.

"The fact is corroborated and irrefutable from multiple sources, including Mallafic himself."

The room whispers in shock.

"You didn't tell them?" I glance at Ashley.

She sticks her tongue up under her lower lip, giving me a long look. "No, I didn't tell them. It's not our god."

I shake my head. "Mallafic lives in this world yet. The stories of our creation are not as we know them. Beenin is not the graceful, righteous beauty you believe."

Several faces turn acrimonious. A woman calls, "That's not possible. Beenin tore him to pieces for what he did."

I ignore her. "You all know Natalia…"

Shadows race into existence, Mallafic materializing among them. "Yes, I know my plaything quite well. A lovely face, and… *tsk, tsk, tsk.* Come here, pet." He motions with two fingers.

The room whispers, the loudest asking who has arrived.

He rolls his eyes, waving at me as he faces the room. "Who am I? Insulting at best and demoralizing in truth. Your pathetic existences are too narrow to begin to comprehend, so allow me to introduce myself. I am Mallafic, a god." He spins. "Now, darling toy of mine, come here."

I grip her waist. "No."

He shies his head back and to the side, laughing at me. "Now, now, no need to be jealous. You'll have my attention soon enough. First," he drags out with a grin in slow motion, "this odious attire must be rectified. Perhaps you can convince him?" Malaaifc's gaze shifts to Sterling.

I look at him, eyebrows raised.

He twists his lips to the side, then stands. "You might be able to persuade me into assisting if your intentions are visual only."

"But of course. I'll not be here long. To suffer the presence of her is a torture I will not bear. Nay, I came to speak in quick, efficient words, but that appearance of mine is unacceptable."

I squeeze Natalia, glaring at Sterling.

He leans over, meeting my eyes. "Do it, Firefly."

I show my teeth, curling my lips in and crinkling my nose, enraged that he would be callous with her safety.

Sterling leans his head to the side, half a smile pulled back on his full lips. "Trust me, Mate."

I peel my fingers back. "All right."

Sterling offers his hand, Natalia taking it. She grips his hand hard. "I'm so pissed at you for this."

He leads her toward Mallafic, stopping several paces short. "As good as you get, even if you are my god."

"Oh, very well." Mallafic chuckles, snapping his fingers. He dissolves, shadows streaking around my star.

They clear, passing by her and leaving her swathed in black haze that glitters, Mallafic reforming from them as he steps toward me. "A throne of white. Such a lack of imagination. How odious."

I stretch a zealous frown. "I agree."

His face wrinkles with mirth as his shoulders shake. "You got one thing right and two wrong. She was...graceful," he says, his voice a breathy whisper in the air, surrounding me. "So...fluid in her movements...tedious almost in how she moved. The allure... ah, the way she knew to use her figure... Beauty, that word itself created for her." He claps.

I jump. The whole room does.

He laughs, bursting into loud hysterics. "Of course she was, you fools. How else do you ensnare a god? Righteousness? No. More of a backstabbing whore with a vile penchant for lies." He faces the room. "I may have been ripped asunder, torn to pieces, but it was not her doing, nor am I dead. Have your vain stories for now. They, like all things, will come to an end."

Mallafic turns to shadows that drop to the floor and spread across the surface.

Sterling grins at me like an excited boy, pointing to our mate.

Her white dress has been altered to black glittery material. She turns, the train slinking in a circle around her feet. It still closes around her neck, leaving her back exposed. The front is a deep plunge to her navel, the skirt fitted through the hips and thighs with a high slit.

She jabs a finger into Sterling. "I am not happy."

He wiggles his eyebrows. "I am. I don't know why he does this, but I enjoy it."

My Dark stretches through the air, snaking around her and pulling her to me. As she gets closer, I get a better look. The fabric is as sheer as a single layer of gauze, her body on display.

It reminds me of another dress, one I purchased for her. I'd had her wear it on the last night of Gathering Shadows. I'd sat next to her over dinner for the course of two runes, behaving myself. The struggle to keep my hands and my Dark off her had been agonizing. Waiting had been well worth shredding it off her body in my bed that night.

Ashley presses her finger to the space between her eyes. "Oh Adontis, that is even less appropriate."

Sterling sits on the armrest of the throne again, smiling ear to ear.

I try to contain my glee. She does look best in black, and every tantalizing detail is on display for me.

Swallowing my excitement, I say, "Natalia Swan is the Dark King, by proof of strength, and my mate." I thumb at Sterling. "Sterling Wellsly. The three of us hold a union contract."

More whispers and shock.

"We will rule together as equal partners. Our intentions are first, to stop the Ancients attempting to destroy our race, and second, to unify our kind."

A man tries to leave.

I send my Dark to slam the door shut, then drag him forward.

Everyone gasps and moves out of the way as he flails across the floor. Layla shakes her head, whispering to a man next to her.

I retract my Dark, asking, "Anyone else want to be a pain in my ass? No? Then I'll remind you all that the Ancients threaten our existence. They intend to destroy the Seraphinus because we can't get along. Too many have died for hatred. It ends now. Dark and Light cannot exist without each other, so we learn to live with each other. Your ways will change. The Dark's ways will change. You can stand with me and my mates, have a say in those changes, or you can be a problem I deal with. The choice is yours."

The man shoves up, glaring at me. "It's impossible, and I won't stand for being an animal."

Jacques laughs. "We very recently learned what you think we are. It's fucking hilarious."

"You have no standing to speak in present company."

I smirk. "His name is Jacques. When he speaks, I am speaking. The same goes for Zander. They are contracted as my right hand, and they act on my behalf. Decide what you want to be, dead or alive. If you want to live, stand with the Dark in a new world."

"You threaten us?"

"I'm telling you how it's going to be. I don't care if you like it, just that you do it. Light Law dictates that you conform or have your Light destroyed. I'm simply abiding by your ways to honor Pierre Bordeaux's wishes."

They all stare, the man turning his head away.

My Dark snickers. *"Sometimes you're not such a stupid host."*

"In that case..." I shrug. "Ash."

Ashley offers a special blend of Rizvor in celebration. Vassals serve up gold plates with the drinks prepared.

I take one, handing it to Natalia and kissing her head, then give the second to Sterling before taking one for myself.

I head down the short steps of the round dais to approach the others. I want to get this over with.

Kristopher intervenes. "Your Majesty."

"I don't like you. I don't like being used or manipulated, and you used a child."

He laughs. "Miss Bordeaux, you looked exceptionally brilliant. This new attire... Was that truly Mallafic?"

Natalia turns into me, sliding her arm around my waist. "Yes."

"Amazing. Callahan Barraco was the one who contracted you, was he not? We were all so quick to judge you for the act and now give him our crown."

A woman approaches my kin. She kneels, speaking to Fallon. "Young Hallow, sir, you look very neat."

"My name is Fallon."

"A strong name choice, but curious. I'll believe nothing about you based upon that name."

Galain puts a hand on Fallon's shoulder. "I don't understand. Fal means story, and Fallon means heroic tale."

"Not quite." She stands and bows to Galain. "Fal means lie."

Fallon's eyes get wide, and his face turns red. "I'm not a lie." He turns to his father, pulling at his shirt. "Dad, I'm not a liar. I'm not." He starts to cry. "I'm not. I'm not."

I scan for Ashley. I need to know if I'm allowed to punch someone for making Fallon cry. Probably not, but I'll ask the price at least.

Galain pulls his son closer. "No, you are neither a lie nor a liar."

Falsion steps between Galain and the woman. "You have

your facts wrong. Fal means story, made up, yes, but legendary in nature. Fallon is the word of Eternums for a story of a hero."

"I do believe my education far outweighs yours."

"Your education on the Eternum language is laughable at best."

The woman scoffs.

Tony joins Falsion, offering up his hand. "You want to argue, Ma'am?" Soris crawls out of his ear, growing to consume Tony's hand. "Meet Soris, the fatum of present times. She knows the language of Eternums better than anyone because she used it for millennia, and she says fallon translates to heroic tale." Soris takes a bow before crawling back into Tony's ear. He ducks his head, wincing as he rubs his head against his shoulder. "Hate that feeling."

Someone approaches Tony. "We are so honored to be in the presence of a fate."

Tony points to his ear. "Don't make her crawl out again. It tickles my brain."

Kristopher straightens his shirt. "Straight for a child in hopes of corrupting innocence for use." He shakes his head. "Be wary, Your Majesty. Smiles hide intentions."

I eye him, but he smiles, moving toward Fallon.

The woman bows again. "I see my education has failed me."

Kristopher shoulders past her and Falsion. "Fallon... May I call you Fallon? You called me friend, after all."

"You taught me to lift the cup," Fallon says, rubbing one eye with a closed hand.

"Yes, I did, and I am honored to be your guest."

"My guest?" His ruddy face fills with surprise, the insult laid being forgotten.

"Why, of course, Young Man. Why else would we all be here?"

I look to Natalia. "I don't trust him."

She pats my arm, leaning in to speak low for my ears only. "Of all those in this room Kris is the only one who asked why I held a contract of the Dark, curious, but not malicious. Interestingly, I don't recall him insulting the Dark either. His establishment was the one place I felt comfortable here."

I frown, pulling her closer.

Fallon looks around. "Me?"

Kristopher drops to one knee, Falsion moving out of the way to glare down on him. "You harm that boy and I harm you."

Kristopher waves him off. "Now, Fallon, you are much too young for a glass of Rizvor, and I doubt you'd like it much anyway, but would you have a cup of tea with me?"

"Can my dad come?"

"I would certainly hope so. He'll want to be a proud father in the way you manage your cup."

I look to Falsion. He jerks his head. He'll keep an eye on that mess.

I face the rest, the gold crown heavy on my head. I need cooperation and fighters.

CHAPTER 51
CALLAHAN

The second coronation ceremony at least involves food. I sit on a cushion at a low golden wood table with my mates at my side. My kin, Zander, Ashley, Tony, and Jacques are the only others at the table. It's a relief that doesn't last long as Ashley instructs me to mingle.

As I raise, I scan the room. Several faces are familiar from Wyham to Layla and Flora. One stands out in particular.

Frowning, I head toward the table, eyeing Palak. He sits next to an older man of the same height and build. As Natalia and I get closer, Palak meets my eyes and then ducks his chin.

The flash of his face in clear view displays a swollen cheek and split lip before he hangs his head. I stop at the table, my hackles rising.

Wyham rises, bowing to me. "Your Majesty." He motions down the table. "May I introduce you to other crown contracted? It would be my pleasure."

I detangle Natalia's arm from mine. "Go heal Palak."

Wyham's face twitches like he wants to smile, but he maintains a straight face. "You know Palak, so allow me to introduce

Louis Delacroix." He motions to the man next to Palak. "He is the eldest of the Delacroix heritage and will speak for his heritage as is our custom."

Natalia kneels, pushing between Palak and the woman next to him. I eye her, realizing it's not Hailey. I scan the table, Hailey at the opposite end. She has puffy red eyes and a red nose, like she's been crying.

I return my focus to Wyham. He waves at others, providing names.

Natalia flickers, her Light pulsing while her hand rests on Palak's chest. Others peer with curiosity until some flush of color returns to Palak and her hand falls away.

She turns to me with ire in her eyes.

I cross my arms to stop from acting. "Palak, I thought you were remaining in Ilbuio."

Louis waves a hand with dismissal. "He is my nephew. I called upon him to be present for your coronation, and he will not be returning to your wretched city."

"Why?"

"He will be here to serve the throne as our heritage is to do."

"The Ancients demand attention. That is serving."

"I'll not risk my heritage seed."

"Then I expect you to take his place."

"I am far too old to fight. I serve better in Izul as a pillar of Light to enforce our laws." He coughs into a balled hand.

Wyham clears his throat. "Louis, you are a crown contracted heritage. Callahan is our Queen of Light and can call upon any of his choosing. You cannot refuse."

"My health is a consideration."

Natalia snorts through her nose. "Please, your health is only a consideration because you seek to hide from possible injury or death, which, by very nature, is hazardous to your health."

Palak turns his head away. A vacant stare stretches across his face. He's not the same man I know.

Louis turns acrimonious. "The Dark has no business—"

"You forget I am a Bordeaux and carry a seed of Pierre's heritage."

"I forget nothing, Dark King." Louis fakes a laugh. "The Dark has done enough damage to this boy. I'll see no more of it."

I raise my eyebrows. "Why was he injured?"

"He returned to me in that condition."

"You're a liar. Alexander would have healed any damage without hesitation."

"My business—"

"Palak," I say, cutting Louis off and raising my voice, "has earned respect through his character and his actions. He survived one of the Dark's toughest trials to ensure that our unification wasn't opposed by Mallafic at great personal cost to himself, and you harmed him. Why?"

Natalia stands. "I know why. Hatred." She lifts her right hand, splaying it open with her palm down, then curls her index finger to pick at the ring on her thumb.

Wyham steps away from the table, offering his arm to Natalia but holding my gaze. "Your Majesty, please allow me to introduce you to the rest of those contracted to the crown."

I look to Palak and then back.

Wyham strains his eyes and inclines his head.

"We aren't done, Louis. Wyham, make the introductions."

Wyham leads Natalia around the table, and I join him. He moves us further away before he speaks, keeping his voice low. "Palak called me for comfort and guidance last night. He had been ordered to return, and when he did, he confronted Louis about the death of his father."

I grind my teeth.

"Louis..." Wyham sighs. "He made it a point to remind Palak

that he is above all else, the Light and will respect the ways of the Light. Palak has been forced to terminate his union with Hailey until he has relearned proper behavior and becomes a man who is worthy of a mate."

I growl, "That—"

"It is a heritage matter not even the Queen of Light can embroil in."

"It's fifty years for attacking another in this city."

He halts Natalia between tables out of earshot of others. "What happens within a heritage is the rule of the eldest seed."

"Natalia was locked up for punching Ashley."

Natalia tries to hide her grin, fighting with her face and rubbing the bridge of her nose.

Wyham nudges her. "That was in front of a Light Queen." He shakes his head at her, smiling with his tone sour. "You were lucky Pierre could provide aid at all for that display." He grimaces. "I support your attempts to interfere, but there is no legal avenue you possess to help Palak. Lingering will spark inquiry. Come."

Several tables later my mind is overloaded with names and faces I will not recall. I didn't try to retain anything with much sincerity. Palak needs help, and it's a puzzle my mind and Dark won't abandon.

I search for Sterling. He's smarter than I am. He can find a way to step in and dig Palak out of the mess.

I move through the room with Natalia on my arm toward him. The Lights avoid or ignore me.

The doors burst open, a man stumbling through them. I startle with everyone else, looking for the cause.

Matthew Bernine points at a Light standing in his way as the other finds balance. "I ain't hurting you or the rest. Now I've done your bows and your words, but I flew all night, and I'm in a piss poor mood. I ain't standing here waiting or saying it again. You have no right to refuse me from my king."

Natalia lets go of me, striding toward him. "Matthew."

He steps into the room. "Natalia, I want to speak with Louis Delacroix."

She bobs her head. "Understandably, but—"

"Louis!" He glances around. "I know you're here, you cowardly rat."

Ashley storms forward with Zander. "Excuse the glow out of me, but this is—"

"I'm not welcomed, but I'm welcoming, now stay out of it, Lady." Matthew sticks a finger in her face and motions her away.

She jerks back, blinking at the end of her nose with an open mouth.

He turns away. "Louis Delacroix? I know you're contracted to the crown of Light and you're the head of your heritage, which means you're here. You're a rat but you'll show to save face."

Wyham clears his throat, rubbing his ear as he looks toward the table with Palak and Louis.

Matthew stomps forward, patting Wyham on the shoulder on his way past. "Good kid."

Wyham fights a smile, looking to the ceiling.

Sterling steps to me, propping his arm on my shoulder. "Are we...?"

"No blood, but otherwise..." I smirk. "I can't do anything. I won't stand in Matthew's way."

"The fuck is going on?"

"*Shh.*"

Matthew stops at the table. "Louis. I never could forget your rat face. Get up. You're going to face me, and there's nowhere to run this time."

Louis rises, a head shorter than Matthew, brushing away wrinkles as he sneers. "You have no business being here or addressing me." He rounds, looking in my direction. "Have this animal arrested. He murdered my brother."

"Jean Paul saved my life," Matthew snarls. "I lived by his strength and was a better man for his friendship. I cherished him so much I named my first seed after him, and he shed tears the day I told him and let him hold my son. Don't you fucking lie *to me* about what happened."

"N–no. No! You did it. You tried to kill me." He waves at Matthew, stumbling a pace away. "He tried to kill me," he yells at the room.

"I did try to kill you after I found you standing over Jean's body, and you ran from me."

Louis gapes, flapping his mouth in the silence permeating the room.

Matthew scoffs. "A coward and an idiot. I ought to wring your fucking neck."

Scampering away, Louis trips over his feet and cowers behind an arm.

I hold my breath against laughing. Sterling doesn't bother muting himself, bursting into laughter.

He wraps his arm around my shoulders. "Tell me I'm seeing things."

"Can't."

Palak stands, helping his uncle upright. "Matthew, please, stop."

"No. I'll go to the afters and take him with me if that's what it takes. I'll have another drink with your father and tell him what a good man he raised, but I won't let him do this to you or that sweet mate of yours."

Palak shakes his head. "This is the Light."

"This is smoragon shit."

"I'll be okay."

"Did you just lie to me, Boy?" Matthew crosses his arms.

Blanching Palak looks to the floor. "Maybe."

Matthew shakes his head. "Get in here, John."

A brunette man enters, taller than Matthew with the same face. He pulls a tri-folded piece of parchment from his inner suit pocket as he approaches Palak.

He stops, bowing in proper form to Palak. "We haven't met yet, but I am John Paul Matthew Bernine." He extends the page. "You have a place with us. Lukette is yours. It's mildly profitable. It can support you and your mate."

Palak's jaw drops.

Louis tries to grab the document, and John slings his hand into Louis's throat.

The room gasps as a collective.

Louis chokes and splutters, hitting the floor.

A woman steps forward, and Wyham moves in her way. He shakes his head.

Zander puts a hand to Ashley's shoulder, jerking her back and whispering something.

John straightens his sleeve and glares down on Louis. "Fuck your selfish ass," he says. "You are to take care of yours, but as you seem to be a pathetic excuse of a man, my father and I will see to the betterment of the son of a man who gave me his name and my life."

Palak looks to the page. It begins to shake in his hands. "You–you... This is the deed to Lukette. I can't... This is yours."

John shrugs. "Now it's yours. You gave my father a fair chance to prove himself honest and earn respect. For that, I would have you stand with me like a brother."

Louis tries for the page again. "No. That is—"

"That," John spits, waving at Palak, "gives him freedom from you."

"He would have to turn his back on me, on this heritage, and step away from the estate. I'd offer him nothing."

"You also couldn't stand between him and his mate and if you touch him again, you'll be unable to claim it a heritage matter, and Callahan will no doubt enjoy enforcing your laws."

Matthew faces Louis, standing toe-to-toe with his arms crossed. "You're going to let Palak do what he wants, trusting him to be a representation of your heritage that Jean would be proud of. You're not going to lay a finger on him for standing with the Dark in peace, and you ain't going to separate him from his mate, or I drag us both to the afters. Do you hear me, rat bastard?" He pokes Louis in the chest.

Ashley throws her hands up. "Someone tell me what is happening. This is unacceptable disrespect to the proceedings of Callahan's coronation and entirely out of place for this event."

I shake my head. "Ash, I couldn't be happier. Let it go."

Palak turns his head. "Hailey?"

She runs to him, throwing her arms around his neck. Fabric rips as she jumps to wrap her legs around his hips. "Follow your heart, My Brightest Light, and I will follow you."

He laughs, spinning her in a circle. "Then I accept." He faces Matthew. "Thank you."

Sterling mutters, "Oh, look, a happy ending." He bites my shoulder. "Huh, not that happy, I guess."

I chuckle.

Louis glares at Palak. "You can't do this. You'll have nothing and no one."

John steps next to him. "He'll have us, and you can rot with Jean's body."

Setting Hailey down, but wrapping his arm around her, Palak lifts the page at John. "Are you certain..."

John looks to the ceiling with a revolted huff. "I handed it to you myself. I said it, now you make me repeat myself as if I am a liar?"

"Wh—why? You owe me nothing. I'm not your sibling seed."

Matthew snaps at Palak, warning him with his eyebrows raised in a stern face. "Young Man, if we are doing this, you are going to make me quit repeating myself. I don't like it."

John smirks. "Ah, the Light. For the sake of your need for words, I will clarify. Your uncle killed your father for having the audacity to set aside prejudice and maintain a friendship with a Dark, then lied to you about the act. Despite your belief that a Dark killed your father, you had the courage to come to Ilbuio, surrounded by Dark, in pursuit of peace and survival, unaware you'd have friends."

Louis waves his hands. "No! No! He killed Jean!" He directs a finger at Matthew. "He did it!"

John, glaring at Louis, goes on. "I live because of Jean Paul Delacroix, and for that he gets respect. Palak proved himself in the maze and actions. Callahan intends for us to merge our societies. I will stand with my king and queen because Jean proved the Light can be a friend to the Dark. If I am to lose something in these pursuits, let it be a sacrifice Jean Paul would be proud of as a way to honor his memory."

Zander smiles. "A more appropriate response for you, Ash? We are witnessing history being made as Pierre would want." He steps toward Matthew. "Thank you for helping my friends." He extends his hand.

Matthew scoffs. "I ain't doing nothing for you. This is for that boy, his sweetheart of a mate, and Jean."

Louis straightens his shirt. "Palak, you're a disgrace to the name Delacroix, and I'll have nothing more to do with you."

He tries to leave.

Natalia steps in his way. "Louis," she starts with a sweet smile, his name dripping with venom. "You haven't been excused, and as you are a crown contract, any unauthorized departure would be seen as refusal of your contracted duties. Sit down and perhaps reflect upon Matthew's example of how things can be better."

"Better? This is revolting."

"Sit or I send you to the afters."

Yanking on his lapels, Louis stares her down.

"Try me," Natalia bats her eyelashes. "Blood and shadows look lovely together."

"You are an abomination and a disgrace to the Bordeaux heritage." He pivots and stalks back to the table.

Sterling hums. "My father used to tell me that if ever there was a way to find a mate, it was to wish upon the stars and ask Adontis for love mirroring her own." He chuckles. "When I wished upon the stars for a perfect mate, I did not realize how fucking terrifying she would be."

"My father had told me the same."

Long ago, and far away, I had wished with every tendril of my Dark crisscrossing in hope that I'd have a mate before I gave up wishes as mythical nonsense and accepted being alone. A mate had seemed so unlikely.

I snicker. "I didn't realize wishing on the stars would send me two."

"Thanks for wishing." He pats me on the shoulder. "Such a good boy."

CHAPTER 52
CALLAHAN

I have never spoken so much in my life. My throat is raw. There are too many faces for me to account for names, my limits for retaining information overwhelmed.

Some smile. Some sneer. Some offer words of support in twisted tones. Others offer veiled disdain. Kristopher Heatherton might have played a game, but he is the only one who seems to speak with honesty.

I keep Natalia and Sterling close through the third ceremony. Natalia guides me through every custom, and Zander gives aid when she flounders.

Tables are cleared by nameless, silent vassals. They keep their heads low, avoiding eye contact.

Music begins, and Zander nods at me from the left side of my table. "You move first."

I don't want to. I'm fed up, stretched thin, my Dark threatening to snap itself and destroy my mind if we must endure another long-winded speech of insults disguised as flattery.

Natalia has always pushed back with a sharper tongue, beating them at their games. I'm better with punching.

I stand, and Natalia follows me up. "I'm fucking tired."

"Stay with Sterling." She hesitates, but I shake my head. "Zan."

He stands, motioning me forward.

As we move from the table, others rise. Several collect together, some approaching me.

I leave Zander finagling open displeasure at my stature from a couple.

Kristopher appears at my side. "Stephanie Meraw," he says with a bow, "a pleasure to see your face and behold your exquisite glow."

I blink at the woman bowing to me, not sure where she came from.

She laughs. "It's not often we are in a presence to draw it forth."

"Ah." He raises his hand, checking front then back. "I see no reason to call it forth in front of a Hallow, do you?"

I frown at him. He's not wrapped in gold the same way as the rest.

"Well." Stephanie claps her hands together. "A marvelous surprise to see your face this evening, Heatherton. Who offered you the honor of bringing you as their guest? I believed you had lost touch with us."

Kristopher holds a level hand and swings it toward me. "Our very Hallow, in fact."

"The list for invitations must have been provided from an old record."

He chuckles, low like a warning growl. "If so, you'd have been forgotten."

Her eyes flash with hatred.

Pivoting to me, Kristopher says, "I do believe it's customary that you speak with all. Stephanie seems to be at a loss for words, and you have many to hear waiting yet."

She sticks her nose in the air. "The pleasure to stand before a Hallow is not something I believed would ever happen."

"It is a pleasure, is it not?"

She bristles, her glossy appearance wavering. "Yes, a pleasure. Excuse me, please."

With a bow, she walks away.

Kristopher shakes his head with a sigh. "Loraine's mother. I introduced her to those of rank. She gave me my daughter, and for that I will always be grateful, but she clawed her way into rank and discarded any attachment when I was cast out."

"You used me to claw your way, as you say, back."

"Mutual benefit. I saw my opportunity and disclosed in honesty that which I did."

"Why were you removed?"

"For daring to recommend rank is utter nonsense. We discard some who may prove worth, but they are given no chance. I was in favor of freeing our Light, as well. I supported many changes from the old ways of rigid structure that serves the select few, and as too progressive, I was cut out. It's a blight upon my heritage, but I saw you as a way to correct my overstep."

I narrow my eyes.

"Why lie when the truth serves me best? You can make inquiries. Zander will confirm." His chest stretches and then caves. "Once Pierre and I were friends. Ah, Dale Wilburn comes. Shall we see if we can get him to admit his hatred of the Dark?"

Dale is a short, stumpy man who wheezes as he talks. He's over a thousand years old, taking advantage of the fact to refer to me as a boy.

My Dark wants to send him to the afters to show him we are no child. I pull on it to keep it under control.

Dale scoffs. "Might I recommend you address that reprehensible and repulsive display?"

I look in the direction he nods.

Natalia flickers, not fully glowing, but tipping on the edge, her silver Light illuminating from within as Sterling leads her across the open dance floor.

I meet Dale's eyes. "I see nothing vulgar."

"We're aware of her adoration of animals, but that thing is unsuitable for our company. Your servant is far too bold to be allowed proximity. Remove the animal and control your mate. A change of attire should be your first business."

My Dark hisses and thrashes.

I yank on its reins. "*No.*"

"*Mates look delicious. That thing is stupid.*"

"*Very, but I want bodies to fight. Play their games for our gain.*"

I look to Sterling and Natalia again, her Light shining steadily, a dim glow from within. It sets the shadows stretching across her body glittering brighter.

I understand Sterling being persuaded by Mallafic. It's hardly fabric, the material soft and cool to the touch no matter how long it adorns her. She says she has two others hanging in our wardrobe. I'm irritated I wasn't made aware or graced with seeing them.

Sterling grins as she laughs. He's coaxed her into relaxing, and I'll not dampen the glow in her.

"Natalia is my mate, as is Sterling, the man she is with. What she wears for our enjoyment is not your concern. Your voice annoys me, as do your insults to my mates. Go."

I point away from myself, watching Sterling dip Natalia. Her leg bends and lifts through the slit against Sterling, so much of her on display.

Sterling runs his hand along her thigh, saying something.

"*Lucky fuck.*"

Dancing was never a skill I learned, but Sterling is always

quick to sway or twirl and dip our mate. I've never had the pleasure of watching them truly dance before.

Voices and laughter have swelled in volume, the room full of mingling bodies and music in the air. It's not different from the welcoming dinner that begins Gathering Shadows, other than the illuminated company and word games. Most contractors get drunk and try to enjoy themselves, knowing imminent death lurks.

Kristopher helps to expel another few conversations. He's quick at dispelling remarks, quips I can't understand stirring fury in the others.

He might be a useful tool. I have to give credit where it's due as a unioned pair skitter away.

I turn to him. Natalia seems to trust him. "What mutual benefits do you offer?"

He smiles, turning to watch others dance. "Did she speak of me?"

"Only today. She claims you were the only one who didn't damn her for her contract to me."

"What effect did it have on me for her to hold it? None. She is a Bordeaux, and that meant leverage to me if I were to be a friend. Am I to be a hypocrite? I cannot push for us to allow our magic freedom while spitting at those who do. Simple logic, no matter how I approached the situation."

The room grows louder still over several more conversations I don't invite upon myself.

Natalia and Sterling linger across the way. Sterling looks in my direction as Natalia chats.

My skin tingles as I hold his gaze.

Someone approaches, another boring conversation to come.

Sterling exaggerates a face of annoyance. I smirk.

The man bows, offering words I don't hear. I'd rather be across the room with my mates. This is nothing but tedious.

The one bright spot of the day had been Palak telling his uncle to go to the afters. I'd given him and Hailey free rein to go with Matthew and John to manage the paperwork with glib remarks.

Kristopher grunts and shoves me to the side. Pain blossoms in my stomach. I stumble, refocusing.

I gape at the hilt protruding beneath my ribs.

"Cal," Sterling roars.

The world turns vivid yellow, the hairs on my body standing up as the smite drops.

I blink to see Kristopher on the floor, the other man turning tail to run.

Grinding my teeth, I yank the blade free, hurling it into his back.

He falls face forward with a yell, the blade embedded between his shoulders.

I press my hand to the wound, my Dark churning and filling holes left by the sharp edges. I can't breathe well, too deep, and pain racks my ribs, twinging the muscles, but I'm under no imminent threat of demise.

Natalia runs to me.

Sterling latches onto the man.

"Babe," Natalia says, pressing her hand to my stomach. "Fuck, don't move."

The wash of energy through me focuses and collects around the throbbing hole. The pain lessens, and I can take a full gulp of air.

Natalia steadies me, eyes glistening.

I smirk. "Little Star, if I couldn't survive that on my own, I'd never have lasted through a single Gathering Shadows."

Sterling drags the man toward me. "Fucking pathetic rat. That's against the rules of engagement, and even you Glow Fucks follow those."

Loraine crumples next to Kristopher. "Father?"

Natalia kneels. "Let me."

Light pulses through her arm until Kristopher stirs.

He sits up, Loraine throwing her arms around him. "Father."

He pats her back, looking around. "May I inquire what happened?" He furrows his brow at me. "Oh, good. You're unharmed. I'm not an avenger, but not that weak."

My Dark pokes through the hole in my shirt, waving tendrils at him. "Something like that."

Loraine sobs. "Father, are you all right?"

Luca grimaces, standing next to them. "What a prick. He had to go and ruin a good time."

At least someone's been having fun.

"They say he's a glutton if ever there was one." My Dark laughs.

I smirk at him, then face the man. Zander stands next to Sterling, though my mate needs no help.

He sneers. "You do it or I will. I don't care about their laws. It stuck you."

The man shows his teeth. "Animals. You can wear a mask, emulate our ways with a crown on your head, but you'll never be one of us."

I glance at Falsion and Shawn standing close. "I'm curious," I say to the attacker, "even if you killed me, highly unlikely given my skill and that of my mates, what did you expect would happen?" I point at my kin. "There are others who carry the Hallow heritage right here. What kind of idiot are you?"

He spits at me. "You think I'm the fool? Everyone here wanted it done, and you exposed your back. I really thought driving a blade into you would be more difficult."

"I expected you to at least honor your ways, including rules of engagement."

"It's a matter of time until Heatherton succeeds."

I cut my eyes at Kristopher.

He turns furious. "I tried to push you out of the way."

The man on his knees laughs. "To play the hero and win trust. He forced my hand, seeking your favor."

Loraine snaps her heeled shoe to the floor. "My father would never do such a thing."

"What better way to regain what was lost than to eliminate the threat to our way of life?"

Kristopher shakes his head. "The final hand you play, and you drag me down with you, Oliver. I'm not surprised, but that stings."

Ashley pushes to my side. "There will be a trial, Callahan. We will determine the truth."

Sterling snarls, "Trial? We all saw what happened. We don't need a fucking trial."

I close the gap between Oliver and me. "You held the blade. A claim that one who was removed from rank could force your hand seems laughable at best given your ways, and you pissed on our rules of engagement."

Sterling leans over, digging his claws into Oliver's shoulder. Oliver yells with pain, but Sterling sneers. "Not even animals ignore rules of engagement or the laws of hospitality."

"You're right. I'll never be a Light. I'm a Barraco, descendant of a Renfair and a Hallow, and I don't intend to pretend otherwise. I made myself clear. I'll be following your law, so conform to my rule or your Light will be destroyed."

I send my Dark into him. Sterling holds him as he thrashes, his Light trying to defend its host. I drag the seed of Light from his chest, throwing it to the side at Luca.

"As a Hallow, I can conjure flames. As a Renfair, I wield the Dark, able to shift to a predator. As a mix, I have one very useful skill to ensure your compliance."

Oliver twitches, gurgling. Sterling lets go, and the body drops to the floor, limp.

I nod at Luca. "Don't waste it."

He wraps the Light, trying to crawl along the floor back to its host. Luca's Dark turns brilliant blue then it extinguishes.

He licks his lips. "Tasty."

"We are Mandolux, Light Eaters. We can dig your Light out and consume it. I'll say it again for those hard of hearing. Conform, or have your Light destroyed." I kick Oliver over, lifting an eyebrow at the body. Tears leak from his hazy, white eyes. "You won't die, not right away, not until you wither, unable to speak or move."

I glance around the room. Most won't look me in the eye as I pass over them.

"Any questions?"

Tony laughs.

I glare at him.

He waves a hand, doubling over in humor. "No, not you. It's Soris. You know she tells me everything that's happening as it happens, and that man just pissed himself when you looked at him."

I lift my eyebrows, glancing toward where he waves. A blond man ducks his head and runs from the room. I presume he needs a change of clothes.

I move my gaze to Kristopher. "One chance to tell me the truth."

He scratches at the back of his head. "Dig my Light out if you want, but I had no part in this."

"I will if someone hands me proof you did."

"Your Majesty, I may be conniving, I assure you, but had I orchestrated this, I would have killed him myself before he could speak so as not to reveal me. The very fact he had the chance to speak my name should declare my innocence."

"Zan."

"Your Majesty?"

511

"Was Heatherton a friend of Pierre's?"

"Long ago, but the connection was severed."

Kristopher smiles. "Ah, but who shared my establishment with his daughter?"

Natalia frowns. "Pierre."

Ashley jerks to life. "That must be a lie."

Kristopher smiles at her. "It is not. I learned everything I know from your father. You'll not find my hand in this mess. I'd never tarnish Pierre's wishes. Use them, yes, but not to diminish his memory. He's always known my beliefs. The webs brought you to me through his actions, no doubt through the strange foresight he always seemed to possess, as if Saris held his ear."

I cock my jaw. "You're like him."

"High, *very high*, praise indeed, Sir, albeit unfounded. I'll not claim to be as prolific in any skill."

I met Pierre in my second century. I tried to kill him for what he'd done and failed. I've been unable to escape his radius since.

Someday, in the afters, I'm going to wring his neck until my rage is abated. I think my hands will lose grip strength before I achieve that feat, but I'll try all the same.

"I hate that fuck."

"In jealousy or spite?" Kristopher asks without missing a beat.

I point at Oliver. "Someone just tried to kill me because of him."

"I am so sorry, Your Majesty. I had no idea what an ordeal it was, given your words and assurance that it was a pathetic attempt and a waste of time. Please, allow me to have a cushion fetched."

Natalia snorts and covers her mouth, covering the explosive giggle as a cough.

Sterling runs his hand up the back of her neck. "I think he meant someone put a hole in his shirt and he's cranky."

I glower, exasperated. "He put a dagger in my lungs."

Sterling drops his chin, staring at me from the tops of his eyes. "Baby, I've done that flirting with you."

I am not going to laugh at that. I won't.

Kristopher smiles, and I'd swear it was with a mouth full of fangs sharper than Jacques's. "You are capable. Of that, we have been assured. Pierre would not have handed this burden to one who could not carry its weight. A simple stab, nothing but a ruined shirt. That is the greater crime, is that a Delorna design? A tragedy."

I look at my chest, curling my lip.

He laughs. "As always, Pierre had more insight and knowledge than any of us. He was, without doubt or question, brilliant and methodical even when we lacked the ability to see his reasons."

Ashley smooths her skirt. "Thank you, Kristopher, for the kind reflection upon my father." She blinks, tears rising, then moves, bending over to lift the crown of Light.

I didn't realize it slipped. I hadn't missed that curse upon my head in the least.

She offers it to me. "Your Majesty."

I grasp it, closing my hand around the simple band to slap it on my head.

She bows. "Perhaps we have all had enough excitement for this day. If you'd like to announce your ministers, we can all retire to settle our nerves."

CHAPTER - Callahan

I COLLECT those present for my coronation, including Kristopher and his daughter, in a group. Then I collect those who were invited to the welcome brunch to the side.

I have Ashley and Zander confer to determine from those two groups they'd preselected, which of them could be chosen.

As they do, I stick two fingers in my mouth and whistle. "Those who served drinks and food at all three ceremonies come here."

Ashley gapes at me. "Callahan, I'll inquire as to your reason for addressing them."

Five step forward without a word, three women and two men. They keep their heads low, hands clasped at their backs like broken mules.

I point at Oliver. He's the man who tried to walk out this morning that I'd dragged back into the throne room. That's enough reason for me to do things my way.

Vassals present for private affairs are the most trusted and valuable resource. They see and hear everything, and are given access to information and entrusted to remain loyal. They were selected with more care than anyone else given an invitation. Invites could be swayed by numerous obligations or personal feelings, but those who serve are consistent in being measured to higher degrees.

"I'm doing things my way as I told you I would. Quit making me repeat myself. Who do you suggest?"

Ashley presents nine offerings.

I point to the woman who claimed the know the meaning of Fallon's name. "You made Fallon cry. Fuck no."

She opens her mouth. Ashley drops her face in her hand, and Zander turns his head away, against displaying a smile.

"You," I say, pointing at a man, "called my mate an animal-loving whore." He opens his mouth, and I push on. "Yes, I heard you. No."

I study the others, stepping to stare down another man. He flinches.

I smirk, looking to the one next to him. "Did he say anything?" I ask, jerking my head at the one before me.

"You'll need to be more specific."

I smirk. "Your name?"

"Corey Marose."

"You'll be fine." I face the man in front of me. "Anything you want to share?"

"You're an animal engaging with another one in a grotesque display of sharing a mate. You're vile, without manners, and I doubt your comprehension of my words as they are more than crude and four letters. Natalia is a Dark-loving stain upon her heritage, but that's not new, and Oliver was my brother. I despise you, feeling nothing but repulsion in your presence."

I wave a finger between them. "Go stand with them." I wave at the vassals.

I have five more, four women among them. One is a tall brunette. I recall her charming smile and tongue of acid.

The man I'd dismissed steps forward. "Why would you select him when the words I spoke were far less insulting?"

"You did it behind my back. He looked me in the eye."

He sneers, and I turn my back to him to face the brunette. "Your name?"

"Brynn Perry, Your Majesty." She smiles wide, eyes flashing.

"Oliver claimed everyone here wanted a blade in me. Do you agree?"

"No, or you wouldn't be here. A Bordeaux and a Fairly protect you and bow to you. They want you here."

I have no idea what to do with that, but it's enough to put her with the others. I'm fucked in word games. Someone needs to manage them.

I focus on another woman, pressing my palms together and holding her gaze.

She stares back, lifting her chin. "How ever may I serve you, Your Majesty?"

I laugh. "Fair enough. Go with the others." I step in front of the woman next to her. "Why would I trust you?"

"Allow me to offer you advice as you are new to our ways. You shouldn't. I have given no word or act to give you any other impression, and I loathe the Dark for it stole my parents."

I step back, waving her toward the others.

Two remain.

"Do either of you know what the purpose of an alpha is?"

The man laughs. "Layla is my sister. I can recite your words if you'd like, or you can accept I know your meaning, while Raine would offer insult." He motions to the woman next to him.

Raine startles, looking at him. "I don't understand."

The man bows. "You have my sincere appreciation for bringing her home."

"Then I expect not to ever have to repeat them for your ears. Go," I tell him. "Raine, why were you selected?"

"Why do none of us get the same test?"

I laugh. "Sterling."

"Games vary to ensure players do not have an advantage over others. If you all got the same question, then others have time to prepare and may change their response based upon previous success and failure."

I stare her down, waiting. I scoff. "If you haven't realized I don't repeat myself, then I have no use for you."

"My heritage is one rank below Bordeaux."

"That makes you part of the trinity now?"

"Never. The trinity is and always will be the Lamonts, the Hallows, and the Bordeauxs."

"The Lamonts are gone."

"Their honor—"

"You'll stand next to Ashley, given your heritage, and help me, but not as a minister."

Ashley presses her lips, turning her head to the side and rubbing the space behind her ear.

I have two designated families to work with mine, keeping their trinity structure. The group I have selected consists of three men and three women.

Zander bows his head. "You need one more to avoid even splits."

I glance across at the others, Kristopher smiling. I'll deal with him, but not give him what he was after.

Brynn says, "If I may, there is still Logan Malloy to consider. He would be a wise choice."

"Who is...?"

Ashley shakes her head. "He is not present, though it is not out of disrespect. He's in mourning and sequestered with his two daughters, they are but one and two. His mate was sent to the afters in the attack on our city."

"I'm not dealing in unknowns. You're here, suspending your ability to mourn because we don't have time. If he can't do the same, I won't bother with him."

Raine shakes her head. "You are as cruel as we've always believed."

Natalia steps forward. "He's not asking of anyone what he doesn't offer of himself." She presses her hand to my arm, leaning against me. "I know you miss Massimo."

I keep my eyes low, swallowing the words I know. Dead is dead. Mallafic, a god, couldn't even bring back Natasha, only create a version. There is no return from death. I push it away, pretending like always that the sting of having one ripped away is a fact.

I slide my arm around my mate. "He'd put a fist in my face if I wallowed over him instead of putting use to his death."

Jacques waves. "I'll do it for him if he ever needs since he's not here."

Sterling joins Natalia. "We don't know any of these Glows. Leave space open for when we do."

"Fine. Six for now with three to come." I step to them. "Vassals, heads up and look at me."

The five shift, glancing at each other and one brave man lifts his head. "Sir, Your Majesty, it is against our rank."

"Those who serve me usually hold their heads high in pride that I've accepted them as mine." I point at Jacques. "Like that. Who are you contracted to?"

"N–no one, Sir. We don't hold rank to be entitled to that honor as lowborn."

I look to Ashley. "Lowborn are mandated to be contracted."

"Some ranks can. Contracts are not mandatory and are an honor."

"That makes this easy. I'll offer you five contracts."

Brynn rattles and slashes the air. "They are unsuited—"

"They will decide if they accept." I face their open mouths.

"They cannot. It is not their place, but ours." She rests her hand on the neckline of her gown. "It's an honor only a select few have the right to, and you've dismissed much better options without due cause, placing these worthless—"

"'Worthless?'" I snarl. "You were served by them. Without them, you have nothing to stand on, and you insult them?"

She pulls back, mouth flapping.

The crowd shifts, and a man walks forward. "Interesting perspective." His lean shoulders are low, his demeanor bleak. He stops, bowing to me. "Your Majesty, my apologies for my tardiness. I intended—"

"You," Sterling shouts.

I turn toward him, or where he'd been. Sterling launches at the man, claws out. Moving past my eyes as I pivot.

I rush forward to dig him off the man. I don't reach him before his Dark clouds around them. A sharp yell comes from within as I send my Dark in to find our mate.

It hisses and yanks, dragging him back as he growls and thrashes, covered in flickering firelight.

I grab him, moving us away.

"Talia. Tony," I order. One of them can deal with the other, any wounds that need tending while I wrestle Sterling.

He claws at my torso, ramming his elbow into my jaw.

The world spins, my side stinging.

I throw him to the floor, following him down. He snarls and struggles, pure rage adding strength to him as I try to pin him without injury.

"Sterling, stop."

"That's the fuck."

"Stop."

He shoves his leg between mine hitting my balls. I growl in pain, the air knocked from my lungs.

He's going to pay for that cheap shot later.

He flings me to the side, and I round on my knees, tangling my Dark around him.

Natalia steps between him and the man, lifting her hands. "Babe."

"Get the fuck out of my way."

"No."

He points over her shoulder. "That's the fucking animal."

I get up, wincing with a hand against my belt and spit a mouthful of blood to the floor.

Sterling makes a quick move, trying to slip past Natalia. She trips him and shoves him back.

He snarls. "Move, Tal, or I move you."

I laugh. "You don't stand a fucking chance, baby." I get to him, putting my hand on his shoulder and leaning forward. "Fuck, you got me good."

"You shouldn't have gotten in the way."

Tony pulls the other man up as he stands. "Good as new aside from the clothes. Can't fix that."

Sterling tries to move past Natalia, and she spins, stepping in front of him and kicking off her heels. "I adore you, so please don't make me hurt you."

He snaps his teeth.

She lifts her fingers, wiggling firelight at him.

I grab him and shove him back, squaring up to him. "Stop."

"He—"

"I told you we can't," I say. I know who he is, and I can't fault Sterling. "I would let you. I would help if you wanted. If. We. Could."

Sterling screws up his face, the bridge of his nose wrinkling with fury. He takes a step toward me, and my Dark gets ready to defend.

I grab him by the back of his neck, pulling his face toward mine. "I'd drag his Light out and let him die broken and slow locked in his head, but I can't."

"You really fucking can. You just won't, so get out of my way."

"Is it worth it to you? You know what's at stake. You decide. I'll throw this crown away and kill him slowly if you think it's worth the Dark and the Light."

"Fuck the Glow Whores."

I shove a hand to his chest, pushing him back. "Zander. Ashley. Palak. They went through the maze to earn this. Fuck that? Wyham and Hailey standing with us? Fuck them? Pierre's life? Fuck that too?"

He grips his fists, raising them to watch them shake.

"Is that your choice?"

He drops his hands, opening them to hang at his side. They snap and shrink, his skin lightening from black to brown. "They earned respect." He takes a shaky breath, his black eyes glistening. "I fucking hate you."

He turns, walking away.

I rub my face, rounding toward the rest. The man is covered in blood stains, his clothes ripped to shreds.

"I know who you are, now give me a name."

Ashley steps to his side. "Callahan, this is Logan Malloy, a very respectable gentleman and dear friend of my father. His heritage is extremely powerful and has always been honorable. He is my mother's brother."

"For fuck's sake." I clamp my jaw. I take a deep breath, holding it to subdue my rage, then exhale slowly. "All right."

Ashley crosses her arms, face stern. "Callahan, this is my family. You cannot tolerate what just happened. It was vile and—"

"And he murdered Sterling's father," I snap, stepping closer. "Burned a Dark alive in front of his young son then gave him a mark for life to never forget it. He said it was to remind a dumb animal it's a dangerous world."

The woman who made Fallon cry sneers. "That's a fallon."

"Get the fuck out of my sight." I point behind me toward the doors. "Now."

She looks around, no one making eye contact with her. Shrugging she moves past me. "*Hmph*! So much for honesty."

I make a fist, my Dark preparing to rip her open. My fingers break and grow, my skin turning black.

"*No.*"

It whines and I shake my hand back to human. "Logan, speak."

"My regrets for the lack of my appearance at your coronation

521

ceremonies. I intended to dine with you in order to make one small gesture of respect and your acquaintance, but I was delayed. My youngest would not stop crying. I fear she misses her mother, too infantile to understand no matter how long she cries her mother will never again hold her."

I raise an eyebrow. "Fine."

"The proper response is to offer empathy to my situation."

"You murdered Sterling's father. My empathy is allowing you to live. You dragged your ass here despite your ordeal and assurances you wouldn't. Stand as the seventh minister."

He inclines his head. "Ashley, what do you think?"

She shakes her head. "I think I am tired. My father was impeccable, never wrong, but I fear what we have done."

"Then allow me to help in pursuits of Pierre's vision." He turns to me. "I will accept the contracted position."

"Cal," Natalia says, shaking her head with disbelief. "You can't."

"This isn't about what he wants. It's not about you or me or him at all. I'd fucking put the bastard in the afters myself if it were."

She folds her lips between her teeth and looks away. She's miffed, but I won't bend on this, not even for her.

"I don't care about past disputes. What's done is done. The dead are dead. The webs of the past are weaved and unchangeable." I look to Ashley, then decide to screw everything. "Pierre's mate died because she chose to engage in a relationship with a Dark."

Ashley's face of melancholy turns to shock and ire.

The burning fury I had at seeing Sterling's mating mark on my mate was unparalleled to any I'd experienced, even my hatred of Pierre was less.

Sterling was at least another Dark, a man I held in high regards. He'd earned my respect, and I'm thrilled in retrospect, but in the moment I wasn't. I can only imagine what Pierre felt in his mate's betrayal for something he already hated.

I have to admit to myself Pierre was right. I understand now that I have a mate.

"If there was a valid reason to hate the Dark, Pierre had one," I say.

Her features pull to confusion.

"He still made this choice. I didn't ask for it, want it, or even know of it until he was in the afters. I didn't even get a choice. He gave his life for mine. He knew he wouldn't survive and still chose to set me free in exchange for death. He handed this crown to me in belief that I could follow what he hoped for, that I could union with his daughter, the Dark King, and take my place as a Hallow and the Light Queen to end the divide between Dark and Light. The Ancients believe we should die because they don't share Pierre's belief. Who is right? Pierre Bordeaux, a man you respected, or Ancients who have watched us kill each other for millennium. Can you set aside the death of a father to prevent another death? I did. I broke a tenet of the Dark, choosing to put something ahead of my desires. I decided protecting was more important than revenge. The Ancients think you're incapable of doing the same. Pierre thought it was possible. Now you all need to make the choice."

I take the crown of Light off and toss it to Ashley. She catches it, gaping at me.

"Louis hurt Palak in several ways for his willingness to change. Oliver put a blade through me. I've been insulted numerous ways without the ability afforded to me to earn respect, and my patience is at an end. In one day, I've had more problems from the Light than the Dark has presented with a glowing Dark King or welcoming the Light into our city." I shake my head. "The Light is too full of hate to see beyond the end of its own nose. I won't waste any more of my time."

"You are a Hallow. You must—"

"My name is Barraco. I am not the Dark or the Light, but born of both, and I would have accepted this responsibility Pierre handed to me if the Light hadn't refused it."

Ashley gawks at the crown, then turns toward Falsion.

He flips her a rude gesture. "It's that young man or none of us."

Luca slaps Falsion on the back with a wide grin. "Damn straight."

I step to Oliver's body. "You don't fucking deserve this, but I'll not make your brother do it." My Dark snaps his neck, ending the suffering.

I stare around the room, then at Natalia. I extend my hand, and she takes it. We'll find Sterling together.

"Callahan," Ashley squeaks. "You cannot—"

I whip to face her, rage burning in my veins. "I never wanted this. I never cared about Dark and Light. I had every reason to abhor the Light when Natalia came into my life and I still accepted the truth that she saved my life and that warranted respect. I hated Pierre more than you'll ever understand and not because he glowed. I had Natalia hidden from me the day I learned she was Pierre's seed afraid of my temper and what it might do to his seed in a thirst for vengeance. I'm not the fucking problem, and Pierre knew it."

Natalia squeezes my hand. "Love you, too, babe."

I drag her out of the great hall into the corridor. "I do love you, Mate, but I still hate that fuck."

No MATING MARK exists between Sterling and me, but he has my worn contract. It acts the same, providing an echo for me to follow.

We track him in the direction of the tower but find him pacing in an alley. Natalia drops my hand, moving to Sterling.

He warns her with a display of teeth. She ignores it, hugging him.

I move closer, standing at her back. I run my hands up her sides then back down, squeezing her hips as I meet Sterling's eyes.

"What are you doing?" I ask.

"I'm fucking lost."

I nod. "Not our city."

"City, place, fucking kind. Not our fucking problem. What are we doing here?" He throws his arms out, bellowing, "This isn't us. We fought to survive. We earned the right and our respect, and we've been spit at, sneered at, and insulted in every fucking way I can think of by these Glows."

"Do you want a name?"

"Fuck no. I want blood."

"You got it. He bled."

"Not enough."

I sigh, resting my chin on Natalia's head. "Baby," I warn him.

Sterling shudders. "How..." he starts in a broken voice, not his rich tone. "How did you do it?"

"The same way you did. You walked away."

"For you, because your insufferable nobility makes me feel like a piece of garbage, and I want to deserve my mate."

I smile, removing one hand from Natalia to rest it on his side instead. "You earned us."

"You let that fuck in your home."

"Self-preservation."

"Fuck you." He almost laughs, emitting a sob. "You chose to

put protecting others before self-gratification. You always do. You're impossible."

"Literally." I chuckle. "A Shadow Beast and a Hallow managed to enjoy each other enough to fuck at least once."

Natalia giggles. "Wonder if it was because she was sassy."

I kiss her head. "Maybe. Maybe she liked that he was shiny."

Sterling shakes his head, a tear sliding down his cheek. "Fuck."

"Talia, do you know how to get us back to the tower?"

"*Mhm*." Her head rocks.

"Let's go. I think our mate needs some appreciation."

I step away, giving her room to move. She spins, pressing her back to Sterling and lifting his hands, wrapping his arms around her shoulders.

"Come, Mate." She tips her head back, smiling up at him.

He stares back, visibly cracked. "I don't hate you." Lifting his head, he blinks, then rubs his face. "I think I meant it when I said it, but I don't really."

"Good, because you're bound and fucked for life. That would have made things awkward." I whistle, motioning ahead of me. "You're still going to pay me back for kneeing me in the balls, though."

He laughs. "That's fair." He takes one step forward, pushing Natalia toward the way out. "What do I and a snowman have in common when we throw a tantrum?"

I fall into step. "What?"

"We melt down."

I shake my head, seeing the humor but annoyed that I find that funny.

Natalia doesn't hold back, laughing freely and real. "You did kind of lose your mind."

Squeezing Natalia, Sterling lets go, moving to her side. "I'm not going to get to kill that fuck, am I?"

I don't have an answer. If the Light accepts me as their Light Queen, no. If I'm free of that crown, I'll drag Logan Malloy to Sterling and slap a bow on his head for my mate.

"How do two cats end a fight?"

He looks over at me. The haze in his eyes clears as he smiles with half his mouth. "How?"

"They hiss and make up."

"That's fucking awful."

"It's the only joke my father ever told me. I was less than a decade old, and a cat bit my hand. That was his response."

Natalia does a little skip, taking my hand. "I have one my dad told me every time I'd complain. What's the hardest tea to swallow?"

I give her hand a pulse. "What?"

"Reality."

Sterling chuckles. "Fuck both of you. I liked my father."

CHAPTER 53
CALLAHAN
2ND NIGHT'S DAY, BLOOMING, 4050, 6TH MILLENNIUM

I have Natalia lead me back to Heatherton's establishment for breakfast. I manage to avoid everyone else, lingering in the embrace of my mates, just us in our own little world as we move through Izul.

Loraine is frosty as we enter.

It's better than I expected. "Have your father join us."

She leads us to a table, and Kristopher turns up. He scowls at me. "Your Majesty?"

I smirk. "I don't like being used."

He scoffs.

"Sit." I point. "I have mutual benefits to discuss."

He raises an eyebrow, slithering to the floor. "Very well."

"I need someone I can trust. You've been far more open and honest than the rest from the start."

"And yet..." He props his elbow on his knee, strumming his fingers on the table.

"I'm offering you a contract of service."

He goes still, picking his head up. "I see. You wanted to

528

punish me by making me wait and receiving an offer of an open slot in private."

"No. You annoyed me, and I decided I'd use you how I wanted, not giving you what you used me to obtain."

"Tried."

"What?"

"I tried to use you to obtain. Without the word, I can infer I succeeded."

He's as bad as my father. I shake my head. "I want someone between me and them. They'll stab me in the back."

"You expect me to take the blade instead?"

"I expect you to be eyes and ears for me. I expect you to speak for me with the interest of all, not yourself, and I expect you to serve all, not yourself. In exchange, you get your rank above them."

"Ah." He chuckles. "Interesting."

"I have Jacques and Zan for my immediate disposal. I need someone to manage day to day without my direct order."

Food is delivered, Loraine bowing as she backs away. Kristopher brushes teacups and works through the process of pouring tea, then arranges food.

He sets a cup in front of me, then Natalia, and Sterling last. He lingers, his fingertips on the rim of the cup as he lifts his head. "Young Man, I offer sympathy for you in regard to your father."

Sterling scoffs.

"I am sincere." Kristopher retracts, sitting with his hands together and resting his wrists on the edge of the table. "While it is true that Logan—"

"I didn't need to know that thing's name."

Kristopher looks to me.

I look to Sterling. "He's a minister."

Sterling flings his teacup at me. Hot liquid slings across my chest, but my Dark catches the cup, righting it and placing it on the table.

I pour him more and slide it across the surface to him. "Strategic placement to appease others while maintaining eyes on him at all times."

Kristopher laughs. "You learn quickly, Your Majesty."

"Everything is hypothetical at the moment, given I handed the crown over to Ash."

"Ah, the turmoil you left in your wake was exciting. You'd be surprised how many stood for you to remain our Light Queen."

"What was the decision?"

"You mean, was it enough? The answer is yes. You played your hand splendidly, far better than I thought you could after one of yours tried to send Logan to the afters. I see why Pierre instilled such belief in you."

I sigh. I needed to break them to my will. I've never tried to break that many simultaneously. It was a gamble on the success. My available tools to force their acceptance were limited and emotional, and mental manipulation was my best chance.

"Clever," Kristopher says, "twisting them with their own blades of belief to suit your desires."

"I was motivated." I lift my cup at him, draining it. "I hate tea, and I have limited days to find a way to send Ancients to the afters."

"Did Pierre not confide that knowledge?"

"He didn't know."

"Ah."

"Do you?"

"No."

I twist my mouth to the side. "Fuck."

"We have company." He stands and bows.

Ashley sinks to a cushion, setting the crown on the table

between us. "Yours, Your Majesty." She adjusts, getting comfortable. "Sterling."

"Ash."

"Logan is my mother's brother."

"Quit saying that fuck's name."

Kristopher chuckles, looking behind me toward the door. I glance behind me and then snort into my hand, hanging my head. "No."

"Yes," Ashley says.

I pick my head up to see her motioning forward.

This is a disaster waiting to happen, and all I can do is try to stop it. "Ash, no."

Logan steps around the table with Tony, bowing. "Good morning."

"Like fuck it is," Sterling slams the heel of his palm into the table, shoving it away. "You are in front of me. There's nothing good about it."

Natalia crawls into his lap, sitting on him with her back to his chest. "Breathe, babe."

He snakes one arm around her, growling into her neck. "Fuck this fucking fucked fucker."

She giggles. "I know, but you know why."

"Says the woman who would kill him anyway."

"That's why I have Cal and you." She shrugs. "You stop me from doing stupid things."

I reach over, stroking the side of her face. "Do we, though?"

Sterling shifts her, turning his head to the side, his chin on her shoulder as he stares at me. He's begging for free rein, pleading that I let him finish what he started.

Logan and Tony have taken a seat. Kristopher walks away.

Logan laces his fingers together and sets his hands on the table, similar to how Kristopher sat. "Sterling, is it?"

He clamps down on Natalia. "You don't get to fucking say my name."

Ashley slaps her palm against the table. "You will show respect."

Logan holds a hand to her. "Callahan, you made quite the speech."

I lift my chin.

Ashley rolls her eyes. "Logan is why you still have the crown of Light. Give him manners at least."

"I didn't ask for it."

"My father—"

"Pierre, yes. He wanted this." I sigh.

Logan shifts his weight, rocking back and forth before settling. "You made a valid point. I cost the life of a father. For that, I could have been killed by the son, which would have left my girls abandoned in this world."

Kristopher returns with a tray, more teacups and pots of tea. He sits and begins to prepare the cups.

Logan continues, ignoring him. "They could have grown to take another father in a vicious, never-ending cycle. I could have defended myself and removed the threat, undoubtedly causing another to seek my death as he seems to be cherished." He motions at Natalia and Sterling.

"You take him from us, and I don't care who you are, you go to the afters with him."

Sterling picks his head up. "I can take care of myself."

My Dark snickers, stretching around him. *Hosts are fragile. I'll keep it safe for my loves.*

I smirk. "My job, baby."

He shakes his head, burying his face in Natalia's hair and neck. "Make it leave, Firefly." He strains, arms flexing around her.

Kristopher serves the tea, picking up his own cup for a drink.

Natalia pats Sterling's arm across her shoulders. "You're strong, babe. You can handle anything, like Cal."

Logan frowns. "To end the turmoil and become one would bring an end to the cycle of death. I support that idea and if Pierre believed in it so much that he gave his life, I will do all that I can to give my aid. I'd like a world where my daughters do not have to live in fear or pain." He stands. "I came to share a meal, but I can tell I am causing discomfort. I'll leave you to rest and enjoy."

"Sit down. My mate isn't delicate. He has a temper, gets dramatic, and no, he's not docile, but he has more strength than you give him credit for. Don't piss me off."

Sterling chokes on a laugh into Natalia's shoulder. "Fuck, the Light fuck was being nice. My mate's the one torturing me."

"You're fine." I focus on Logan as he retakes his seat. "I want fighters. I don't care about rank. I need skill and bodies to deal with the Ancients."

He inclines his head. "That can be arranged."

"Get them to that building, the..." I look to Natalia.

"Arena," she says with a nod.

"We'll decide who is good enough to go. Make arrangements for you and the other six, plus the five lowborn who served to meet us there. I'll sign contracts while we determine strength and options. You come too, Kristopher."

Tony's eyes roll back into his head, glimmering pure white.

I watch and wait.

He slumps, rubbing his eyes. "Ugh, that's awful." He shudders. "I know, parasite, but it's still like floating outside my body and I don't like it."

He shakes his head, stretching his shoulders back and expanding his chest. "Fuck. Ness absorbed another codex. Mallafic said there was only one more before she got to write the ending of her story then she'll be ready."

Natalia leans forward. "Ready for what?"

"I don't know."

"Hey, stupid spider, what purpose?"

Tony shakes his head. "She gets really offended when you call her a spider."

"Eight legs, spins webs, that's a spider. It's got to be better than parasite."

He laughs. "Oh, she's really mad at us, fuming about how she is a god and shouldn't be treated this way."

Clicking her tongue, Ashley picks up her tea. "As is her right. You need to show more gratitude that you were selected to be a host and give her proper honor. I would adore being picked to give a fate my ear."

"She likes you and is willing to accept a host who will treat her with dignity, but you have to kill me first. Wait until we've finished dealing with the Ancients, sweetheart."

Logan narrows his eyes at Tony. "You will refrain from my niece starting immediately. I care not that you hold a fate. You are unsuited to a Bordeaux."

Tony snickers, toasting him with his cup. "Pierre tried that too. It didn't stop Ash."

"Young Lady," Logan warns her with a stern expression.

"My father mated with a Magia, producing her," Ashley argues, motioning at Natalia.

"His dalliance is noted and still frowned upon. She was given stature at his behest, although her associations with the Dark raised eyebrows. Going forward that can be of no consideration, but she is not a Seraphinus nor true Light."

Natalia throws her hands up. "Now I don't have the Light?"

I shake my head. "I fed on you, Little Star. You have the Light."

Logan shakes his head. "Pierre was insistent that she was his daughter, but the color is wrong, and she is not our kind. He presumed she was an Ancient."

"Ancients don't have wings. She does."

Tallie gets smaller. "What the fuck am I?"

Sterling rocks her. "Ours."

I grin. "Right answer, Mate."

WITH GREAT REGRET, I purchase clothes after breakfast in a shop within Izul. I don't have time for anything else. I'll make do with the available offerings, but everything comes in shades of my least favorite color palette.

Sterling and I settle on the darkest shades of gray we can find, dull versions of Natalia's Light.

He gets the simple shirt on, the thin material stretching across his chest as he collects the thick ropes of his locks and ties them back.

The lighter fabric provides clear shadowed definitions of his torso. My Dark whispers at me to trace them.

Natalia steps forward in tight gold pants and a white, short-sleeved top. She wrinkles her nose at Sterling.

"Firefly, I'm begging you. Having my mate look at me like I'm gross physically hurts."

She laughs, reaching for his shoulders and jumping up. "It's just wrong."

He catches her, his magic wrapping around her. "It feels wrong, too."

"Never had that." She tilts her head to the side. "Pierre swore I needed to wear brighter clothes. You don't look like you."

He hugs her, looking to me. His eyes narrow. "Cal's still pretty."

She giggles. "He's always pretty." She taps his shoulder. He slides her to her feet, and she turns, checking me over. "You look better in shades of black, though."

I lift my eyebrow, scanning the low scoop of her top. I slip my finger under it, pulling it away from her skin to steal a glance beneath. "You look better in nothing."

She shakes her head, her face scrunching in disgust. Not the response I was hoping for.

She shudders. "I'd wear that dress for you, but when he does it..." She winces, squirming in place.

I kiss her forehead. "My little star."

We return to the tower, and I rouse Jacques and Zander to raid the library. I want anything on the hysterium tree they can find.

Falsion volunteers to help, but I send Galain with Fallon and Maria instead for their ability to comprehend the old language. I need Falsion, Shawn, and Luca to weed out the weaker fighters.

We collect at the arena.

Luca turns in circles as he moves inside, staring up and whistling in a steady, long, low tone.

I'm inclined to agree as I look toward the glass dome. Floor after floor, the building rises.

Sterling gapes up like he's offended, then shoves me. "The fuck don't we have one of these?"

Chuckling, I rub my mouth. I might need to reconsider where we train.

Luca takes off, spreading his wings as he heads upward. "Day-um!" He laughs. "You've got to see these weights."

Heading for one of the dozens of mats roped off with red cords, I survey the area.

Sterling joins me, slipping between the ropes to jump on the mat. "Fucking prissy bitches. No wonder they're so soft. Hitting this has to be like landing on a cloud."

Curious, I hoist myself over the ropes. I jump, testing the surface. All the times I've slammed into hard dirt and stone, floods through me. This would be a dream.

"Come on." Sterling lashes at me with a hand and several strands of Dark. His magic wraps around my arm and yanks me closer to him. "You and me, baby."

"You sure?" I stretch my neck.

"I haven't swung at you once since the dining hall."

"Come get me," I say, puckering my lips.

He laughs, lifting his hands and coming closer.

I give Sterling something to beat on for a while, swinging full force with him. It feels good to let loose, and he can take it. He gives it right back until we're both panting and wincing.

I lean on the ropes. "Talia."

She drops her handstand and perks up. "Yes, Boss-Mate-Owner?"

I chuckle. It's been a while since she's referred to me like that. Hearing it makes my Dark bounce. "Heal me."

Sterling shoves against me. "Me first." He puckers his lips at her. "You know you wanna be sassy and annoy him."

I push my fist against his shoulder. "She's been behaving. Don't encourage her."

She slips between the barrier ropes and giggles. "I should fix that."

I yank her to me, crushing my mouth to hers, opening to taste her. It seems like it's been months of crushing expectations and responsibility since I've enjoyed her, even if I was inside of her last night.

Sterling leans into my back, chuckling in my ear as I twist my tongue with hers.

I can't recall the last time I was this at ease. I'm not staring down another Gathering Shadows. I'm not trapped by a list or the contest set, wondering what challenges I'll face, grappling with the thought of sending Sterling to the afters.

He's not dying in the games or the contest. I have an equal partner in him and a friend.

I don't have to worry about losing Mass—that failure has already come to pass. Natalia will be at my side, she's stronger than ever as a weapon and tool. As a woman, she's the perfect mate.

I tilt Natalia's head, deepening the kiss. Dark and Light twist around me. Sterling runs his hand up my side and chest to grip my shoulder, his arm beneath mine as he presses into my back.

Natalia pushes against my front, kissing me back with a hand on my jaw.

The Light is going to bend to me. I wear their crown and the crown of Dark. I have a sassy star full of raw power unmatched by anyone.

I possess two mates who fit perfectly with me and each other. I have Tony, and a fatum. Two Fairlys, a Bordeaux, and the strongest fighters of Dark and Light will come together.

I have my kin out of the mountains, secure with plenty of Lights to feed them. Fallon can grow up with a father who's proud of him. Galain won't die young, starved to death. My son has a woman.

I have hope we can win for the first time and believe that two sides can blend together as shadows instead of contrasts.

Hope. It's a strange elation in my chest. I've known the definition since childhood, but I have never felt it in all my years.

Pulling back, I brush my mouth against hers. "My little mate and guiding star."

She grins. "My alpha."

I clear my throat. "Heal me."

"Don't move."

When I'm healed, I head for Ashley. Several of the ministers have already gathered. I have contracts to sign, and I crack my knuckles. It'll be a tedious process, but my long list of things to accomplish is shrinking.

NATALIA IS UPSIDE DOWN AGAIN. I don't know why she's disregarding my orders. Shawn, Luca, and Falsion are sparring with Lights.

Sterling speaks with another.

A swarm of Lights gathers around the arena, most standing still. She could be working. She's not.

I can't get her cooperation for morning training, either. She's always upside down every time I turn around after taking my eyes off her.

She has sheer, raw power and incredible agility, but she lacks true finesse. She's the only one to kill an Ancient in hand-to-hand combat, though, so I can't get too cranky. After all, if she put as much time into being a weapon of death as she has into being able to bend and flip, she'd be terrifying.

Sterling steps to her, encouraging her legs to bend from vertical and wrap around his hips as he laughs, his mouth moving to speak words too far to hear.

I should put an end to it. We don't have excess time. Lingering, I waffle between knowing what's right and what I want. They're happy right now. I can't bring myself to burst the bubble and remind them why we're here.

Ashley steps to my side.

I hum, Sterling lifting Natalia, pressing her against his chest. My Dark stretches, murmuring with contentment as we view our mates. I wouldn't have ever chosen to share Natalia, but it's proving enjoyable.

A star and the bird who would chase her, daring to try to steal her from the one who possessed her, would make a beautiful myth about bringing a lonely god to his knees in love.

I laugh at myself. After all these years, I have an imagination. Maybe, just maybe, my father will have something to not criticize.

Ashley tilts her head with a confused scowl. "That is an abhorrent display. You should do something about it."

The demand doesn't warrant a response.

I call Sterling mate, but it's a name. The affection runs deeper, albeit not woven into me like Natalia. I formed the bond of mates with her, not him. I want them both.

Without taking my eyes off my Natalia and Sterling, I ask, "How did she do it?"

"Who? What? Be clear in your language."

"Aurora. She mated twice, my father and yours."

"She mated him?"

"You didn't know?"

"I wasn't aware she mated him, only that he mated her."

"How did she do it? You can only mate once."

"Gods, you of all should know that's not true. We can mate multiple times."

I turn to her, scowling. "No. I don't know how she managed that."

Ashley blinks at me. "Where did you ever hear that from?"

"All the Dark knows that fact."

Natalia leans over backward, bending her body in a half circle, gripping Sterling's shins.

He runs a hand along her abdomen, pushing her shirt up, but she unbends her legs from him, spreading them apart and holding her weight as her back bends further into an arch.

It lowers her hips level to his. My Dark pants in my skull, dripping with desire. There's nothing but thin layers of cloth between them. I want the fabric gone. I want to watch them work into a frenzy of need, then make them beg me for their pleasure.

Ashley sighs. "I saw the mark of your father on my mother. He mated her."

"He did."

Sterling wraps his hands and Dark around Natalia's hips, holding her. Sterling is getting firsthand experience with the position. I'll ask if it's worth trying later.

Ashley huffs, motioning in front of her. "Then why the insistence that it cannot be done? If you know my mother mated both my father and yours, you know it can be done."

I tear my gaze from my mates. "I don't know how that is possible. That's why I'm asking."

"I don't understand. My mother mated your father and mine. Your father mated my mother and yours."

"He never mated to my mother, only Aurora."

She stares at me so long I question if I forgot how to speak the common tongue. When she opens her mouth, her eyebrows come together, no sound emitting.

She presses her lips, facing forward. "I was of another belief."

"He loved Aurora more than the breath of his life. The way he spoke of her was in the highest regard with passion in every word, and every word was a shadow of his affections."

"My father confessed to sending her to the afters, but I presumed it was a vain effort to keep my distaste for you from poisoning our interactions and ruining his intentions."

"He did it." I shake my head, tipping it back to stare up. "She was growing my sibling seed, ours, I suppose. My father never could have brought himself to hurt her."

"The Light can mate multiple times. I presumed the Dark

could as well." She runs a hand over her hair. "I have no idea what you are or are not capable of."

"Fair enough."

She hums. "It's seen as reprehensible and deplorable to take two at once." She shakes her head. "Unforgivable, even. You'll not find support for this in Izul. The ability is implemented only after one mate has died, and another is found. We see it as a twist in the webs, one fated to die and the next to be found."

"I don't care about what others think."

"You did well with the others. In my humble opinion, that is."

"There is nothing fucking humble about you."

"Why, thank you, darling."

I chuckle. "I put Raine with you to keep your structure of a trinity, but keep an eye on her."

"Be careful of Heatherton."

I lift my hand. "I'm wearing that one for a reason."

She laughs. "I'm not certain that is enough."

"I'll give him enough rope to hang himself or prove us both wrong." I shrug and move to my mates.

Sterling looks to me as I approach, grinning. "I have an idea."

My Dark wraps around Natalia, lifting her to face Sterling, her chest to his, and then I press to her back, running my nose along her neck, inhaling her with my hands on her hips. My Dark purrs, wrapping around both of them, tethering them to me as I draw strength from them.

"Everything go fine?"

"*Mhm.*" I nod against Natalia. "Everything will run here through the ministers until we're finished with the Ancients. No changes until then, and they've agreed to be open to discussing collaborative adjustments when the time comes in pursuit of peace. It's getting better already."

"I'll watch your back but watch yourself all the same."

Natalia sighs, relaxing into me. "I promise to cover your front, your back, your dick..."

I chuckle with Sterling, kissing the top of her shoulder. "Good girl."

She purrs.

Sterling laughs.

I drift in ease. I run my hands up Natalia's sides, and she lets her head fall back to my shoulder.

Sterling drops his gaze to our mate with the faint hint of a smile. Contentment lingers in his face, Natalia's arms loose around his neck as she leans into me. Meeting my gaze, he smiles, the wince lazy.

If I can mate him too, I will, binding him to me and her for eternity. He's mine as much as she is, and it smolders as a possessiveness in my veins. I have Light heritage, maybe I can.

Natalia can. I'll share that with her later when Sterling isn't around. The choice will be hers, without Sterling demanding or pressuring her.

Sterling sighs, grabbing my hips to yank me closer, pinning Natalia tighter. "You two are going to be the death of me yet."

He kisses Natalia, and I close my eyes. Not to avoid seeing it, but to enjoy and partake in the moment as much as I can, her Light and his Dark twisting around me and pulling us together as one, as much as we can be.

Sterling says, "All right, loves. Let's go find some more strong fighters."

"What are the options like?"

Sterling shrugs. "Not bad, as much as I hate to admit it. There are some damn good ones."

CHAPTER 54
NATALIA

"I'm hungry," I say, slipping through the ropes to join Cal on his mat. I wrinkle my nose, collecting my hair into a ponytail. "Can we eat?"

Cal nods. "Dinner."

Someone smacks into a mat hard, drawing my eyes. Sterling kneels over a man, shaking his head. He stands, offering his hand to help the Light to his feet.

Cal whistles.

Sterling perks, looking in our direction.

"Dinner."

Returning to the Light, Sterling shakes his head, talking.

Cal tugs my hair. "Little Star."

I beam at him. "Yes, Mate?"

He trails the back of his knuckles over my cheek, running his fingers around my ear to travel along my jaw. I close my eyes as he tips my head back.

His lips brush against mine, sending sparks across my whole body. Tension winds through me, my Light coiling with desire.

He pulls back. "We need clothes."

I open my eyes. "That's what you're thinking about?"

His gaze fixates on my mouth as he runs his thumb beneath my lower lip. "I was thinking that we could go find a store that sells nothing but straps and lace that my claws will tear off your body."

I shiver with excitement.

"Do you know how breathtaking you are?" His lips curve, sliding across mine to my ear. "I've seen her now—Sasha."

Her name, with the heat of his breath, sends goose bumps racing across my skin.

"I'd choose you." He nips my ear. "You're beautiful." He kisses my neck below my ear. "Absolutely gorgeous." He kisses again, lower.

I grip a fistful of his shirt, ready to snap. My body pulsates, my skin burning with a need for his touch—only his.

Two large hands rest on my shoulders, another mouth pressing to the other side of my head. "Every time I see you two together, I lose my fucking mind."

Sterling draws his hands along the tops of my shoulders and down my arms, making my stomach flutter and my skin burn hotter.

It's not only Cal's hands. I need them both—four hands gripping tight, wrapping around me.

"Mates," I manage, panting for air, begging in that single word. Heat pools between my legs, an ache winding tighter in my core.

Cal growls, wrapping his hand around the back of my neck and crushing his mouth to mine.

I whimper into his mouth as Sterling slips his hands around my ribs.

I have two mates, two very real, very honest mates. I have love just like I always dreamed, more than I know what to do with. I'll write our love as stars in their Dark.

Sterling rumbles with a possessive noise. "I was thinking…" He nips at the shell of my ear. "We're going to need fresh clothes, and I would love to take you shopping for something I can tear off you after dinner."

Cal swirls his tongue against mine, chuckling into my mouth before pulling away. "I had that very same thought."

"*Mm.*" Sterling grips my hips, rocking his hard shaft against me. "I'm thinking lace." He licks my neck over their mating marks.

My eyes roll into the back of my head as all that tension snaps and spasms through me as spiraling pleasure.

I sag into Sterling, tugging at Cal.

He chuckles.

Luca pops into view at Cal's back. "Are you three going to fuck on this mat or are we going to get dinner?"

I moan, trembling. "Maybe?"

Cal chuckles. "Dinner."

ASHLEY HAD STEPPED IN, commanding me to join her for fresh attire. She's made arrangements for dinner among our closest supporters for a respite this evening from the strain of infighting. It sounds well and fine, aside from the disappointment of not shopping with Cal and Sterling for lingerie.

Ashley and Hailey had squabbled about which store to choose. I'd remained silent without much care.

I stare at myself in the mirror of the dressing room. I'd picked out a lace dress with the words of my mates in mind. I press my fingers to the pendants hanging around my neck, a star and a firefly resting above the sweetheart neckline.

The curtain rips back, metal hoops screeching along the bar to reveal Ashley. She surveys me. "Honey, you look fabulous."

I run my hands down my stomach, smoothing the cream-colored lace over my hips and following the full-length skirt to the floor.

She points. "Heels will be required."

I bob my head.

Clicking her tongue, she comes to stand at my back, almost a full head taller than me in a shimmering gold and white gown.

She eyes me in the mirror. "Well, as I said, flawless, so what is your problem?"

I let my hand fall away from the necklace, curling my index finger to rub against the ring adhered to my right thumb.

Ashley rolls her eyes, gripping my wrist to tug me from the mirror and out of the curtained area. She forces me to sit in a chair positioned in front of a vanity.

"Sit." She waves off a clerk coming closer. "Out."

Instead, she picks up a comb, working to detangle my silver strands and part my hair into sections.

She secures the top section, then a second portion, then a third, starting a war-braid. When she's finished, she taps the mating marks overlapping on the side of my neck.

"Do you intend to mate Sterling?"

I cover the marks with my hand. "Cal says you can only mate once."

"His idiotic notions on the matter are incorrect." She fusses over my hair. "Knowing that, what is your answer?"

I swallow hard. "I don't know."

"Do you think it's possible to have two mates?"

We stare at each other in the mirror. I have an eerie sense she's not asking about me.

"You and Tony?"

"Amusements to distract myself." She lowers her gaze,

pulling on another piece of my hair as she blinks several times. "I have not been allowed to mourn."

"Pierre and I... I barely knew Pierre, but..."

She looks upward. "If you'd been less volatile and crude, you would have found father to be exemplary and comforting."

Hailey walks into the room. "I found these." She shows me dangle earrings of long gold threads decorated with stars. She grins. "Palak mentioned the nickname."

I run a strand through my fingers. "They are beautiful."

Ashley shakes her head. "Absolutely not. I doubt I'll be able to rip that necklace from you, and the metals will clash."

Hailey shrugs, tossing them aside. "I overlooked that." She turns to the mirror, checking her lipstick. "This might be the last new dress I can afford for a while."

Ashley hums. "Palak has turned his back on his heritage."

Hailey bobs her head. "He has, yes." She sighs, leaning on the counter to face me.

I ask, "How did Matthew even know?"

Flicking her wrist, Hailey sighs. "My mate, ever proper, called Matthew to offer goodbyes and show appreciation toward him for the truth as well as the friendship offered. I believe he—Matthew—demanded details, and upon my mate's compliance, there was quite a bit of foul language and a quick end to the conversation."

I smile. "That sounds like the Dark."

"*Mm.*" She flexes her thick eyebrows. "Yes, indeed, how vulgar the inability to be clear in words. However, Matthew and his son were generous. They've relinquished everything about Lukette and its profits to Palak. He has very little coin to his name and it will take time to increase his accounts. It's dreadful."

"The Delacroix estate is far larger and offers more than Lukette ever will," Ashley reminds her.

"He chose me," Hailey snaps back, smacking the counter

with a flash of vinegar. "I will not fault my mate for reducing our wealth in exchange for our union. Matthew has been nothing but kind, affording me an opportunity to be happy. Palak chose me. He chose this." She waves at me. "Merging our kind as Pierre demanded, and you'd mock the decision?"

Ashley steps around me, sorting through makeup. "Not in the least. I was stating a fact. I'd trade the Bordeaux fortunes for my mate without hesitation." She lifts a palette and sets it down with a sigh.

Hailey reaches a hand toward her. "I am so sorry about Akash."

Ashley nods. "Everyone claims to be."

"You glowed at his side."

"Yes." Ashley picks up the same palette and finds a brush, turning to me. "What do you think? Can someone have two mates?"

Hailey gestures at me. "I see the way she looks at them, and more importantly, the way they look at her. How did you manage that, darling?"

I look to her, only for Ashley to grab my chin and pull my face forward.

She taps the end of my nose with the brush. "As always, Sister Mine, you try my patience."

I roll my eyes, keeping my head still as she applies makeup to my face. "I didn't do anything."

"*Psht.*" Hailey laughs. "I do not believe that. Tell us, what wiles did you use to convince them to share you?" She leans closer, her white eyes gleaming with excitement.

"I really didn't. Sterling did it. He wanted to share first and Cal..." I smile. "They love each other."

"What's it like?" Hailey lifts her eyebrows. "You know, two men? Do you do it together or..."

Ashley jabs the brush at Hailey. "You are making her blush and it's interfering with my ability to finish."

"Oh, please. You can make anyone look amazing with your eyes closed." Hailey smirks at me. "So?"

I laugh. "Yes."

"Yes?" Ashley picks up two lipsticks and shows them to Hailey. Hailey taps one, and Ashley tosses it to the side, opting for the other. "What does 'yes' mean?"

"Sometimes it's one or the other, sometimes it's both."

"I'm picturing two Palak's and do not know if I could handle that much." Hailey laughs. "My mate is insatiable."

She flickers, her golden light shining beneath her skin. It glimmers, turning her fair skin to a translucent gleam of sunshine.

I smile at the way she gleams. "Cal and Sterling are too."

Ashley steps around me to review her work. "Tony is as well. The stamina he has—"

I retch. "Please, please, I beg of you, do not tell me. I saw him fuck my sister more times than I can count."

Ashley leans over, smiling at me with a devious light to her face. "It's incredible the things he can do with his tongue."

I shudder, screwing up my face in disgust. "Oh Mother, I do not want to know."

"You were a fool to turn him away." She stands and shrugs. "As much as my heart belongs to Akash, Tony's ability to provide multiple orgasms is unparalleled to any partner I've had."

Hailey gives her a mischievous look. "Maybe not a fool. Palak turns me to mush. The mating bond only increases the pleasure, and he's one." She holds two fingers up. "Tal has two, and I saw Callahan lift his shirt earlier." She fans herself.

Ashley shakes her head. "You have a mate."

"Palak is strong, and so is his body, but not like that. Where do all those muscles come from? Is it because they're animals?"

I narrow my eyes at her. "They're men."

"No, darling, they are animals. It is a fact. While I accept, they aren't my enemy anymore, that has not changed. Oh...can they fuck you in their true form?"

My face burns. "They can, but not me. I'm too small. However, Cal's tongue in his true form is massive."

Hailey screams with laughter, covering her mouth.

Ashley wrinkles her nose. "Ew."

Hailey smacks at her. "Ignore your sister. She has no imagination."

I smirk. "I fully intended to. That tongue..." I roll my eyes to the ceiling mocking pleasure.

There's a knock, and Hailey rolls her eyes, going to answer the door.

Palak's voice slips into the room. "Mate, you look incredible."

She glows. "As always, right?"

"As always." He pulls her out of sight.

Ashley has her chin tucked to her chest, a crease forming between her eyebrows.

"Tony gets it, you know?" I tell her. "Having your heart ripped out and destroyed. Trying to figure out how to live like that and be okay again."

Ashley lifts her gaze to mine in the mirror. "How can you love two?"

"I don't know, but I know you can."

CHAPTER 55
CALLAHAN

Zander assists in where to find proper clothes for me and Sterling. We both grumble about the lack of color in options.

Zander shrugs. "We are the— We are in Izul, where the options are suited for the Light."

A clothes rack tumbles.

Galain sighs under the frigid glares of shop assistants. "Fallon, act like a young man, not a wildling. We are not in Avengart."

Turning to aid the clerks, Zander rights the rack. "He's a youngling." He smiles. "I made messes as a boy with too much energy."

Falsion cringes. "Never thought I'd miss the cheap itchy sweaters I stole."

I opt for slacks and a buttoned-down shirt. Zander suggests a coat. I decline. I'm already uncomfortable and struggling to breathe.

He leads us to a taller building, straight to the top floor.

The dining room is empty except for one very long table set with plate settings and chairs for a few dozen. The room is swathed in shadows and the glow of the moon from the wall of windows overlooking the city. Candles send the darkness dancing, mixing with the white décor.

This is the definition of *ifferentiti*. Bellasom had warned me my translation was crude, but the delicate balance of this room, crafted to celebrate illumination bathed in the starkness of night, brings sharp relief to her words.

Wyham, Matthew, and John step toward us.

I nod to Matthew. "I would have thought you'd have run from this city by now."

"Eh." He shrugs, leaning his head toward Wyham. "This boy gave me and mine a place to stay. Jean taught me the proper customs of Light, so I can navigate this white hole better than you think, and I want to keep an eye on Palak to know if Louis gets bold."

Wyham sighs. "I cannot state enough my appreciation for what you've done for Palak. My home is yours as long as you desire."

Matthew rolls his eyes at me, jerking his thumb at Wyham. "If I hear that one more time, I might stand in one place and let someone kill me in the next Gathering Shadows. Teach them better. It's embarrassing."

I laugh behind a smile. The Dark is hard and unforgiving as stone, but it lives and breathes to make alphas. Not everyone can survive by sheer strength, and those of us who can push harder tend to those who need shelter. I'll break my body and scar my soul to protect. It's a trait engrained into my bones, the surfaces etched with deep carvings of what an alpha is supposed to be.

I won't shy away from violence, cull the rotten and weak for the better of all, but when I'm done, the world remade, it will be better for everyone still standing.

Sterling nods, his thick, rope locks loose about his head. "We make new laws. We teach them our ways. We prove to them the same as any other that we take care of ours."

Matthew jerks his chin at something behind me.

I turn, Natalia walking toward us with Ashley, Hailey, and Palak.

She's wearing lace. I grin, my Dark giddy and bouncing at the idea of getting our claws out later to tear it off.

Palak guides Hailey to me. "Callahan, Sir. I'd like to offer my services at your earliest convenience."

Hailey places her hand on Palak's shoulder. "We both will."

I incline my head and sidestep them to my mate. I had wished for a mate, and Adontis gifted me a piece of herself. She's more beautiful than any night sky or woman I could have dreamed of.

I cup Natalia's face and kiss her forehead, inhaling her sweet scent. "Mate."

"My alpha."

Grinning, I lead her toward the table. Both ends have a single chair available, so I opt to pull one from the middle, helping her sit.

Sterling drops into the chair next to her with a heavy exhale. "Chairs. Thank fuck. How are we the animals but they're the ones who like being on the floor?"

Natalia giggles, and I take the place on her other side.

I turn to drape my arm over the back of my chair as Galain guffaws. Others have arrived, the overlay of conversations increasing the volume of the room.

Falsion points at my kin one at a time, then shrugs and moves toward the table.

Maria speaks with Layla and Flora, stepping closer toward them as Logan enters, cradling a bundle close to his chest, a strand of gold wrapped around the wrist of a young child like it's holding the child's hand.

Ashley greets him, cooing at the bundle and then lifting the second into her arms.

They approach the table, not for seats, but looming toward me and my mates.

Logan stops, bowing. "Sterling."

He twists in his seat and gapes.

"I wanted you to meet my daughters, Amelia and Emily."

Sterling shoves his hand through his locks. "Fuck, come on. That's not playing fair."

Ashley lifts the toddler's hand, waving it at Sterling. "Can you say hi, Sterling?"

"Hi, Star-ling."

He growls in his throat, pushing up out of the chair. "This is fucked up of you..." He reaches for the girl in Ashley's arms. "Come here, sweetling. Gods, you're precious."

Logan's jaw clamps as Sterling holds her in his arms. "That's my eldest, Emily."

Sterling flashes that perfect grin. "Look at you. You're beautiful."

"So was her mother."

I scratch at my chin with a lazy smile. Seeing the child wrap her hand around one of Sterling's long fingers melts my heart. Someday, it'll be my pup. Mine or his...egg? I have no idea what young birds are called.

Ashley steps to his side, leaning against him to brush the brown curls of the child from her round cheeks. "What do we say?"

"Welcome an...and welcomed."

Sterling chuckles. "You teach them young."

"As if you wouldn't have already given yours a blade."

"Fair enough, but it would be wooden. We do not give sharp things to little ones, do we? No, we do not. They are dangerous. Gosh, you are adorable."

Emily shakes his finger. "It's so big."

A strand of Dark wraps around her wrist.

Logan twitches.

"Uh-oh." She stops moving to stare at it. "What is it?"

"My magic," Sterling tells her. "It's curious about you."

"Daddy, Daddy," she lets go of Sterling's finger to raise her hand, the Dark extending as a long, translucent shadow. "Look."

"I see," he says, his voice tight.

She giggles. "It's cold." She pokes at the shadow. "It's so funny."

Ashley smiles wide. "That's Dark. Can you say Dark?"

Emily's eyes stretch wide. "Daddy," she wails, bursting into tears and flailing. "Daddy, help."

Sterling jerks his head back. "What?"

Ashley takes Emily, shushing her. "*Shh*, it's all right, Emily. Let me see."

Sterling's wide nose crinkles with ire. "I didn't do anything."

Ashley rubs Emily's wrist. "There's nothing there, honey. See," she shows Emily her own wrist, running her fingers over it. "Nothing there."

"Monster," she cries, clinging to Ashley. "Monster. Monster."

Natalia shakes her head. "Happy as can be and not afraid until you tell her it's Dark, then all of a sudden Sterling's a monster. Cute."

Logan sighs, shaking his head and shifting the bundle in his arms. "We teach our young the Dark is dangerous for precautions." He hesitates, glancing at me, then bundles Amelia before threads of gold wrap around the child. He extends his hand toward Sterling. "Give me a piece."

Sterling crosses his arms, rocking back on his heels. "No. That," he says, pointing at a sobbing Emily, "it won't hurt. You..." He mocks a frown. "I can't always control it."

I stand, offering a coil of shadows from my palm.

Logan wraps it around his finger.

Ashley pries Emily away, turning her in her arms. "Look, look." She wiggles a finger at my Dark curled around Logan. "Look, see? See, it's not hurting your father."

Emily quits crying, her chubby cheeks pink. "Oh."

Logan pulls my Dark closer to his daughter. "You can touch it. It's not going to hurt you."

Emily goes to poke at my Dark, moving closer, then pulling away several times before the barest tap echoes in my Dark. She yanks away in a hurry.

Her big eyes focus on me, a solid silver ring glistening in them.

I cock my head. "Do all your young have eyes like hers?"

Ashley nods. "Yes. The ring fades with age. Our oldest loses it altogether when the sickness sets in, and they go blind."

"We lose it then too, but ours is never that visible."

Emily taps my Dark in a quick motion as an attempt by a child to be sneaky. "Dark."

"Dark," Logan nods.

"Monster?"

I lift an eyebrow. "Maybe."

Logan gives me a withering look. "Counterproductive, Your Majesty."

"I'm not going to lie." I fake a grin. "I'd give her nightmares if she saw me."

Natalia laughs. "That's the truth."

My Dark whines.

Logan frowns. "I have never seen a Mandolux."

Natalia stands, smoothing her skirt. "Think apex predator of bone and fire with very little weakness. Now make it big." She slips her arm under mine, hugging close and grinning up at me. "They're amazing."

Emily pokes at my Dark again, and it splits, raveling a strand around her small hand. "Dark." She shakes her hand. "Daddy, Dark."

He smiles. "Yes, sweetheart. That is Dark."

"Dark." She pushes against the strand. "It's cold."

I retract my Dark, and Emily grabs at it. "No, Dark. Dark, come back."

Logan chuckles. "We need to eat first." He nods. "Will you be sitting here, Your Majesty?"

I hate that term. It makes me feel trapped, but the reality is I am. "Yes."

He scans the table.

Ashley adjusts Emily on her hip. "I'll fetch suitable seats for the girls."

"Thank you, Ash."

She walks away. "Did you have fun?"

Sterling sticks a finger at Logan. "That was low."

Logan chuckles. "But effective." He cradles the bundle again. "This is Amelia."

"You already won. What do you want from me?"

"A world where my daughters do not live in fear and will be there to raise their daughters or sons."

Sterling points at me. "That's his job."

I smirk. "Equal partners bound and fucked for life, baby."

"Fine." Sterling huffs. "I'm not killing him, all right?" He rubs his face, turning to sit down with his face in his hands.

I nod at Logan, turning to stand behind Sterling. I grip his shoulders. "There are worse things than letting a father live."

He scoffs.

"You'll have a seed of your own someday, and you'll get the same opportunity."

Picking his head up, he twists his face over his shoulder with a frown. "You said—"

"I changed my mind."

"Really?" He spins to the side, reaching for Natalia. She goes willingly to sit in his lap.

"Really, really, Mate." I clap him on the shoulder. "Now convince our mate."

She looks between him and me, then wrinkles her nose. "No."

Sterling wraps his arms around her with a lazy smirk. "We'll change your mind."

She drops her head back, glowering at the ceiling. "Probably." She rights and stabs a finger into Sterling's chest. "But I'm not a baby machine."

He chuckles, pressing his fingers between hers. "I know that, but I want one, a boy of my own to raise."

She rolls her eyes and focuses on me. "This is so not fair. He's on your side."

I smile. "We'll have a fuck trophy sooner or later."

She sighs. It's better than an adamant refusal.

I lean over and press a kiss to the top of her head. Someday Sterling and I will wear her down and fuck her into giving us seeds. I can't wait for the day when his and mine are like brothers. They will be brothers even if they aren't the same. I won't care whose lineage it carries. Anything my mate gives me will be a son of mine.

CHAPTER 56
CALLAHAN

Jacques sits on my right, sipping Rizvor with a grin. "Damn, this shit is good. Maybe not everything about the Light is awful."

Across from us, Palak grins. "If you like tea, wait until the Harvest when we have the Bisinfoil Tea Festival. The special blends are always the best."

Jacques shakes his head. "No, but Thames is going to lose his mind. He wouldn't shut up about the tea Zander gave him."

I look to Jacques. "Did you find anything today?"

"Not yet." He sets his flute down. "They have an entire floor of one wing dedicated to horticulture and botany that we have to search book by book. I was doing that and missed all the fun."

"A whole floor?" As Light Queen, I'll have full access to the Light's library. I try not to drool. "How large?"

"Larger than all of Ilbuio's library."

My chest aches. My collection of carefully cultivated and nurtured trees was destroyed when the Magia blew up my home. Every trunk bent, every branch either damaged or pruned away, every root trim and repotting a waste of my time, but I had loved my trees, my friends. I miss them.

"Izul is a well of knowledge we never even knew existed. No wonder that gorgeous specimen knew so much after her time here."

Natalia cants her head. "Ness?"

"Vanessa." Jacques grins. "When she gets back, I plan to sink my fangs into her now that Mass is in the afters. That woman is built right and has the brains to match. What more can a man hope for?"

Natalia slowly smiles, the expression tinged with an ache. "You'll be thrilled to know she loves snakes. She calls them fun noodles."

Jacques flares his narrow eyes wider. "I'm a fun noodle?"

I shake my head. "You're a Vyper, not a snake."

"Bring her snakes." Natalia bobs her head. "She'll love you for it."

"Count on it." He laughs. "I attract all the scaly worms in this world. They curl up in my boots and I've woken up to them curled up on me. I was the one who drew the shadow serpent to Basileus for—ah—never mind." Wincing, he scratches behind his ear.

I glare. "I assumed a Vyper managed that thing for him. No one else would have gotten it in a box."

"Yes, yes," he says, motioning with a limp wrist to wave me off. "I was under orders from Basileus. It wasn't my idea to give the poor baby to Natalia. She was barely a decade old, and I felt awful putting her in the box knowing she was going to end up dead. Even if the poor girl hadn't been smited, Basileus would have had her killed." Jacques hangs his head, fidgeting with the base of his glass across the tablecloth.

Natalia stiffens. "You put that thing in the box that I opened?"

"It wasn't my idea. It's Gathering Shadows. Even I hate those games some days." He shudders. "I was Mar's contracted, a Vyper Basileus had access to and a player."

"I will not be putting in a good word with Ness." She laughs, but it stops short as she begins to frown. "Although telling her you almost killed me might work in your favor. She hates me now."

My Dark wraps in tendrils around her, one rope twisting around her forearm to stroke over her wrist. The news of Vanessa's behavior struck me as odd. I'd brought her into my world at the behest of Natalia, keeping her safe from the threat to her life from the Magia, given my blessing to Massimo, and granted their union while pouring coin into the sea in a wasted expense for a union ceremony not of my ways, and helped her connect to her Dark.

My ire is overshadowed by my mate's torment. Vanessa's betrayal of Natalia is as infuriating as much as confounding. Natalia had put Vanessa above everything, even me, several times. I am her mate, and still Vanessa was more important. Vanessa is my concern as far as Mallafic's interest, but otherwise, I'll throw her to the wolves when I've dug her out of his clutches. As long as she isn't used against us, I have no more concerns for her.

Mallafic. The name sends a ripple down my spinal muscles. We know myths, legends, and bedtime stories for children. None of our information is valid for determining what he wants, but his interest in Vanessa is simple. She has pieces of his soul bonded to her. The problem is I have no idea what that means or what Mallafic plans.

"How long will it take to find information on hysterium?"

"Maybe another day or two. That library is massive, and the catalog system is nonexistent for what we are searching for. Some books appear to be missing as well. An entire row of books on the Ancients is gone." He snaps his fingers. "Poof. Vanished.

And I don't mean a row on a bookshelf, I mean a row of book-shelves is empty. No one seems to know how or where the texts went."

I rub my face. "Don't waste your time searching for them. Vanessa had mentioned meeting Aydian, Lucius's brother, here in Izul, in the library. He likely took everything."

Jacques laughs. "Smart. Fucking annoying, but smart."

Zander leans around Jacques. "Vanessa should have immediately notified Pierre. When he granted her access to our library, he had no knowledge of her lack of loyalty."

Natalia twists toward him and laughs. "Why would she be loyal? You all called her my pet, and you treated us like prisoners."

"She was here at your request or wouldn't have been given entry to our city at all otherwise. That is a pet."

Tony whistles, waving two fingers. "Buddy, if you ever want a woman, quit calling them pets."

Natalia jabs a finger at me. "Cal never treated her like a pet."

I frown. "No, I used her as leverage to assure your coopera-tion." I stretch back, pressing into the seat. "Pierre did much the same."

Tony laughs. "I called that shit. Tal, everyone knew if they wanted you, they needed Ness. Even the Magia tried that. You were never, ever going to turn your back on Ness or let anyone hurt her, no matter what it cost you." He waves a hand at me. "That's why he had Mass—"

"No," I snap. "I brought her into my world, I took care of her as mine, I gave her a contract, yes, but I did not embroil Mass's affections. No order, not even a discussion of what you're accusing me of transpired."

Jacques toasts Tony with his glass. "Trust me, friend, that wouldn't have been necessary, and no man would mate someone for that reason."

The meal passes in languor with plenty of drinks and laughter. When the last course of a cinnamon apple and fresh cream dessert is cleared from the table, Ashley stands.

She lifts her glass, smiling at me. "Callahan."

I rub the back of my neck. "Yes?"

"Thank you."

"Don't thank me yet. We may all be in the afters very soon."

"You have already begun the impossible act of repairing the bridge between our kind."

"It's not impossible. Diona and Renave did this once to form the council. They brought others together much like this, I suspect. It's where my kind came from. Before that, our kind came together to nearly eradicate the Ancients. This isn't impossible. This is repetition. The impossible is making it last."

She frowns, lowering her glass. "My father believed in your ability to do just that, Your Majesty. We," she adds, gesturing along the table, "believe in you."

I shrug. "Don't. I already had a mate that's Light and a mate that's Dark. I already possessed the ability to set aside hatred. I can lead by example, but in truth, I can't control this. It's you who's doing it. You choosing to stand with the Dark. Palak choosing to accept the truth and turn his back on his heritage in favor of one who earned respect instead of going along with blind belief and tradition. It's Logan showing his daughter the Dark isn't a danger just because it's the Dark and she is the Light. It's not my doing. It's yours."

I take a breath. "It's Pierre's doing, giving his life for mine and the belief he holds in my ability to lead, setting aside the disputes we had. It's Sterling choosing to let two daughters keep their father instead of stealing him as his was stolen." I shake my head. "I'm not responsible for those acts. Do not give me credit for another. If this happens, it will be merely because I forced you to stop killing each other. For us to build the bridge is entirely dependent on others following the acts of everyone at this table."

Shifting the sleeping baby in his arms, Logan toasts me with a teacup. "Every time you open your mouth, you reaffirm Pierre's belief in you, Young Man."

Falsion stands, lifting his Rizvor flute. "Fuck Matteo. You're a damn good man, Callahan." He chugs his glass.

Toasting Falsion, Matthew laughs. "It's about time someone said it. Matteo was a fucking prick larger than a smoragon."

I scowl. "My father—"

"Ah!" Falsion points at me. He sits with a warning glare. "Don't you dare defend that cold bastard."

Sitting down, Ashley wraps her hand under Tony's bicep, her fingers digging into him, wrinkling his shirt sleeve. "What was Matteo like?"

I shake my head, rubbing my forehead and reaching for my drink.

Falsion sneers. "He was an arrogant pup. He thought the world of himself, the opposite of Cal, who finds fault in everything about himself. Everything Matteo did was amazing, and he let you know it."

I drain my glass. "Fal."

"He—"

I fling my glass at Falsion. Ashley is thinking of her mother, and I'll spare her any concerns I might. While I can't openly communicate how much Matteo loved Aurora, I can at least shield her from Falsion's low opinions.

Light from Zander ensnares the glass, setting it right side up on the table.

Falsion gives me a grumpy scowl. "Kid, he was a shit father and not that good of a man."

I face Ashley. "Matteo held high expectations, but they were fair, as was he. He held himself to the same standards that he held everyone to."

"Except Matteo was blind to his own faults."

"Fal." I sigh, rubbing my face. I sit up, leaning forward toward Ashley across the table. "He was honest to a fault, more so than the honor code we have. If it was a fact, it didn't matter how cruel, it was a fact. The day my mother died of the sickness, he told me to accept dead is dead and move on."

Natalia rests her head on my shoulder, her Light winding around me.

"My father operated on logic alone. He always told me to set aside my feelings for the truth. He was strong. He was capable. He challenged his contractor and won, fought to earn highborn rank, and then earned a spot on the contender's list his first year at Gathering Shadows. It was unheard of. Everyone knew his name before he even arrived for his first games. People still talk about him with awe for the way he conducted himself with strict adherence to our tenets, polite manners, and the strength he had."

Matthew shrugs. "Cold prick."

I give him a long look, then meet Ashley's eyes again. "He loved knowledge and obscure words. His favorite myth was the '*Brothers Three*', and he collected every version in existence. He kept it in his personal library in the library at the Obsidian Palace alongside every rare and special book he could get his hands on."

She turns her head away, her lips pressing. "I understand."

Zander slides my flute across the table to me. "Pierre maintained exceptionally high standards as well. There were days it seemed impossible to hold his respect without failure."

Ashley and I lock eyes. I wonder what traits my father and hers shared, if they were as similar as Sterling and I, if that's why Aurora mated both.

A small voice behind me says, "Dark."

I jerk and twist, searching for the girl.

"Dark. Dark." She grabs at the shadows stringing between me and Sterling.

Logan whips toward the empty chair next to him, then stands. "Emily?" He cranes, jostling the baby and hushing it as it begins fussing.

Sterling shifts, picking her up. "What are you doing wandering around on your own, Little Lamb?" He sets her in his lap.

"Dark." She grabs one of the locks of his hair, pulling on it.

His head jerks down. He blanches, trying to free himself. "Hair."

She yanks like pulling the rope of a bell over and over. "Dark. Dark."

"No," he grumbles. "Hair. Hair! That's hair."

Natalia shakes, lifting a hand to her mouth to stifle herself.

"Dark. Dark." Emily keeps pulling.

Sterling grimaces, but I roar with laughter as the table dissolves into humor.

Logan takes his seat, shaking his head. "My sincere apologies."

I wave him off. "He's fine."

Sterling shoots me a glare, trying to stop Emily from tearing his lock off. "This is worse than getting stabbed. I can't fight back. She's too cute."

"Lesson learned for when we have ours."

He chuckles, managing to get Emily to let go, wrapping shadows between her fingers and around her arm. He rubs the side of his head. "She's got a grip for such a small thing."

She claps her hands, playing with the shadows as she giggles.

"Dad," Fallon whines. "Why does she get to do that, but I can't eat the Light?"

Galain drops his chin, trying to rub away a smile. "You bite, and we do not eat people."

Luca wiggles his eyebrows. "Not until we're older."

Ashley snaps and cuts the air with her hand in a slashing motion. "That is inappropriate."

Tony laughs. "He's got a point, sweetheart."

A chagrin smile claims Logan's face. "Exactly where do you think your nieces came from, Ash?"

"Oh, Adontis." She turns pink, turning her face to the ceiling. "Please, I beg of you all, find some manners."

CHAPTER 57
CALLAHAN

I pull my shirt off and pick up Natalia by the waist to toss her onto the bed. She squeaks, then giggles as I straddle her, running my hands up her sides. "Mate."

Sterling settles on the bed, sitting up against the headboard with his long legs stretched out straight.

I look to him, and he grins as he adjusts a pillow behind him and slumps lower. "I want to watch you break her."

My Dark twists with exhilaration at the idea, several ideas already forming.

I help Natalia sit, staying on top of her though. "This," I tap my chest. "Take your magic back. I'm healed and you need it."

"Oh," she runs her fingers over it. She pinches the silver strand and pulls. As it starts to slip free, my lungs sear, pain radiating through my chest.

Sweat beads at the nape of my neck, and I grab her hand, trying to stop her as I pant for air as the world sways. Warm, sticky, wet beads roll down my chest.

Sterling puts a hand to my shoulder, steadying me. "Cal?"

I gag and splutter for air as my chest spasms. Pain wracks my mind, blurring my vision. My Dark screams, thrashing in my skull, both of us confused at the sheer, overwhelming agony splitting us in half.

Sterling's fingers dig into my shoulder. "Put it back, Firefly. Now!"

She presses her palm to my chest, energy coursing through me. There's something else, stabbing and weaving within me. It tickles the back of my skull, goosebumps racing across my flesh. I shudder, cold gripping me.

My eyes cross, and I collapse to the side into Sterling. "Fuck," I rasp.

He forces me upright, smacking his hand to the side of my face to wrap his thumb under my jaw and force me to look at him. His brow furrows, his thick eyebrows contorted with rage. "Cal?"

Natalia runs her hand over my shoulder, drawing the other down my torso. "Babe? Babe, talk to us. Tell us you're okay."

Sterling snarls silently at me, then twists toward her. "The fuck did you do?"

"Nothing! I was just pulling my Light out."

"He started bleeding and couldn't breathe."

"That wasn't me. I didn't do anything. I wouldn't."

I slump into him, face planting into his chest as the misery dwindles enough for me to get enough air to whisper, "Mates."

Sterling pushes me up, grabbing me under my jaw again. "We're here, and that shit is staying in you. Do you hear me? Both of you stubborn idiots need to accept this: It stays."

Natalia sighs, her voice faint. "I didn't mean to."

Sterling relaxes his grip on my face and exhales, deflating. "I know. I never thought you would intentionally hurt him, but I think it was killing him."

I struggle to push away from Sterling and end up face down on the bed between them. Groaning, I give up. "What the fuck?"

Natalia runs her fingers up the back of my neck and into my hair. "The stars... Adontis wove herself into Nehil, maybe she couldn't ever take the pieces back? That's why we have stars?"

I shudder, the pain less but lingering. My chest throbs and my mind reels. "What did you do to me?"

"Esme is effective against balanced souls. Wounds inflicted by the crystals or shards of Esme can't be healed."

Sterling says, "We know that."

"Maybe we don't understand what that really means. Maybe...maybe you can't ever heal the wounds?"

"You cut your arm, and that healed."

"It took days."

"It's been days," Sterling snaps. "He should be healed."

Digging deep, I find the fortification to roll to my back. I stare up at Natalia through half-closed eyes. I sometimes forget how beautiful she is.

Sterling runs his thumb over her forearm in his hand. "See? You healed."

I rub my chest. I'll keep this piece of her for eternity. "It doesn't matter if she healed or not. I'm obviously not."

They frown down on me.

I lift my eyebrows. "What?" I reach for Natalia, resting my hand on the side of her face.

"It's just..."

"Just what?" I circle the mating marks overlapping on the side of her neck. "It doesn't matter."

She whimpers and shifts. "Babe," she whines, batting my hand away. "Stop, we need to figure this out. This is bad."

I let my hand drop, wheezing on a laugh. My muscles shake with fatigue as I force myself to sit. She thinks this is a fault. It's not. It's a blessing in my webs. "I will never live a day without you by my side."

"Babe," she leans over, pressing her mouth to mine.

571

Ecstasy races across my skin, seeping into my soul. I'm never going to be without her. That sends my Dark soaring. Our life is tied together forever to our woman, our mate.

Sterling wraps an arm around my shoulders, leaning into us. "Fuck, you two give me anxiety. I don't want to lose either of you."

I pull away from Natalia, smiling. I take her face between my hands, meeting her silver eyes. "I know damn good and well you won't see the afters until you are ready."

She wrinkles her nose. "What if something happens to me?"

I turn up one side of my mouth, humor lessening the lingering twinges and angry pulses in my chest. "My life, whatever is left of it, is yours. I tethered myself to you for eternity, my soul bound to yours as mates, and now my life is bound to yours as well. However long I live rests with you, in your hands, and I couldn't ask for more. If you die, then I will follow you to the afters. You have always been my fate."

"Oh." She stares at me.

I glance over my shoulder at Sterling leaning against me. "And we're keeping our birdie." I jostle him with my shoulder.

He snorts through his nose. "I dare you to try and get rid of me. I have a contract that says I'm bound and fucked for life." He flashes a wide grin at us. "And I'm not going to let you burn it either."

"It'll rot in the back of the drawer."

"No, it won't. I moved it."

I give him a hard look. "Where?"

"Piss off. I'm not taking chances. I'm not going anywhere and there's nothing you can do about it."

I chuckle, shaking my head. I focus on Natalia. "I think our birdie needs a reminder of his place."

"No," Natalia presses her palm to my chest, her fingers splayed. She's so small.

"You're not allowed to say that to us." I tap the tip of her nose.

"I almost killed you fractions ago. You need to rest."

I scoff while Sterling opens his mouth against the crook of my neck and drags his teeth across my skin as he starts laughing.

"He's had way worse injuries during Gathering Shadows and still kicked my ass. He's fine."

I don't know if I kicked his ass, but I survived. He probably went easy on me. The thought registers like a sharp, rude jab of a blade in my side. "How many times did you let me kick your ass?"

He snickers but doesn't answer.

I hang my head and groan. "Baby."

"Mate."

I tip my head back and stare at the ceiling even as I pull Natalia against me. He's always been my mate. I might have refuted our bond, ignoring the call of his soul to mine, but it never mattered. No amount of time was ever going to change my webs.

My Dark sings with euphoria as it winds around our mates. I'm going to revel in them tonight and for the rest of eternity.

CHAPTER 58
CALLAHAN
3RD THISTLE'S DAY, BLOOMING, 4050, 6TH MILLENNIUM

The walls are closing in as days slip past. These white buildings and strict columns stifle the air. I work with my mates to weed out fighters, sending the best of them to Ilbuio to join the rest.

Ashley insists on a morning meal each day with the magistrates. Those breakfasts are as tedious as they are painful.

Hiro assures me the contractors in Ilbuio are obeying the rules. The world seems stagnant, these available days slipping through my claws.

Every evening we dine, I see more and more faces, the laughter louder and the conversations freer.

Logan brings his daughters, and Emily has Sterling wrapped around her finger. It sends an ache through me for days beyond these when it won't be a girl with brown curls but a daughter with white-blonde hair and eyes like Natalia's. It reminds me why I fight, why I'm here.

Tonight, we dine in yet another establishment vacant of any other rabble.

Natalia stands on the open balcony with Hailey and Ashley, the three of them never far from each other.

Palak and John laugh with them, Hailey glimmering beneath Palak's arm.

Matthew and Falsion have found a vantage point at a bar, sitting facing each other while angled outward to survey and watch.

Luca chats with a pretty woman with black hair. Even from here, I can see the glaze of excitement in him, like a boy in love. Maybe he is. I doubt he's spoken to many women.

Sterling cradles Amelia, playing with Emily using blocks and his Dark. Logan is nowhere near them.

That makes my heart lighter. Sterling will be an amazing father to our pups.

I don't know several faces, smaller groups collected about the room full of smiles.

Maria brings Fallon to Sterling and Logan's daughters to share the building blocks.

Jacques slips toward me, lifting a book in his hand. He extends it to me, stopping short. "Hysterium."

I take the book, mostly a pamphlet, and flip through the pages. There are sketches of the trunks, thick and warped with blue ink lines worked through. Detailed flowers and petal documentation spread across several pages. On another set of pages, tree limbs stretch across two pages, different in depiction.

I brush my fingers over one, frowning. There are buds and sprouting new limbs. I've never seen it grow, but the image is clearly denoting such.

Closing it, I ask, "Anything else?"

"No, and Kazez says nothing else even looks promising."

I bob my head, turning it over and over in my hands. "We get those crystals, and we'll be ready to face them when they come back."

Jacques stretches his arm over his head. "Can we leave this city now? I'm suffocating."

I laugh. "Yes. Drink all the Rizvor you can tonight. Tomorrow, we go home."

"Fucking finally."

I move toward Logan and Kristopher, lifting the book. "I have what I need."

Kristopher reaches for the book. "This?"

"Best and only option. If that's not it, we're fucked to the afters and back."

Logan presses his lips. "There will be a day, Young Man, when your language becomes acceptable."

"Or a day when you tolerate my language." I cross my arms. "I'll be returning to Ilbuio, Heatherton. Your contract will be in full effect. I expect compliance, and if you overstep—"

He stops me with a sharp look. "Will you ever forgive my ploy?"

"Not a strong skill in my repertoire."

He shakes his head, offering me the book once more. "You read Seraphin?"

"I know a significant amount and what I don't, my kin are excellent at deciphering. They lived with an Ancient in the Avgora Mountains."

Logan takes half a step closer to me. "They did?"

"She was family to the Mandolux who lived there."

"Can she assist?"

I shake my head. "Mallafic killed her."

Logan frowns. "I'm still reeling that Mallafic exists in this world yet, and not merely for the tales of our origins. He is old, very old."

Kristopher smirks. "One might say ancient."

I glance around, the hairs on the back of my neck standing. "Do not toy with Mallafic. I wouldn't suggest opposing him for any reason."

Logan takes a drink from his tumbler. "You fear him."

"In due cause, I assure you, and I am not easily rattled."

Kristopher exchanges glances with Logan.

Angling toward Logan, Kristopher furrows his brow. "How can we help?"

"With Mallafic? You can't. We have no idea what he wants. We don't even know the truth of what happened. If you see him, I feel pity for you. And whatever you do, do not praise Beenin."

"I gathered the notion when he presented at your coronation, but otherwise, he seemed—"

"Don't finish that statement," Sterling says as he steps into our circle with Emily at his side, gripping one of his fingers in her tiny hand. "Don't insult him. Don't goad him. Don't— Don't do anything. He will play some game and you will not win. The only one strong enough to survive him is Tal, and I mean survive. I'm not certain even she can handle him."

Emily lets go of Sterling to hug her father's legs. "Daddy."

"Hi, sweetheart." He smiles down at her. "Did you have fun with your friend?"

"Ash took Amelia, but Emily wanted you."

Kristopher sighs, a fondness to his sharp features as he stares down on the girl. "I remember Loraine being that small. It seems like days ago I was her hero."

Logan puts a hand on Emily's head. "I think I've already lost that position. She's infatuated with this one." He waves his hand at Sterling.

He grins. "She's a cutie."

I knock my fist to his arm. "Say goodbye. We go home tomorrow."

Logan bends over, hoisting Emily into his arms. "Emmy, can you say goodbye?"

"Bye." She waves at him.

Logan points. "Sterling."

"Star-ling."

"Say bye, Sterling."

"No."

Sterling chuckles. "She's going to break so many hearts." He sighs. "I hope you know she's the best thing about you."

"I do, and for what it's worth, I will say sorry."

Sterling bares his teeth.

I put a hand on his shoulder. "Do you know why the Dark doesn't apologize?"

Kristopher takes a drink. "I imagine it's because you lack remorse."

"It's because saying sorry is a way to alleviate your guilt. It's a pathetic, empty word designed to assuage you while offering no resolution to the individual you wronged or the mistake you made."

Logan hugs Emily tighter. "I had just lost my brother to the Dark. I offer not an excuse, but a reason for my cruelty. I was drowning in grief at the loss when I saw you and your father. I wanted revenge. Take the apology as a confirmation of the guilt I hold. It was a dim moment in my life and one that has brought pain."

Sterling grips his fists, turning away. "Fuck you. You have no idea...what you did, the amount of agony. It wasn't just losing my father. It was this," he spits, pointing at his neck. "Every fucking day I relived it when I looked in a mirror. Every fucking year I stepped into the maze, and it burned around me. Every nightmare— You don't get to say sorry and rid yourself of guilt."

"Thank you," Logan says in a low voice, "for my daughters, for adoring my daughters despite everything."

"She's cute. You're not, and I still hate you."

Logan smiles. "Understandably."

Sterling points at me. "He's why I backed down. Do whatever he wants, anything he says, and stand with him whatever comes, or I have no reason to let you live."

He pivots, walking away.

Emily reaches for him. "Star-ling, come back."

Logan takes her hand. "He will, sweetheart. He'll be back. He's your Light King. He won't be gone forever."

Never, I think. He'll never be gone. He's half of me.

I still need to talk to Natalia and let her know she can mate him. It's on my list of things to do when I get her alone, but there always seems to be time for it later when I achieve that in rare moments. I tend to lose my mind when I have her close.

CHAPTER 59
VANESSA

3RD THISTLE'S DAY, BLOOMING, 4050, 6TH MILLENNIUM

The last codex. I hold it in my hands, memorizing the weight and texture of its scales. I have loved every new piece, every page, but this will be different. It pulses and vibrates with me in excitement. Almost. Almost...

Collecting the pieces, painstakingly searching for the source of the echoes, plagues me. The need to be whole gnaws at me almost as the need for the truth.

I'm going to get the truth from the beautiful, perfect one. She is going to confess before I tear apart her soul.

She took my heart. She had ripped it away from me for her own selfish desires. The pain had been unimaginable, deeper than the body, ripping apart my soul.

She took from me, and I will take in turn.

I hug the codex closer, inhaling the scent of decay and death. She might have ruined everything, but my salvation is nigh. She can't take this from me.

Once she might have been dear to me. Once I might have done anything she asked, followed her everywhere, but no more.

The broken parts of me are together, the frigid rage and bitter resentment grow stronger with each memory.

It wasn't my fault. None of it was my doing, and the blame is not mine to accept. The perversion was her even as they reviled her.

I sit back on my heels as a wolf howls. The cover of Nehil is dense tonight, the stars burning brighter than I ever recall. Adontis must be with her lover this night. They are always strongest when they are together, even their quarrels disrupt the world and reshape it with each disagreement. I've never questioned their love. Far be it from even me to do such. It's too potent, too powerful, and the stars remind us as much as guide us in warning.

It's impossible for such magic to exist in this world or the next, for mere children to grasp. I know that now, but the bile taste of my failed attempt has left me hollow.

Except it does, because my mother imparted a thread of herself to a child born. Her magic is infectious, magnetic even. It's grown day by day, stronger now while it thrives with the very magic that is life itself. I can feel it pulsing, the mirroring echo of myself.

I question everything, sitting under the canopy of my parents, considering what I'm about to do, what must be done. It's daunting, but the anticipation is sweet.

Shaking my head, I consider what the world once was. I miss the time before. I had friends, so few but they were true. The woman I loved changed everything from this world to me, but she has never faced retribution for her brash acts.

"But it wasn't Tallie. It was you!"

I smooth over the wrinkle in my mind, hushing the inner voice. That's the difference I feel, staring at a shade of myself. It's not a pure echo, the missing link between him and me. I need a bridge between us to finish my work.

He tasted blood in a glorious moment of retribution, and I will have my turn. The one who gambled my life, who ripped up my world and tore my heart away, will pay. I will have blood and vengeance for the misery she caused.

I will take from her what she holds dearest, what she longs for. She doesn't deserve what was stolen from me.

Love, so impossible to grow and yet...

My foe to defeat is a piece of Adontis herself, glimmering silver in the shades of black threading around her, that for her love may flourish. Even I must admit she belongs where she is, in a sea of black as a little star. It's not poetic. It's truth.

How fickle the webs to weave such a tale for my knowledge. It's cruel, but such is fate.

My darling has given me everything I need. Her ability to burgeon such an impossible magic and to curate it with devotion brings a fickle resolution.

I squash that voice again. It matters not. I know the truths of this world. Cormag had no idea he'd be so consequential, so damning. My story is tied to this vessel, just as we are tied to Cormag's thread. I can see it now with radiant clarity, as easy to read as Adontis's love for Nehil in the stars.

If everything goes to plan, I'll fix the imbalance and then I will re-write history to immortalize the truth. Maybe I'll carve the words into mountains or reshape the world to spell out the truths.

"Once upon a time there was a monster," I whisper, then laugh.

That will be the first line of my tale, but I must to finish the story before I etch it in history. First, I need to be whole, and that, oh yes, that is coming to pass very soon.

CHAPTER 60
CALLAHAN
4TH EVERGREEN'S DAY, BLOOMING, 4050, 6TH MILLENNIUM

I've settled back into Ilbuio. I've gotten to enjoy my mates and sleep well for the first time since I left this city. It's ironic, given I've never once slept deeply or smoothly in this damned city, but the big bed, black sheets, and full darkness soothes me.

I've pissed away precious time sorting out room arrangements and restructuring duties of the crown and my personal estates. Natalia brought nothing into our union, but Sterling's lineage empire is larger than mine, and life isn't waiting for this war to conclude. It's been headache after headache, paperwork to sign and negotiations made along with settling disputes between Dark and Light. Tensions are ratcheting higher every day. The forty days are nearly over, and we still haven't harvested the crystals or found an alternative weapon.

I have a book to read. I move that to the top of my priorities for today as I lounge in my chair at breakfast, watching those around me.

Natalia laughs with Tony and Ashley. Sterling grins. Jacques waves his hands as he speaks words I can't understand over the thumping of my heart.

Hiro joins in, Thames grinning wide as Zander throws his arm around Jacques's neck, dragging him sideways into him, and they shove, feigning discord and grinning. Alexander points at Zander, his mouth moving. Zander gapes as the others laugh.

Hailey cuts in. Palak turns pink. Matthew and John roar with humor.

Wyham speaks and Oscar leaves everyone howling in turn.

I've rebuilt my little world, and this time I won't take it for granted. I don't make the same mistake twice. These friends I will hold onto.

I frown at the book on hysterium. I've kept it with me, skimming the pages, but now it's time to sit and read. I whistle sharply.

Sterling yells for quiet.

When the table is full and the Seraphinus are silent, I call out, "On behalf of the Dark King, welcome to Ilbuio all those who have arrived from Izul. If you need anything, see Sarina, Raz, or Tam. If you need healing, see Alexander, Tony, or Natalia. If you have a dispute, see Hiro, Oscar, Jacques, Zander, Palak, or Wyham. Training is at Sun's rune behind the palace and is mandatory for all. Dinner is at Thistle's rune and is mandatory for all. No attacks will be acceptable between our kind, and retribution will be swift. For the Light, that is having your Light destroyed. For the Dark, your king will send you to the afters any way she pleases. You're all excused."

The room bursts to life, chairs screeching and dragging across the stone floor.

I have missed this palace, the stone and shadows a blessed change from Izul.

Jacques takes a drink from his coffee mug. "What is the plan?"

"The plan is to figure out the plan after I read this." I lift the book. "If we can rip the crystals off the hysterium, we use those and go to war."

Zander asks, "If not?"

Jacques laughs. "We prepare to die."

THE LAST DAY I had to spend reading an entire book was when my father was alive. Those days are faint in my memory, long lost dreams I walked without the comprehension of reality, swaddled by my father in comfort and luxury of every kind as the seed of a contractor.

I had no cares, no responsibilities, no weight. I would read for runes, from breakfast to dinner, on occasion missing dinner and catching the displeasure of my mother. She's the faintest thing of all, forgettable and unremarkable.

My father is the most solid of the shadows in my past. He was the most shaping and damning moments of my life from his wisdom imparted to his death. He instilled the belief that reading was as important as learning to throw a punch and spin a blade, something Chiara never gleaned.

After I sent him to the afters and took over our lineage estate, everything got delegated as I had contracts and responsibilities to tend to, instead of the time to devote to reading. It's been centuries since I've had this ability, but reading is the most important task of all, everything else delegated in its favor.

I look up from the book, rubbing my dry eyes and stretching my stiff neck. Thames, Hiro, Jacques, and Tony are going through fighting combinations, trying things and laughing. Falsion and Galain are watching from the ground, taking a break from sword training, sitting side by side and yelling out pointers, everyone focused on improving combat skills.

Luca and Shawn are still following Zander's lead, whacking wooden swords together. The extra training is necessary. None of the Mandolux are familiar with weapons, having relied on sheer strength and hand-to-hand skills for the purpose of feeding. The ancients will require more than their current skill set despite their strength.

I get up, heading for Falsion. He claims our translations of the language are crude, and his understanding will be better than mine. I need confirmation that I understand what's in this book.

Ashley and Falsion both offer their assistance, and I return to the steps to review my findings. It's a bleak confirmation of what I suspected.

She runs her finger over the book cover's edge. "We need two willing to sacrifice to the hysterium to release the crystals."

"That's the way I understand the spell." I roll forward, bracing my forearms on my thighs. "It's the only way I can think of to have weapons against the Ancients. I don't see another way of having a weapon to send them to the afters with."

"The only question is who dies?"

Standing, I move to my mates.

Sterling looks to me as I approach, grinning. "Done?"

My Dark wraps around Natalia, righting her from the handstand. "Yes."

"Good news?"

I press into Natalia's back, forcing her face into his chest as I run my nose along her neck, inhaling her with my hands on her hips. My Dark purrs, wrapping around both, tethering them to me as I draw strength from them.

I meet his gaze, tired. "Hysterium, the Ancients called it *Gremalvis*. It was the *coranima*. Falsion can best translate that word as the life of the heart. The hysterium was revered and protected, honored once a year by the sacrifice of two lives, and it would shed its crystals to bloom again, growing."

"Fine. We sacrifice two lives, and we grow the cursed thing, and get the crystals."

"There are words in the book that if the *Gremalvis* were to ever die, this world would die with it." I kiss the side of Natalia's head. "You were right to not tear it apart. We don't know what's real or myth, but something we don't understand shouldn't be destroyed. Hysterium is all one plant, every sprout is connected to the others, one root, which is a play on the idea that it's the *coranima*. I've tried to cultivate and plant it before, taking clippings for my garden or collection, but they would never take root, so there's credence to the myth."

"Or you're not as good as you think you are."

I run my hands up Natalia's sides, and she lets her head fall back to my shoulder. "I cultivated every other species I wanted, and I enjoyed the most difficult of species to work with for the challenge it offered."

"I want just one—*one*—thing you're bad at."

Natalia giggles. "Sexual innuendos."

Scoffing, Sterling asks, "Who are we killing?"

"There's a ritual that's done. Two individuals have to be willing to give their life, so we can't just drag them to the tree and kill them."

"That makes things more of a challenge. Anything else?"

"That's not enough?"

Chuckling, Sterling drops his gaze to our mate with the faint hint of a smile. "You two are more than enough."

He kisses Natalia, and I close my eyes. Her Light and his Dark twist around me, pulling us all together as much as one as we can be.

Sterling says, "All right, loves. Let's go find out who we are killing."

I press my fingers between Natalia's. "Neither of you speak up when I ask for volunteers."

He snorts through his nose, smiling and resting his forehead to mine. "I can do anything I want with our contract."

"I know you can," I growl in the back of my throat, baring my teeth. I hate admitting it. He's mine, and I protect him.

He grins wider. "I'm not your contract, so I don't take orders."

"No, you're my mate." I shove him backward. "Walk."

I throw Natalia over my shoulder, striding past Sterling. She has legs. She could walk. This way I get to grab her butt, and I keep a good handful as I approach the others.

Stopping in front of them, I roll Natalia off my shoulder into my arms and set her on her feet in front of me. Sterling moves to my back, Dark twisting around me as he drapes his arm over my shoulder.

Between them, I feel invincible. Hiro catches my eye and smirks.

I take a deep breath. "We need two willing sacrifices for the crystals. Two willingly give their life to the tree, and it sheds the crystals to re-bud and grow. That's how we get our weapons."

Palak gapes. "Why not simply pick the crystals off?"

"The hysterium tree," Ashley answers for me, "is the tree of life or the soul of the world, depending on the author. Either way, damaging it could damage the world."

Hiro says, "I plucked two, and it shook the world. We do it their way." He looks to Thames. "We could volunteer."

Jacques locks an arm around Tony's neck, dragging Tony over in a headlock with a laugh. "My friend and I volunteer first."

Tony pushes free, ducking his head as he rubs the back of his neck. "I'm Soris's host and have a better chance against the Ancients. Ash is the last Bordeaux." He looks at her.

Zander says, "I'm a Fairly. I do more good fighting than dying."

Falsion opens his mouth. I flip him off. "I'm not wanting any of you. You all are the strongest of us, and we need you to fight."

Palak shrugs, mocking a frown. "I'm valuable like most shiny things."

Sterling chokes on a laugh.

Zander looks to the palace. "We should seek other options beyond this circle."

CHAPTER 61
CALLAHAN

The dining hall is packed full, no more empty room, tables shoved in tightly to accommodate the accumulation of the Dark and Light.

I make the announcement of the ritual, asking if there are any willing to sacrifice themselves, and am met with silence.

Falsion stands. "I will."

I glare. "Sit down. I need you to fight."

Galain stands next. "I will be the second."

"Fuck no," I yell. "The two of you—"

Falsion cuts me off. "We both have lineage seeds, which we will do anything to protect. Maria and Fallon will be taken care of in return for this act. It's as willing as you'll find, and no others are speaking up."

Ashley stands. "I'll go finish the setup."

I stand. "You two, with me."

I head into the hall, glowering at them. "What were you thinking?"

Falsion shrugs. "That my little girl needs a future. I came

here for her, agreed to fight this war for her, and that I will die for her."

Galain bobs his head. "Shawn and Luca have agreed to watch over them, help them."

"I'll take them as my responsibility as well," I say, hanging my head. "I'll take them as head of the Hallow heritage, give them places of respect."

Falsion extends his hand to me, and I grip it, embracing him as he thumps me on the back. "Thank you. Thank you for bringing the Mandolux into the Dark, for fighting for our respect."

Galain says, "Raise my boy right. Teach him everything you know. I'll be honored if he's anything like you."

I push away from Falsion, struggling to breathe. "I didn't bring you fucks into society intending to watch you die."

Galain knocks me with a fist to my arm. "I'm going to say goodbye to Fallon." He saunters off, and I look to Falsion.

He's got me in strength and age. "I never did put you down."

He grins. "Maybe in the afters you'll get another chance."

"Fal..."

"Don't. I watched a brother of my lineage bring us into society with respect to be given. I got to have a perfect pup who grew into a pretty girl, then a beautiful woman. I've had the time of my life with you for these last days surrounded by new friends. My webs have given me the best final days it possibly ever could, and a blessing from them that my daughter won't have the same misery and pains I did in those mountains." He steps closer, a hand on my shoulder to stare me in the eye. "I got to see you spread your wings for the first time and fly. I thought Matteo was strong, but when I saw you fly for the first time, I knew no matter what Matteo did, you'd be stronger than any of us ever would."

I blink stinging eyes, my throat constricted.

"I got to meet your mate, and she is a perfect match. They both are."

I swallow the ball of emotion. "I know. I didn't intend for two."

"I like him as much as Tal."

"I love them both."

"I know," he says with a smile. "You three will bring the Seraphinus together, and you'll be as breathtaking as you were that day you took flight. I believe in you so much I am willing to wait to hear all about it in the afters."

"I'll take care of Maria."

"I know. You raised that boy Thomas, and you did a fine job." He drops his hand and turns away as the door opens behind me. "I'll say my goodbyes to Maria and meet you at the tree."

I watch him walk away, turning to my mate. She steps to me, Sterling at her back and following, both closing in on me to hold me. Neither says anything to me.

Sterling moves first, asking, "Is it ready?"

Ashley says, "Yes."

I look to her, taking a deep breath. Natalia takes my hand, leading me forward a step. I take another, then another.

I stand at the tree, dirt orchestrated in circles and runes, several hysterium blossoms dotting the spell layout. It looks right as far as I can tell.

Tony wipes dirty hands together, dusting off the loose debris. "Ash is going to walk Falsion and Galain through everything while I perform the ceremony. Soris can help with translations." He points to his ear.

I lift my chin in response. The hysterium scent is all around me, the scent of my mate. It's going to taint the pleasure—a bitter reminder of Falsion and Galain's sacrifice every time I smell her.

Falsion and Galain stand where Ashley tells them, Tony

speaking words and Ashley directing Falsion and Galain to cut their hands with crystals on the trees and press their palms to the trunk.

Tony speaks again, closing the book.

I hold my breath, Falsion and Galain exchanging glances with raised eyebrows before looking to me.

I shrug, and look to Tony, who has eyes of pure white, his lips moving.

His head hangs and he says, "Bad news. It didn't work."

"What does the fatum say?"

"Why don't we have the spell right? We're missing something. She doesn't know what, just that a piece is missing, and when I try again with..." He pauses, clearly listening to Soris again. "If I try again with 'different will work,' but she can't see the webs of what will be clear enough to know more."

"She knew about the child of Mallafic."

"She did, but it's the same as 'different' will work." He glares at the sky. "She can only see pieces and nothing with clarity."

Ashley takes the book from him, and I turn to Falsion and Galain. "You can go until we figure this out."

"Come now!" a man calls out, laughing behind me. "I wouldn't be so quick to dismiss them. Perhaps I can be of assistance?"

I turn, fear dripping down my spine as I stare down Mallafic. Vanessa stands off to the side, one pace behind with a wide grin.

Natalia steps forward, putting herself between them and the rest of us. "Do you know what we are missing?"

"Hello, Plaything." He flourishes a bow to her. "Have you reconsidered your falsehood yet?"

"No. Tell me what we are missing."

"A game, perhaps? Yes, perhaps..." He laughs, turning to Vanessa and offering his hand. When she accepts, he spins her forward toward Natalia. "A game. If you play, I will tell you that which you seek."

I step to my mate's side. "We'll play."

Mallafic appears before me, so close I can smell the stench of rotting wet leaves and death. "Oh, now, you." His hand presses to my chest, his claws pricking my skin through my shirt. "I dreamed so long of playing with one of your kind. Am I to truly have this treasure?"

He grabs my shirt, yanking me forward and sending me toppling to my knees before I have much comprehension. I catch myself before my face hits the stone and lift to my knees.

There's a snap of fingers behind me, and Sterling is on his knees at my side. Natalia stands before us, Mallafic at her back.

A hand rests on my shoulder, decorated brown skin with runes of black from fingertips to elbows and onward. I follow them to glance at Vanessa. I narrow my eyes at her, looking to Sterling, who kneels with her other hand on his shoulder.

My Dark quivers.

Facing forward, I ask, "What's the game?"

Mallafic runs his hands down Natalia's arms, pressing his face into her neck. She goes stiff, then blurs with shadows. Her clothes have transformed into sheer shadows, a low-cut dress with a high slit, her body in brilliant display.

Sterling chuckles. "I hate to say it, but I like his choice of attire, Firefly."

She scowls at him, but Mallafic rests his chin on her shoulder, his arms around her waist. "Such a wasteful shame she's one of my lover's things, but not even I could rip that seed from her when I remade her for what was given at birth is even beyond my ability to steal." He bites her shoulder, and she twitches, face flinching.

When Mallafic picks his head up, bloody marks are left behind, his lips stained red.

Natalia shoves her elbow into him, rounding on him. Her fist goes through shadows, and he laughs. "Oh, my darling, not yet." He twists her toward us again. "We have a game to play before I am whole again and can feel your sting."

Sterling turns his head to me. "I fucking hope you know what you're doing."

I cut my eyes to him. "I'm going to play a game."

"Cal, no. We can find another way."

"We have a way."

"I don't think—"

"We've played more games than we can count individually and together more than we know. We might bleed, but I'm betting we win."

He sighs, "Cal."

"Play the damn game. We're running out of time."

"All right, fair point. I'll play."

Mallafic laughs. "Darling?" He turns his face into Natalia, nuzzling her ear. "Will you play my game?"

"I hate this game already," Sterling mutters.

Natalia stares at me, and I incline my head. "Play the game. We'll get what we need."

She starts to shake. "Fine," she whispers. "I'll play."

Mallafic whisks between us, clapping his hands. "Wonderful. I do enjoy being entertained."

Tony yells, "Cal, no! He's going to—"

Mallafic flicks his hand, whispering words. Cracking stone fills the air, and I turn my head, checking over my shoulder. Tony, Ashley, Falsion, and Galain are on the other side of a barrier, Tony's throwing his body against it. His face contorts, his mouth open, and he slams his fist against it. Muffled sound comes through, but I don't know what he says.

Chuckling, Mallafic says, "I do so hope you enjoy the game as much as I do, but alas, please remain spectators. I'll have to insist, in fact, that you do not interfere with the show."

I glance at Sterling, who cuts his eyes at me. "That's not good."

"Ominous. That's the word you wanted."

He chuckles, muttering under his breath. "Bloody fucking Barracos."

"Complain later."

Mallafic turns his back on me, taking a step toward Natalia. "Will you confess your lie?"

"I love Cal."

My Dark winds around me, queasy with delight. No matter how many times she says those words, I'll never get tired of hearing them.

Mallafic steps behind her again, collecting her hair and running his thumb over my mating mark on her neck, Sterling's bite overlapping it.

He looks to me, staring me in the eye. "How many teeth do you have?"

Natalia winces as I lick my front teeth, and I glowering from the corner of my eye at Sterling.

He grimaces. "Not that many."

"*Tsk, tsk*, such a beauty, and yet so false in your affirmations." Mallafic clicks his tongue. "You tell a man you love him, then torment him with another? Inviting him with the same lies, no doubt."

She closes her eyes as they well up.

A growl rips from my chest. "She made it my choice."

Sterling shakes his head. "She didn't know I intended to do that to her. I abused her trust."

Mallafic sneers, closing his hands around her throat and lifting her jaw. "Open your eyes, Plaything. See them on their knees."

I try to stand, but Vanessa leans on my shoulder. I struggle against the weight, and she whispers strange words, pain wracking through my legs and abdomen.

Sterling snarls as she drags us to sit back on our heels. "What the fuck is this? What's the game?"

Natalia opens her eyes, holding my gaze. I bolster my spine, trying to display calm for her.

Mallafic twists his lips with a wicked glee. He tightens his hands around her throat. "Which did you lie to?"

Sterling says, "Neither of us. She loves Cal. I know that. He knows that. She knows it. Everyone knows it."

Mallafic chuckles, whispering something in her ear. She twitches, gripping her fists.

"A heart divided cannot be one in love. Which did you lie to? Choose, darling, who dies to be spared from your lies?"

My stomach and Dark squirm. "I quit."

I try to stand, but Vanessa's fingers crush my shoulder, bones snapping. I bite off my snarl of pain, trying to round on her. My Dark rushes toward her, contacting an invisible barrier around me, contained no further than a hand's width from my body.

It snarls and slams into the nothingness that prevents it from defending us.

She grins at me, grabbing me by the hair and then slamming my head into Sterling's. He groans, and the world spins.

Mallafic says, "Now, now, we can't have that. You agreed to play the game, after all."

"This isn't a game."

Sterling laughs. "This is fucked, but so are we." He lifts his chin at them. "It's me."

Natalia warbles, trying to step forward. "No."

Mallafic sinks claws into her shoulder. Her shrill scream is muted behind closed lips as she jerks to a halt.

Sterling tries to stand, but Vanessa forces him to the ground with a hand on his shoulder again.

He glares at her. "When did you become so strong?" Shaking his head, he says, "It's all right, Firefly. We both know it's me. Her choice of who dies is me. Send me to the afters."

Natalia's eyes flick to mine, begging me to do something. My mate is bleeding, her heart breaking. I can feel it, the echoes of her pain filling my head. I stare back, pleading with the gods for a way out of this with my whole heart.

I want my mates together, safe and happy in my Dark. I can see them wrapped in my shadows, laughing as we languor, waking up together in early morning illumination, still humming in pleasure before seeking more.

I lay on the bed as Natalia and Sterling straddled me while she played the guitar, her soft voice singing words of home and sugar cures. She sang of love. Every new song had made her shine brighter. I'd known then.

Too many days. So many memories. It's not enough. I want more.

"Tal," Sterling starts spouting stupid again. "Just say my name, Firefly. We both know your heart is his. He dug it out of you that night, and it's been his ever since. You never lied to me. You never told me you love me. I always knew I was just sharing your bed, and I got longer with you than I expected."

I snarl, "Shut up."

"I knew when I sank my teeth into her that she was yours and I didn't care. I didn't care because I wanted her, wanted to share her even for a fraction. I wanted to feel her as my mate, and force you to see me. I wanted you both and wished on the stars. I got my wish."

"Then shut the fuck up!"

"It's me. You know it. She knows it, and I know it. I shared the perfect mate with you—you, my god of bone and ash. I've worshipped you for centuries, and I never thought I'd taste you, but I did. Our mate glowed for us and begged for us. She's stronger than we'll ever be, but still wanted us. I got everything I could hope for, but she's never loved me."

One tear rolls down Natalia's cheek, and it breaks something deep in me. I can't look away from her, my chest tearing apart as if every word he speaks pulls the thread of her magic looser and looser. "STERLING, SHUT THE FUCK UP!"

"Me," he says, looking to our mate and Mallafic. "The choice is me."

Natalia nods, and fissures crackle through my chest. "Sterling."

I try to jerk out of Vanessa's grasp but fail. "No! There's no choice. This isn't a game, it's sick. She fucking loves you. I love you."

Sterling looks to me with confusion.

I glare. "You're a fucking idiot as much as I was."

"What?" He gapes. "You two...?" He looks to Natalia.

She smiles, blinking out tears. "Will you at least allow me to say goodbye?"

Mallafic retracts his claws, licking at them. "Oh, very well. Say your final words. I'm a god, not a monster."

She walks to Sterling, dropping to her knees and taking his face between her hands. "Babe."

I twist, facing them, trying to dislodge Vanessa in vain. My shoulder screams and throbs, so I give in, letting the arm hang useless. "Talia, you can mate him." They turn their faces toward me. "Mate him. We can find him again."

She kisses him, her Light unraveling in threads of silver. There are so many, glittering brightly.

I'm half Light, even if I don't glow. I am a Hallow, a heritage of Light mixed with a lineage of Dark. *"Can we have them both?"*

My Dark hisses. *"We can try."*

I drop my head to Sterling's shoulder, my Dark emptying out of me and leaving me hollow.

I sink my teeth into his shoulder, my Dark releasing a shrill hiss and tightening into my bones, anchoring its hooks while sealing itself to Sterling.

He's mine. A mate I share with my mate. Ours.

I pull back, my voice gruff. "We'll find you again."

Sterling sobs, choking in the back of his throat, "You two are the death of me." He remains leaned into Natalia, grabbing the back of her neck to pull her in for a kiss. "I don't mind. I love it. I love you, my wicked, burning firefly. Cal...not sure if I hate you or love you right now. Take care of our mate." He meets my gaze. "Find me again."

"I will." I smirk. "Baby."

He chuckles. "I regret—"

Vanessa lets go of his shoulder, grabbing his throat and ripping it. Blood flings, Natalia shrieking, and the spray splattering across my face. I wince and blink, the gore on my cheeks and lips, thick blood clinging to my eyelashes.

Sterling's body flips to the side, more blood spilling out of him. I stare, my chest mounting with pressure.

Natalia presses her hands to Sterling, her Light pulsing as she tries to bring him back.

Mallafic drags her away. I can't move, can't look away. His eyes are open, his head flopped wrong on a neck that's half gone.

Natalia screams and thrashes, crawling back toward him.

He's already in the afters.

Hanging her head, she turns glossy eyes to me, blood spray covering her face and torso.

Gritting my teeth, I try to stand, but pain racks through me, my eyes rolling into the back of my head. I gasp on all fours, but my shoulder can't support the weight and I fall on my face as my lungs catch on fire.

Natalia screams, "Cal!"

Mallafic's voice fills the air as I try to breathe. "Darling, do quit fighting the inevitable. I gave you a choice, who died for your lies."

Not lies. The words burn in my brain, but I can't get enough air to manage them. I know the truth. I know my mate.

She was always willing to break her heart for me and I never questioned that she would sacrifice Sterling for me. If I had, I might have sent Sterling away. I wouldn't—couldn't—break her heart.

I'd danced around Sterling my whole life, too afraid to let him close. It never mattered. I already loved him. We'd fallen in love over centuries from afar.

He'd known before I did. He'd seen the truth. He mated my mate to force me to acknowledge what he already knew.

"Sterling," Natalia says, her voice shrill. "We made a choice."

"Ah, yes. You looked at the two of them but never yourself. You could have saved them if you had been willing to sacrifice yourself. That is love."

My Dark howls, my body twitching. There's no air in the world, or my muscles won't work to draw it in. Either way, the world is gray.

"Let go of me! Cal!"

My throat sings with a fire like burning flames of agony. Wet slips down my chest, pooling in a dark puddle beneath me.

"Cal!"

My Dark whimpers and dissolves in my head as everything goes black.

"Cal!"

I fall. I fall forever through a rush of frigid nothingness, inky black and ringing silence surrounding me as a yawning eternity of death.

CHAPTER 62

NATALIA

"Cal!" I scream, thrashing against Mallafic as Vanessa leans over and rips a chunk of flesh from Cal's throat. "Cal!"

I set myself on fire. Mallafic loosens his grip with a snarl as I grab at the air, Cal going limp on the ground, blood leaking from him too fast, too much, there's so much blood pouring out of him.

I round with my elbow, trying to break free. The only solid portion of Mallafic is the claws digging into me, anchoring in my flesh to hold me in place as I fight.

So. Much. Blood.

So. Many. Fractions.

My knees give, my Light wailing in my head as our second mate dies. I can't breathe, can't see through the tears. I cry on the ground, no longer fighting, staring across the stone at Sterling and Cal, both dead.

Dead.

Gone.

In the afters.

I stare, my Light slithering through the air in search of them, pain filling my skull as a numbness spreads through me.

Mallafic rebuilds as a swirl of shadows in front of Vanessa. He lifts her bloody hands, smiling down on her. Lifting her hands, he presses his lips to one palm, then the other.

"Finally," he chuckles, stepping into her. He disappears, shadows wrapping around Vanessa as she tips her hand back and laughs.

I stare, blanketed in confusion, too numb to move.

Vanessa reaches up, plucking a blossom from the hysterium, smelling it, and twirling it in her fingers. "Alas, my sweet darling, our time has come to an end."

She sets the flower on the ground, drawing circles around it. Drawing runes in the dirt, she mutters to herself.

I can't move. I can't even comprehend what is happening. Nothing matters.

She reaches toward her chest, plunging her hand into herself and yanking her heart out. She grins at me with fangs and pure black eyes. "I'll take from you, my darling, but I leave you with this parting gift. Our webs are not yet finished and you have so much more to write."

It's not her voice. I've learned every tone in her arsenal, and that snarling rasp is not her.

She nestles the heart onto the flower, then rests her hand on top. Shadows rush forth from the gaping hole in her chest, around her shoulder and down her arm. The dirt swirls, intermixing with shadows and cascading upward in a torrent around her.

Vanessa crumples to a pile of limbs, but the cyclone rages on, dirt and blossoms spinning around in the shadows, a body forming beneath the surface, and then it explodes, radiating outward to leave behind a man.

I stare from my knees, numb and dazed.

Mallafic turns to me, his skin still pale but tinged with life, his black hair thick and glossy. His face is younger and less gaunt, his eyes a deep, dark green.

Stepping to me, he extends a hand. "Darling."

I gape at him.

He lifts neat eyebrows, set narrow across an upticked nose. Wiggling his fingers, he whispers, "We aren't done with our game."

Game. Sterling. Cal. My ribs squeeze, tightening down further and further, threatening to snap as the bones seek what's no longer there. That thing is in the afters with my mates.

I scream and lunge at him, swinging even as I take him to the ground.

He throws me to the side. "You are volatile yet."

I roll to a stop, scrambling as he rights, straightening his clothes.

I rush forward, but he disappears. I stop, whipping around at his chuckle.

"You are a delectable treat. I'm so glad we'll have eternity together."

"I'm going to kill you."

He grins ear to ear. "I offered you a prize in return for playing my game. Would you care for your answer?"

"That wasn't a game, you sick, mutilated, twisted bastard."

He makes a face of exaggerated frustration. "You lack fore-thought, darling." He snaps and appears before me, rolling his shoulders. "Right for—"

I swing, and he catches my wrist, shying his head back to stare down his nose at me, one eyebrow cocked.

"Darling, you're emotional. It's distasteful. Nevertheless..." He takes a deep breath, his chest inhaling. He's slender and sleek, of delicate build. "You played the game perfectly, and I won. It was courteous of you to grant me this win after my previous loss.

It makes our next game much more exciting. Oh, the anticipation..."

I grab a crystal, swinging it in my left hand toward his neck.

Snatching my wrist, he gives me a long, disapproving glare. "I will not be so close to having come so far for you to end this here."

My Light stretches in me, warming me. "I don't care about anything other than sending you to the afters, and I'll gladly send myself with you." The air buzzes with my fury.

"I came for one and one alone, so a boon in turn for the misery. Rules were meant to be broken, my darling. You and I are the exception, for a gift of gods, their very souls given, imparts a special gift, one my lover never had for her theft."

"I hate your stupid words, your fucked games, and your dumb face!" I kick at him, trying to wrench my hands free. "I wish Beenin had killed you."

With a laugh, he throws his head back and muses at the sky. "Oh, darling, that temper of yours need curbed. I see now my words will fall on those deaf ears you possess this night, so I will leave you with that which you've earned and nothing more. That which you seek for your spell is the impossible. You need two linked by it for the sacrifice." His grip releases as flashes of Light in the air buzz louder and faster.

Mallafic disappears. I clamp my jaw, screaming behind closed teeth. I glance around, searching for him, but he's gone. I'm left alone with living statues and three bodies on the ground.

The others rattle and move. Tony reaches toward me. "Tal."

"Cal..." I stumble to him.

I fall to my knees, sitting back on my heels and hanging my head. Moving to press a hand to his back, I hesitate, afraid that if I touch him, he won't move, that this will be real. If I don't touch him, there's still a chance I can wake up from this nightmare.

Someone yells my name. Others rush around, blurs of

shadows too distorted for me to comprehend. Someone flips Cal over, voices shouting.

Someone shakes me. "Tal! Tal!"

Blinking, the world rushes over me like a tidal wave of color and sound. I blink at Thames. He grimaces.

I push him to the side, leaning forward on my knees, reaching out for my mate. "Cal?"

Thames grabs my wrist. "He's in the afters."

Pulling away from him, I hug myself, staring at his body.

Hiro crouches next to Thames, blocking Cal from my sight. "We know what happened. We won't ask."

Dazed, I meet his eyes. "What?"

He flicks his fingers to the side, and I follow the motion to Tony standing between Ashley and Vanessa.

Vanessa.

I get to my feet, lunging at her. Dark wraps around me and Tony steps in front of Vanessa as I'm yanked away, back into something solid.

Hiro says, "Mallafic was using her, and she wasn't in control of herself."

I bare my teeth. "Liar! You wanted him dead. You wanted to hurt me."

Tony holds his hands up. "Tal, you're feeling a lot right now."

I throw my hand at him, sending a blast of Light his way. I'll take him down to send her to the afters if I must.

Tony holds his arm out, bent up to show his forearm, shielding from the attack. "You're pissed, you're hurting, you're blaming, you're broken up, and want to hurt something as much as you hurt. You want revenge. You'll do anything to go back and fix it. I know."

"Shut up!"

"No. You just lost the love of your life—both of them."

I scream and send another blast of Light at Tony.

He blocks, stepping closer. "You had love. It was real, true love. Everyone saw it. You just lost everything, and you want to die. You don't care about anything else, but you can't do that right now. Think, Tal." He stops in front of me, pulling his features together. "This isn't over. The Ancients are coming back."

"I don't care," I sob. "I don't care about anything."

He sags, shoulders dropping. "I know." Dragging a hand down his face, he turns his head away and sighs. "Do it for Cal. He would want you to save the Dark. Hold on to that. Hold on to what he would want. Let that be your crutch."

Hiro says, "The Dark needs you, Tallie. We need our king, and you are the strongest of us."

I scoff, the snort of disbelief bubbling into a choked laugh then hysterics as I laugh and cry together. "I couldn't save Cal. I didn't save either one of them."

Falsion says, "You didn't even have a chance. Mallafic orchestrated the trap and played his game in a rigged fashion to get what he wanted."

Tony says, "Mallafic gave you the answer to what we need for the crystals. I didn't understand, none of us do. He said the impossible—two linked by the impossible. That must have some meaning between you two."

I blink clumped lashes, sniffing through my nose. "What?"

"He said we needed two linked by the impossible for the sacrifice."

"What's impossible?" I wipe at my face. "I don't know what... I don't know." I fall to ground between my mates—what were my mates.

Blood soaks into my clothes, and there's still a lake of it stretching between the two. They're gone. I lost everything. The men I love were stolen from me.

Mallafic said love doesn't exist. He's been bent on proving I don't love. He thinks it's a fallacy.

Rubbing my eyes, I whisper, "Love. They have to be in love."

Galain nudges Falsion. "Guess my love for you doesn't count."

"You're like a brother. Wrong kind of love, I guess."

Hiro sighs, letting go of me. I shift to watch him pull his shirt off, tossing it at me. "Clean yourself up." He steps to Thames. "Sugar Bear."

Thames looks at him then laughs. "Are you ready for the afters already?"

Hiro tries to smile, the expression stuck on his lips. "If I'm with you."

I jerk. "No!"

They both look to me with confusion.

"No," I repeat. "No, please. I need you. I can't run the Dark— run anything. It'll all fall apart without you. Without— Without — With..." I can't even get the words out.

Thames smiles. "You'll have help."

Jacques whistles, waving his fingers. "I've got it covered. Me and Oscar, although I seem to be a curse for contractors. I've had two die on me in the last few months." He winces. "Not my best joke."

I bury myself into Hiro's shirt, trying to stop the tears.

Vanessa's voice floats through the air. "Has anyone tried to heal Cal?"

I turn with putrid rage, but Tony puts a hand on my shoulder. "Seriously, Tal, clean yourself up." He turns his back to me. "His throat is ripped out and it's been near half a rune, maybe more."

"He has a soul lock. Unless you break the lock, it'll keep the soul trapped. Cal's soul might still be locked in his body. I would try."

I throw Hiro's shirt at him and run to Cal, pressing my hand to his chest. My Light wraps around him, and I center.

His voice echoes in my head. *"Together."*

I squeeze my eyes shut, sending a prayer to anything listening, and send Ki into him. It thuds back as a hollow echo.

Dead.

I press harder, pushing more. It comes back, bouncing like a rubber ball on pavement until the thuds blur together in my ears as dull whacks, the Ki reverberating into my arm like hammer strikes.

My Light snarls, but a slip of Ki skips away, then another small beat, before the thuds turn less harsh, Ki flowing smoother out of me into Cal.

It burns, dragging from me in droves, and then a hand rests over mine. I stop, hanging my head. It's pointless. Dead is dead, and no amount of Ki is going to bring my mate back to me.

I lift my head, opening my eyes expecting Tony to be waiting to tell me to give up, but there's no one there. I look to my hand, the hand on top of it attached to a wrist, an arm, a shoulder— Cal's body.

Cal lifts his head off the ground as he twists his lips. "Usually you're a lot gentler with healing."

His Dark wraps around my arm, threads twisting with my Light. My eyes haze over as I laugh, throwing myself on him.

He catches me, holding me close as I sob in relief. "Cal."

"Mate."

Jacques yells, "You fucker! I thought you were dead, and I was out a contractor again."

Cal rumbles with humor. "Least important concern I had." He sits with a grunt and a wince, keeping me close as he presses his nose to the side of my head. "You're covered in blood."

I pull back. "So are you."

He lifts one corner of his mouth, then glances around. "Where did you all come from?"

Tony answers. "You've been dead a while."

"You brought me back from the afters?" He meets my eyes, lifting his eyebrows.

Clearing her throat, Vanessa says, "You have a soul lock. I thought maybe it would have kept your soul in your body rather than letting it go to the afters."

Reaching behind him, he rubs the back of his neck and down between his shoulders. "I guess we know what I did to myself now." He turns his head toward her, features tightening with rage. "Give me one reason I don't send you to the afters."

Tony steps between them, crossing his arms. "She's already explained she was under the sway of Mallafic. That shit that was in her from the books? It all ended up in her. She wasn't in control."

Cal relaxes. "Are you in control now?"

"Mallafic took all of it and remade himself. Apparently, he needed Ness to kill you. It's a long explanation. It's just Ness again, and we all know she's...no threat."

"Ha," Vanessa fakes a laugh. "I'm weak, useless me again."

I push away from Cal, rocking onto my feet and standing, offering him a hand up. "If she had to kill Cal for some reason, then she failed. Is she going to try again?"

"No," she says. "No, I wouldn't—won't. I don't want Cal dead."

Falsion says, "You ripped his throat out. I don't care what you say, what excuse you have now, you get anywhere near him again and I send you to the afters."

Cal leans against me, hugging me. "Did we at least get what he promised us?"

Tony says, "We need two linked by the impossible. Tal seems to think that's love. Hiro and Thames have volunteered."

Cal turns toward Hiro and Thames. He grimaces, and I hold onto him tighter.

Hiro shrugs. "I serve the Dark. This is the best I can offer, and I have a guarantee I stay with my mate."

Thames laughs. "We'll go together and stay together. I'll be your best little vassal forever."

Hiro drags Thames into a kiss, shoving him back to say, "That's going to die with us in this life, Sugar Bear, or so help you the gods."

Thames grins with his tongue between his teeth. "I hope they have tea."

"If they don't, I'll make tea." Hiro pulls Thames's head lower, pressing their foreheads together. "Anything for you, Mate."

Ashley says, "I need to reset the spell. Someone," she glares toward Vanessa, "made a mess of it."

Vanessa hugs herself, shrinking back and growing smaller, hanging her head.

Cal asks, "Are you sure about this?"

Hiro nods. "I am. This is how I serve the Dark." He bobs his head to the side, smirking. "Slightly self-serving. We won't face the Ancients. I won't risk living without my mate or leaving him behind. We both go together, now."

Thames grips Hiro's hand, Hiro wincing. "Sure thing, baby."

CHAPTER 63
CALLAHAN

Ashley moves to reset the spell.

I drop to my knees, falling into a pool of congealed blood. Sterling gazes up at me with glazed over eyes turned gray.

I reach for him, hesitating. My Dark whimpers and whines. My fingers tremble.

Finding strength, I force his eyes closed. I hang my head, resting my hand on his, the thick twisted locks of his hair coarse against my palms. He'd been proud of his locks, something relating to his lineage. It was a fashion developed in the time of clans, something chieftains in his lineage wore. I heard all about them and the tradition one night.

He was the last of his lineage.

I'd longed to see him with a daughter of his own. I'd wanted brothers, his seed and mine.

I'd wanted a life with him. I wanted him almost my whole life, avoiding this moment in fear and wasting so much time.

"Cal?"

I wipe my face, my nose stuffed, and my throat clogged. Rising, I face Hiro.

He nods to me. "He was a good man."

"An even better mate."

Thames hugs Natalia with a sad smile. "Lightning Bug, don't waste this. Send those fucks to the afters."

She sniffles, nodding. "I'll miss you."

Hiro punches her in the shoulder with a limp wrist that lacks force. "You're the worst Dark King that's ever been."

She covers her face with her hands and sobs into them.

"But I'm damn proud to have stood with you." He steps away. "Ready, mate?"

Tony reads the words as Hiro and Thames follow Ashley's instructions. They press their palms to the tree, the bark glowing.

Thames winces. "I'm fucking terrified, Honey Pot."

Hiro yanks his face to his as the blue starts to glow in their hands, racing up their arms. The glow intensifies, blocking everything from view even as I squint, trying to keep my eyes on them.

The glow stops suddenly, the tree sparkling brighter than I've ever seen. The branches shudder, and the crystals tinkle like a delicate rain of glass, falling around us.

I press Natalia closer. My chest aches. Hiro and Thames are gone, nothing but a twinkle in the air.

The others start to move away, feet shuffling in the silence. Jacques tucks Vanessa under his arm as they move past.

I hate that woman.

Tony nods at me, his arm around Ashley. "We'll find others to pick these up, put them somewhere safe."

I nod, squeezing Natalia. "Go."

Falsion and Galain move closer. Falsion stops to pat me on the shoulder. "Take your time. Take all the time you can."

Galain picks up the corpse, his head dangling by thin flesh.

I turn into Natalia, pressing her close to avoid seeing more. The scent of hysterium mixes with metal.

Blood. Sterling's blood.

I hold her closer, one of us trembling, maybe both. We played a game and we lost. It's the first time she and I didn't win. We've managed to find a way to survive, but the cost was high.

I lost another friend. I lost a mate, maybe both. Natalia and I will both be cracked from Sterling's vacancy.

I told her to mate him in urgency, acting on emotion alone. I'd been focused on not giving him up. She mated him, at least tried. I mated him.

We're forced to live with that, live without our mate. It's going to be difficult. I won't regret it, ever. I'll find him in the afters and we'll have more time.

"Cal?"

I pick my head up and meet her eyes. They are darker than I've ever seen. "Talia, I... I failed you."

"I failed," she mewls, blinking to send tears down her cheeks. "I couldn't save him."

"I said to play. It was my choice." My voice is raw, the words dragging out of me in a confession that cleaves my chest open.

She shakes her head, gripping my shirt. "We needed—Ster–Ster... He..."

I rest my chin on her head, holding her tight as she shakes and sobs.

Tonight, I'll bite my tongue. I won't be my father's son and chide her for her pain. She doesn't have to swallow this and pretend it's not real. For this evening, I will let it consume her and me.

Tomorrow, we have to stand again. We can't wallow. We have to focus on the truth. The Ancients are still a threat and one bearing down on us with ferocity.

Not tonight.

Nightmares the morrow will bring will be faced then. I won't consider or manage them before they arrive.

My father would be disappointed, but I don't care. For one night, I am going to mourn what I've lost, the broken heart I share with my mate ripped open and pulsing with longing.

Matteo Barraco never let anything hurt him, not that he showed. I'm not him, no matter the expectations I stare down at carrying his name.

He had been flawless and proud. He had known so much.

If only myths were more than ink on parchment. The Brothers Three was my father's favorite myth, all different versions, some variation of a doorway built to bring back one from the afters. The stories of the Ancients are fantasies of the tongue, suiting the purpose of teaching lessons.

Mallafic thinks love isn't real, that he could play with my mate and smash her heart without comeuppance. I'll teach a god a lesson. I'll do more than make him bleed for hurting my mates.

I'll prove to him he's wrong. I love them both. Her heart, my heart, they aren't divided. They are shared with more love than I thought possible.

The love is real. I can feel its bite knowing I won't endure another riddle from Sterling or watch him laugh with Natalia.

"Cal?"

I take her face between my hands, tipping her head back and kissing her forehead. "We will find him again in the afters. Together, Little Star. We'll hunt him down and bring him back to us again."

"I... I love..."

"Him and me." I rest my curved mouth to her brow.

"You—you knew?"

"Yes." I stroke her hair, tucking it behind her ear and

following the line of her jaw to her chin. "Did you really think I wouldn't notice my star glowing for him?"

She sniffs, her lashes falling as she lowers her gaze. "I..."

"Talia," I whisper. "It's okay. I love him, too."

Her eyes snap to mine. Adoration shines in them.

"Were you able to mate him?"

She nods, crestfallen and meek.

"I mated him too."

Her lips part as she gasps. "But..."

"He is our mate."

"I didn't think you would be...okay with..."

"Do you love me?"

"Yes." She buries her face in my chest, holding so tight my ribs might crack.

"As long as you love me, I can do anything. I can steal a star or kill a god. I can love our mate with you and enjoy it. I can do anything with your love." I dig her face free, trying to smile. "We finish this. We send the Ancients and that fucking god to the afters. We bring the two together, and then we find him again. Will you do that with me, mate?"

"Yes."

I might not measure up to my father. The failures I have made are too numerous to count. I have my faults and weaknesses, but I am not done fighting.

The crushing, daunting fact is that if I fail this time, my entire race will pay for my lack of strength. I've failed so many times before.

Natalia will help me. She is my star, my god, and I worship her, trust in her, and believe in her.

I have no more patience with petty disputes. I will bend them into whatever society I create without mercy. I will remake this world, and any who stand in my way will feed the soil with their blood and bones. I'll send the Ancients to the afters. I'll hunt

Mallafic to the ends of this world and until the end of time for my revenge if I have to. I'll keep my star close then we'll find our mate when I've avenged him.

Tomorrow. It all waits until the suns rise in the morning.

Tonight, I have a star to mourn with.

NATALIA & CALLAHAN'S STORY WILL CONCLUDE...

ACKNOWLEDGMENTS

As always, I have to thank you, my lovely reader, for taking the time to read my book. Without you, this story would never be known, so thank you.

Now comes the obligatory appreciation nods:

1. My poor, suffering husband Eric has had to fund this endeavor, put up with me talking to myself and my imaginary friends, and has listened to me bemoan the last few chapters for quite some time. He deserves a round of applause for not divorcing me, if I'm honest.

2. Renee and Amanda should be nominated for saint hood, reading this book and providing feedback to me, but were forced to endure waiting for me to write book six after that ending.

3. Gina (KillingItWrite), my editor does her best to fix my grammar and tighten these books. I know they're long...

INDEX

SOUL LOCK

*CALLAHAN'S PROTECTION SPELL

THE SPELL

The traditional soul lock spell is three parts.

1. create a sigil on a vessel

2. create a sigil on a body, the soul's vessel

3. cast the spell that will transfer the soul to the marked vessel, removing the soul from the body

---

CAUSE & EFFECT

After Cornu was sentenced and his soul ripped from his body in 9 pieces, those responsible deemed it was too harsh a practice that should never be implemented again, however it became common practice to create a soul lock sigil on yourself to prevent the ability to have your soul removed.*

*Callahan's "protection spell" is a soul lock

GREMALVIS

"HYSTERIUM"

Every sprout of the Gremalvis is connected to the original sprout through a network of roots that spans the world.

The roots and original sprout reside near the serpent river's head, swaddled in mountains in which the city of Vallemon was carved.

As the tree of life/the soul of the world, if the Gremalvis dies the land will come apart and life will end.

FEEDS ON THE LIGHT OF ADONTIUS & THE DARK OF NEHIL

BLACK BARK, THE CRACKS GLITTERING BRILLIANT BLUE

PURPLE-BLUE FLOWERS ON LONG THIN BRANCHES

CRYSTAL SHARDS MIX AMONG THE FLOWERS, DANGLING FROM THE VINE-LIKE BRANCHES

THE RITUAL OF REBIRTH

When the Gremalvis is in full bloom, lush with floral sprouts and crystals, typically once every ten years, a spell is cast to release the crystals.

Two souls linked by the purest, true love willingly give their lives to the feed the world, as Nehil and Adontius created the world in love.

When the crystals are released, they can be planted and watered to release a new soul, creating Eternums.

The crystals are pure balanced energy, made up of Ki.

I'll find you in the afters.

MATES

TETHERING ONE SOUL TO ANOTHER

The first mates were Nehil and Adontius, their mating transpiring when Adontius strayed, enamored with another. Her betrayal shattered Nehil, and as he began to unravel Adontius sewed their love story into the fabric of his existence, creating the stars and giving a piece of herself to Nehil, binding them together as one for eternity.

Eternums and Seraphinus hold the power to follow in the way of their gods and mate. They accomplish this through weaving a piece of their soul into another/another's soul. They bite the intended mate, branding their mate with their unique bite mark.
*The bite must break skin to create holes for magic to fill.

The bite mark is referred to as 'the mating mark' and it is permanently sealed into the mated with a piece of the mater's magic. The mating mark is sensitive to the mated when touched by the mater, capable of delivering pleasure or encouraging it.

The mating bond is permanent and cannot be undone. It can be a conscious choice or an impulsive action in the heat of a moment. Those intending to mate but have reasoning to wait can inscribe their name into their future mate with a piece of their magic.

The mater's magic has to agree to the mating bond & desire it to. Each magic has its own voice & its own echo. The mater's magic will choose a mate that has an enjoyable echo.

The mating bond is believed to allow two souls to remain connected even in death so that the two souls can reunite in the afters.

TRAITS OF MATES

The mating mark is sealed with a piece of the mater's magic - it will echo to allow the mater to find its mate

The touch of a mater for the mated individual is intensely pleasurable & heightens sexual experiences

The scent of a mated to the mater is overwhelming & correlates to a personal, happy moment or a shared happy moment between the mater & the mated

LOSING A MATE

When the mater loses it's mated, it's an agony. The mater's magic has lost a piece of itself and constantly seeks it, withering away from the loss of itself and its loved one. The mater's magic will slowly give up, become unruly, then unravel into death.

www.ingramcontent.com/pod-product-compliance
Lightning Source LLC
Chambersburg PA
CBHW031018030726
47497CB00004B/909